D0346811

Paris,
He Said

C333826153

By the same author

Little Known Facts
Portraits of a Few of the People I've Made Cry (stories)

Paris, He Said

CHRISTINE SNEED

BLOOMSBURY
LONDON · OXFORD · NEW YORK · NEW DELHI · SYDNEY

Bloomsbury Publishing
An imprint of Bloomsbury Publishing Plc

50 Bedford Square
London
WC1B 3DP
UK

1385 Broadway
New York
NY 10018
USA

www.bloomsbury.com

BLOOMSBURY and the Diana logo are trademarks of Bloomsbury Publishing Plc

First published in Great Britain 2015

© Christine Sneed, 2015

Christine Sneed has asserted her right under the Copyright, Designs and Patents Act, 1988, to be identified as Author of this work.

This is a work of fiction. Names and characters are the product of the author's imagination and any resemblance to actual persons, living or dead, is entirely coincidental.

All rights reserved. No part of this publication may be reproduced or transmitted in any form or by any means, electronic or mechanical, including photocopying, recording, or any information storage or retrieval system, without prior permission in writing from the publishers.

No responsibility for loss caused to any individual or organization acting on or refraining from action as a result of the material in this publication can be accepted by Bloomsbury or the author.

British Library Cataloguing-in-Publication Data
A catalogue record for this book is available from the British Library.

ISBN: TPB: 978-1-4088-6807-2
        ePub: 978-1-4088-7390-8

2 4 6 8 10 9 7 5 3 1

Typeset by RefineCatch Limited, Bungay, Suffolk
Printed and bound in Great Britain by CPI Group (UK) Ltd, Croydon CR0 4YY

To find out more about our authors and books visit www.bloomsbury.com. Here you will find extracts, author interviews, details of forthcoming events and the option to sign up for our newsletters.

For Adam Tinkham,
and for Kate Robes Soehren,
who got us to class and on many very early
trains when we were students in France

"The bird of paradise alights only upon the hand that
does not grasp."
—John Berry

Contents

PART ONE

Jayne, Summer

CHAPTER 1

Flight

As Jayne made final preparations to leave New York for Paris during the first few days of June, a heat wave turned the sky ashen with trapped pollution and unshed rain. The people she passed on the street seemed more short-tempered than usual, and no one met her gaze other than schoolchildren who glanced up at her with innocent apathy. For a long time she had assumed that poverty or loneliness, or both, would force her to flee the city, but instead she had met an older man who invited her to trade Manhattan for his home in Paris. She said yes with little hesitation.

The air was dry and the sky free of glowering clouds as her plane landed in the gray northern sprawl of Paris's exurbs at seven thirty in the morning, the highways already pulsing with cars and brightly painted tradesmen's vans. She had not slept on the flight from JFK because she was thinking of the man who waited for her on the threshold of tomorrow morning, someone who sold other people's art after finding it impossible, years ago, to sell much of his own. She was leaving her friends, her native language, her family, her doctor and dentist, her library card, the purposeful little dogs, some dressed in sweaters and plaid coats on winter days, that she saw walking with their doting owners on the streets near her apartment.

For six independent but mostly hand-to-mouth years she had lived in Manhattan and had not been to Paris since college, nine years earlier, but she had thought of it every day, as if it were someone important she hoped without reason to become indispensable to. Each quarter had its own manicured parks and public squares, and thousands of Parisians walked or rode bicycles or took the train to work and to the narrow-aisled stores where they often shopped at the end of the day, filling net bags and small wheeled carts. When she first saw them as a student, the stately, weathered buildings with their stone facades seemed to encourage romance. She found Paris more serenely beautiful than the other cities she was familiar with, many with fuming smokestacks and superhighways driven like a stake through their thundering hearts.

One of the first things she intended to do after her arrival was visit Sacré Coeur and the hilly northern quarter it presided over and look upon the miles of rooftops descending like stair steps, its spires and soot-darkened chimneys and riverine belt at the middle. At twenty she had stood on the same hilltop and believed without question in her right to everything she desired: prosperity, love, the admiration of friends and strangers, a long and healthy life. She had been in Paris with a group of four or five other American students, sharing a bottle of red wine, its plastic Monoprix bag poor and slippery camouflage. They were all confident in their glamorous futures as playwrights, painters, concert pianists, and dot-com entrepreneurs, but they remained as unknown now as they had been then—one had become a speech therapist, two had married and started families, a fourth had moved to Peru to work for his aunt's tourism business.

Liesel, her closest friend, saw her off, pretending on the long cab ride to JFK from Jayne's apartment on East Second Street that she fully supported Jayne's move overseas. But as they said good-bye a few feet from where the security line began, Jayne was startled to see that her friend had started to cry.

"Liesel," she whispered, her own throat threatening to close over. "I'm not leaving forever." She stared down at the dirty floor, its dull white surface streaked with black slashes from the thousands of rubber soles that had already shuffled over it that afternoon.

"You don't know that," her friend said softly. She wiped her eyes, embarrassed. The last time Jayne remembered seeing Liesel in tears was at another friend's birthday party three summers earlier, when someone had slipped in a DVD of The English Patient, thinking it high comedy to couple the film with the party's Pogues sound track. The prankster had underestimated the movie's appeal to some of the drunken guests, Liesel especially, who in high school had seen it in the theater five times. Jayne herself had seen it three.

"Of course I'll be back," said Jayne.

"You don't know when, though."

"No, but you can come visit me, can't you? And I'll be on the other end of the phone anytime you need me."

"Six hours ahead of me."

"Yes, but I'll still be there. We can Skype and e-mail too." She took one of Liesel's small hands in her own, noticing that the freckled skin of her friend's arms had turned to gooseflesh inside the over-air-conditioned airport. "For all I know, I'll be back next week."

Liesel shook her head. "You won't be."

"So come see me. Or I'll have to fly back and kidnap you."

"I'd better go before it gets any later. I have another hour or two of work left at the office," said Liesel, trying to smile. She hugged Jayne one more time, hard, as if to hurt her a little, and fled. Jayne stood blinking after her friend, bereft. When she turned to look back a moment later from her place at the end of the security line, Liesel had already disappeared, her brown ponytail and yellow blouse no longer visible in the crowd of harried travelers.

Two redheaded children complained to their father about sore feet, neon-green backpacks slung over their narrow shoulders, one of the packs stuffed to sausage-like rigidity, the other limp as an airless balloon. Near them, a woman in pink shorts and a black tank top was snickering at something a man in a Yankees cap had whispered, his mouth hovering at her ear. He had an overgrown blond mustache, and Jayne wondered if the woman sometimes dreaded kissing him—probably not, considering the way she was leaning into him. Jayne heard her phone chime, the sound almost lost in the cacophony of departure. It was a text from another friend, Melissa, who had not been able to find a sitter for her six-month-old son and ride with Jayne and Liesel to JFK. *Miss you already. I'm jealous & would do what you're doing in a second if I could.* Melissa had been married for two years to a man she'd met on a backpacking trip in Colorado. She had not intended to have a child so soon, but as she sometimes said, this was nothing to be sorry about. She was nuts about her adorable son, who was healthy and a frequent smiler, and who, to Melissa and her husband's surprise and relief, had begun sleeping through the night at three months.

The image of Liesel in tears stayed with Jayne as she passed through security and settled at the gate in the Air France concourse. That her friend would miss her terribly—or the opposite—had not been foremost in Jayne's thoughts as she'd made plans to leave New York. Until they'd said good-bye a few minutes earlier, Liesel had not seemed very upset by Jayne's move to Paris, only a little wistful that she wasn't going too. Jayne didn't believe, in any case, that she would remain in France for the rest of her life. A year, maybe two or three at most. Any duration beyond this was difficult to fathom.

On the plane she had a window seat, the two passengers on her right an older couple, a woman with voluminous iron-colored curls in the middle seat. More than once her elbow grazed Jayne's arm, her head also drifting down several times to rest on Jayne's shoulder until she twitched awake and righted herself, mumbling her excuses in accented English. Her husband snored next to her, his gray head nodding forward, chin sinking into his chest. Jayne wondered where they lived, and if, like Laurent, the man who had invited her to live with him in France, they were residents of the eighth arrondissement, which she knew was one of Paris's toniest quarters. Maybe they were Laurent's neighbors, or else had purchased paintings from his gallery on rue du Louvre?

No, not likely. He usually flew first or business class. They were in coach. She said nothing about the reasons for her trip, and they didn't ask. They didn't try to talk to her at all. Aside from the flight attendants who moved briskly up and down the aisles, smiling as they asked for beverage and dinner preferences and later offered hot towels and bottled water, the plane was hushed, a sealed, speeding vessel, hurtling them at five hundred miles per hour far above the cloud-cloaked earth toward the week or month or years—maybe the rest of their lives—they would spend in France.

CHAPTER 2

In New York

With a partner, Laurent owned two galleries, one in New York, the other in Paris, both named Vie Bohème. Jayne had been doing office work since graduating from college, first in Washington, D.C., and later in Manhattan; she was also an artist, but not a successful one, in part because for the last several years she had not been a very productive one either. She knew that some of her friends believed that her relationship with Laurent was one of calculation, of mutual unspoken checks and balances—she the pliable young woman with hopes, he the older man, more than twenty years her senior, with money and different hopes (one being that he not grow old too fast) and a gallery's walls to offer her if he decided to do so. The fact that she had not asked him to show her work and he had not suggested it did not, as far as she could tell, keep people from speculating.

What had kept them together past the first date were the same things that she assumed kept most new couples together: curiosity and lust, and with luck, shared interests. Laurent listened when she spoke and often remembered more details from their conversations than she did, something that had never happened to her before: it was spaghetti squash that her mother grew in the garden, not zucchini—didn't she remember telling him this? They agreed about many of the things she had sometimes argued about with other men she'd dated, most recently Colin Fuller, whom she was seeing when she met Laurent. As she did, Laurent thought that a well-made American potboiler was preferable on occasion to a lugubrious documentary at the Film Forum; that trains should be as efficient in the States as the ones in Europe, but he doubted they would be in his lifetime, or in Jayne's; that the best time of day was the morning, although she liked to sleep in, because with the two jobs she'd had to work to stay clear of an eviction notice, she had only been able to sleep past eight on Sundays.

"Will you miss your life in New York?" he asked the morning before she planned to fly to Paris. He had already been home on rue du Général-Foy for several days, having left a week earlier to prepare his apartment for her arrival.

"Some of it," she said. "But I won't miss my neighbors, that's for sure." The offending neighbors were two New York University MBA students who lived above her and her roommate Kelsey. Kelsey was also a graduate student at NYU, but her area of study was Clinical Psychology, not Being Assholes, as she and Jayne had renamed the master's program of the unreformed frat boys upstairs. Kelsey was much quieter than Drew and José too, who once or twice a week could be counted on to clomp drunkenly up the front staircase at three or four in the morning and, after much cursing and muffled laughter as they fumbled with their keys, continue the drunken uproar in their apartment. The ceiling was old and flimsy, and on some bleary mornings Jayne found paint flakes on her desk and in her hair and bedside rug.

"It will be quieter here," Laurent assured her. "You will almost never see or hear my neighbors."

"That sounds like heaven."

"But there is a little noise from the street, Jayne. You should know that."

"As long as it's not someone banging around above us, I'll be fine."

"No, don't worry about that," he said. "You will sleep soundly."

"I can't imagine sleeping without earplugs. It'll probably feel strange for a while."

"You will get used to it. One less thing to worry about, and one step closer to nirvana, yes?"

It had been Laurent's suggestion that she move to France to spend more time making art and working in his Parisian gallery, but her first impulse was to refuse. She assumed that he had made the offer solely out of pity.

He laughed at this accusation. "Do you think I am so stupid?"

"No," she said, taken aback. "But if you're asking me because the job in D.C. fell through and you're worried that I'm thinking about jumping off a bridge, you needn't."

"Needn't?" he repeated. "What a strange word."

"You need not," she said. "I did want the job, but it's not the end of the world that I didn't get it."

"It was not a good one," he said firmly. "You would have been doing someone else's work, and she would have all the credit. Assistant director is not so good."

"It's better than what I'm doing now," she said. For the last several years Jayne had worked full-time as an administrative assistant and office manager for a small accounting firm on West Fourteenth Street that employed three CPAs, one part-time webmaster, a college intern, and herself. A few evenings a week she also worked at a women's shoe store on Elizabeth Street. The job she had almost been chosen for, the source of what she assumed to be Laurent's pity for her, was an assistant director position in the international programs office at the Washington, D.C., college where she had minored in studio art and French and majored in international business—more practical by far than her minors! her father had insisted—but post-college, her business major had not helped her find a job for which she needed more than a high school degree. For the international programs job, however, she had hoped to have an advantage over the other candidates because she had been a work-study student in the office for the two years that bookended her junior-year semester in Strasbourg.

And probably she had had an advantage: a week after the initial phone interview, the hiring committee paid for her to take the train down from New York and put her up in a room in the campus hotel. She was told by the smiling director, who claimed to remember Jayne from eight years earlier, that she was one of two finalists. The interview lasted an entire day, and with little ceremony, she was handed off from one group of encouraging or distracted university bureaucrats to the next. It had seemed to go well, despite her embarrassment after she bumped her coffee cup with a gesturing hand while talking to the second wave of interviewers, spilling the flavorless, lukewarm liquid onto the table and her skirt.

She had returned to New York thinking that professionally, at last, things might be aligning: she would soon have the chance to move back to Washington and start over, with optimism and good health insurance. She'd have more time to draw and paint, and to prepare food that hadn't come from a can or a frost-furred box because she was too tired on the nights she wasn't with Laurent to make any real effort to feed herself. The cookbooks she had held on to since college, picture-filled hardcovers that she had studied closely before her first uncertain attempts to bake bread, to roast a pork loin to the point of perfect tenderness, and to make a pan of spinach lasagna that didn't emerge from the oven a watery morass, would be opened more than a couple of times a year. She would have to leave Laurent behind in New York, but he was returning soon to Paris and had not yet asked her to move across the Atlantic with him. They had been dating for a little more than four months when she interviewed for the job in Washington, and although he'd said he admired the work she'd shown him, a series of small oil paintings she'd made of old photographs found at a flea market near Liesel's apartment on the Upper West Side—some of unoccupied rooms, others of strangers' unsmiling faces—he had not mentioned anything about putting her work in a show and launching her career as a New York artist, something Liesel thought he should already have offered to do. Jayne dismissed her friend's complaint. "It doesn't work that way. Laurent is running a business, not a charity."

"Your work is as good as just about anything we've seen at Vie Bohème," said Liesel.

Jayne felt the sororal warmth of her friend's indignation, but she doubted she was as talented as Liesel insisted. Her friend had long been prone to exaggeration: if they were held up in traffic for more than a few minutes, Liesel would later say that the delay had been interminable; or if she'd seen a movie she liked, she'd proclaim that she had just been to the funniest/most brilliant/best movie ever—something that seemed to happen every other month.

"I'm not going to ask him to put me in a show," said Jayne. "He gets that all the time and doesn't need it from me too. If he wants to represent me, he'll suggest it."

Liesel was undeterred. "You're dating a guy who owns two galleries. Good galleries too, not some bullshit place that's hardly better than a poster shop. If you don't make an effort now, you never will."

"That's not true."

Liesel opened her mouth but closed it again.

"What," said Jayne.

"I just think you're cheating yourself. He has to know that you want his help."

"He probably does, but there's no rush, is there?"

"I don't know, is there?" asked Liesel. "How many years have you been saying that to yourself?"

On the night she met Laurent, Jayne had plans with Colin, who she'd been seeing for three and a half months by that time, but earlier in the afternoon he'd had to cancel their dinner date in order to stay late to finish a job for a demanding client. His boss was working overtime too, and Colin knew that he couldn't leave at six as he'd been planning to do. He offered to take Jayne to a late dinner instead, but she was sure that by nine or ten o'clock she'd be too tired to fix her hair and makeup again and step out into the chilly night to meet him.

While Colin was eating carryout Thai at his desk and staring at his computer screen, she intended to stay in to finish an overdue library book and call her parents. Her mother's tone in her last message had been more aggressive than usual: "I won't take up much of your time, Jayne. Ten minutes, maybe twelve. Can you spare that for your mother?" Jayne's sister, Stephanie, two years younger and her only sibling, had told Jayne that their parents were having trouble—Mrs. Marks was sleeping in the guest room, and she had stopped cooking for their father, saying that he could eat frozen dinners and peanut butter sandwiches until he started doing more of the dishes and picking up after himself. Yet when Jayne had last called home, her attempts to get her mother to talk about any of this had been sidestepped. Mrs. Marks would only say that she and Mr. Marks were fine, tired but fine.

"You and Stephanie don't need to worry about us," her mother said. "Everything's the same, I suppose, except that he wants to get a new dog, and I don't."

"Why don't you want to?" asked Jayne. "It's been six years since Clemmie died."

"I know, Jayne. As if I could ever forget. Your father reminds me almost every day."

Jayne's sister lived in Los Angeles, down the bottlenecked 110 freeway from their parents in Pasadena, but Stephanie saw them infrequently—only a few times more than the two visits Jayne tried to make each year. Stephanie called home a little more often than Jayne did, and also kept closer track of their parents' health, schedules, and grievances. The year after Stephanie started college, their mother had left their father, though she only stayed away for five days, and neither Jayne nor her sister heard anything about this rift until a couple of years later, when their father let it slip over the Christmas holiday. It was only the four of them at home, no gossipy relatives to worry about, but her mother had not wanted to discuss her short-lived defection. Jayne and Stephanie looked on with apprehension, feeling wronged to have been told nothing of the situation until their father saw fit to spoil that year's Christmas, as their mother accused him, fuming.

Before Jayne had returned her mother's call on the evening of the Vie Bohème opening, Liesel texted and begged Jayne to go with her. She had a crush on one of the three featured artists and was desperate to attend.

Jayne had read about the opening, but there were dozens of artists, playwrights, and musicians debuting their work in New York every week. Within a year after moving north from D.C. she had stopped going to galleries most weekends, feeling herself excluded from Manhattan's art world in a way that seemed impossible to breach. The desire for recognition, the fear of being ignored, the barely suppressed competitive urges—all these undercurrents in almost every gallery crowd—now enervated her more often than not. Liesel had never been an artist and so did not feel the same way.

The eight or nine group shows Jayne had been a part of before meeting Laurent, most of them taking place while she was still an undergraduate, had attracted few people other than the artists' parents and roommates and the people the artists were having sex with. At twenty-two, then at twenty-three and twenty-four, her college diploma still in its envelope and buried in a desk drawer, how she spent the bulk of her days had less and less to do with boar's-hair brushes or charcoal pencils or tubes of acrylic or the more precious, eternal oils. Her bedroom was hardly bigger than a hall closet; there was no space for her easel, and she had to resort to taping unstretched canvases to the wall. Or else she painted on heavy butcher paper, also taping it to the wall next to her room's one drafty window.

Since college, she had winnowed down the contents of her heavy, paint-encrusted metal chest of art supplies, everything inside once as important and intimate to her as the contents of her wallet. Some of her brushes and cheaper paints, the acrylics and watercolors, she sent to her parents' house in southern California or sold to former classmates, but she held on to the best brushes, her charcoals and oil paints, and a few of her smaller sketchbooks, keeping them in a tiered red plastic case beneath her desk. During the weeks when she did less work than she expected to, she could still hear the smug voice of a star classmate, a guy nicknamed Pepper who had gotten into Yale's M.F.A. program in painting on his first try: "If you have time to make excuses, you have time to do your work."

She had not applied to M.F.A. programs, doubting that she was ready to compete with applicants as good as Pepper, and if she had gotten in, she'd have had to take on more student loans. Instead, she found what turned out to be an exhausting job as a paralegal near the same campus where she had so recently been a student greedy for the pleasures of adulthood. Some of her classmates had to take temping jobs after graduation, but those positions seemed almost enviable after the paralegal position took over her life. She worked overtime nearly every week, and one of the lawyers thought nothing of calling her after hours and bombarding her with requests and complaints.

After two years of sixty-hour weeks, she moved to New York to try to find a job as a gallery assistant and to live with Liesel, who had begun her third year of law school. By then Jayne had trouble imagining her work hanging on the walls of some acquisitive stranger's home, or in the galleries all over Manhattan where for a year she'd fruitlessly applied for jobs. Imagining her work on someone else's walls had once been almost as effortless as putting on her shoes. Her one real commitment after college was to getting by, to sending out, even in the leanest months, the payment due on her student loans; this made her feel respectable when other facts of her life did not: the wretched frustration over a lost subway card recently reloaded; the muffins and fresh fruit stolen from hotel conference rooms where she was meeting an out-of-town friend; the neighbor's Halloween card with ten dollars inside, sent by an Aunt Ginny in Salt Lake City and mistakenly put in Jayne's mailbox, which she had kept.

An hour after Liesel's call, Jayne dutifully appeared at Vie Bohème, her friend already there, looking very pretty but anxious in a black-

and-white sleeveless dress she had bought especially for the opening. If Liesel's new crush, Bernard Ferriss, a painter from Boston who had moved to Brooklyn a year earlier, ignored her, Jayne would be surprised, though he might tease her too—the gallery's binary decor matched her dress exactly, something he couldn't fail to notice. Jayne could see this ruining the night for Liesel, who was very sensitive, especially around men she was attracted to. The walls were white, the cement floors lacquered to a hard, bright sheen, and black ceramic vases of stark, velvety calla lilies had been arranged on tables stationed throughout the long, narrow space. Light fixtures that wouldn't have been out of place in an oil-spattered garage dangled from the ceiling. Also on display was the compulsory crop of unfriendly red-lipsticked women and skinny men with nicotine-stained teeth, their laughter erupting every minute or two in jittery gales.

Some of the paintings were so good that Jayne wondered, as she almost never did, whether she would have bought one if she'd had the money. The four paintings she liked most were photorealist oils of handsome college-age boys, each canvas three by three feet. The portraits turned out to be Bernard's, a new series she hadn't seen when she'd searched online for his work after Liesel mentioned meeting him through Bernard's cousin, who was one of her law school friends. But it was Laurent who ended up being the most memorable sight in the gallery. She knew as soon as she saw him that he had to be one of the owners. He looked relaxed and calm among the people who stood near him, a few glancing at the paintings mounted at even intervals before them. His face did not shine; his shoes didn't pinch; his soft gray suit and loose cotton shirt, its mint green the same color as the ice cream Jayne had liked most as a girl, had likely been tailored precisely to his measurements. It seemed as if he believed he had nothing to prove to anyone, though of course he did—it was his taste, after all, that he was selling, his idea of what good, possibly great, art was.

She kept an eye on him, tracking his movements across the half-filled room; after her third or fourth furtive glance, she found him staring back at her. It was November and rainy, but his skin glowed as if he had recently returned from a beach vacation. He was beautiful to her shy, starved gaze. She glanced behind her to see if he was looking at someone else, but his eyes were still on her when she turned around again.

A week later, after their first night together, he spoke the words *coup de foudre*, his breath warm against her ear.

She couldn't meet his eyes. Love at first sight was a fantasy she had tried to stop believing in during college, when the boys she thought might like her too were as likely as not to be more interested in her roommates or each other or their professors. "You're being silly," she said softly.

She felt guilty too; she had not yet told Colin that they were through. On the surface, she knew he seemed a better match for her; Colin was only a year older than she, American, a Manhattan resident. He was a CPA and liked his job most of the time, although some of his firm's wealthy private clients did get on his nerves, and Jayne's too, when they interfered with her and Colin's plans to see each other. He played basketball two nights a week and tennis every other Saturday morning with a college friend who lived off a trust fund, which Colin did not appear to envy. Sometimes she admired this; at other times his broadmindedness about his rich friends irritated her, as did his uncritical love for New York, which seemed at times to verge on idolatry. ("The traffic, the noise, all the crowds," she'd grumble. "Well, it's New York," he'd say. "You have to pay to live here. But everything you need is only a block or two away. How could you not love that?")

Still, his optimism was also one of the things she found most endearing about him, along with his sweet tooth, bigger than her own, which was a first for a boyfriend; also, the fact that he took stand-up classes at a comedy club near his apartment. He was always trying jokes on her, some of them so awful (*Did you hear about the blind horticulturalist? She got arrested at a funeral for trying to deadhead all the bouquets!*) she found herself laughing harder at the whoppers than at the good ones. She admired too his habit of visiting used bookstores, where he looked for the scruffy old biographies and novels that he kept in a bookcase in the dusty living room of his apartment on East Twelfth Street, which he shared with another friend from college, this one without a trust fund. A first edition of *Catch-22* was the book he valued most, one he kept intending to reread, but it was Jayne who did, on the sly at the shoe boutique when her boss wasn't there.

After they'd been together for three months, Colin gave her two books that she'd had on her to-read list for years, *Anna Karenina* and *Endless Love*. ("*Endless Love!*" cried Melissa when Jayne told her about the gift. "That book broke my heart. Colin must be in love with you. But what's he trying to say? It didn't end so well for David and Jade. Or for Anna.") One thing he hadn't said was that he loved her. She hadn't said it yet either, but the week before she met Laurent, Colin had talked about introducing her to his parents when they would be in town over New Year's.

Melissa and Liesel thought Colin was good-looking and sweet, and if he made her happy, this was what mattered most, but didn't it bother her that he wasn't interested in going to art galleries with her? He might tolerate museums, but wasn't this true of most of the people she knew?

She didn't mind very much because she didn't go to galleries as often as she used to. If she hadn't met Laurent, she would have continued dating Colin, even if she wasn't sure he was the man she'd been waiting for. That man seemed to be Laurent.

The sky outside Laurent's bedroom was cloudless, the west-facing window open a few inches, its dark blue curtains parted to let in a breeze tinged with cold humidity from the nearby river. She would be late for work but didn't care, her heart buoyed by this defiance of a rule she had always observed without question. They were still in bed, the mattress smaller than she'd expected, but Laurent was subletting an acquaintance's apartment and had explained unprompted that he hadn't bought a bigger bed for his brief stay in New York because there was no space to store the owner's. A queen would also have crowded the room more than it already was. That he worried about this at all touched her.

"I'm not being silly," he said, kissing her bare shoulder. "Only honest. I must be one of many men who have told you they are crazy about you, un vrai coup de foudre, Jayne."

She shook her head, lacing her fingers with his. "No, no one I've gone out with before you spoke French, at least not very well."

His laughter was subdued. "Whatever language they spoke, some of them must have said the same thing."

"Wouldn't you like to know?" she said, smiling. His unshaven cheek scratched her as he kissed her shoulder again. In his hair were the commingled scents of a grassy cologne and smoke from the Gitanes he bought expensively at a tobacconist near Grand Central ("They must be fresh, or I cannot smoke them," he'd told her. "They are not always so good where I buy them in New York. In Paris, they are never stale."), an addicting masculine perfume.

He already occupied a larger place in her life than she wanted him to, but she wouldn't tell him this, not even in the languorous tones of postcoital flirtation.

"I haven't had that many boyfriends," she said. "Not serious ones, anyway." Maybe it would be smarter to lie, but Laurent would likely sense it if she did.

Men of his pedigree—wealthy, European, sophisticated, quite a bit older but not perversely so, she didn't think—their paths did not often cross her own, except when they came into the boutique where she and her Florentine boss, a woman close to Laurent's age, sold Italian shoes marked up by three times their wholesale price. Men like Laurent invariably were accompanied by girlfriends or wives. They might smile and look her over when their wives' backs were turned, but they did not do more than this. If they had come back later to ask for her number, she would have been suspicious. She did not need a married man in her life with his guilty conscience, or worse, his rich man's sense of entitlement. She hoped Laurent wasn't married. He had told her over their first dinner together at a restaurant in Midtown— no prices on the menu and a wine list nearly an inch thick—that he was divorced and had been for years. She'd believed him, but later, riding in a taxi back to her apartment after declining his invitation to go home with him (on their second date a few nights later, she did not refuse), she realized that it would not be difficult for him to lie about his marital status, his wife conveniently in Paris, leaving him free to seduce girls their children's age in New York.

The night of Vie Bohème's opening, however, Laurent was not with any woman—wife, mistress, or worshipful, pretty assistant— that she could see, and he eventually made his way over to where she and Liesel stood talking to Bernard, Laurent touching Jayne's shoulder lightly from behind. She nearly upended her champagne glass when she turned and saw that it was he, the beautiful man from the other side of the gallery, her first flustered thought that he wanted her to make room for him to pass.

"No," he said, taking her elbow. "Don't move. I wondered if you would like more champagne." He nodded toward the half-empty flute in her hand. "Are you enjoying it?"

"It's so good," Liesel interrupted. "What kind is it?"

Jayne thought that her friend was already a little drunk. The champagne bottle's telltale orange label was clearly visible.

"It is Veuve Clicquot," said Laurent. "I will tell the *maître de cave* at the vineyard that you like it. We are friends."

"Really?" said Liesel. "You know him? I hope he gave you a good deal."

Laurent chuckled. "Oh, no. He doesn't need to. His champagne sells itself."

Jayne glanced at Bernard, blond, tall, remote. He did not appear to be listening; he was staring beyond Liesel's shoulder, a look of studied blankness on his handsome stubbled face.

"I'd better not have any more," said Jayne to Laurent. "But thank you." The thought that this man was too old for her arrived and was turned away. "I get a headache if I have more than one glass."

"Ah, all right," said Laurent. "We have Perrier if you would like it instead. No one will notice if you switch."

(The next morning, when Jayne called to rehash the party with Liesel, her friend would say, a little jealous but also genuinely irritated by Laurent's presumption, "Why should he or anyone else have cared if you didn't want to drink? It's not like we're in high school." And in the next breath, "Do you really want to go out with that guy instead of Colin? At least Colin was born in the same decade as you.")

"No, that's okay," said Jayne. "I'll just stick with this one glass."

"Stick with this?" he said. "American expressions are so funny. Mind your own, what do you say, beehive? That's the one I like best."

"Beeswax," she said, laughing. "I don't think I've heard that one since third grade."

"I read it somewhere," he said. "I had to look it up. In France we say 'Occupe-toi de tes oignons.'"

"Mind your own onions," she said.

He nodded. "Alors, vous parlez français."

"Un peu, c'est tout," she said.

He smiled, his eyes still pinning her. "Only a little? Vous mentez, c'est mon soupçon."

She didn't think she was lying, not exactly, but before she could decide how to reply, he took her hand and at last introduced himself as one of the gallery owners, he and his partner both from Paris. He shook Liesel's hand, bowing slightly over it, and complimented her on her good taste. Liesel looked uncertain. "These paintings," said Laurent. He pointed at the college boys on the wall. "Aren't they astonishing? Bernard is very talented, yes?"

"Oh my god, he's amazing," cried Liesel.

At her side, Bernard reddened but looked flattered. "Thanks," he said. "I think I like them too."

"Good," said Laurent. "Because they are extraordinary."

"I agree," said Jayne. Bernard's work was very good, but it annoyed her that he kept looking around while she and Liesel tried to talk to him, searching for someone more important to ingratiate himself with. She also sensed that he had no real interest in Liesel. He would sleep with her and let her buy him dinner from time to time, but Jayne doubted that he would offer Liesel the commitment her friend was hoping for. She was being grouchy, Jayne supposed, and Liesel would have said that Jayne was jealous because Bernard was in the show, and she was not. Probably she was jealous, but this didn't negate the fact that he was about as charming as a stubbed toe.

They were interrupted by a hovering couple that Jayne thought she recognized from another opening a year or so earlier. They were art collectors, not penniless gallery rats there for the free wine and artisan cheese; the woman was a highlighted blonde in a short orange dress; the man, his baldness partially hidden under a golf cap, wore a gray cashmere sweater and black wool pants. Each kissed Laurent on both cheeks before leading him to another corner of the gallery, the whole space now crowded, the air having grown warmer and heavier with laughter and heightened conversation in the last quarter hour.

Laurent circled back to Jayne an hour later when she was on the verge of slinking home to eat cereal alone in the kitchen, her room-mate already out for the night with her classmates, as Kelsey often was on Fridays. In their apartment with its mice in the walls and the noisy upstairs neighbors, Jayne would stand with her cereal bowl and stare out the window at the faded brick building across the street, replaying in her head the brief exchange with Laurent.

While Liesel flirted and leaned as close to Bernard as he allowed, Jayne was wondering if she had the courage to return to Vie Bohème to catch another glimpse of its owner, even if he would know what she was up to, and think her foolish or else easy prey. But I suppose I am, she thought.

Now he was at her side, steering her away from the door. "If you're free," he said, "I'd like to take you to dinner. This Tuesday? Because I read the other day that this is the night when many restaurants serve the freshest fish. You like fish, I hope."

It was Friday now. She worked Tuesday evenings until nine, but already she knew that she would call in sick if neither of the other two part-timers could be convinced to take her shift. She might be fired over this man, but the thought was not so terrible. She'd been thinking of looking for a part-time job that did not require her to stand for hours, even when no one was in the store.

"I do like fish," she said. "I think Tuesday should be okay."

"Is Monday better?" he asked, smiling, she thought, at her hesitation.

Monday would be better. It was one of her nights off. But if she said yes, she might seem too eager.

Still, did it matter? They were adults, even if she didn't often feel like one.

"Monday is probably okay too," she said.

"The fish won't be as fresh," he said. "But we will have steak instead. If you like it."

"I do, but I don't eat it very often."

"Good for you. I don't either. Only four or five times a week."

She blinked. "Four or five times? I'm not sure that's a good—"

"I am, how do you say it? I am kidding you," he said, his eyes crinkling. He had a lot of wrinkles. She had some too, especially when she smiled, which she had been told since childhood by her mother and grandmother to do often because it made every girl a little prettier. Jayne had never heard anyone apply this rule to the boys she knew, and sometimes she had frowned fiercely when ordered to smile.

"Do you remember my name?" she asked. The question exhilarated her. Maybe she was trying to punish him. Why did he think he could tease her?

"Of course I do," he said. "Julie."

This was probably another attempt to tease her, but his face gave nothing away. "No, it's Jayne."

"Ah, even better."

• • •

A few days after she learned that the job at her alma mater had gone to someone else—the news coming in a cowardly letter, the director's name probably signed by her secretary—Laurent suggested that Jayne leave New York with him. It was an easy decision, once she understood that his offer was sincere. He had been encouraging her for several months, within days of their first date, to spend more time making art, and even though she hadn't admitted it to Liesel or Melissa, she had begun to wonder if he was considering putting her in one of Vie Bohème's shows—and if it were in Paris?—she could hardly stand to complete the thought.

There was also her suspicion that she had fallen in love with him. She didn't want to be with anyone else, this much she was sure of. She still cared for Colin and regretted that she had hurt him, but her feelings for the assured, worldly Laurent were stronger. And the job rejection had stung: they had hired a recent graduate, purportedly one with more experience in international programs. She had a hunch that her rival was also a man, which she later discovered was true, the smiling face of the turncoat director flashing through her mind. She wondered what she had done wrong in the series of campus interviews—maybe it was the spilled coffee?—but in calmer moments knew this to be ridiculous. "If it is not for the reasons they stated in the letter," said Laurent, "you will never find out why. Do not waste more time thinking about it."

"I know you're right, but it still bugs me," she said.

"You must learn to live with uncertainty."

"Or else I will be miserable." She paused. "Yes, I know." He sounded like her father, but she didn't tell him this.

"Six weeks will give you enough time to prepare, I hope," he said.

A moment later he added, "Please understand that I am not proposing marriage. But I do not want you to bring home other men. You are with me, yes?"

"I am," she said, surprised. "I wouldn't think of bringing home another man. I'm not like that."

He held her gaze, trying to suppress a smile. "You say that now, but it isn't impossible that you will change your mind. Beautiful women often change their minds. I have seen it happen more than once."

Did it happen to you with someone else? she wondered, but didn't ask. Did he really think that her desires and allegiances could mutate so quickly? Maybe he thought this of all women. "What about you?" she asked. "Are you going to bring home other women if we're living together?"

Or men? But she didn't think he slept with men.

"No," he said. "No question. But what you do and what I do outside of the apartment, that is not for the other person to worry over. All right?"

"What do you mean?" she asked, staring at him. She felt the first steely hint of a bad headache. "Are you saying that you plan to go out with other women even if you're not bringing them home?"

He shook his head. "No, that is not what I am saying. Maybe it is my English, the way I am trying to express this."

"You speak English just fine," she said. It was dizziness that threatened her, not a headache. She could feel the months they had spent together, she with the warmly embraced belief in their exclusivity, crumbling away. "Tell me what you mean," she said. She wondered who was waiting for him back in Paris. Because now it seemed as if someone was.

He took his time replying, as though he really did need to find the right words. "You are getting upset over nothing," he said gently. "I know I did not say this properly. What I mean is that I do not want you to worry when we are not together. I was once close to a woman who always assumed I was seeing someone else if she could not reach me on the phone or if I had an appointment in the evening for the gallery that went longer than I expected. She was very jealous, and it was a shame, because she had no reason to doubt my feelings for her."

She didn't reply. If he was telling the truth, and he seemed to be, she felt embarrassed for jumping so quickly to the worst conclusion.

"But I will not be a prison master either, Jayne. You are free to come and go as you like. You do not need always to tell me where you are going or who you are seeing."

"Why wouldn't I want to?" she said. "What would I have to hide?

"Nothing, I am assuming, but I am not going to ask for a detailed list of your every move."

"And you'll expect the same from me where you're concerned."

"Yes, and I do not think that is unreasonable. You must not worry about me, Jayne."

How confident was she supposed to feel about this arrangement? How badly, she could hear Liesel asking, a cynical but concerned edge in her voice, did she want a show at Vie Bohème? Then she heard herself say okay and saw him nodding in approval.

"This will be something nice for both of us," he said. "We don't need more reason than this."

"But you do understand that it is a big deal for me to move overseas."

He touched the top of her hand. "Yes, of course."

"You might want me to leave after a week."

"I won't. What you are wondering is, what if you want to leave after a week? You are free to stay for six days or six thousand. As long as you would like to." He paused. "Barring the unexpected. Chaos, I am speaking of. Other than that, it is up to you."

Or Eros, she thought. The two forces did not seem so different to her.

"All right," she said, letting him take her hand and press it to his lips.

"Do not worry that there are other women," he said. "I have never brought up Colin, have I, even though you have told me that he has called you and sent you e-mails?"

"That's true," she said. "But he's not a threat."

His gaze did not waver. She wondered for a second if she was telling the truth and didn't allow herself to blink.

"I know he isn't," Laurent finally said. "That is why I do not ask about him."

She had not intended to for it to happen, but she'd ended up in bed with Colin on the night she broke up with him. She did not tell Laurent, nor did she think he needed to know; it had happened only a few days after their first night together, and they hadn't made any commitments to each other yet. On the valedictory night with Colin, she was morose and moody; he kept asking what was wrong until she confessed that she wanted to see other people. Hearing this, he sat up suddenly in bed, a stricken look on his face with its dark smear of whiskers. His pale chest rose and fell erratically as he stared at her, and she had the urge to hide her face against his shoulder but knew it was selfish to try to draw comfort from the person she was hurting. She could not meet his eyes and rose from his bed, groping for her clothes, saying lamely that she was sorry and she understood if he would not want to talk to her again, but he shook his head.

"Maybe we should just take a little time off?" he asked. "What if we talk again in a few days?"

"Colin," she said quietly. "I think I need more than a few days."

"I know that my work cuts into our time together. And that I probably like sports too much. I used to get in fights with a girl I dated in college about it." He let out a laugh that sounded like a knife scraping a table. "I could play a little less basketball," he said hopefully. "Instead of two nights a week, I could just do one if you wanted me to."

She felt guilt roiling in her chest. Why wouldn't he simply let her go, or else force her out the door, half clothed and contrite? She would have preferred this to his sweet, futile efforts to make her stay. "I don't think you need to—I don't—"

"Let's not decide anything now. Let's talk in a week," he said, his face gray in the dim room; he was trying to smile, but his lips were trembling. She couldn't look at him.

"All right," she said softly. "In a week or so."

What she did not say as she finished dressing in the darkened bedroom with its miniature basketball hoop on the back of the door, her eyes on his moon-white, mournful feet, was that she had already met someone else, and this man was so at ease with himself, so thoroughly charming and in command each time she'd been out with him. Colin often told her to decide what they should do when they went out, and if she insisted that he choose a restaurant, they sometimes spent an hour texting back and forth before they ended up in one of the same three places they always went to because they were both half starved by the time they finally made up their minds. Laurent also knew how to make money and spend it luxuriously; he knew to put his arm around her and pull her close, as if sheltering her from splashing cars or strong winds, as they walked from the cab into the restaurant and later when he summoned another cab after dinner. He reached for her hand across the table while they waited for their server to appear, and again as they waited for dessert, something Colin had never thought to do, or had been too shy to do.

There was also the fact that being in bed with Laurent was like riding a boat through a storm—she wanted alternately to hold on and be tossed into the waves. Afterward, it felt as if she'd been washed ashore, naked and dazed, mutely euphoric.

CHAPTER 3

No One is an Island

I n the year before Jayne met Laurent and moved to Paris, she experienced a number of more or less commonplace events that, like new neighbors who incrementally grew more intrusive and obnoxious, began to encroach on her peace of mind in a way that she realized might before long become unendurable.

Her anxiety flooded out in a feverish verbal stream one evening in an e-mail to her sister. Jayne had just returned home from seeing a movie with Colin, one with a profane talking bear, a movie so brainless and obvious that she had left after the first hour and walked home alone while Colin stayed in the Union Square cinema to watch the remaining hour. Her sister saw a lot of movies too and worked as the assistant to the owner and CEO of a small record company that seemed always to be wobbling on the edge of bankruptcy, which was due in part to the owner's habit of signing musicians who made little money but ran up large bills for producers, engineers, and studio time.

What if I died tomorrow? Jayne wrote to her sister. *What if you died tomorrow? What do you think people would say about you? What would you want them to say about you? Why am I living in a city I can't afford and spending large portions of my never-to-be-repeated life on dumb jobs I can barely get out of bed for in the morning? I came to New York to be an artist, and all I've done so far is watch other people do it instead.*

Instead of answering the e-mail, her sister called and left a long-winded message, which Jayne didn't listen to until the next morning because she was up late arguing with Colin about why he hadn't left the stupid bear movie too and had let her go home alone to write furious e-mails to Stephanie. "Existential crisis" was the term her younger sister repeated three times in her rambling voice mail. "Cliché" was another, though Stephanie laughed a little as she said it, apologizing for making light of Jayne's bad mood.

Some of the events that Jayne connected to her increasing sense of disquiet:

— One Saturday afternoon in late September, she'd gone with Kelsey to a free lecture at the New School titled "The Ideal and the Idealized: Sex and Love in the Age of Instant Celebrity," which was held in an austere, overwarm auditorium. Dozens of people huddled in chairs with poor lower-back support and peered warily at the speaker, a media critic known for her brilliant, pitiless screeds on contemporary sexuality and societal selfishness, and who spoke with frightening fluency about Facebook, pornography, and personal ads. *More people than ever before are spending their lives alone, whether they want to or not. Despite our supposed connectivity, we have never been more miserable and closed off . . . The obscene number of choices, of immediately available pleasures, have made us, paradoxically, restless and dissatisfied!* Jayne left feeling as if she'd sustained repeated blows to the back of her head. Though much of what the speaker said was old news, and spoken in a tone of practiced gravity, her words nonetheless burrowed into Jayne's consciousness like a poisonous tick that could not be dislodged. She went home and sulked in her light-deprived bedroom, her neighbors upstairs pounding around as if practicing for a *Stomp* audition. At frequent intervals, she heard them shouting with laughter. Feeling murderous, she made herself leave the apartment again for a yoga class. She would be late, but if she didn't go, she knew that she would march upstairs and scream at her neighbors; both Drew and José were twenty-six, but they resided within what seemed an interminable adolescence. They were probably already drunk and would laugh in her scowling face before suggesting she join them in their sock- and trash-strewn apartment for a threesome. They had done this before, to both her and her roommate, and to the overly talkative, middle-aged widow who lived next door to them.

— A nuclear power plant had melted down, disastrously contaminating the nearby ocean and the land on which it sat. More proof that the world could not possibly be an endlessly renewing and self-mending resource.

— Close friends from high school and college had gotten married or announced their plans to marry suitors who, in a few cases, they had known less than a year. Jayne had other friends who were already married, one of them within eight months going through a rancorous divorce, but the more recent weddings and engagements seemed more serious, more adult and deliberate. Some of these friends had also earned enough money as lawyers, software engineers, or café owners to buy not one but two homes in desirable cities and oceanside resorts. She didn't think it was envy she felt so much as self-lacerating regret at having neither the kinds of interests nor the ambition to earn for herself what these friends already had.

— Jayne's father tripped on a rolled-up newspaper in the driveway, fell on his face, and broke one of his front teeth. The newspaper was there every morning, but on this day, Mr. Marks was carrying a big watermelon that he'd grown in his garden, one he planned to share with his coworkers, and did not see the paper because the watermelon was blocking his view of his feet. Up until then, her father had seemed to Jayne all but invincible, even after her mother admitted to deep-rooted feelings of restlessness, which she finally confessed to over the winter, when Jayne was newly in the thrall of her romance with Laurent and more insulated from unhappiness than usual.

"We're not getting a divorce," Jayne's mother had assured her. "But after so many years together, you have to expect that one of us is going to want a change of scenery from time to time."

"What does that mean?" asked Jayne.

"I don't know yet," said her mother. "We'll see, I guess."

"That's not very reassuring," said Jayne.

Her mother paused. "No, I suppose it's not."

Her father's injury, his clumsiness, his ensuing depression, all seemed to underscore the illusoriness of his life's permanence, of her mother's, of Jayne's and her sister's lives too. About his wife's midlife crisis, as he called it, his voice tinged with irony, he would not say very much to Jayne or her sister. "Your mother doesn't want you girls in the middle. We're keeping it between her and me," he said, dogged and embarrassed. "And our therapist. It shouldn't be a surprise that we've hit some potholes on the road."

Jayne was surprised to hear that they were seeing a therapist. "Mom got you to go?" she asked.

Her father's laughter was caustic. "No, Mom did not. I got her to go."

—   Most of an island in the South Pacific, inhabited for centuries by a small, peaceable population of fishermen and their families, had been submerged by rising water levels. The islanders were forced to flee to New Zealand, whose officials did not want to offer them asylum because they had troubles of their own—strained public aid and health-care systems, general agrarian woes. Jayne had understood this, but still thought it unkind and unfair. Why was a country as big as New Zealand, at least compared to the beleaguered, submerged neighboring island, being so ungenerous? Surely there had to be some mercy in the world. It was Australia that eventually agreed to help the islanders, but they were vague about how long they would be able to offer these homeless people food and shelter, something that Jayne woke up very early in the morning worrying about more than once, unsure why these strangers were so often in her thoughts when plenty of people were suffering within shouting distance of where she was lying in her bed, with its twisted sheets and coffee-stained comforter.

She could foresee bigger, more populated islands flooding, their bewildered inhabitants fleeing for their lives. No one was mentioning the other living creatures on these islands either. Who knew where they were going, other than to a watery grave?

• • •

PARIS, HE SAID **37**

Other indignities small and medium stepped out from the consoling camouflage of her daily routines and rituals. Strangers dialed her phone and yelled at her when she told them they had the wrong number. People let doors close in her face as she tried to enter stores, restaurants, and post offices on their heels. If she made a disapproving sound, the offender might turn on her and tell her to get a life, furious to be called out on a thoughtless act. If all she had to worry about was someone forgetting to hold the door for her, she was pretty damn lucky!

"You live in New York," her father said when she complained to him over the phone. "What do you expect? Rose bouquets and parades in your honor?"

"Common decency would be nice," she said.

"Common decency," he repeated. "What exactly is that, Jayne?"

It was in the month before she left for Paris, long after the e-mail to her sister and the breakup with Colin, that she received alarming news more personal than the nuclear meltdown or the drowning island. She had known it would come one day, but nonetheless she wasn't prepared for it.

Pepper, the college classmate who had gone on to Yale's M.F.A. program, had been hired to teach painting classes full-time at the San Francisco Art Institute. This fact she supposed she could live with, set it aside, and move on mostly unencumbered, but the next line of his updated biography revealed (he had a Wikipedia page already, another blow) that one of his paintings had just been chosen for the Venice Biennale. Who had plucked him from oblivion? One of his Yale instructors? Someone he had met at an artists' colony? Or possibly, more distressing still, one of their undergraduate instructors?

"But you're going to Paris," said Liesel over drinks the day after Jayne had made these discoveries. They were at KGB, where they had once gone every Thursday night for two beers each—three if it had been a difficult week—when Liesel was finishing law school and Jayne had first moved north from D.C. "Fuck Pepper and that Venice show. Does he really still call himself that? It's such a stupid nickname."

"I don't know," said Jayne. The bar's red lights made Liesel look both sexy and a little demonic. "His Wikipedia page lists his real name. Gary Lentz."

"He has a Wikipedia page?" said Liesel, doubtful. "I want a Wikipedia page."

"I'll start one for you if you start one for me."

Liesel shook her head. "You have to be famous. Or sort of famous. Wikipedia has gatekeepers."

"We'll get one," said Jayne. "If he's got one, I'm getting one."

Liesel glanced at a black-haired guy with a fussy goatee on the other side of the bar. She had been gazing at him experimentally for the past hour, and he had started to return her looks. "That's the spirit," she said to Jayne, her eyes still on the goateed man. "Nothing like a little old-fashioned jealousy to get you off your ass and into the future."

CHAPTER 4

City of Cities

*L*aurent's apartment on rue du Général-Foy, a few blocks from one of the city's busiest train stations, Gare Saint-Lazare, took up the entire third floor of his building, which in New York would have been considered the fourth floor. Jayne was struck by his apartment's spotless opulence when he unlocked the heavy oak door that opened onto the landing and led her inside for the first time. The rooms were bright and startlingly spacious, accustomed as she was to New York's claustrophobic domesticity; most of the apartments she knew there were so cramped and dim that even her friends' feline companions looked crowded in their little velour beds, let alone the bigger-than-purse-size dogs that a couple of her friends kept as roommates. Her friends Daphne and Kirstie had two border collies squeezed into their six-hundred-square-foot condo, and also had a baby on the way. Jayne had no idea how they would all survive in the aftermath of the baby's arrival.

She especially admired the tall French windows in Laurent's home, which she would soon be in the habit of opening in the mornings to let in the day's freshest air. He'd bought the area rugs on the hardwood floors in Ankara, he told her with some pride, while on a long-ago vacation with his ex-wife and their children,

Frédéric and Jeanne-Lucie, who were both around the same age as Jayne and already married. The thick wool was very soft, the pile almost pillowy beneath her feet. On the walls were oil paintings of urban landscapes, several pastoral watercolors, and figurative drawings, along with a half dozen looking glasses in gilded or carved wood frames. Laurent kept houseplants too, African violets and pink and white orchids in porcelain pots—had his daughter Jeanne-Lucie cared for them in his absence? Or some other woman who might one day step toward Jayne from among the strangers on the street to say that she was Laurent's friend, her emphasis on the word making it clear that she was something else entirely? The sofa and upholstered chocolate brown armchairs in the living room— the *salon*, she had been instructed to call it during her profligate college semester in Strasbourg (her Visa bills so alarming during those months that her father canceled the card)—were large, over-stuffed, and modern. The wide sage-green sofa looked as inviting as a bed.

"Do you think you will be comfortable here?" he asked, watching her stare at everything with what she was sure was an awed, covetous gaze.

"Yes," she said, her voice breaking. "Thank you for asking me to come."

"Oui, chérie. C'est mon très grand plaisir." He smiled. The fine bones of his face moved her so deeply that she had to turn away.

Included with the apartment were a *chambre de bonne*, a small room two flights up on the building's top floor, where a domestic servant had once lived, and a shared bathroom down the hall. Laurent rented these tiny quarters to a student at the École Normale de Musique named Philippe, a dark-haired cellist, pale and tall. His parents lived in Lille and sent care packages every few weeks, filled with sweets and other small gifts their son seemed rarely to want and often left in the hall for the two other students and the retired bachelor postal worker who inhabited the floor's other three maid's rooms. Laurent had laughed quietly, and with a trace of sadness, as he told Jayne about the chocolate bars, the pots of raspberry jam, and the lemon-scented hand soaps that Philippe placed in the corridor for his neighbors. "His parents must not know that he does this," said Laurent. "If they did, they would probably be upset and might stop paying his rent. I'd be hurt by this too if he were my son."

"If they stopped paying, you'd evict him, wouldn't you?" she asked.

"It isn't likely they will find out. I don't think they visit."

"Maybe that's why he throws out their packages."

"Maybe, but it might also be that he has told them not to come," he said.

Jayne rarely saw Philippe or the building's other occupants after she had settled in, her suitcases emptied of the neatly rolled layers of clothes and plastic-bagged shoes. By container ship—its transatlantic passage, Laurent warned her, slow as a sleepless night (une nuit blanche, she remembered from a distant French class)—she had sent two trunks from New York, books and more shoes, some scarves and coats, though Laurent had said that they could shop for new clothes when she arrived. He had never stated it directly, but she knew that he had family money.

What he had told her was that his parents were in their late thirties when he was born, and died within seven months of each other when he was thirty-five. They had been the proprietors of a vineyard in the Gevrey-Chambertin collective of winemakers, an enclave not far from Dijon; the business was now in the hands of Laurent's younger sister Camille and her husband Michel, Laurent having announced at nineteen that he wanted to make art instead of wine. He had not succeeded as an artist though, and had stopped painting with any seriousness at twenty-five. Instead, he had decided to try selling the work of other artists, and at this, he'd been successful.

Much of the art Laurent sold in the Vie Bohème on rue du Louvre consisted of narrative paintings, lithographs, and figurative pastels and charcoals. He and his partner André also sold small-scale sculpture, most of it in marble or bronze, which reminded Jayne of Rodin and Brancusi. It was all very skillful, often arresting and beautiful, though Laurent had hesitated when she compared several of the artists he represented to more famous ones.

"Not everything is derivative," he insisted. "Some things are original."

She nodded, but on the whole, the art he sold did seem derivative to her, though she would never say this outright.

"I know what you are thinking," Laurent said before Jayne could reply. "That it has all been done, but this is not true. Each painting is new because each person will paint in a different way, even if some of the paintings look alike. You might make a sculpture or another work that looks like someone else's, but it is not someone else's. It is yours because you do not have the same process as the other artist."

She couldn't really say that he was wrong. His was only another way of seeing, albeit a convenient one, considering that he earned a comfortable living selling art that sometimes resembled other, more celebrated art. He had painted this way too; the few canvases of his own that he eventually showed her reminded her of Monet's, technically sound but stiffer than the most famous impressionist's as if the master had asked his students to copy one of his cathedral or Giverny paintings while looking at its image in the mirror instead of head-on. Depth, something spiritual? Jayne wasn't sure, but some vital element was missing.

"Love," said Laurent. "I did not love what I was painting the way it needed to be loved. I did not have the heart yet. It will sound strange, but this is true. I kept worrying that I would not be good enough, and so," he said with a self-deprecating look, "I was not. I needed to love the experience of painting more—the way the brush felt in my hand, the scent of the paints. And myself too, maybe, but perhaps you will help me with this."

"Do you want to start painting again?" she asked.

He shook his head. "No, no. I want only to learn to be a better lover."

She smiled. "I'm serious, Laurent."

"So am I," he said.

Two days after he'd met her at Roissy, on the other side of the sliding glass doors that separated orderly, martial customs from the anarchic rest of the world, the weather was so clear and mild that her happiness felt almost unbearable: seventy-five degrees, a few cotton-ball clouds, the sky a deep, luminous blue. Laurent went in to the gallery for a few hours, and Jayne left the apartment and walked the few miles east to Sacré Coeur. She was feeling the pressure exerted by the sketchbooks, two canvases, and tubes of oil paint she'd bought the previous evening at a store on rue Bonaparte, where she'd seen a few students from the École Nationale Supérieure des Beaux-Arts buying their supplies too. She had entered the shop almost dumbstruck with pleasure at being in the city where an art history professor who claimed Picasso as a distant relation had argued that the Western paradigm of beauty had been defined. Jayne remembered taking frantic notes during his lectures on early Impressionism, her hand cramping painfully near the end. The peppery mix of scents in the store, the pigments and gessoed canvases, the oil crayons and paints and drawing tablets—the sight and smell of so many colors and textures and possibilities continued to exhilarate her, no matter how many times she'd stood staring covetously at overflowing rows and racks of art supplies.

The boy at the register had a thin, impassive face but spoke in a friendly mutter. His blue eyes grazed hers as he rang up her purchases, and finally he smiled a little as he took her credit card. His nails were painted metallic silver, and two studded black leather bracelets encircled each wrist. On one hand was a tattoo of a stoplight.

"C'est mignon," she said, pointing at the tattoo. She was so happy her voice nearly shook. "Très bon, votre feu rouge."

She sounded like a simpleton. *It's cute. Very nice, your stoplight.* She winced inwardly.

"Merci," he said, glancing up at her again. He had something in his mouth that seemed to make it hard for him to speak—a new tongue stud, or maybe a huge wad of gum? Not chewing tobacco. Did the French use that foul stuff? She hoped not.

She wished she had kept her own mouth closed, but she'd wanted so badly for him to know that she was like him, that she was an artist too. She had also tried, she realized now, to look like a student; she'd pulled her dark brown hair into two long pigtails and was wearing a tight black T-shirt and a short olive-green skirt. In the mirror behind the register, she could see that her face was still flushed from the hot, humid walk across the Seine. When she was done with her errand, Laurent planned to take her to dinner a few blocks away at a café that he'd started going to many years earlier, when he was trying to be an artist too.

Now that she no longer had to answer to an alarm clock Monday through Saturday, to the deadening demands of nine-to-five and, on some evenings, six-to-nine, she intended to draw and paint every day for at least three or four hours, no excuses permitted short of a coma or full-body traction. Apart from the hours she spent working at Vie Bohème and exercising her artist's eye and hands, she could do whatever she wanted—a fact her sister had grumbled over in a recent e-mail: *Why are you so lucky? Why am I the one who's stuck with the insane boss who bitches every single day that he should never have sold his inventory to iTunes because those bastards are making all the money?* "There should be laws . . . there should be a revolution! Where have all the revolutionaries gone?"

When Jayne told Laurent she felt guilty, he said, "If it were your sister instead of you, do you think she would have turned down an offer to be here so that you would not be upset?"

"No, I know you're right. But I'm not used to having something that other people are jealous of. It takes a little getting used to." She paused, smiling. "Not that I won't get used to it."

He smiled too. "Oh, I am thinking that you will. It is not so hard."

At dinner, her bag of art supplies hidden beneath the white-cloth-cloaked table, Jayne ordered the poached sole, but when their food arrived, she realized that she didn't have much of an appetite; jet lag had descended, her earlier giddiness flattened by fatigue. Laurent was hungry, however, and while she nibbled at her fish, he ate all of his steamed mussels and French fries, the café's signature *plat principal*, and drank a beer served in a gleaming Pilsner glass.

He watched her fight to keep her eyes open. The café was loud; they had to raise their voices to be heard across the table, but she still had trouble staying alert. Among the tourists and middle-aged couples, four men in dark gray and midnight-blue suits pointed at each other and laughed aggressively at a nearby table, their faces shining with prosperity and confidence.

As he excavated a mussel from its shell, Laurent said, "You have changed your life, Jayne."

She looked at him, her heart pounding. "Yes, I guess I have."

"If you work hard, you will have everything you want," he murmured. "And then we will see who you will become."

"Do you mean if I work hard at my art?"

He nodded. "Yes, of course that is what I mean."

She glanced down at her napkin and was surprised to find herself twisting it in both hands. "You mean you're going to put me in a show?" she blurted.

He nodded. A tiny french fry crumb dotted his chin. She fixated on it, not sure if she should tell him or brush it away herself, but with his unwavering gaze pinning her, she was reluctant to do either.

"Yes, of course," he finally said. "You knew that I would put you in a show before you decided to move here with me."

"I actually didn't know that, Laurent," she said, taken aback. Was he serious? She supposed he was. "I didn't come to Paris because I thought—" She stared at him.

He batted away her words with a dismissive hand. "You had to know, Jayne," he said. "You were counting on it. Some part of you was, and that is just fine." He gestured to the waiter for the check, which arrived on a small black platter instead of inside a leatherette case. Laurent took a few bills from his wallet and settled them on top of the paper.

"I really wasn't," she insisted, her body tense with nervous joy.

"I can see that you are very excited," he said. "But I know you must be very tired too. We will take a taxi home instead of walking back."

She nodded, still stunned.

On the ride back to her new home, she held Laurent's hand tightly and rested her cheek against his shoulder. He smelled so good, even after the cigarette he'd smoked outside the restaurant before summoning a cab; she was used to the harsh smoke now and had grown almost to crave the scent on his clothes and hair. She was so tired, luxuriously at peace for the first time in weeks; she wanted to keep her eyes open, to feel everything that was happening to her, to stare at the golden light reflecting off the ancient stone buildings along the Seine. The Eiffel Tower was glittering in the distance as if fairy dust had been tossed onto it, its lights an undulating cape of gilded, winking flecks. She closed her eyes for a second, and when she opened them again the taxi had pulled up in front of their building on rue du Général-Foy, the street emptied of all its daytime occupants; its nocturnal lighting, soft and a little spooky, reminded Jayne of a set where a vampire film might be shot.

Laurent was gently shaking her awake. "Chérie," he whispered. "You're home now."

Laurent's words from the previous night still dominated Jayne's thoughts as she moved through the crowded, noisy streets to Sacré Coeur, a walk she had planned since long before she stepped off the plane. She peered into the boutique and department store windows on boulevard Haussmann, its sidewalks clogged with tourists, the bulky shopping bags at their sides making it difficult for anyone to pass.

She had not sent an e-mail bursting with the news of Laurent's offer to Liesel or Melissa or to the one art instructor she still kept in touch with, Susan Kraut, whom Jayne had worked with eight years earlier, and had seen again four years after that summer when she passed through Chicago on her way home to Los Angeles from New York. During the long layover she'd arranged between flights, she had taken the train into the city and gone to the gallery on Wells Street where her former instructor was exhibiting new paintings—moody, unpopulated interiors of homes that looked haunted by benevolent ghosts. Jayne had taken an intensive painting class with Susan, having begged her parents for the money to enroll in the three-week summer course. During those rainy, hot June days at the school that sat like a sullen gray fortress on the western periphery of Grant Park, Susan taught her to work with light and focused more on composition than any of Jayne's previous instructors. The portraits Jayne first began to paint in the class, most in color, the somber interiors, the more chromatically vibrant exterior landscapes, formed the core of her portfolio. She had been working with these subjects and the themes of absence, longing, and dream-like loneliness ever since.

When she showed some of these early paintings to Laurent, the few she'd hung on the walls of her apartment in New York, he looked at them closely for what felt like a long time. Her stomach tensed as she watched his face for some hint of his thoughts. Finally he said, "You were twenty-one when you painted these, Jayne? Why have these not already been sold? Because they would sell."

Nothing anyone had ever said to her had given her more pleasure than those words. Now, her legs moving her toward the domed Parisian cathedral a couple of miles from her new home, she realized that she should have felt more confident that Laurent intended to release her work into the world.

But on that evening, as they stood peering at her paintings together, she hadn't believed him. "I don't know," she'd said. "There's a lot of competition. You know what New York's like."

"There are galleries in other places, Jayne. You don't have to start here."

"I didn't. I started in D.C."

He gave her a droll look. "Do not say you are like me, Jayne, that you do not have enough talent. It is clear to me that you do. But you need to keep working and seeing what comes to you. Paris will have a good effect, I am sure. In France we like to think we have the answers to all the most important questions."

She laughed. "Such as?"

"Such as, what is nineteen o'clock? Such as, why do tourists stop suddenly in the middle of the sidewalk?"

She laughed again. "I already know the answers to those questions."

"So tell me why tourists stop in the middle of the sidewalk."

"Because they've just realized that they've been pickpocketed."

He was laughing now too. "Yes, very good. Exactly."

The streets around the Anvers and Barbès-Rochechouart Metro stops were almost impassable. Throngs of slow-moving women and impatient men rummaged through piles of cheap shirts and plastic-wrapped cosmetics and toiletries on the tables in front of Tati and the other bargain stores that populated the quarter. The massive dome of the sun-bleached stone church loomed above the commercial melée. On the winding gray staircases and terraced lawns, bedraggled parents and young couples huddled together, drinking soda and bottled water bought from North African men who fished the drinks from scuffed blue plastic coolers filled with melting ice.

Sacré Coeur and the merchant-lined streets looked very much as Jayne remembered them when she and her friends had visited nine years earlier. She stood on the plaza in front of the cathedral, watching the curious or the devout disappear through the entrance into the cool, hushed gloom; a sound halfway between a gasp and a sob escaped her throat. A few feet away a middle-aged couple, the man in a Lakers T-shirt, the woman in a baggy green sundress, glanced over at her before quickly averting their eyes.

It was all still there, an immense quilt of bold, fantastical human will: the faded tawny golds and grays of the descending rooftops and scorched chimney pots, the cold steel-blue river with its fabled Left and Right Banks, the towers and steeples and crooked cobblestone streets, bisected by wide, brutish boulevards. As seductive as a mirage, but every slab of stone, every silent or uproarious inch of it, real. She had not returned triumphant as a brilliant painter or a self-made woman whose only worry about money was how to spend it. She was eight years out of college and past her dewiest youth, living off the largesse of a man she had known less than a year, but she had come back to Paris anyway. It was hard to imagine being unhappy here.

CHAPTER 5

Chez Laurent

Mornings in her new home, even four stories above the street, were full of bleating horns and people calling to each other in strident voices, laughter erupting from deliverymen on motorbikes or from students on their way to the nearby lycée, their giggling flirtatious, their cries of feigned adolescent indignation.

"Why does there always have to be so much noise in the morning? It's not as bad as New York, but it's louder than I expected," Jayne complained groggily while Laurent put on the gray pants and the blue pullover he kept on a hook on the back of the bedroom door; he always managed somehow to look well dressed, even in his casual clothes. Each morning around eight he dressed and disappeared for a half hour to buy a copy of Le Figaro and drink an espresso at the tabac he favored on rue du Rocher. "It's always men shouting too," she said. "Never women."

"Women do not shout in France," said Laurent, smiling down at her as he pulled open the shutters that they closed each night at dusk. Their bedroom windows overlooked the street; the windows in the living room faced the courtyard, where it was quieter. She read in there on some afternoons, stretched out on the sage-green canapé with its unyielding plum pillows that smelled of cinnamon.

("Couch?" Laurent had said when she'd first used that word. "How strange it sounds. Like someone clearing his throat! *Canapé*, Jayne, use that word instead.") She sometimes carried her laptop into the living room ("The *salon!*") and answered e-mails after breakfast, or she wrote in her journal after Laurent had left for his espresso.

"I'm sure that Frenchwomen shout if a man is attacking them," she said.

"Frenchmen are gentlemen," he said. "We do not attack our women."

She raised herself on her elbows, rolling her eyes. "Really? What about Dominique Strauss-Kahn?"

"He is a rare case," he said. "You must get New York out of your head to live fully in Paris."

"And Chicago and L.A. too, for that matter."

"One day we will go to Los Angeles, and you will show me where all the film stars live."

"I don't really know where they live," she said. "You'd have to pay for a tour that would take you to their neighborhoods."

He did not look convinced. "You couldn't take me?"

"I really don't know where their houses are. I told you that my dad's a lawyer and my mom's a high school teacher, didn't I? We don't hang out with movie industry people."

"Yes, I remember."

"My parents live in Pasadena, not Beverly Hills. Their next-door neighbor owns a dry cleaner's. They have a nice house, but it's not a glamorous neighborhood." She hoped they would continue to live in the house far into the future, but if her mother did leave her father, Jayne knew they would likely have to sell it. (When she'd mentioned her worries about her parents' marriage to Laurent, he had hardly blinked. "It is not easy. I was not a success as a husband. I don't think that many men are." "My dad isn't like you at all," she said, not realizing until the words were out how offensive they likely sounded. But Laurent had not looked offended. "I have never thought that he is, and to be frank, I would hope we are not at all alike.")

"I can show you where President Hollande lives," he said.

"Everyone knows where he lives. It's not a secret, is it?"

He laughed. "You are supposed to be impressed."

"You're being silly, and I'm still tired." She lobbed a pillow at him. He dodged it and laughed again, tossing it back onto the bed.

It was the beginning of her third week in Paris, the first official day of summer, and she did not feel at all homesick. No longer having to share a 450-square-foot apartment with walls so thin she could sometimes hear her roommate snoring, no longer having to rely on the wan light that filtered in through their unit's four windows, if the sun was out at all—she did not miss this. She did miss her friends, but even that wasn't so bad. They had e-mail and Skype and texts; she talked to them almost as much now as she had in New York.

The light in Laurent's apartment was the most pure of any place she had lived—not as bright as Pasadena's, but more flattering, softer. Pure was his word, but she thought it fitting. "It is a mood," he had said, "and the most important element of any room, of any work of art too. I knew when I first saw this place that I would buy it. It is not very close to my gallery, but it was too beautiful not to have."

"You raised your children here?"

He shook his head. "Frédéric was living with a friend from the university when I moved in. It was a year or so after the divorce. Jeanne-Lucie lived with her mother and visited me two nights a week. She was only a year away from university too."

The light in the morning was the strongest of the day, flooding in from the northeast-facing rooms until it grew more muted and golden in the early afternoon. Even when the sky was overcast, the pearl-gray and ivory walls still seemed to glow gently. Laurent had hung paintings in every room except the bathroom and the kitchen. "Humidity is very bad if you want your art to last," he said. "And no serious art should ever be hung near the bathtub or the bidet."

"Of course not," she said. "Only art that isn't serious, but in those cases, I suppose you can't really call it art."

He laughed. "No, we call it commerce."

Even if most of the intricate paintings Laurent favored weren't unforgettable—the landscapes, the still lifes of laden spring and autumn tables—there were six scrupulously detailed family portraits (the artist's signature not entirely legible, S. Bau—), four children and their parents, that hung at eye level in the hallway leading from the bedroom to the salon and her cherished canapé, and they were all as good, better, Jayne thought, than any painting of Pepper's.

"We have fairy light in Paris," said Laurent. "La lumière des fées dans la Ville Lumière."

Being here with him really did feel as if she had stepped into a story of enchantment. She had no idea how long it would last, but she tried not to dwell on this. For once in her life, she would live in the elusive present.

At a farewell dinner at Liesel's place, Melissa and Liesel had both asked Jayne what she thought Laurent was getting out of the bargain. Presumably, without much trouble, he could find another pretty girlfriend in Paris, another destitute artist. "You're beautiful, Jayne, and I know he thinks you look like that French actress, Audrey Tattoo or whatever her name is," said Liesel, "but think about it, he'll be supporting you over there. You're sure he won't change his mind after a few weeks?"

"Audrey Tautou," said Jayne. "Not Tattoo."

"You really do see a future with him?" asked Melissa. Most of the time Jayne could count on her to be more tactful than Liesel. In college Melissa had gotten a degree in social work but after graduation had veered off to enroll in culinary school. She'd dropped out after five months to take a human resources job at Chase, where Liesel also worked as a tax attorney. Melissa had once confessed after three large glasses of wine that she'd only slept with two men besides her husband. Liesel had offered her condolences, but Jayne had told Melissa that she shouldn't regret it. If Joe, her husband, was good in bed, she wasn't missing anything. "He is good in bed," said Melissa, momentarily grave. Then she shrieked with laughter. "On my birthday."

"I do see a future with Laurent," Jayne said now. She knew her friends meant well, but she felt as if she were under interrogation. "We're a real couple, if that's what you're asking. As far as I can tell, neither of us is biding our time until someone better comes along."

Shorty, Liesel's cat, a fat black male with white-stockinged legs, loped into the kitchen and began meowing imperiously. They'd already opened a second bottle of wine and were eating carryout spaghetti puttanesca——Liesel had made lemon pasta but added too much salt to the sauce and had to order in Italian. The cat tried to jump onto Melissa's lap, but Liesel shooed him away by threatening him with a spray bottle filled with water.

"You're so mean," cried Melissa. "The poor cat probably has nightmares about that bottle."

"He can handle it," Liesel said flatly. "Otherwise he'd think he's the boss. I got up one morning and found him in my handbag, trying to open my wallet."

"You probably left a doggie bag in there overnight," said Melissa, snorting. "You're still mean."

Jayne looked down at Shorty, who had settled on his haunches next to her feet. He stared up at her, sniffing the air. She had not told Melissa or Liesel about Laurent's insistence that she not worry where he was or what he was doing when he didn't come home on time —her friends would doubtless have read even more into this hedge than she had been willing to let herself do. If the situation turned out to be unlivable, she could always return to New York. If she were a different kind of woman too, she later realized, she would probably have felt grateful for the license to run amok in Paris.

"I know you're a real couple," said Liesel. "But despite the fact you're giving up your whole life here to move to Paris with him, I'd say you're getting more out of the relationship than he is."

"Is it supposed to be quid pro quo?" asked Jayne. "He's not keeping a balance sheet of all he's doing for me, as far as I know. Maybe he is my patron, in a sense—he said he wants me to spend more time making art while I'm there, which is one of the main reasons I'm going—but he's also my boyfriend."

"Good," said Liesel. "Tell the bastard to cough up a show."

"Liesel," said Melissa. She glanced at Jayne. "That's so exciting. I'm really glad he said that."

"Bernard needs someone like that," said Liesel.

"What are you talking about?" said Jayne. "Laurent and his partner already represent him."

"No, no, I mean, he needs someone who'll pay his bills, so he can spend more time painting and less time doing other jobs."

"But he teaches at Pratt now, doesn't he?" asked Melissa. "I thought he was happy about that."

"He is, but it's only part-time. He still has to work a few shifts at the frame shop."

"I thought you weren't seeing Bernard anymore," said Jayne.

Shorty let out a desperate meow and rubbed his face against her shin. She was still eating but reached down to pet him. He started purring, the sound loud and gravelly.

"Shorty, leave Jayne alone," said Liesel. "He knows he's being bad." She bent down and aimed the spray bottle at him again. Shorty only looked at her and blinked his Halloween green eyes, still purring.

"You're a shameless beggar," Jayne scolded softly. He meowed again, more plaintive.

"I don't want to see Bernard anymore," said Liesel, setting the spray bottle next to her wineglass. "But it's not like lots of other men are calling."

"Robby Ortiz, the cute guy down the hall from me you're always giving the eye, asked about you last week," said Melissa. "I told you that."

Liesel shook her head. "He makes a lot less money than I do. Eventually he'd resent me for it. I don't need another Bernard situation."

"Robby would never resent you," said Melissa. "He's so nice."

"He's also twenty-four."

"So? He likes older women."

"He'd hate me for being an old bag after a while too."

"Liesel, you're not an old bag," said Jayne, laughing in a shrill burst. "You're so cynical."

Her friend glanced at her, her expression sheepish. "Actually, I was wondering about Laurent's business partner. Is he single?"

"He was dating someone, but I'm not sure if they're still together," said Jayne. "He also lives in Paris."

"So does your boyfriend. I could move over there too." Liesel glanced at Melissa. "Wouldn't that be cool?"

"You'd leave me here by myself?" said Melissa.

"No, you, Joe, and Josh could move to Paris with me."

"We're not going anywhere," said Melissa, morose. "Probably not until Josh grows up. We have our dog to worry about too."

Jayne thought about the little she was taking with her to France: only clothes, a few sketchbooks and brushes, some of her books. Her three plants, an aloe, a cactus, and a persnickety orchid that Laurent had given her not long after they started seeing each other, she was leaving with her roommate, who promised to water and talk to them.

"No one's going anywhere but you," said Liesel. "Good for you, but you still suck for leaving us."

CHAPTER 6

Beauté, Plaisir

Vie Bohème in Paris had one large showroom that overlooked rue du Louvre, a wide north-south street that led to the Seine and the museum with which it shared its name. The gallery looked much like its black-and-white counterpart in New York, but the floors were hardwood instead of glazed cement, and its showroom had more windows and square footage. It also had a back office with three desks, two black walnut, one black Formica—the two in wood for Laurent and his partner André, the smaller Formica-topped one for the bookkeeper who came in once or twice a week. This was the desk that Jayne used, too.

The gallery also housed a slightly dank WC—she had yet to encounter a French toilet, including the one at Laurent's apartment, that did not have a hint of the swamp about it—and a storeroom to which Laurent, on her inaugural after-hours visit to Vie Bohème, had led her. Without preamble he'd pulled up her skirt and pressed himself upon her with an urgency that reminded her of the first few times of her life, her senior-year high school boyfriend showing the same ardor, barely more than a virgin himself. When it was over, she'd rested her cheek against Laurent's chest and inhaled his earthy smell; she could feel his body's damp heat through the silky cotton of his shirt and pulled him closer.

"Tu es merveilleuse," he whispered, tilting her chin up to kiss her.

She smiled up at his shadowy face in the dim light leaking in through the gap between the door and its gently warped frame. After that day, each time she went back to the storeroom to look for a file or a roll of paper towels, the fusty smell of woolen coats and cardboard boxes would remind her of what she and Laurent had done on her first visit. "I've never had a new employee orientation anything like this one."

"I am thinking that you will do many things here that you have not done before," he said, his smile sly.

"Really," she said. "I await your instruction."

That evening after dinner, she spoke with Liesel on Skype and told her that Laurent had given her a very thorough orientation at Vie Bohème that afternoon. Liesel grasped immediately what Jayne meant. "Degenerates!" she cried. "I'm calling the French morality police as soon as we hang up."

"There's no such thing," said Jayne, laughing. "Not from what I can tell."

"In that case, I'm booking my ticket as soon as we hang up," said Liesel. "And one for my new underage boyfriend. He's fifteen, and he adores me."

Jayne laughed again. "Sounds like an improvement over Bernard."

"Well, yes, but that's not saying much," said Liesel.

Not long after they began dating, Laurent had told her that he planned to turn her into a sensualist. She'd admitted that despite her job at the SoHo shoe boutique and frequent proximity to pricey goods, she did not have the means to treat herself to fancy clothes and pricey baubles, nor to culinary delicacies. "No caviar, ever?" he asked, surprised. "No *terrine de canard*? Not even the occasional bottle of Dom Pérignon?"

She shook her head. "My parents didn't buy those things when I was growing up. I never got used to having them. It's not like my friends were eating that stuff either. You've seen what most Americans eat—hamburgers, pizza, and potatoes."

"And something called a Cheeto," he said dryly. "Pauvre fille. We'll taste them together. You will love them too."

"I don't know," she said, wary. "I love to eat, but I've never been particularly adventurous."

"You will see," he said. "The flavors are so magnificent. Even better than a slice of pepperoni with a side of Funyuns."

He was partly right: the duck terrine she sampled was rich and smoky, much more agreeable than the Russian caviar that Laurent wanted her to love too, but its texture was too alien to her unrefined taste buds. She liked the Dom Pérignon, although she awoke with traces of a headache the next day, after drinking only a glass and a half. "My parents knew the vintners at Moët et Chandon, the house that produces Dom Pérignon," Laurent told her. "They were friendly because, I think, they were not competitors. Not in the sense that they would have been if my parents also made champagne. But pinot noir is our grape too. The best burgundies and champagnes are made with it, including my family's wines."

His parents' wine was sold under the label Maison Moller, and the collective of vineyards they were a part of produced one of the few grands crus, which he explained was the most sought-after designation for Burgundy vintners.

"It seems like all French people are expected to drink wine in order to be considered truly French," she said. "Some parents let their kids drink it, don't they?"

"Some do, yes, but with moderation. Anne-Claire and I did not let our children drink until they were older, except on special occasions. Then they could have a very small glass. I think there is probably more drinking in your country. La quantité de bière, mon dieu. We don't drink nearly as much beer in France."

"People do drink a lot of beer in the States," she said. "It usually starts in high school and gets worse in college. But I was never that interested. I suppose I was afraid of losing control."

"Do you still feel that way?" he asked, curious.

His scrutiny made her hesitate. "I suppose I do," she said carefully. At the time, they had only been together for a month. She knew that he would remember her answer, that it mattered.

"I will not get you drunk and take advantage of you."

She laughed. "You don't need to get me drunk to take advantage of me."

"There are alcoholics in France too, of course. We have the same problems that you do here. Drugs, poverty, racism. If you go to the periphery of the city, you will see the big, ugly buildings where many immigrants are forced to live."

"I'm aware that not everyone in Paris shops on rue du Faubourg Saint-Honoré," she said.

"No, they do not."

Some of the patrons of the boutiques on rue du Faubourg Saint-Honoré were also the people buying art at Vie Bohème. Jayne had noticed that the work in the gallery's catalog wasn't political, or in some cases, only obliquely so, though she knew that unless an artist was already famous, art with a radical agenda was usually a hard sell. Good for museums, not so good for attracting private collectors. Few art buyers wanted a painting of a bound and naked man, the contents of his skull leaking onto the side of a road, or a black canvas with the word RAPE slashed across its center in ferocious red capital letters.

"Look at the name of our gallery," said Laurent, shaking his head, when she asked if he and André had ever tried to sell angry, edgy work. "This is not Vie de Douleur, or Vie de Tristesse. This is Vie Bohème. Vie de Beauté, de Plaisir."

Of course he wasn't interested in sadness and suffering; beauty and pleasure were so much more profitable. She'd known this about him from the night they'd met: the paintings at the Chelsea opening had all been very sexy.

"Whether or not anyone wants to admit it," he said, "most people live to pursue pleasure, one pleasure after another."

She smiled. "Yes, and sometimes many pleasures at the same time."

He nodded, returning her smile. "Good, so you are already aware of this."

Twice more during her first two weeks in Paris, Jayne returned to the art supply store near the École des Beaux-Arts where the boy with the stoplight tattoo worked. She saw him again on her third visit and realized as he rang up her purchases—tubes of cadmium yellow and viridian green, another of alizarin crimson, and three featherweight boar's-hair brushes for detail work—that despite the painted fingernails and black leather jewelry, he looked a little like Colin. She had not yet told her ex-boyfriend she'd moved to Paris, in part because he had stopped calling at the end of February, when she'd admitted that she was seeing someone else and had been for a while. With no detectable malice or sincerity, Colin had said he was happy for her. He had also all but stopped e-mailing her by the time she packed her suitcases and left her roommate behind with her plants, a stained caramel-colored ottoman, a forest-green area rug, and the heavy-drinking MBAs upstairs.

She had seen Colin twice after their breakup. They'd met once for coffee a week before Christmas, and he'd given her a poinsettia plant that she later brought to the office, where it still lived, and a Coach wallet that she had felt uncomfortable accepting. She had only brought him a card and a bar of his favorite dark chocolate, one studded with hazelnuts, not expecting him to arrive with expensive gifts. He was nervous and seemed happy to see her; he had dressed up for their meeting in new jeans that fit him well and the navy lamb's-wool sweater she had given him for his birthday in late October. This was the first time they had seen each other since the breakup, and he looked good; he'd had a haircut and was clean-shaven, no missed whiskers below his eyes or near his ears. And yet her thoughts kept drifting to Laurent, to what he might want to do that evening, to the fact that he would be returning to Paris over Christmas while she flew to L.A. to see her parents and sister for five days. She wanted Colin to return the wallet but was afraid of hurting his feelings. She ended up keeping it and thanked him but felt resentful of herself and, unfairly, she knew, of him too. Later, when Laurent noticed the wallet and complimented her on this new acquisition, she did not say that Colin had given it to her.

The last time she and Colin had gotten together, for breakfast on the Sunday after Valentine's Day, when Laurent was in Paris again, this time on gallery business, it had not gone so well. Colin seemed hungover and spoke heatedly for most of the meal about his job and his older brother, who was cheating on his wife. When Jayne tried to pay the check, he looked offended and insisted on paying. When they parted ways a few blocks from her apartment, he had trouble meeting her eyes. "I know we weren't seeing each other for that long," he said softly. "But I thought, I thought you were—" He couldn't finish the sentence, and the sight of his face, red from the cold and his warring feelings, made her throat close over.

"I'm so sorry, Colin," she said, reaching up to put her arms around him, her nose pressed to his warm neck. He smelled like honey and cold wind. He mumbled good-bye and didn't look at her again before he turned and walked hastily away. She stayed where she was, watching his retreating back. When her phone began to ring, she knew from the tone that it was Laurent calling from Paris, as if he sensed the sad tension she was feeling on the other side of the ocean. With conflicting pangs of guilt and pleasure, she answered. She looked once more in Colin's direction, but he had disappeared.

CHAPTER 7

Dans la Rue

Jayne's sister wanted to visit later in the summer or in the early fall, as soon as she had saved enough money to buy a plane ticket. Stephanie was desperate for a few days' escape from L.A. and from her record executive boss, who was in the middle of a contentious divorce and had lately gotten into the habit of sharing with her every detail of this unhappy experience, no matter how personal. Laurent had told Jayne that of course Stephanie could stay with them, her parents too if they wanted to visit, but Jayne wasn't ready to invite anyone in her family to France. She didn't yet want them to know the extent to which she depended on Laurent, nor did she feel like fending off the questions she imagined her mother asking, and not for the first time: *What are Laurent's intentions? What are yours? Which classes are you teaching? What? I thought you told us you planned to teach classes at an art school in Paris!*

And whether her parents would be willing to get on a plane together remained to be seen. "You're in Paris now, Jayne," said her mother, "living what sounds like a fairy tale. Please stop worrying about us." At breakfast the next morning, Laurent had said the same thing, adding that she and Stephanie hadn't lived at home for years anyway, and their parents' private life really wasn't any of her or her sister's business.

"You say that because you're divorced," said Jayne. "But I'm sure Frédéric and Jeanne-Lucie weren't very happy when you and Anne-Claire announced that you were separating."

"No, maybe not, but they knew it was coming. They'd known this for years. I think it was a relief for them, in the end."

"I wouldn't be relieved if my mother left my father," she said. "I doubt they'd know how to live without each other." If they did separate, it would probably feel as if some appalling truth about herself or the world had suddenly been revealed. (*All marriages are a mirage, Jayne. Didn't you already know that? Or, I didn't give birth to you, honey. We found you alongside the highway in a cardboard box!*)

"They would know how to live, Jayne. They are adults, yes? And they brought two children into the world and provided a good home for you, if I'm not mistaken. I am sure that they could figure out how to move on."

"I don't want them to have to figure it out," she said, petulant.

"You want to live in the world as if you were a child," he said. "But you cannot."

"Is it childish to want my parents to stay together?" she asked, her voice rising.

"No, but expecting them to stay together for your sake is."

Once she'd been in Paris for a while, she was sure that she would want to show her parents and sister around the city, lead them to the base of the Eiffel Tower, to the Pont Neuf, to Notre Dame—they were the first Parisian monuments that she had ever seen. M. Keller, her junior high French teacher, had taped posters of those landmarks to his classroom walls. Oui, he was an American, but a Frenchman at heart, and the owner of a Peugeot, he'd proudly announced. He was also well dressed and handsome, and every girl in the room seemed to have a crush on him. "Paris, c'est ma ville préferée du monde entier," he'd told her class, Jayne listening with smitten attentiveness to this tall man in the blue pinstripe suit, his silk tie green paisley, dizzyingly elegant. She later repeated his words to her mother and apathetic sister. His favorite city in the entire world! It would become her favorite city too, six years later, when she first stepped off the train from Strasbourg at Gare de l'Est, directly onto Parisian earth.

"Un merveil," he'd also said, translating it for the students who stared at him dully. "A marvel, mes élèves. A marvel!"

Now that Jayne lived in Paris, she could see these monuments every day if she walked southeast from the apartment toward the Seine. Whenever she did, she would pause to watch the river traffic, the sound of the boats and rushing water filling her with an unaccountable surge of hopefulness. From the north end of the Pont Alexandre III, she could look across the swift, murky river to the immense golden cupola of the Hotel des Invalides, Napoleon's remains interred beneath it.

If she turned to the west, there was the wide, gray traffic-choked expanse of the Champs-Elysées, the unearthly Arc de Triomphe in the near distance, clusters of tourists shuffling over the sidewalks, their heads raised in tired or exclamatory wonder. Sometimes Laurent was with her, his hot, strong hand holding hers, but she preferred to walk by herself, especially in the morning, after the rush-hour traffic had dwindled, when he was either reading the paper on the sage-green sofa or already at the gallery, meeting with a private buyer or with André to discuss the images and queries they had received from hopeful artists.

The air near the Pont Alexandre III smelled of exhaust and dust and sometimes of rain. During her first few weeks, she crossed the bridge several times and twice walked to the Musée Rodin, one sculpture inside the museum luring her through the gates more than the famous ones stationed in the gardens, The Thinker with his

noble, weather-scarred face and the ornate, imposing *Gates of Hell*. It
was *The Kiss*, an embracing couple carved from pale, buttery marble,
that she wanted most to look upon. The sculpture was so personal
and seemed to Jayne an image smuggled from a young girl's dream
of what ideal love was.

Sometimes she sketched the sculpture, solitary visitors and tour
groups shuffling past, a few inquisitive people glancing at her, but
only children were bold enough to ask to see her sketches. (One
afternoon when her drawings were not turning out well, she wrote
a note to Rodin on the back of a botched page: *Were you thinking of
Camille Claudel while you worked on* The Kiss? *Why did you not come to her rescue
when her mother and brother locked her in that asylum? She died there, so many years
later. Were you ever jealous of her talent?*)

A third French artist Jayne admired and had discovered not long
after she began studying art was Marie-Joseph Vallet, who changed
her name to Jacqueline Marval after her application to exhibit her
paintings in the Salon des Indépendants was rejected in 1900. The
next year, applying under her new name, she was accepted. She
worked closely with Henri Matisse and Kees van Dongen, and was a
frequent visitor to Gustave Moreau's home in Montmartre, and in a
coup that Jayne suspected was wholly unanticipated by Marval, she
was declared the most interesting painter in the 1911 Salon
d'Automne by poet and art critic Guillaume Apollinaire.

When she was still in high school, Jayne had found Marval's
paintings in a heavy library book redolent of mold and neglect—so
few of her classmates, as far as Jayne could tell, spent time browsing
the dusty stacks where the art books languished—during a study
hall when she should have been preparing for a trigonometry final.
The Frenchwoman used color with an aggressive energy that immediately seduced Jayne. It made no sense to her that Marval was not as
well known as the male painters who had been her friends and

whose work was frequently exhibited with her own. Was it because she had been a woman, and like the forsaken Claudel, could be dismissed with little more than an unheeded cry of protest?

At the time she found the library book, Jayne had been sketching rooms filled with objects. Her chairs and lamps and sofas were meant to seem on the verge of animation, but they were defeating her. Seeing the interplay of color and light in Marval's paintings, she realized that she needed more depth in the contours if she hoped to make her objects appear possessed.

Later, during the summer class in Chicago, Susan Kraut also taught her to think more about composition, to place her objects within the rectangle of the page or canvas in ways that generated both stillness and energy. In college, she realized now, most of her favorite instructors had been women, though Susan was the only one with whom she had stayed in touch for more than a couple of years after graduation.

When she told Laurent about Jacqueline Marval, he had had to look her up. "I'm not sure how I missed her," he said, apologetic and a little embarrassed. "Her work is very striking. We could go to Grenoble to see some of her paintings in the museum there, if you'd like. You've seen the ones in Paris, I'm guessing."

"Yes, but I should go back and look at them again. I'd love to go to Grenoble too. I intended to go during the spring I was in Strasbourg, but I never made it down there."

"You were busy having love affairs with young Frenchmen instead, I am sure."

She smiled. "Yes, of course I was."

When Jayne was alone, she sometimes looked at the framed photographs Laurent kept in the apartment, unable to stop staring at these images of his very handsome past selves. Her favorite photo was on an end table next to the *canapé* in the salon, a picture of him and a school friend, taken in Saint-Tropez, both men smiling and shirtless, deeply tan. Jayne often looked at this photo when she was reading and fighting drowsiness on sunny afternoons.

In photographs or paintings, strangers' exotic faces inhabited almost every room of the apartment, the six family portraits in the hallway sometimes flitting into her consciousness as she dropped into a nap. When she asked Laurent if he'd ever displayed the artist's work, he said that he had, but offered little else, except that Sofia had also worked at Vie Bohème as an assistant for a little while.

"Where is she now?" she asked.

"In Italy," he said casually, but did not meet her curious gaze.

She felt a twinge of jealousy but didn't feel she could pry. She said again how skillful the portraits were, how full of feeling the faces seemed to her on some days, on others, only passive acceptance.

"Yes, Sofia's talent is very special," he said.

"I want to be that good."

"Yes, of course you do," he said neutrally.

I will be, she thought, resentful.

CHAPTER 8

Commerce and Art

Jayne had kept to her plan of sketching and painting for a few hours in the mornings or afternoons, sometimes both, every day since her arrival in Paris. She began working at the gallery a week after she moved into Laurent's apartment, and it was on her second Wednesday at Vie Bohème that she met Laurent's daughter and also had a disconcerting encounter with Laurent's business partner, André. She'd seen him four or five times in New York, but they had never spoken for more than a few minutes at each meeting. André was only ten years her senior, and she almost matched him in height when she wore heels. He looked like some of the soccer players, all coiled energy and grinning cockiness, that she had seen Laurent watching on TV on Saturday afternoons in New York, his mania for the game at first making her laugh, but he was resolutely serious about it. French males of all ages loved soccer, he'd told her, his tone reproving when she gave him a funny look. "It is the same way that many American men feel about baseball and much more barbaric football," he said.

"But not much happens in soccer other than a bunch of guys chasing a ball around," she'd said. "It's worse than watching baseball!"

"No, no. Soccer played well is very beautiful. If you start watching matches with me, you will see."

"I don't know, Laurent. I'd probably fall asleep."

"Oh, Jayne," he'd said, pained. "You cannot mean that."

André had always been an art dealer, never an artist, she knew. "He is practical in ways I am not," Laurent told her. "We are a good pair. It was his ex-wife who brought in some of our best clients. Her father was a painter, and he knew many people who have been helpful to us." Laurent paused. "I liked him very much. He died four years ago in a car accident in Nîmes while visiting his mistress."

"Did his mistress die too?" asked Jayne.

"No, nothing so dramatic. She was at home. He had a heart attack when he went out to buy wine for their dinner."

André's smile was friendly each time he shook Jayne's hand or kissed her cheeks in greeting, but his direct, appraising looks unnerved her a little. Despite her desire to turn a neutral eye on him, André's confidence and his muscular, compact body impressed her.

In New York, after she first met André, Laurent had said, "He is charming, but he is like a dangerous animal. He moves very fast and bites hard when he decides to bite. I will have to keep an eye on him. And you too." He laughed as he said this, but Jayne could not tell if he was joking.

André dressed much as Laurent did, in fine wools and silks and linens that required dry cleaning, but André had his clothes tailored a little more closely to his body's contours. He was also more tightly wound than Laurent, not having been mellowed by years of childrearing, of diapers, temper tantrums, teenage anarchy. She wondered too if André used a bronzer or a tanning bed. Laurent's color was natural; he had a Sicilian grandmother from whom, he'd said more than once, he had inherited his skin tone and sanguine personality.

"Paris and you are getting along well?" asked André now. "You must be speaking more French now."

"Some, mais pas beaucoup," she said, her voice cracking. God, she thought. What is wrong with me?

"But you are trying?" he said. "Tu essais?"

"Yes," she said.

"Tu n'as pas le mal du pays, Jayne?"

She looked at him, silently groping for the translation. Was she homesick? "No, I love it here," she said. "It's very beautiful."

"New York is also very beautiful," he said. "I miss my time there."

"It is," she agreed. "But it'll be waiting for you whenever you want to go back."

"And you too. Unless you decide not to go back."

She nodded but said nothing.

"Do you think you will stay here forever?" he asked. "Especially if you can convince Laurent to marry you?"

She hesitated. Was he kidding? It didn't sound like he was. "I don't know if I'll stay forever, and I'm not thinking about marriage either," she said coolly. "It's not something that Laurent and I need to decide at this point."

"No, no, of course not," he said. He smiled, baring his teeth, the tip of one of his incisors pressing into his lower lip. "Laurent is very generous, yes?"

"He is," she agreed, wishing that Laurent would get off the phone. He had been talking on it in rapid, animated French for almost an hour. It was possible that André had meant no harm, that he was trying only to gauge whether or not she was a trustworthy employee. After all, she had been welcomed into his and Laurent's professional lives without, as far as she knew, Laurent having asked for André's approval. It seemed wise to remain wary of him.

He was sweating, the scent of his cologne rolling off him in a soapy wave. Jayne shifted her weight from one hip to the other; she was uncomfortable but hoped he couldn't tell. They stood less than a foot apart, close to the gallery's entrance, a taxi pausing directly in front of them to pick up a man in a beige suit. Passersby glanced in the gallery's large front windows, an older man and woman in shorts and tennis shoes—tourists, Jayne thought; few Parisians over the age of twenty-two wore shorts or athletic shoes if they weren't in fact exercising—stopping to study a painting of a teenage girl in a green bikini, supine on a white towel, full summer: JEUNE FILLE À CANNES, HUILE SUR TOILE. The price was five thousand euros, but this was not posted on the painting's placard. André and Laurent kept the price list in a slim black folder on top of a filing cabinet behind the gallery assistant's desk; it was one of the first things Laurent had shown her when she started working at Vie Bohème.

"I have known him for twenty years. He is like a brother," André said, an edge to his voice that had not been as noticeable a moment ago. "Maybe more like a father. You might see him this way too."

She looked at his canny, perspiring face. Laurent had told her not to trust André, but until now, she had found herself wanting to. "I don't see him that way," she said. "He's nothing like my father, and I don't have a brother."

He put a hand on her shoulder, the pressure heavy and admonitory. He stepped closer, his soap smell tickling her nose. She stiffened but didn't back away. "Laurent is my very good friend," he said. "We have lived through many, ah, many moments together, not all good things, but I care about his well-being."

"Yes, I'm sure you do. I do too. You don't have to worry that I wish him harm, André."

"We should have a drink one evening and talk some more away from here," he said. "Laurent has told me about your paintings. I am guessing that you are here in Paris because you expect us to exhibit your work. I know that Laurent has likely made promises to you already."

She stared at him, but before she could reply, he spoke again. "I must sound rude," he said, "but I am only being honest." He let go of her shoulder and turned away to greet a dark-haired woman in a white hat who was entering the gallery with a bored-looking adolescent girl. Jayne could hear the girl speaking to her mother in a high, whiny voice. André addressed the woman by name and offered his hand. Jayne stared out at the street for a few more seconds before retreating to the back office, where Laurent was still on the phone. He glanced up when she entered and made a comical face, either unaware of or deliberately ignoring the irritation she was sure could be read on her own face.

Of course she wanted a show. What artist wouldn't? And André's unvoiced scorn made her want one even more.

What an asshole! He was trying to intimidate her, to make sure she watched each of her still-tentative steps, but later, after she had cooled off, she realized that she had no idea who had preceded her—maybe Laurent had been involved with another young artist and given her opportunities like those he seemed to be offering Jayne, and it had gone badly.

Laurent wasn't a fool though, nor did she believe that André was wholly innocent. She had access to the gallery's check register and had noticed a number of bank drafts with his name on them in the last several months, most of the checks in the high-hundred euros. Maybe he was using the money for gallery business, but she had not found any receipts on file with his initials, like the ones Laurent turned in when he made work-related purchases. One of her currents tasks—likely to change, she guessed, if she questioned André's expenditures too closely—was to pay the bills sent by caterers and the occasional florist for openings or the private-viewing receptions they sometimes hosted for their best clients, and for the cleaning crew that arrived every Wednesday night to buff and wax the floors and remove the densely woven black wool rugs near the front door and in the office, bringing them back the next morning, freshly aired and beaten.

The gallery's bona fide bookkeeper, a bearded, unsmiling man named Armand, with springy gray hair he parted with limited success down the middle, took care of the other accounts: the utilities, the lease, the business taxes that were disbursed on a strict schedule, the salaries paid to Laurent and André along with her own wages, which were generous, five hundred euros a week for twelve to fifteen hours of work. What the accountant thought of this, she didn't know.

The gallery also employed two assistants, François and Nathalie, both attractive art students in their early twenties, who split the week's hours, their schedules rarely overlapping. Nathalie sometimes knitted on the days André wasn't there to disapprove, her blond curls bobbing lightly as she clicked the needles and pulled more yarn from her skein. They sat on a stool at a desk made from an old door and an iron trestle that looked to Jayne like the undercarriage of an antique sewing machine. From this perch they nodded to the people who trickled in to gaze at the work and ask questions, some of them smart and informed, a few verging on the idiotic, but the assistants never smirked, Laurent having trained them not to—the person who asked the witless question might turn out to be a serious buyer. It had happened before. "You don't have to be a genius to appreciate a fine painting or sculpture," he told Jayne. And, "There is no rule that says a person with money must also be intelligent."

"No, that's for sure," she said.

"In France we are more foolish with love than with money," he said, reaching for her hand.

"Good thing that abortion is legal here then," she said, giving him a wry look.

"Oh, Jayne," he said. "So serious all the time."

"I was kidding," she cried, laughing.

He was happy with himself, a fact she'd understood from their first meeting. He was a success in the most obvious ways, and even his failure to become an artist, he seemed to have accepted and left behind, adapting himself to another, related career that made him less vulnerable, personally if not financially, to art-related trends and the mercurial tastes of critics and collectors. He was nothing if not easygoing and adventurous, qualities that she found very appealing. "I am an opportunist," he had declared one night not long before they left New York. "I have a nose for business. That is the American expression?"

"Usually we say head instead of nose, but yes, I think you do," she said.

"I have both maybe." He grinned. "And feet? Because I now have galleries in New York and Paris."

Within a week of the Vie Bohème opening in New York, he and André had sold all but two of the twenty-one paintings mounted on their walls. The remaining two sold by the end of the following week. Bernard and the other two artists were not yet well known, but after their successful show at Vie Bohème, Laurent expected that they were on their way to greater renown and prosperity.

His instincts proved correct, as Jayne learned was often the case: in the weeks after the opening, Bernard was offered the part-time faculty position at Pratt, and not long after Jayne moved to Paris, Liesel told her that RISD had called to ask him to teach two painting classes during the next school year. "He'll be able to stop working at the frame shop once he starts at RISD next fall, but between the commute and his own painting, I'll never see him," Liesel said grimly. "And if I have to go out to his dump in Queens one more time because he won't make the trip to my place, that's it."

"You've been saying that for months," said Jayne.

"I know." Liesel exhaled dramatically. "I know!"

Bernard lived in a basement apartment and used an adjacent storage room as his studio; his place was in Woodside, not far from LaGuardia, his neighbors with their small, screaming children and domestic unhappiness almost as hard to ignore as the roar of the arriving and departing jets. Liesel had a comfortable and, by New York standards, spacious one-bedroom on West End Avenue near the Seventy-Second Street subway stop, but Bernard claimed to feel out of place there. Jayne suspected the truth was more likely that he didn't want to spend the time getting to her place from his studio in Queens.

"What does Melissa say?" asked Jayne.

Liesel rolled her eyes. "You know exactly what she says. I should have dumped his ass a long time ago. But she's married. She doesn't remember all the BS you have to put up with when you're single."

"I think you need to take a break and come visit me."

"I still have to renew my passport, but I did get my picture taken for it, and I have the form. Are you sure Laurent wouldn't mind me staying with you?"

"No, he'd be happy to have you. We have a guest bedroom. This place is pretty big. You've seen it."

"Skype tours hardly qualify," said Liesel. "If I come for a visit, what about setting me up with Laurent's partner?"

Jayne was sure that such a pairing would be a disaster for her friend, probably for most women. "I think he's seeing someone," she said. She looked away from the screen and Liesel's hopeful face, out the living room window, where she could see down into the courtyard. On some afternoons a small black-haired boy rode a yellow bicycle around its perimeter until his mother called him inside or an elderly neighbor yelled out his window at the boy to be quiet, though he made very little noise. "I'm not sure if he's still dating the woman he was with in New York when he was there to open the gallery. I can ask Laurent." She paused. "He's kind of slippery, Liesel. I don't recommend pursuing him."

"Then he's exactly the kind of guy I'm used to."

"I'm serious. I don't trust him."

"What guy do you trust?" said Liesel. "Do you trust Laurent?"

Jayne nodded. "Yes. I do."

Her friend glanced away from the screen for a second before turning back to meet Jayne's eyes. "You don't look like you mean it."

"I trust him as much as I've trusted anyone I've dated," she said. She didn't really know if this was true, but it seemed a futile exercise to spend more time considering Liesel's question. She was here in Paris with Laurent, and on the whole very happy that she was. Unless something terrible happened, she intended to stay, at the very least until after her show at Vie Bohème opened.

CHAPTER 9

Daughters and Other Women

At six thirty, a half hour before the end of Jayne's second Wednesday shift, a ponytailed woman in a sleeveless red dress and beige sandals entered the gallery with a little girl in a stroller. It was a windy day, the occasional crumpled piece of trash pinwheeling by in the street, and the woman smoothed down her dark hair as the front door closed behind her. Jayne had come to the front to slip an updated price list into the binder and glanced over at the door as it opened, past gangly red-haired François on his stool, long legs splayed, preoccupied with something on his laptop. Jayne knew as she called out a greeting, which assistants rarely did—André had instructed them to nod hello and smile at visitors as they arrived but to let them browse in peace—that this slender, well-dressed woman had to be Jeanne-Lucie. She looked so much like her father, even more than she did in the photos of her in the apartment. A few feet past the entrance, she stopped with one manicured hand atop the stroller. She looked over at Jayne but didn't return her smile; Jayne was reminded of her childhood cat Butternut's narrowed eyes before she shot out her paw and whacked a passing human on the shin.

"Bonsoir," she said to Jayne's "bonjour."

Jayne felt her smile stiffen. Was Laurent's daughter correcting her? "Bonsoir," she said. She knew that she should introduce herself, but in that moment she didn't feel like being friendly.

Jeanne-Lucie continued to study her, still not smiling. "Mon père, il est toujours là?"

". . . Votre père, c'est Monsieur Moller?" asked Jayne. Ill-tempered Butternut came to mind again; she couldn't resist baiting Jeanne-Lucie. But Laurent's daughter had to know by now exactly who Jayne was and what sort of relationship she and "Monsieur Moller" shared. Laurent had no reason that she could imagine to keep her a secret from his children, especially if one of them lived only a few miles away.

Jeanne-Lucie seemed to be struggling to keep a straight face. "Oui, Monsieur Moller."

"Il n'est pas ici." Jayne wasn't sure when he'd be back either.

"Où est-il allé?"

"Je ne sais pas," said Jayne. "Il m'a dit que . . ." She paused, groping for the words to finish the sentence. "Il m'a dit que . . . He said he had an errand to run, but that he'd return by seven."

"We will be in the office until he returns," said Jeanne-Lucie. She spoke British-accented English, brisk and precise. When Laurent had told Jayne that his daughter had studied for two years at the Royal Academy of Art in London, she'd been both impressed and intimidated. Jeanne-Lucie's English husband was not an artist, but Jayne couldn't remember what he did—importer of textiles? of construction materials? Something commercial, that was all she could recall.

"I'm Jayne Marks," she said, offering her hand.

Jeanne-Lucie looked at her for a moment before shaking her hand. "Jeanne-Lucie Moller," she said.

So she hadn't taken her husband's name. Jayne wondered how many Frenchwomen kept their maiden names now after marrying. Most of her married friends at home had taken their husbands' last names.

Jeanne-Lucie pushed the stroller toward the back of the gallery and nodded to François, who straightened out of his slouch and greeted her politely as she passed. Jayne noticed that he also said bonjour, but Jeanne-Lucie did not correct him.

Moodily she followed Jeanne-Lucie to the office, remembering that her daughter's name was Marcelle, and that she'd turned two in May.

André had gone home just before Laurent left to do errands, and Jayne was alone with Jeanne-Lucie and Marcelle in the back room, François the only other person in the gallery. Jeanne-Lucie smoothed her skirt and positioned herself in her father's large black leather desk chair, unbelting her daughter and raising her onto her lap. The little girl turned her curly-haired head and peered up at Jayne, smiling shyly. She was dressed in a lemon-yellow pinafore and a white collared blouse, white lace-fringed anklets and pink sandals on her feet. She had chin-length brown curls and brown eyes that looked at everything with curiosity. Her tiny hands, each clasped over a knee, were so perfect that Jayne found herself staring at them.

"Salut," said Jayne, breaking the silence. She waved at Marcelle.

"Salut, madame." She giggled softly and looked up at her mother, who nodded at her.

Jeanne-Lucie glanced at Jayne. "Has my mother come by to introduce herself?"

"No, she hasn't," said Jayne. "Does she plan to?"

"I'm sure she will soon. She likes to meet my father's girl-friends."

Jayne regarded her. What did that mean? Did Laurent have other girlfriends now? They had that so-called agreement, after all. *Don't worry about me when we're not together. Everything's fine.* But she had been with Laurent in Paris for almost three weeks now, and so far had seen no indication that he was having sex with someone else, unless he was such a skilled deceiver, having perfected over the years since his Bohemian youth his technique for delivering a whopping lie. He might be silver-haired and no longer young, but Jayne doubted that he would ever lack for amorous companionship.

"He's the same age as George Clooney," Melissa had once pointed out. There was a resemblance between the two men too, which had pleased Laurent when Jayne mentioned it, but she was sure that he had heard it before. If he dyed his hair, he would probably also have looked ten years younger. A part of her was grateful that he did not.

"My parents have been divorced for a while, but they're still friends," said Jeanne-Lucie. "I'm sure my father has told you."

"We haven't really talked about it."

"That's not surprising, I suppose. He's a private man." She paused. "That is what he likes to say. But I would say instead that he is a secretive man, which is not quite the same thing."

Jayne hesitated. "That hasn't been my impression."

"But you haven't known him very long, have you," said Jeanne-Lucie.

All Jayne knew about Laurent, her feelings about his trustworthiness, her assumptions and prejudices, favorable or not, were each bound up in the present and very recent past: his age, his profession, his marital status, and the terms of his fatherhood; his slightly fallen arches, which required expensive running shoes as well as handmade dress shoes that he ordered from a Florentine atelier; his impatience with other drivers, though he drove infrequently; his black

Jaguar, garaged two blocks over from their apartment; his prefer-
ence for red wine rather than white. Red, he thought, demanded
more from its admirers, more of an educated palate, and of course
he had grown up in Burgundy, where his family had been vintners
for several decades—though about this, admittedly, she knew little,
only that he thought the region beautiful (but becoming too
crowded), and his sister Camille and her husband hardworking.

He didn't speak often of his parents but had told Jayne that his
mother's name had been Karine, his father's Dominique, and that
only his mother had gone to college, but she had left after two years
to get married; they had hired seasonal workers for the harvest,
some of whom had migrated north from Spain, others from Italy—
or if the time for the harvest had come upon them suddenly, which
had happened during seasons with stormy or otherwise unpredictable weather, they hired anyone they could and begged friends and
family, near or far, to help. Other facts that Jayne knew: he did not
like to sleep late, even if he went to bed late; he loved dogs but did
not want to devote the time necessary to care for one. He loved his
children and grandchildren too, and was in frequent touch with
his daughter, his son a little less so.

"My father told me that you are an artist too," said Jeanne-
Lucie. "He said that you have shown him some of your work."

"Yes, Laurent—your father, I mean—has been encouraging."

"He said that you are very good."

Her tone was conversational and friendly enough now, but
Jayne perceived herself to be outclassed. It was the first time since
coming to Paris that she had felt this way so strongly, although in
New York she'd sometimes had similar feelings. It was money,
mostly, the people who visibly possessed it; they made her aware,
whether they intended to or not, that she did not really belong to
their caste, despite her pretty face and college education. If she had

been an established artist, or more fashionable, would the class divide have been less wide?

Jayne glanced at Marcelle. The little girl was watching Jayne and her mother closely, her expression animated and inquisitive. Like her mother, she resembled Laurent: the thin but shapely lips and nose, the dark eyes, and the brown hair Laurent had had before he'd gone gray. Jeanne-Lucie's skin was olive-toned like her father's but as yet unlined. She also had the Frenchwoman's typical figure: slender and small-boned, not very tall nor markedly athletic. She looked as if she would be swallowed whole by Laurent's chair if she hadn't been balanced on its edge, Marcelle on her knee. Jayne was a couple of inches taller than Jeanne-Lucie; her arms and legs were more muscular too. In France she sometimes felt ungainly, though she was as fit as she'd been in college from her walks around the city and the runs she took along the Seine every few days, usually early in the evening, when Laurent was still at the gallery.

"He's kind to say that about my work." Jayne smiled at Jeanne-Lucie. Did his daughter know that Laurent had dangled the possibility of a show before her? He'd told Jayne that he'd never displayed Jeanne-Lucie's work, though she wasn't sure if this was because his daughter had refused his offer or if Laurent had never made one. "You're an illustrator, aren't you?" she asked. "I think your father told me that you teach art too."

"You can call him Laurent. It won't upset me."

Jayne felt the same flare of annoyance that she'd had when Jeanne-Lucie had corrected her bonjour. Before she could say anything, Laurent was pushing open the office's heavy steel door. His thick hair, which he hadn't had cut in more than a month and a half, was tussled from the gusty day. How surprised she still was that a man like this had brought her to France to live with him. ("You lucky bitch!" a woman who had bought several pairs of shoes from her at the boutique exclaimed when Jayne told her why she'd be leaving the store. "Yes, that's what I keep saying too," Jayne said, though she was a little shocked by this wealthy, well-dressed woman's crude familiarity.)

Laurent paused on the threshold and stared at the three of them, his expression guarded before it brightened.

"Ma chou," he cried. For a disoriented second Jayne thought that he was talking to her. *My little cabbage*—she'd always thought it such an odd endearment. His granddaughter climbed down from her mother's lap and charged toward his outstretched arms, almost tripping over her sandaled feet.

"Attention, chérie," Jeanne-Lucie cautioned.

Laurent as grandfather and father—this was Jayne's introduction to him in these roles, the latter defining him for more than half his life, but until now she had known him only as lover and gallery owner. The intimacy Jeanne-Lucie and Marcelle shared with him, the long-standing claims they had to his affections, made her a little jealous.

She looked over at Jeanne-Lucie, but she was watching her daughter kiss her grandfather on both cheeks, Marcelle clinging to his neck like a lemur. Laurent caught Jayne's eye and smiled. Every female in the room adored him, circumstances he had probably long been accustomed to.

He's so smooth, so confident, she wrote later in an e-mail to Melissa.

> How comfortable he seems to be with taking the things that
> women give him. I don't want to worry about this, but sometimes
> I do, and there are times when everything feels a little perilous,
> like I'm walking on a patch of ice and if I'm not really careful,
> I'll fall and break something that will take a long time to heal.
>   But in fairness to him, he's very giving too.

Of the many things Laurent had said and done that had made an impression on her, she thought particularly often about a conversation they'd had after seeing two men, one skinny and middle-aged in a baggy gray suit, the other younger and burly in jeans and a black sweater, shouting fiercely at each other in the street near Laurent's apartment. The curses erupting from their mouths made her want to flee, but Laurent seemed almost hypnotized by the scene. She finally had to grab his arm and pull him away. She wondered if he was recalling some fight from his past. Did someone hate him as much as these two men seemed to hate each other? The argument was about a woman—the middle-aged man's girlfriend, who was also the younger man's mother, from what Jayne gathered.

As they turned away from the arguing men, Laurent said something to her in a low voice that she had to ask him to repeat.

"If you are not taught kindness and good manners as a child," he said moodily, "it is hard to learn them as an adult. Maybe impossible. I worry more and more about how angry people are. Your country has too many guns, Jayne. The younger man had one. I'm sure I saw its outline under his sweater."

"What?" she cried. "If you thought that, why were we standing there so long?"

"It was only a few seconds, Jayne. I do not want people to be so angry all the time, but each year, when I look around, this possibility seems less and less likely."

"You're an idealist," she said.

He shook his head. "No, I don't think so, because I don't expect the things I wish for to happen."

Laurent insisted that they have dinner that evening with Jeanne-Lucie and her daughter, at a quiet restaurant near the gallery, their table in a room lit by candles and wall sconces that looked like miniature gaslights. Marcelle was so well behaved that Jayne kept checking to see if she had fallen asleep, and at one point it did look as if she might drop off, her chin easing toward her chest, but a man's laughter at a neighboring table roused her, and she turned back to her plate of buttered noodles. When they said good-bye on the sidewalk in front of the café, they exchanged air kisses on both cheeks, Jeanne-Lucie not appearing to hesitate before she offered them to Jayne.

After their taxi deposited Jayne and Laurent on rue du Général-Foy, he said, "My daughter likes you." They were walking into the courtyard, he half a step behind her.

"Really? I couldn't tell," said Jayne. Jeanne-Lucie had seemed only to tolerate her; she had not been particularly warm.

He reached for her hand, slowing her down to his pace. "Why do you say that?"

Jayne looked at him, surprised that he sounded concerned. Had he actually expected them to become friends so quickly, if at all? "I kept wondering if she thinks that I'm trying to take advantage of you. She barely smiled all night."

"She knows that you couldn't do that, Jayne."

"She does?" How arrogant he was, this man who claimed not to need socks when it was cold but a moment later she'd hear him swearing in the next room as he searched for his slippers. He was confident, he said, not arrogant, something they had discussed early in their courtship, he often gliding into a crowded Manhattan restaurant without a reservation but managing to acquire a table without a debilitating wait, and sometimes, with no wait at all.

"My daughter knows that I know how to look after myself," he said.

"Why did she say that her mother is going to stop by Vie Bohème to inspect me?" The question had been buzzing insistently in Jayne's head throughout dinner, put there by Jeanne-Lucie, whether she'd intended to or not.

Laurent gave her a blank look. "My ex-wife? Anne-Claire? I don't remember Jeanne-Lucie saying anything about that."

"She said it to me earlier, before you got to the gallery. Is your ex-wife really planning to come by?"

He grimaced. "That is ridiculous. No, no, I doubt it."

"She told me that Anne-Claire likes to introduce herself to all your girlfriends." They made their way through the hushed courtyard that smelled of damp soil into the tiny elevator designed to accommodate at most two adults and a small child, though three adults sometimes tried to squeeze into it. Twice since Jayne's arrival the strain of three grown bodies had caused an alarm to sound in the elevator's narrow glass box, a high-pitched, angry beeping that had summoned her from the apartment to check on the cause of the noise, one of the passengers chuckling and cursing as he got out of the elevator to take the stairs the rest of the way up to his own floor.

Laurent laughed as he jabbed the button for the third floor with his middle finger. On it he wore a gold signet ring that had initially seemed like a dandy's affectation, but she had grown used to it, and now his finger looked naked and vulnerable when he didn't wear it. "I don't know why Jeanne-Lucie would have said that. You're my only girlfriend, and I don't think you will meet Anne-Claire anytime soon, though maybe she said something to make Jeanne-Lucie think so. I really don't think that my daughter is trying to cause problems." He put his hands on her shoulders and pulled her toward him. On his breath she could smell the wine he'd had with dinner, and the garlic from his roast chicken. She'd had a salade Niçoise and had noticed that Jeanne-Lucie gave her a peculiar look as the waiter took her order. Perhaps she wasn't supposed to order a salad for dinner, but why did it matter? Sometimes her ignorance exhausted her. It would get easier, she hoped, and it wouldn't have mattered at all if Jeanne-Lucie hadn't been there to give her a disapproving look. The only time Laurent had commented on something she ordered was on one of their first dates. She had asked the waiter for a Coke, not a glass of wine, to go with her salmon filet. That he could not condone. ("You are an adult woman," he'd scolded, a little incredulous. "A Coke is a child's drink!" "I don't drink that much wine, she said." "I never really have." He raised his eyebrows and said, "Probably because you have not had enough good wine.")

"I hope you're right about Jeanne-Lucie," said Jayne. "I'm not expecting us to be best friends, but I do hope we can be friendly."

He pressed his nose to her hair, pulling her closer as the elevator labored up to their floor. "We may not tell you our life stories and invite you to our birthday party the day after meeting you, but the French are not as unfriendly as some people think we are," he said. "Jeanne-Lucie will probably ask you to lunch soon." A moment later, he looked over his shoulder at Jayne as he unlocked the door, his key a blunt, blocky object much sturdier than the thin, notched keys she still had from home, stashed in the back of a drawer with the lace bras and underwear she had picked out and Laurent had paid for at Galeries Lafayette a few days after her arrival, along with two dresses, one black, the other mauve. Both fit as if they'd been tailored for her, and their fine-spun cotton and silk fabric was so light against her skin she would have been happy to wear them every day.

"Do you really think she will ask me?" she asked now.

"Yes, of course."

She didn't reply. What a long day it had been, first André accusing her of using Laurent to get a show at their gallery, and then an impromptu meeting and dinner with Laurent's aloof daughter, who apparently wanted her to come over for lunch.

Laurent locked the door behind them and bent down to take off his shoes, arranging them on the coarse wool mat where she sometimes left her shoes too. He stood up and took both of her hands in his. "What are you thinking about?"

"I don't know," she said. "Nothing, I guess."

"Don't look so sad," he said. "Everything is wonderful, no? Je t'aime, chérie." He put his arms around her and drew her against his chest. He was strong and slim; she liked that he did not carry weight around the belly that so many other men his age did.

She was conscious of her breathing, of his breathing too. "Moi aussi, Laurent," she said softly, both reassured and buoyed by his tenderness. "Je t'aime."

For weeks these words had only inhabited her thoughts; it was both unsettling and thrilling to hear them spoken aloud now. He pulled her closer and kissed her before stepping back a little to press his forehead to hers. She leaned into him. Before Laurent, she had told three other men that she loved them—Henry, her one serious boyfriend in high school, and a college boyfriend, Nick, who eventually hurt her badly by cheating on her with one of her former dormmates during the spring semester that Jayne had studied in Strasbourg. The third man, Sebastian, was someone she had dated after college, although they had known each other since high school. He'd lived in Chicago the whole time they dated; by then, she had moved from Washington to New York. Their relationship ended after thirteen months, in part because she had trouble affording the frequent trips they took back and forth to see each other, and he wasn't ready to move in together. She believed that she was, and his reluctance and the breakup had taken a while to recover from. She had never told Colin that she loved him, though at times she had thought she did.

Laurent was holding her against his warm, familiar body, one, like her own, that had only a finite number of years in the world to make an impression, to do good or harm or nothing at all other than sleep and eat and spend many hours each week at a job that wore it down and emptied it out. And what had her life been so far? What had she done other than sleep and eat and plod to work after she left behind college and her adolescent longings to be someone who positively influenced the way other people thought about and moved through the world?

"Come to bed," Laurent whispered.

She followed him down the hall, past the portraits of the family that stared out at them noncommittally, into the bedroom, where they undressed and he touched her almost reverently before lowering himself onto her, his heat blanketing her body as he moved inside her. She closed her eyes, and the person she imagined was him, but as a younger man, as he looked in a photo taken with a boyhood friend in Switzerland, where they'd been hiking on a summer trip with their girlfriends, Laurent a year and a half from marrying and another year from fatherhood. He had told Jayne that he and his wife had been faithful to each other for more than ten years, but then suddenly they were not. She'd wanted to know more, but when she asked who had strayed first, he shook his head and said that neither of them had been blameless. "But who cheated first?" she had asked again.

He'd looked at her, weariness registering in his expression. Do we really need to go over this again? Jayne could almost hear him thinking, even though she had never before asked what had happened. "I suppose that I did," he'd said. "But Anne-Claire and I didn't exactly compare notes."

Later he had added, "It was going to end. That is what matters. Not who did what first."

He was close to drifting off when she settled her head against his shoulder and whispered, "I'm very happy." She thought she could feel him smiling in reply.

But instead he said, "You will get used to it, Jayne. People always do, no matter how happy their lives are. They get used to it and don't feel so happy anymore."

"Why do you think that? That's so depressing," she said, raising herself up on one elbow to peer down at him. He was smiling, but she didn't think he was joking.

He shook his head. "No, not really. It is good to know this because then it will not be so surprising when it happens." His silver hair stood up in small peaks along his forehead. Women everywhere, even brisk, businesslike Parisian women, found him striking. Jayne had noticed them eyeing him on the street and in the shops and restaurants he took her to. The women also looked her over, trying to decide if she was pretty and put together well enough to be a real rival. Or maybe they were trying to figure out if she was his daughter.

"You invited me to live here with you so that I would be happier than I was in New York, didn't you?"

"Yes," he said. "Of course I did. I'm not saying that you won't be happy here, on the whole, but I suspect at times you will feel some restlessness."

For a second, she thought about bringing up André's withdrawals from the gallery account in retaliation for Laurent having taken a pin to her bubble of contentment, but she was tired and knew he too would be asleep within seconds if he closed his eyes. She felt sure that he had some idea André had written checks out to himself; he'd made no apparent attempt to disguise them in the ledger.

"Good night," she finally said.

"Bonne nuit, chérie," murmured Laurent, reaching for her hand and squeezing it once before he closed his eyes for the night.

She awoke a few hours later, Laurent asleep next to her, his chest rising and falling lightly under the fragrant cotton sheet. She lay there groggily wondering how much malignancy, if any, the invisible force field she had stepped into at the gallery contained. She wasn't interested in driving a wedge between André and Laurent. She wanted to paint and enjoy her life, as Laurent expected her to do. After all, for the first time since childhood, she was freed from real concerns about money. It was foolish, possibly even ruinous, to scavenge for problems.

Around five, unable to fall back asleep, she got up to use the bathroom and checked her e-mail on her phone on the way back to bed. Colin's name was in her in-box, the first time he had written since April. The sight of his waiting e-mail woke her up fully, guilt and nostalgia warring in her chest. Only a couple of days earlier she'd come across a photo of Colin and herself on her computer, one taken at a friend's farewell-to-summer party the previous Labor Day. He was turned toward her, looking at her with openhearted fondness, but her expression was more subdued, her eyes on someone out of view; she couldn't now remember who it was. On the old Epson in Laurent's office, she'd printed the photo in black and white, and later that day she'd begun sketching it.

This was the first time she had chosen Colin as her subject, and she thought that she might eventually paint the photo. Laurent wouldn't recognize him; he didn't know what her ex-boyfriend looked like, and as an artist whose subjects chose her as often as—if not more often than—she chose them (this a line she had heard Laurent himself use more than once), it seemed to be within her rights to paint Colin if she was inspired to do so.

With uncanny clarity, she could still see his retreating back on the frigid February morning they had last seen each other, his shoulders hunched in his black overcoat, hair shaggy and in need of a trim. It was months ago now, but she remembered that last meeting in painful detail, one where he had angrily forked pancakes into his mouth at the breakfast place she had suggested in the East Village, Colin complaining about his job and his philandering older brother.

It was foolish to think so, but she almost felt as if the sketch she had just begun had summoned his e-mail, its subject line "Hey." No greeting, only an immediate leap into the message:

> Heard you moved to Paris. I got a new job a few weeks ago and now will probably have to travel there every few months. Might be fun to meet up for a drink, etc. if you have time. I can let you know when I'll be there.
>   OK thanks, Colin

His "OK thanks," its pretense of casual politeness, made her pause. Omitting his name completely or signing off as just "Colin" without "Sincerely" or "Yours" or "Regards" seemed too abrupt, maybe? When they were together, he had signed his e-mails "The One and Only C," if he was in a jokey mood, or with an assumed name: "Gordon Higgins Poindexter III" or "Jules Whitsunday" or once, her favorite, "Carl P. Sagan (Please do not confuse me with the famous astrophysicist, Carl E. Sagan—I am tired of answering his e-mails!)."

She typed three different replies but didn't send any of them. She would write to him later, after she had some idea of what she wanted to say. Surely she didn't owe him an immediate reply?

And what did he mean by the "etc."? He probably didn't know himself.

CHAPTER 10

Women from the Past

After her unsuccessful attempts to reply to Colin's e-mail, Jayne went back to bed and tried to fall asleep again but couldn't descend into anything deeper than fitful dozing. Laurent got up as usual a few minutes before eight, dressed himself in the clothes hanging on the back of the door, and left for the *tabac* to buy the newspaper and drink his first espresso of the day. The second one he liked to have around two or three in the afternoon and often made it himself on the office machine at the gallery, which Jayne was still learning how to use. It was an expensive Italian model that she knew he didn't like other people to touch unless he had taken the time to oversee their first few attempts at pulling a shot, but typically no one dared, other than André. More than once after André had used it, she had seen Laurent stand frowning before the machine, tsking over the stray grounds and dried drops of espresso his partner had not wiped off the metal plate beneath the portafilter.

When he left the apartment, calling *au revoir* from the main hall, Jayne heard his heavy key in the lock, then the reassuring click of steel meeting wood. She stayed in bed for a few more minutes and listened to the passing cars and mopeds in the street, the latter's buzzing engines, especially as they receded, always more plaintive than ornery to her ear. If Laurent had asked what image brought Paris most quickly to her mind, she would have said it was a sound, not a scene—the insect drone of Vespas and the occasional cough or roar of the motorcycles driven by delivery boys and students, sometimes a well-dressed man or woman, bright scarf flying.

Her sister and Liesel had both asked if she felt lonely in Paris, if she minded knowing almost no one. No, because it was all a strange relief, liberation from the small box she sometimes felt that the people she knew in New York had packed her into: college grad but no money, no husband, no kids, artistic pretensions that so far have led to nothing of note. The box's sides would be marked THREAT LEVEL LOW.

For now, the gallery and its staff and the foot traffic from the busy street, the polite, curious people drifting in and out all day, kept her occupied. She had Laurent and the unexpected promise of Jeanne-Lucie's companionship—but of that possibility, she had no idea what to think.

When Laurent returned from the tabac thirty minutes later, Le Figaro folded under his arm, she was already out of bed but had left a drawing on his pillow, a human heart she had hastily inked, copied from an anatomy guide in the study, the word amour printed under its lower ventricles. She listened for his step from her seat at the desk, her own heart pounding in her ears. Along with the drawing of Colin, she was working on sketches of the study where she worked and of the salon, with its tall windows and comfortable sofa. She had also begun a painting, her first in the apartment, of a faded color photograph her sister had found at a yard sale in L.A. and sent to her with several others the previous year, its back marked Joanie and

Jim, 10/67, Salinas. In the foreground was a young couple, newlyweds, Jayne thought, but there was no confirmation of this. The pair stood by the front bumper of a powder-blue Cadillac, the smiling man's arm around the woman's shoulders, her smile more tentative, her red hair in an expert updo. Laurent stopped in the doorway, watching in silence as she worked. She raised her eyes and smiled at him.

"I love to see you drawing. I've meant to ask if you've been writing in a journal too, Jayne. Isn't this what Americans in Paris are supposed to do? Because then, like Mr. Hemingway, you can publish your memoirs and become famous."

"Or like Martha Gellhorn, one of his wives, did."

"I haven't heard of her."

She smudged a line that was too dark. "I'm not surprised. Hemingway ate women for lunch, but he couldn't digest Gellhorn. He spit her back out, mostly intact. I've only read a little of her work, but I think she was a better writer than he was."

He had come up behind her chair and slipped a hand inside her robe. "You are naked, Jayne? Under your dress?"

She squealed at his hand's coldness. "Yes, I am. But it's a robe."

"In French *robe* means dress."

"Yes, I know."

"Will you spend all day like this?" He put his mouth to her ear and nibbled the lobe, his breath warm and smelling of cigarette smoke. "In your robe, working on your drawing of this handsome couple in the desert?"

She laughed, wriggling away. "That tickles," she said. "Maybe I will. Do you think I should?"

"Yes. How nice it would be, don't you think?"

"Why don't you spend all day naked with me?" she said. "That would be more fun than me being here all day by myself without any clothes on."

"I would if I didn't have to go to work."

"You're the boss," she said. "You don't have to go in if you don't want to. Have you ever spent an entire day naked?" As soon she asked this, she realized that she didn't really want to know the answer.

Without a moment's pause, he said, "Yes, of course."

"Of course?" She could hear a note of censure in her voice.

"I have been to nude beaches, Jayne. Many Europeans have. My favorite one is in Italy. When I was there, I didn't bother to wear clothes for most of the trip."

"Didn't you go to any restaurants?" Her gaze fixed on his left eyebrow, on a long silver hair that jutted upward.

"No, we had our meals at the hotel."

She wondered who the woman had been, if she was an artist too and younger than Laurent. Where was she now? "Did everyone walk around naked there? Even the waiters and the concierge?"

"No, only the guests, but the waiters did not wear very much either."

"Well, that's interesting." She didn't know what else to say.

"We could go there too if you would like to. It is a very pretty beach near Portofino."

"Who did you go with?"

He bent down to kiss her cheek. She smelled the Gitane again. "A friend. It was a while ago, chérie. Not long after my divorce."

She peered down at her sketchbook. The drawing was not working. She would need to start over.

"I lived a lot of years before I met you," he said. "I was never a monk. You know that."

"I know," she said.

"You don't have to worry."

"I'm not."

He looked at her, a half smile on his lips. "No, of course you're not."

She pushed her chair back and stood, one hand holding her robe closed. "I'd better get dressed and go out for some groceries. I was thinking of cooking tonight. I found a recipe for shrimp linguine that looks good."

"I'll be out with André and a new client tonight. Maybe tomorrow for the shrimp? I probably won't be home until after ten. You should eat whatever you would like. Take yourself out to dinner. Treat yourself to something good, like a very big steak."

"Ha-ha," she said. He knew that she did not eat beef anymore, something she had decided to stop doing over the winter when she finally read *Fast Food Nation*, a book her sister had recommended.

His client was probably a woman, a new buyer, or maybe an artist, but Jayne didn't ask. She had realized in New York that if Laurent was meeting a man, he would say so: "I will see Yves-Alain Nagy, the landscape painter, tonight" or "Olivier Denis, the sculptor of our marble dancers, the artist you think has borrowed too much from Degas." A woman's name was rarely offered. Was he, as his daughter alleged, a truly secretive man? But it seemed to her a gesture more circumspect than secretive.

"I'll need to put clothes on if I take myself out to dinner," she said.

He smiled. "Go out in your dress. No, your robe, I mean. But don't forget to put on your shoes first."

She laughed. "No, that's okay. Maybe you could invite me out with your clients sometime."

"We will see," he said. "It is a possibility, Jayne."

"I'd like it."

"You want to be included," he said. "I understand. That is only natural. You're not bored, I hope."

She shook her head. "No, I'm not."

"You will hear from Jeanne-Lucie soon, I think. But I do not want you to ask her to tell you all my secrets if you do become friends."

She turned to look up at him. "I'm sure your conscience is clear," she said, nonchalant.

His laughter sounded forced to her ears. "Oh, no, I wouldn't say that."

CHAPTER 11

Work and Leisure

*A*re you taking care of yourself? Melissa wanted to know, her newly maternal tendencies as clear across thirty-five hundred miles of fiber optics as if she were voicing her concerns directly into Jayne's ears.

Jayne's sister Stephanie also had questions, less tactful than Melissa's. *What if Jayne got pregnant? And what if Laurent cast her out, forcing her to return to New York, a baby on the way or else an appointment scheduled at Planned Parenthood? Who knew how she'd be able to handle all that.*

Pregnancy was unlikely, unless it was some other man's child, because Laurent had had a vasectomy a few years after Jeanne-Lucie's birth. "I saw no reason to risk having another child when the world is already very crowded," he said. "My wife was not happy with this choice, but she understood why I made it."

"You didn't ask her before you did it?" asked Jayne.

"Yes, of course I did. She went with me to the hospital, and afterward she drove me home. She also made sure that I didn't go in to work for a few days, as the doctor had recommended."

"From what I've heard, most men don't want to have it done."

"No, they do not, but this surgery made sense. It should not cause as much controversy as it does, especially with so many people on the planet, twice as many now as when I was a child."

"He could still give you an STD," Liesel and Stephanie both had said later.

"You should use condoms anyway, Jayne," Liesel added. "You never know if some of his soldiers will leap into the breach and make it across. I've heard about that happening."

Jayne pretended to agree. Liesel was hardly a model of scrupulous birth control use anyway; she had taken plenty of risks during their long friendship, the most recent, from what Jayne gathered, with Bernard, but Jayne did not point this out.

Almost everyone Jayne knew from home had ideas about how she should spend her time in Paris. Write a blog about the city's best pâtisseries! The best swimming pools and health clubs ("As if I even swim," she'd told her friend Daphne, who drove her two border collies from Williamsburg to a beach on Long Island as often as she could, but Daphne insisted, "It's probably one of the few things there aren't already five dozen guides for."). The best dog parks, knitting circles, emo clubs ("What are those?" Jayne asked her sister, who then mocked her ignorance over Skype), organic bakeries, gluten-free bakeries ("In France?" asked Jayne. "Yes, of course in France," said Melissa. "Just do a Google search, and you'll see." "No offense, but I didn't come to France to go gluten-free," said Jayne. "Or to write a guide about how to do it here either."), Japanese noodle shops, Vietnamese noodle shops, pizza parlors, yarn shops, bicycle shops, bicycle tours, helmet shops, soccer gear shops, soccer pubs, lamp boutiques, bead boutiques, flower shops, soap stores, all-night pharmacies, all-night wine shops. She could illustrate the blog too and land a huge book deal, like the one the cartoonist who blogged about her suicidal thoughts had gotten.

"If you're not going to keep a blog, which wouldn't even taken that much of your time," said Stephanie, "why not invent something? Like sunglasses for dogs."

"Don't be ridiculous," said Jayne. "Sunglasses for dogs?"

"Aren't people in Paris completely wacked over their dogs? I read that some of them spend two grand on fancy leashes at Chanel. You should invent little dog Ray-Bans and make a billion dollars. You just have to give me half because it was my idea."

"You can invent them and keep the billions all for yourself."

"Maybe I will. That way I can get away from my boss, who told me the other day that his wife used to make him use coconut oil as mouthwash and as a sex lubricant."

"Is he on drugs? Why would he tell you that?"

Stephanie made a noise of contempt. "Of course he's on drugs."

"You can use coconut oil as mouthwash? That's so strange."

"Look it up. It's true."

"That's all right. I believe you."

Jayne did not need advice from friends or her sister on how to spend her time in Paris. She had her job at Vie Bohème. She spent hours every day painting, she read, she went for walks and ran a few days each week. She had the weekends and most evenings with Laurent.

A few days before Colin's e-mail arrived, Liesel had announced that she wanted to visit in mid- to late August. By then Jayne planned to have at least two or three new paintings completed and another underway. She was working mostly with her collection of junk-shop and flea-market photographs, the ones in color, though she thought she might start a series of paintings in black, white, and gray in the next few months. Laurent was letting her use his study as a studio and had moved some of his files and his laptop into the salon, where he kept a small writing desk. She'd bought an easel at the art store off rue Bonaparte and set it up next to the bigger desk in Laurent's study, where she did her sketches before moving to the canvas, her paints and brushes spread out across the desk's newspaper-covered surface when she was painting. Her laptop she tucked into one of the desk drawers or else kept on the kitchen counter, where the Wi-Fi signal was the strongest.

Before she was able to set up her work area, Laurent had asked François from the gallery to come over to help him move a filing cabinet and a bookcase out of the study to make space for Jayne's easel. François had not asked if Laurent was grooming her for a show; his work hadn't yet been displayed, nor had Nathalie's, but other art students who had worked at Vie Bohème as assistants, such as the mysterious Sofia B., had been given shows, though only after they were no longer working for Laurent and André. Laurent had told Jayne that one criterion for how he and André chose gallery assistants was whether they liked the assistants' own artwork. "They must fit with our aesthetic interests," he said. "That way they can better understand what we sell."

When she told Melissa what Laurent had said on her second night in France, that he intended at some point to put her work in his gallery, her friend had screamed into the computer's electronic eye, then clapped a hand over her mouth. "Shit," she whispered, wincing. "I just put Josh down for a nap. But Jayne, oh my God, I'm so happy for you. I knew it!"

"I really didn't know it," Jayne whispered back. "Not at all."

"No, of course you didn't, which is probably one reason Laurent is so willing to help you."

· · ·

About an hour after Laurent had left for Vie Bohème, Jayne was working on the drawing of Colin, his e-mail still unanswered, when the doorbell's stately bong-bong interrupted her. She ignored it, but when it rang again, she got up from her desk, annoyed, and went into the hall. It was a little before noon, and Laurent was often home at midday, but Thursday was his early day at the gallery. He opened and manned it alone until Nathalie or François arrived an hour or two later. She wondered if he had lost his keys and was returning to pick up a spare set, but this seemed unlikely; he would probably have called and asked her to bring them down instead of coming all the way up to the apartment again.

She squinted through the peephole, the face of the man on the other side slowly assembling itself through the tiny distorting glass: Philippe, the music student from upstairs, the one who discarded the care packages his parents sent. She wasn't sure if she should let him in, especially because she was still as naked beneath her robe as she'd been when Laurent had left for the day, but Philippe had probably heard her approaching footsteps. She tied the sash of her robe tighter and opened the door halfway.

"Désolé de vous déranger, madame," he said, blushing pink from the neck up. He wore jeans and a red polo shirt; he was lean and pale, probably at most twenty-three, with a bony, equine hand-someness. His face was unlined and clean-shaven, the hands at his side large and bony too, more fit for kneading bread or maybe for sawing wood than for playing the cello.

"Ça va. Tu ne me dérange pas," she said, even though he was bothering her. "It's okay."

"Alors, il y a quelqu'un en haut . . . for a long time someone is in the bathroom upstairs," he said haltingly. "I hit at the door, but no one will answer. Will you let me use yours and M. Moller's? I am sorry. It would take so long to walk to the music school."

She didn't know if she should let him, but Laurent had never told her to be wary of Philippe. But would he have? "All right," she finally said. "Entrez. It's around the corner, first door on the right, première porte à la droite."

"Merci," he said, his face still red.

She could hear him even after he shut the bathroom door, peeing exuberantly, her own face turning warm now. She had long wondered, without ever being able to answer the question to her satisfaction, why people were so embarrassed by their bodies when their basic functions were all the same. She had known an artist who took on the topic in college, her paintings of urinals and of women and men peeing alongside each other in open stalls impressing Jayne as both funny and smart, but their instructor, a man with veins in his neck that bulged during his frequent aggrieved outbursts, had not been that impressed. Some of her classmates speculated later that he was jealous.

When Philippe reappeared a minute later, wiping his hands on his pants and thanking Jayne several times, she surprised them both by saying, "Why don't you keep the packages your parents send you?"

He blinked, and for a second she wasn't sure if he had understood her. He looked down at his hands and said, "They send too much. I used to be fat. That is the word for very big, yes?"

"Yes, it is," she said, surprised. "But you're so thin now. I can't imagine you being fat."

"I was," he said. "It was very . . . c'était très difficile pour moi."

"I'm sure it was difficult," she said. "I'm sorry to hear that." She paused, her eyes moving involuntarily to his stomach, which was as flat as the wall behind him. "But you give away the other gifts they send too, don't you?" How nosy she was being! But she found it impossible to stop herself.

"Not always," he said. His eyes were on his scuffed black oxfords, the toes worn down to grayness. "They send so much. I don't like to have too many pieces—how do you say it?—in my room."

"Too many possessions or things. I'm sorry. I shouldn't be such a busybody."

He looked at her thoughtfully before turning toward the door. She was conscious again of her nakedness beneath the robe but no longer felt as shy about it. "Thank you," he finally said. His hand was on the doorknob when he glanced back at her. "How do you know I give away the packets from my parents?"

"Laurent told me," she said. "I guess he must have noticed, or else maybe one of your neighbors told him. I'm really not sure."

"Are you his wife?"

She shook her head.

Philippe nodded. "He is not a bad person."

She stared at him. "What do you mean?"

"I have had worse . . ." He paused. "The word for the person I pay each month?"

"Landlord?"

"Yes, landlord. In French it is *propriétaire*. Mais vous parlez francais, oui? Un peu?"

"Oui, mais pas très bien. I studied in Strasbourg for a semester in college, but I hung around with other Americans mostly. Not the best way to learn a new language, I know."

"You will get better if you practice. Like me with the cello. I am better than I was two years ago, even two months ago."

"I wish you practiced here in the building. I never hear you."

He had put his hands into his pockets and was leaning backward on his heels. He shook his head. "My neighbors would not like it. They would complain. I must practice at the school. They

have rooms for this. Je vous laisse maintenant. Merci beaucoup—
thank you for letting me—"

"You're welcome, Philippe," she said. "No problem at all."

She had almost shut the door when he turned again. "You can
go back to sleep now," he said, nodding at her robe.

"I wasn't sleeping, though I'm sure it looks that way," she said,
pausing before she blurted, "Wait, Philippe. One more thing. Have
other people lived here with Laurent before me?"

He considered the question, his expression both serious and
preoccupied. "I have not lived here very long. Only a year and a
half," he said. "There was maybe one woman before Monsieur
Moller went to New York. But I am not sure. She might have been
his daughter. I do not remember."

He turned to face her more fully, his eyes moving to her chest.
She looked down and saw that her robe had sagged open, her
breasts half exposed. She almost scratched the thin skin over her
clavicles in her haste to pull it closed. If she hadn't listened to
Laurent and sat around naked all morning like a dimwit, she
wouldn't be in this embarrassing situation!

"Thank you, Philippe," she said, avoiding his eyes. "Bon après-
midi."

"Merci. Je vous en prie, madame."

She shut the door, waiting until she heard his step on the stairs
before she went into the bedroom to get dressed. She had
spent enough time that day unclothed, and now she wanted
to get out of the humid apartment for a while. Who was the
woman Philippe had mentioned? Not Jeanne-Lucie, surely, but
someone young, maybe Sofia? Laurent had never mentioned having
a live-in lover before her, but this didn't mean that he hadn't had
one; she had never pressed him for information, knowing that he
would have told her not to worry about it—what, really, was the

point? She reached for the skirt and blouse she had worn the previous day to the gallery, not caring that both pieces would have benefited from a washing. In France, she had seen people wear the same clothes several days in a row, and no one seemed to bat an eye.

It was after twelve now; she would go for a walk and find some lunch while she was out. On her way through the building's crepuscular entryway, she encountered Laurent's cleaning woman, Pauline, her hair in a topknot, a red bucket in one hand, pink latex gloves and a gallon of eau de Javel visible inside. She was going up to the apartment, she told Jayne by way of greeting. Jayne had forgotten that she was coming, and Laurent had not reminded her, something he usually did because Pauline, he was sure, preferred to clean the apartment when no one was occupying it.

Pauline was Czech, middle-aged, a graying blond with green eyes and prominent dark eyebrows. She had been friendly but not overly talkative in the few exchanges Jayne had had with her. Laurent had told her that Pauline spoke five languages and had lived in several countries. Why she was cleaning houses for a living, Jayne wasn't sure, but Laurent seemed to think it was because she liked the work—strenuous, maybe, but with tangible results. She could also be her own boss, more or less, and after she'd finished the work, her time was her own. Jayne suspected a deadbeat husband, but Laurent had scoffed at this.

"I don't think it's too messy up there," said Jayne. "But it is a little warm."

"I am used to that, Madame."

"Please call me Jayne," she said, something she had asked Pauline to do twice before now.

Pauline glanced toward the front door before meeting Jayne's eyes again. "Did Monsieur Moller leave a check for me upstairs?"

"I didn't see one," said Jayne. "But it could be that I just didn't notice it."

Pauline sighed. "It should be on the dining room table."

"I could call Laurent right now at the gallery and ask him. It wouldn't be a problem."

The older woman shook her head. "No, no, don't bother him. I will call him if it is not there. He owes me for the last visit and for today's."

"I'll make sure he gets a check to you tomorrow if you don't find one," said Jayne, surprised by Laurent's forgetfulness. It wasn't that he couldn't afford to pay Pauline. "Or I could go to the bank and get cash for you now." She wondered again how Laurent could have forgotten. Something must have been on his mind.

Pauline faltered. "No, no, that's okay. But if you would ask him to send the check to my house today or tomorrow, that would be good."

"I will, Pauline. It's no problem." She couldn't tell if the other woman was embarrassed about having to ask for her pay. Maybe forgetful employers were something she was used to, but what a drag to have to ask for money you were owed. Jayne had never been good at it. Even as a girl, she had not liked asking her parents for her allowance if they forgot to give it to her on Fridays after school, but her sister had not had any qualms, a trait Jayne had both admired and teased Stephanie about, to which her sister retorted, "I'm not being greedy by asking for something I'm owed!"

"Au revoir, Madame," said Pauline, her eyes showing an emotion that Jayne couldn't decipher: anger, resignation? She wondered what Pauline thought of her and Laurent, if anything at all. Did she feel contempt for her wealthy employers? On some days, if she was especially tired, Jayne wondered if Pauline was disgusted by the evidence of sloth and excess she doubtless found in some of the homes she cleaned. Laurent's apartment glowed for a day or two after she'd plied her mop and dust cloths to it. She was the best cleaning woman he had ever had, he'd said. "They are not so easy to find," he'd added. A couple of years before meeting Laurent, Jayne had briefly considered taking on extra work as a house cleaner in Manhattan, but she had managed to find the job at the shoe boutique instead. A woman Jayne had worked with for a year at the accounting firm had a second job with a maid service and earned more than the shoe boutique paid Jayne, but Jayne still did not want to clean houses. It was snooty of her, she knew, and maybe Pauline also had a college degree. Maybe she too had worked in an office for a while but had determined that she could set her own schedule and earn more by cleaning apartments. These circumstances trumped almost any white-collar job, in Jayne's view.

CHAPTER 12

Canvases

A sensory detail Jayne remembered well from her semester abroad: the bacterial smell of French butcher shops and cheese stores, especially in the open-air markets that sprang up in different neighborhoods every day of the week. In Paris, her favorite marketplace was not an itinerant one: the rue Montorgeuil, a cobblestone street with shops that sometimes overflowed into sidewalk stands where Laurent had taken her one afternoon during her second week in France. "It is a very old street," he said. "Très, très vieux, en fait."

He had first seen it as a small boy, he and his parents often traveling to Paris at the new year from their home outside Dijon. Vie Bohème was only a few blocks south on the rue du Louvre, and he walked to rue Montorgeuil often, sometimes buying his lunch from one of the street's many *traiteurs*. "A trattoria," he said, "You maybe are familiar with the Italian word but not the French one. We have traiteurs chinois, italiens, français, many different kinds."

Montorgueil teemed with affable, tireless merchants, some of whom called out as Jayne slipped past, feeling shy: *Mademoiselle, j'ai de bons petits melons, deux balles! Tomates, pommes, épinards!* Of the determined commercial chorus of butchers and green grocers, Laurent said, "I think of this street as the soul of Paris." He nodded to the vendors calling out to them and other passersby, some shoppers pushing two-wheeled carts which she had always assumed were designed for the old and arthritic, but she had spotted one in Laurent's apartment. She had yet to see him take it out of the utility closet though, where it had probably been stashed (by some former female occupant?). "I say this is the soul of the city because we all must eat," he said, pointing out his favorite pâtisserie. Its window display, artful as a museum exhibit, contained two rows of doll-house-size chocolate and vanilla cakes and fruit tartlets, each on a diminutive porcelain plate. Jayne knew only a few shops like it in New York, also French pâtisseries, or American ones trying to look French.

On both sides of the street she noticed men on lunch break, many of them wearing maintenance jumpsuits, street sweepers in lime green, electricians in blue, their eyes following the pretty women who passed as the workmen chewed their falafel sandwiches and gyros. Her thought as she and Laurent walked slowly along rue Montorgueil, admiring the small, symmetrical pyramids or neat rows of green and white asparagus, oranges and lemons, whole fish glistening but lifeless on crushed ice ("You must not touch anything," cautioned Laurent. "Le marchand is the only person who touches the food before you pay."), the plentitude of cutlets and breads and cheeses, was that the teahouses with their elegant displays of cakes and puff pastries, along with the candy stores— the confiseries and chocolatiers—were probably a child's dream of heaven on earth. But the only children present were in strollers, the others likely hidden away in their grammar schools and lycées, to be released after three or four o'clock to swarm the sidewalks in search of bonbons, pains au chocolat, and sablés.

Jayne had mentioned the multitude of Parisian candy stores and bakeries to Liesel during a Skype call not long after her arrival.

"You're so lucky," said Liesel. "I'd get so fat if I were there. But I'm sure you'll stay as skinny as a pole."

"You wouldn't get fat. You run more miles than anyone I know."

"That's so the Hostess cupcakes won't catch up with me."

"I can't believe you eat those disgusting things," said Jayne. "When you visit me here, we'll eat ourselves sick. No more half-baked cupcakes filled with whipped lard."

Liesel smirked. "You make them sound so appetizing. I'm going to go buy some right this second." She got up and disappeared from the screen, Jayne laughing and calling after her.

When Liesel returned a few seconds later, she flashed her breasts at Jayne, who shrieked with scandalized laughter. "I've always wanted to do that," her friend said before breaking into a violent burst of laughter too. "Wasn't that what Skype was invented for, cybersex? If you ever need a new job in Paris, that might be the ticket."

"You're crazy," said Jayne.

Liesel nodded. "Of course I am. You're just figuring that out now?"

The next morning, she saw that Liesel had sent her an e-mail overnight:

> Dear Paris,
> Where are your coffee and donut guys? Why are there only crepes guys everywhere? How am I supposed to get a decent sesame bagel? God help me.
>   Love, Jayne.
> P.S. I have better tits than Liesel does.

Jayne replied,

Dear New York,
If you'd put in some alleys instead of forcing people to put their rancid trash on the streets, maybe you'd be a world-class city like Paris.
    Yrs, Liesel.
P.S. Don't believe a word Jayne says about me. She's on heavy meds.

Liesel wrote back with a question and a retort: *Paris doesn't have any alleys either, does it? And quit talking smack about New York and my tits.*

Paris is more beautiful than New York, with or without alleys, Jayne insisted. *And FYI, I don't need heavy meds, not since I moved to France. You can have all my prescriptions.*

It was a humid afternoon, and Jayne was sweating as she walked across the center of the city to rue Montorgueil. She would buy a sandwich for lunch and drop by Vie Bohème to ask Laurent about the check for Pauline. In the shop windows she glanced at as she drifted southeast across the eighth arrondissement in the direction of the Palais de l'Elysée, she saw many of the accoutrements of privileged lives, the quarter filled with the wealthy and well-dressed: men's and women's highly polished leather shoes, onyx and silver fountain pens, theatrically lush potted orchids, leather satchels, fine porcelain and crystal vases. At a notions store, she stopped to study a half dozen skeins of lavender wool yarn and a row of silver thimbles arrayed beneath a rainbow display of cotton thread, the spools a faithful reflection of the ROY G BIV acronym she had learned in grade school. In Paris no acquisitive whim seemed too trivial.

A few art galleries lived in between the boutiques too, ones with such discreet signage they were easy to miss. Laurent scoffed at his eighth-arrondissement competition, though she suspected that his dismissal was fueled by envy, he the competitor with a less desirable address. The block of rue du Louvre where Vie Bohème was situated was respectable, the rent high, she imagined, as it doubtless was for most storefronts in the better arrondissements, but the area was less fashionable than the quarter where they lived.

To be on her own, to have the license and means to roam a city like this one—she still had trouble believing it when she awoke next to Laurent and looked up at the ceiling on some mornings, a ceiling above which no one stomped with exuberant rudeness in the deadest hours of night. Her new happiness felt vibrant but precarious, as if she had been recruited without qualifications to care for a delicate, priceless object—a fragile glass cup that would shatter if she didn't learn how to hold it with precise amounts of gentleness and tenacity.

Aside from Melissa, who seemed sincere in her happiness, if not also sometimes flattened by the responsibilities of marriage and motherhood, Jayne could think of no woman she was close to who claimed to be happy. Her sister Stephanie? No, brave jokes notwithstanding. Their mother? No, definitely not, despite her attempts to disguise her midlife anomie. Her former boss at the shoe boutique? Taking care of a father dying of throat cancer. Liesel? Lonely and frustrated by her bad luck with men. Her old boss at the accounting firm? College-age daughter struggling with anorexia. Daphne and Kirstie? Both were so nervous about their impending motherhood that Daphne, who wasn't carrying the baby, had started smoking pot after work most days, something that infuriated Kirstie. Jayne was curious about Pauline too; what would this practical woman have said if questioned about her state of mind? She might have laughed and shaken her head. She might have said, "Don't worry about it. Just be. Happiness isn't a right. It's a privilege."

The city, steamy with sun and noonday commerce, with droves of helmeted men on motorcycles—so many more than Jayne remembered from nine years ago. She made her way to rue Montorgeuil, where she bought a can of Orangina and a falafel sandwich and ate it while perched on a curb with other people-watchers near the Saint-Eustache entrance to Les Halles. The area was under construction, and benches were hard to find, the few not obstructed by construction barricades occupied by tourists wilting in the day's humidity. From behind her sunglasses Jayne watched a couple's exchange move from friendly to heated, the miniskirted strawberry-blond woman turning away and stalking off; the man, his light blue shirt open at the neck, lavender tie loosened, staying where he was, a stunned half smile on his dark face. The woman did not look back at him; after a moment, the man, trying hard to arrange his face in an attitude of indifference, went in the other direction, toward rue du Louvre. Jayne soon followed his trajectory down the block to the south, where Vie Bohème and its beach-scene paintings awaited her, and, she hoped, Laurent did too.

At dinner with his daughter the previous night, he had said something that Jayne had not heard him say before. Jeanne-Lucie had asked Jayne what she liked best about living in Paris, and when Jayne replied that there was never any shortage of interesting things to look at, Laurent answered before his daughter could, "Un peu trop, peut-être. But better there is too much than too little. I think that is what a city is, at its heart—a gallery with millions of curators."

His kind dark eyes had fastened on Jayne's as he spoke. He raised a hand and swept it toward the window, an elegant, encompassing gesture. She felt an almost ferocious wave of tenderness for him. "I love that," she said. "That's such a beautiful way of seeing."

"It is nice, Papa," Jeanne-Lucie agreed.

"Paris is always in flux," said Laurent. "New York too. Any city, I would say."

"Yes, and maybe that is why people like them so much," said Jayne.

"Or don't like them," said Jeanne-Lucie with a small laugh. She glanced at Marcelle, who was craning her neck to look at a little boy two tables over who had fallen asleep in his chair. "Do-do," said Marcelle, looking at her mother. "Le petit garçon fait do-do dans le restaurant."

"Yes, that's right," said Jeanne-Lucie gently. "He *is* sleeping in the restaurant."

"I want to," said Marcelle.

"No, chérie. At home, wait until we get home. Then tu feras do-do."

Laurent was not at the gallery, but André was. Jayne found him sitting in a half slouch behind the antique trestle table, paging through an office supply catalog, when she arrived a few minutes after two thirty. He looked handsome in his beige summer sweater, matching loafers, and navy blue pants woven from a fine, soft-looking linen. One of her bosses at the accounting office on Fourteenth Street had had a pair that in her memory was almost identical. She wanted to touch the fabric, to confirm that it was linen and not some convincing counterfeit.

After she'd said hello, but before she could ask where Laurent had gone and when he would be back, André gave her an odd look. Through the forgiving filter of recollection, she would later think that the look was more amused than angry.

"You will have your show, Jayne," he said. "Laurent and I talked this morning and decided that you will be in a spring vernissage with two other artists. No sooner had you and I spoken of it, et alors, Laurent told me that he wanted to schedule it."

How pronounced his cheekbones are, she thought, gazing at him. In the next second, she wondered if she might not be able to breathe, his words narrowly penetrating the haze of her disorientation.

"Jayne?" he said. "You agree, yes?"

She stared at him. His voice seemed far away.

He hopped off his stool. He was smiling, and for a second her eyes refused to recognize him. He took her by the elbow, shaking her arm softly, aware, it appeared, of her stupefaction.

"Jayne," he repeated. She could smell his cologne, cut hay and cloves. "Are you awake? Did you hear me?" he asked, raising his voice.

She noddéd. "Yes. Yes, I would love to be in the show. I don't quite know—I'm—thank you, André."

"How very nice it is when we get what we want." He paused. "It is what you want, isn't it?"

"Yes, it is," she said. "Where is Laurent? I want to thank him too."

"He is with Sofia. They were meeting for lunch, but by now, I am thinking that lunch is over." His expression was mischievous. She could imagine him as a boy, waiting for the girls in his class to sit down so that he could pull the chair out from under them.

"Sofia?" she said. She could hear a clock ticking. It seemed impossible that it might be André's wristwatch, but she didn't know where else it could be coming from. Maybe her ears were ringing in some new, awful way. He wanted to undermine her happiness, she understood absently. "The woman who did the six portraits of the family in our apartment?" she asked.

"Yes, that is Sofia." André smiled. "You have not met her yet?"

"No, I thought she was in Italy."

"She was, but she is back now," he said. "Laurent and I would like you to display four or five paintings in the spring, Jayne, and maybe two or three drawings. Laurent showed me pictures of some of your paintings." Seeing her look of surprise, he asked, "Did you know he had taken pictures of them?"

"No, I didn't."

"They are good paintings, better than I expected, to be honest." He smiled again.

The ground felt strange, almost spongy, beneath her feet. On the heels of the news that she would be given a show, she was having trouble understanding the information that Laurent was out somewhere with Sofia. Or had been with her, if he wasn't anymore. She had been caressed, then slapped. She looked at André but could only say thank you.

He turned and motioned for her to follow him. "Would you help me with the espresso machine?"

"Doesn't someone need to stay up front?" she asked, still trying to recover her equilibrium.

He glanced back at her, a half smile on his lips. "Do not worry, Jayne. It will only be for a minute. We will hear if someone comes in."

She trailed after him into the back room. He left the door open but herded her toward the espresso maker, far enough into the office to be out of view of the gallery's street entrance, she would later realize. The Rancilio machine gleamed reassuringly. Laurent had likely wiped its vented plate and stainless steel sides when he'd opened the gallery earlier that day, using the soft pink cloth that he shook out into the wastebasket under her desk after each use and kept folded neatly in a drawer beneath the machine.

André stopped a foot in front of her, and turned abruptly. He put both of his hands on her shoulders and before she could step away or fully register the warning signals her body was sending out, his mouth was on hers. She did not try to pull back, not fast enough, she dimly recognized. His lips were warm, and when he touched her lower lip with his tongue, she still did not push him away. That evening she would wonder if she'd been too dazed to react angrily, too off balance from the news he had delivered like two subsequent blows to the face: the spring show and Laurent's long lunch date with the brilliant Sofia. Though it was also possible that she had actually wanted to kiss him.

She was aware that from the beginning, she had been both attracted and repulsed by André and could recall almost every detail of the evening they'd met. He had come into Vie Bohème in New York wearing a gray herringbone overcoat, laughing at something the blond woman on his arm had said, her hair pulled tightly back, her lips so plump Jayne thought that they'd been injected with collagen, both the woman's and André's faces pink from the cold night air. Laurent and Jayne had been on their way to dinner, and her own cheeks were burning with pleasure. A moment earlier he had told her how pretty she looked in her green minidress, one she'd bought a year earlier for twenty-two dollars at Uniqlo, though she hadn't told him this.

André had smiled at her for a long moment before enveloping her hand in both of his. "C'est un vrai plaisir, Jayne. Enchanté," he murmured. "You are as lovely as Laurent has said." The blond woman, Tiffany van Something, laughed with forced cheer and hardly acknowledged Jayne when they were introduced.

Later, over dinner, Laurent had made fun of his partner. "He is very gallant, isn't he," he'd said, his smile inscrutable. "'Enchanté, chérie. Un vrai plaisir. Mais oui, un vrai plaisir, chérie.'"

André's hands were now migrating from her shoulders to the back of her neck, his fingers twining in her hair, but a noise from the gallery's main room made her leap back in alarm. He groaned softly and looked at her, blinking. The kiss had lasted at most five seconds, but if Laurent had witnessed any part of it, Jayne knew that he would have been no less angry or disappointed than if it had gone on for five minutes.

"C'est rien," he said, his eyes dilated, his lashes coarser than she'd previously noticed. "That was from the street."

"Are you sure?" she asked. She went to the office doorway and looked into the empty show room. Her breaths were coming in small gulps. She needed to leave before Laurent returned and sensed that something had happened.

"I have to go," she said, glancing at André. Her throat was constricted. He stared at her, his face unreadable, but he said nothing before she turned again and fled into the bright sunlight of midafternoon, out into the stream of people and cars moving on the street with swift, impervious ignorance.

As she walked back to rue du Général-Foy, half breathless with disbelief at her shameful behavior, she was hardly aware of the red lights that her body, as instinctive as a well-trained dog's, knew enough to stop for.

Her mind kept reviewing the same three thoughts:

She would have a show in the spring in Paris.

Laurent had been out with Sofia and had not told her that he would be seeing this other woman.

She had kissed his business partner, who both offended and inconveniently appealed to her. And if he tried to kiss her again, she wasn't sure what she would do. Why didn't she know for sure that she would shout at him or slap his face?

Her phone chimed after she had been walking for several minutes. She disregarded it until it chimed a second time. There were two messages, the first from Laurent: *Just missed you, A said. Everything OK?*

The second was from André: *You did not have to run away. I will not bite you.*

She only responded to Laurent's message: *A show! You weren't kidding that night at the restaurant. How can I thank you?*

A few seconds later he wrote: *I will think of some way, chérie. Do not worry.*

Her reply: *Thank you. Thank you!!*

She wanted to ask what he'd been doing with Sofia, but her guilty conscience, and for the moment, her pride, would not permit it. She'd also forgotten to ask him about Pauline's check.

Something that had happened since Jayne's arrival at rue du Général Foy was that she had never previously felt such uncomplicated joy while working on a painting. At present she was occupied with Joanie in Salinas, the woman's tentatively smiling face enlarged many times to fill two-thirds of a two-by-three-foot canvas. She had started to paint the photo faithfully, Joanie with her husband Jim's protective arm around her shoulders, the light blue Cadillac behind them, but before the end of the first afternoon Jayne decided to focus only on Joanie. Standing a few feet away, her eyes on the woman's sad eyes softly taking shape by her hand, Jayne felt an unexpected but growing certainty that before long she would have what for years she'd believed that she wanted, and from then on her life would become something else, something bigger and louder, its boundaries overlapping with countless other lives.

She would be envied and admired, and at times feel conflicted about these inevitable companions to success. She would have a name recognized by other artists and the people who knew about contemporary art. Pepper, with his Yale M.F.A. and tenure-track teaching position in San Francisco and his painting in the Venice Biennale of a derelict footbridge across an angry river, and with his gallery in Chelsea with exclusive representation rights, would hear her name, and at first he wouldn't be sure if he remembered her, but eventually he would. On one warm Saturday afternoon he would drift in from the street, step into Vie Bohème–New York, where her new paintings, all realist narratives, were on display. She could hear him saying to his girlfriend (not his wife—he wouldn't be close to marrying anyone yet, she didn't think), "Well, I definitely didn't expect this."

It seemed to be looming there before her, a signboard in the distance that became clearer as she drew closer, the letters taller and more vivid with each fraught or tranquil minute:

Joanie, oil on canvas

Vicky and Sheldon at the Brown County Fair, oil and charcoal on paper

Last Night He Said, oil on wood panel

Sarah with Cat-Eye Glasses, india ink and oil on canvas

Owls and Starlings, oil on canvas

Karen and Frank on the Canyon Road, oil on canvas

Jayne Marks (b. 1983, American)

CHAPTER 13

Unreturned Calls

The apartment was warm and a little stuffy, the rooms permeated with the lemon and bleach scents that lingered for a full day following a visit from Pauline. Jayne regretted not remembering to ask Laurent about the cleaning woman's check, but she did not want to call or send him another text. Her hands shook slightly as she turned the bolt on the inside of the apartment's main door and locked herself in. She was having trouble forming a lucid thought after the turmoil of the day's events; she wanted to disappear into a nap but doubted she would be able to calm down enough to fall asleep.

She took a shower to cool off after her hot, zombie-like walk home from Vie Bohème, and remembered as she rinsed her hair that Colin's unanswered e-mail was still in her in-box. In their last e-mail exchange, two weeks before she left Manhattan, he had again brought up his faithless older brother but ended his e-mail with a joke: *What do bagpipers and javelin throwers have in common? They don't have to be very good to get people's attention.* He'd also written, *Text me if you want to have breakfast again sometime?*

Sure, she'd replied. *I'll let you know.* She intended to see him before she left, but in the end, she hadn't. For weeks she'd dreaded the thought of meeting him for another morose breakfast and telling him about her imminent move to Paris, but during her last few days in New York she felt nostalgic and wished she had made plans to see him one more time.

By then, however, she had too many last-minute tasks to take care of, and ultimately it seemed best to leave those embers undisturbed. She hoped now that Colin was seeing someone else. If he wasn't, it had to have been his choice because from what she had observed in their four and a half months together, he had no trouble attracting women.

Working intermittently now on the sketch of his photo from their friend's Labor Day party had made her miss him more than she'd expected to—his texts and voice mails, his mischievous sense of humor; he had once sent an orange-and-green toy frog to her at the accounting office, a note included that instructed her to kiss the frog because it was a species that really did turn into Prince Charming. In return, she sent him a small box of Godiva chocolates at his own office, a photocopied picture of Tom Hanks as Forrest Gump taped to the lid. Her note read, *Life is like a box of . . . well, you know. May your life be much bigger and last much longer than these chocolates undoubtedly will. (Save a caramel for me?)* She hoped he would forgive her for the hasty departure from Manhattan, and that they really could stay friends, though she had never been able to pull this off with any other ex-boyfriend.

Colin! she replied,

> *How nice to hear from you. Yes, you're right—I did move to*
> *Paris. The opportunity came out of the blue and well, as you can*
> *see, I grabbed it (!) and now I'm here. It's great, I have to say.*

If you do come to Paris, yes, of course, let's meet up. I'd like that a lot. I'm sorry I didn't tell you I was moving. There were so many things to do before I left, and I felt so crazed trying to organize everything that I really wasn't sure it would all come together and that I'd get on the plane on time.

It's nice to be back in touch, btw. Be well and congratulations on the new job!

Jayne xoxo

She pressed send and went into the salon, where she drew the curtains, took off her skirt and blouse, and dropped them on the floor before she lay down on the green *canapé* for a nap. When Laurent's landline rang a little while later, she was pulled out of what felt like the beginnings of a deep sleep. She didn't move.

After several rings, the answering machine that Laurent still had not replaced with voice mail clicked on, and the woman who spoke into the electronic silence after the greeting was Jeanne-Lucie. Jayne sat up and looked at the small teakwood table that held the phone, the red eye of its companion answering machine blinking as Laurent's daughter said, "Allô, Jayne? . . . tu es là?" She paused. "Jayne, are you there? Please answer if you are. It's Jeanne-Lucie, Laurent's daughter."

"Oui, allô, c'est moi," said Jayne, nearly fumbling the cordless to the floor when she pulled it off its cradle. "Sorry, I was in—"

"I'm glad I caught you," said Jeanne-Lucie. "Are you busy on Saturday? I'm having a couple of friends over for lunch and thought you might like to join us."

Jayne gazed at the flowery heap of her clothes on the floor. A block or two away, she could hear the scream of a siren. "I'm not sure if your father has anything planned for us that day." She made a face. She hadn't intended to say "your father."

Jeanne-Lucie paused. "No, my father does not. I just spoke to him. He'll be at the gallery." As if you didn't already know that, Jayne could almost hear Jeanne-Lucie thinking.

"Oh," said Jayne. "Then yes, of course, that'd be nice." She felt obliquely scolded, but Laurent had insisted that his daughter liked her. Maybe this was just the way Frenchwomen communicated with each other. "What time would you like me to be there?" she asked.

"Twelve thirty, and you don't need to bring anything," said Jeanne-Lucie, anticipating Jayne's next question. "One other thing. My mother might be coming too. I thought you would like to know."

Jayne looked down at her hands, noticing how uneven her nails were. She would have to file and buff them before the luncheon, or else go around the corner to the nail boutique on rue du Rocher where she'd seen a flashing neon pink sign announcing a manicure sale the last time she'd passed by.

"Hello?" said Jeanne-Lucie. "Are you still there, Jayne?"

"Yes," she said.

"My mother is very nice. You will like her."

Jayne held back a nervous laugh. "Are you sure you wouldn't like me to bring anything?"

"No, I'll have everything we need," she said. "À samedi, Jayne, et bon après-midi."

A Saturday lunch at Jeanne-Lucie's home. Jayne wasn't sure what to think: a friendly gesture, or some sort of hazing ritual for her father's new girlfriend? Jeanne-Lucie and her husband Daniel's apartment was near the Père-Lachaise Metro stop, a couple of blocks southwest on rue Merlin. When Jayne shook off her apprehension and looked at her foldout map of the city, she saw that rue Merlin ran parallel to rue de la Folie—a more aptly named street, if ever there was one, for the surreal state in which she had lately taken up residence. Did Laurent know that his ex-wife had been invited too? Was he also aware that André had just kissed her?

She called his cell phone, but his voice mail picked up. She didn't leave a message, and when she sent a text a moment later— *Pauline needs her ck & Jeanne-Lucie just invited me to lunch*—she did not receive a reply to it either. She tried the gallery line next, but it was André who answered. Laurent had gone out again, he informed her, offering nothing more. "Is he coming back soon?" Jayne asked. She felt almost feverish. Maybe Laurent did know about what had happened in the back room, but she could think of no logical reason why André would have told him.

André sounded amused when he told her he didn't know. "We are meeting an artist for dinner tonight, and perhaps Laurent will go directly to the restaurant from wherever he is now."

"Who are you meeting?" she asked. Was it Sofia again? Twice in the same day?

André paused, and in this moment she could imagine him smiling, his slightly stained teeth bared in the soft light of the rear office. "A painter," he said mildly. "She's very good. Her name is Chantal Schmidt. Do you know her?"

"No, I don't know her," she said without enthusiasm, but she would look Chantal Schmidt up online after she got off the phone. She knew almost no one in Paris. He knew this too.

"Ah, tant pis," he purred. "Why don't you come back to Vie Bohème right now? You can talk to me while you wait for Laurent."

"No, I'm not going to do that, André," she said. She was trembling again very slightly; she held out her left hand, willing her nerves to steady themselves. "Please ask Laurent to call me when you see him."

"C'est important?" he asked.

"Oui, c'est important. Merci."

He waited, but she said nothing more. Finally he murmured, "You don't need to worry, Jayne. Not about me. Bonne soirée." He hung up, leaving her more uncertain than before she called. She wondered if he was being sincere when he told her not to worry. It was difficult to believe that he had anything but his own interests at heart.

At seven o'clock and again at ten thirty, she tried Laurent's cell phone, but each time was routed to voice mail. He did not call back; she suspected that André had not given him the message, but she had to think that he had checked his voice mail at some point in the evening and was knowingly ignoring her calls and the second text she'd sent between them. Intermittently she worked on the Joanie painting that was taking shape on her new easel, but it was hard to concentrate when she kept wondering why Laurent continued to be silent.

She wasn't supposed to worry about what he was doing when they weren't together, but it was ludicrous that he would think such a thing possible, as if he were telling her not to worry about what was in the closet, from which the strangest, most bloodcurdling sounds were emerging. She put her brush in the jar of solvent next to her easel every fifteen minutes or so and checked her quiet phone, which she had placed on a table in the hall, hoping it would distract her less if it wasn't directly under her nose. She paced around the apartment, stopping before every framed picture, Sofia's family of portraits difficult to look upon now without strong feelings of suspicion and jealousy and doubt assailing her.

There were dozens of books in the bookcases in the study to distract herself with, many of them American or English novels in French translation, a few in the original. But Jayne had only ever seen Laurent reading the newspaper, a few art magazines, and sometimes the sports daily L'Equipe, which he purchased for soccer scores and news about player trades, coach firings, and negotiations over their replacements. She looked at the book titles, repeating them to herself to keep her mind off her silent phone.

When he finally came through the door a little after eleven, she was fully dressed and trying not to feel angry and neglected. He was putting her in a show, after all. Wasn't this enough to make her happy, no matter what he'd been doing that day, out of sight and out of reach? And she was hardly one to be casting stones right now either.

Laurent stopped in the doorway, surprised to find her in the hall when he opened the door, a rush of stale air from the stairwell following him inside. He held her unsmiling gaze, his face softening into what looked to Jayne in her grouchy mood a goofy, almost clownish smile. She could smell the cigarette smoke on him from several feet away, and her irritation increased. Juvenile as it was, she refused to be the first to say hello.

He continued to look at her, still smiling, and blinked several times. She wondered if he was drunk; before now she wasn't sure if she'd ever seen him tipsy.

"I had not expected the evening to run as late as it did," he said.

"I guess you were having a good time," she said.

"How was your day?" He stepped closer and put his arms around her. He was acting as if everything were the same as always, as if he knew nothing about her and André, and for this alone she knew she should be grateful, but she was still mad that he hadn't responded to her calls or texts.

"Quoi, Jayne?" he said. "What is it?"

Even in her state of angry distress, she didn't have the nerve to ask why he'd been out with Sofia and what had happened on their lunch date. Instead, she blurted, "Have you ever noticed how few books by women you have on your bookshelves?"

The clownish smile appeared again. "What?"

"Why do you have so few books by women?"

He pulled her closer, but she turned her face away. He smelled so powerfully of smoke, and she could for sure smell whiskey on him now. "What's the matter?" he asked, pretending to pout. "Why are you angry with me? Aren't you happy about the show next spring?"

"I'm very happy about that," she said. "I wasn't expecting it. Certainly not so soon. Thank you."

"You're welcome, Jayne."

"I tried calling you on your cell tonight," she said. "I also called the gallery around five thirty and asked André to have you call me, but I guess he didn't tell you. I texted you too."

He let go of her to unfasten one of his cuffs, but he had trouble removing the silver cuff link. She'd forgotten that he'd left that morning wearing her favorite shirt, a tailored oxford in light blue, made from a cotton fabric so soft it felt like silk. He had bought it at Saks and had let her wear it around his apartment in New York one night on the condition that she go without a bra. Now he had worn it to lunch with Sofia and to dinner with Chantal. "That's my favorite shirt," she said.

He nodded. "Thank you. I like it too."

She said nothing and watched him continue to wrestle with his sleeve before she grabbed his clumsy hand and unfastened the cuff link for him.

"André told me you called, but my phone ran out of power," he said.

"Couldn't you have borrowed André's cell? I told him it was important."

"He didn't offer, and I'm sorry, but I didn't think to ask. What happened?" He blinked as if his vision was blurry. "He did not tell me it was important, Jayne. At least I don't think he did."

"You don't think he did," she repeated.

"I don't remember. I am sorry. It was a very busy day."

"I guess so."

He paused. "Yes, it was, Jayne."

She looked down at his feet. He was wearing the shoes he'd had on the night they met, Florentine-made loafers, very soft black leather. "How was your dinner?"

He put a hand beneath her chin and forced her to meet his eyes. "It was fine," he said. The whites of his eyes were pink-tinged.

She held his gaze. Someone on the street honked twice, the second time long and irate.

"You remember that you should not worry about me when we are not together," he said.

"Yes, I know, and you aren't going to worry about me either," she said, failing to keep her voice from rising.

He ignored her exasperation. "No, I am not. I do not see the point. I cannot control you or anyone else, nor do I want to."

"I guess you didn't see my text either," she said. "I called because Pauline needs her paycheck, and your daughter asked me to lunch today. She said that your ex-wife is also going to be there."

He made a disgruntled sound. "Anne-Claire is—" He shook his head.

"She's what?" she said.

"She is funny."

"I don't know what you mean by that."

"Elle est un peu bizarre," he said. "Strange is how you would say it, I think." He bent down to slip off his shoes.

She wondered if he would want to have sex tonight. She wanted to be left in peace but had only ever refused him once, on a night when she had an upset stomach from the clams she'd had at dinner. He'd had steak and later joked that she really should eat more red meat.

"Your wife is strange," she said. "That's all?"

"Ex-wife," he said, putting his arms around her again. "You are in such a foul mood tonight, Jayne. I am sorry, but I did not expect my phone to die at dinner."

She knew she should say, "That's all right." How many arguments, how many backs turned coldly away, would be avoided if these three words were said instead of some furious alternative?

"You still haven't told me why you have so few books by women either," she said. "Did your wife take them with her when you got divorced?"

"She did take some of them," he said. "Ex-femme, s'il te plaît."

"The ex-femme who I'll be meeting on Saturday."

"You don't have to go if you don't want to."

"No, I'm going. I already told Jeanne-Lucie that I would."

"Anne-Claire will be nice to you," he said, reaching for her again. "And Pauline's check is at the gallery, where I keep forgetting it."

"Why is it there?" she asked, surprised.

"Because, nosy girl—" He paused. "That is the expression, yes?"

"Yes."

"Our accountant does some of my personal bookkeeping too."

"That's nice of him."

Laurent shook his head. "I pay him for it."

"I was kidding," she said.

She stood in his arms, halfheartedly hugging him back. There was nothing wrong, not really. If she were to lay everything out—her fears, the possible problems and self-doubts—if she were to arrange and inspect them like laundry on the line, with its wrinkles and small indelible stains, she would find little more than the occasional inconveniences and minor indignities of being alive. And what were they when compared to the impossible good fortune of a gallery show, of a generous, indulgent lover in Paris?

If she wanted to continue to live with Laurent, she knew that she'd have to trust him. The lunch with Sofia had probably been nothing more than two friends, business associates, really, meeting up after a long time apart, and maybe his phone really had run out of power. She did not know why she was always so willing to assume the worst. Being with Laurent in Paris, working more purposefully as an artist, did feel like the beginning of a new life, the one she had hoped to step into since she'd left home at eighteen and started college.

"Come to bed, Jayne," Laurent was murmuring now into her ear. "Don't be cross with me."

She fidgeted against him, his beard tickling her. "Cross," she said. "You sound so British."

"Blame my son-in-law," he said. "You might meet him on Saturday if he has the courage to stay home for the luncheon."

Instead of the bedroom, he led her by one hand to the *canapé*, their steps silent on the plush rugs. She had given in, she recognized, accepted his evasions, but she could feel a kernel of resentment in her chest, something that might not go away. The bitter heart of the matter, she knew, was jealousy. It bothered her badly that he might be attracted to Sofia and to Chantal, the painter that he and André had met for dinner, though when Jayne had looked up Chantal online after the call with André, she'd found only two photos, both showing a pale, severe-looking woman with thick black eyeliner and a confrontational look—not Laurent's type, as far as Jayne could tell. She had looked up Sofia too, having finally managed to decipher her last name from her signature on one of the six portraits in the hall. Sofia looked beautiful in the pictures that Jayne found of her—a Sophie Marceau lookalike—and this had done nothing to improve Jayne's mood.

She knew that she couldn't expect Laurent never to find other women attractive simply because she was living with him. She herself had not stopped noticing other men, and considering what had happened with André earlier that day, she was hardly blameless. She had been in touch with Colin too, and perhaps even more of a transgression was the fact that she'd begun drawing him in her sketchbook.

Laurent spread the purple throw over the sofa, and Jayne lay down on her back, shivering as he settled on top of her and parted her legs with his knee. She could not resist his lust or the inevitable upwell of her own when she saw its determined, exhilarating glint in his half-closed eyes. They had done this so many times now, almost every day since she'd started seeing him. She wondered when their desire for each other would wane—a year from now, two years? But right now he was kissing her neck, the whole fragrant, sinewy length of him pressing her into the soft blanket beneath her naked back. She did not want to do this with anyone else, but when the image of Colin's face arrived, she felt a confused stab of desire. A moment later, André's face replaced Colin's, and she could again feel his hands on her shoulders, pulling her toward him in the back office. But in the final hectic seconds before orgasm, she saw no one's face, only the dark violet wash of pleasure that emptied her mind of all its ungovernable impressions and complaints.

• • •

After they'd gone to bed, the purple throw folded and smoothed over one arm of the *canapé*, teeth brushed, bodies showered and dried off, Laurent answered a question that she hadn't asked. "She's a lesbian, Jayne."

She was drowsing next to him, but hearing his words, she awakened as if pinched. "Who? Sofia?"

He rolled his head from side to side until she heard his neck crack. "Chantal is a lesbian," he said. "The woman André and I met tonight for dinner. In case you would like to know."

"Oh," she said, laughing a little. "Thanks."

"I like her and her work very much. So does André."

"Then I'm sure you're both very happy that she's interested in working with you."

"Yes, we are." He yawned and covered most of his face with his hand. "Chantal is three years younger than you are, but she has already been painting seriously for twelve years. You and she will be in the same show, Jayne, along with one other artist. It might be my daughter, but I don't know yet."

She was so surprised that she laughed in a choked burst. "Jeanne-Lucie?"

"Yes."

"What does André say?"

"He doesn't know yet."

"What do you think he'll say?" she asked.

He moved his head to meet her eyes, his own eyes dark hollows in the faint light filtering in from behind the curtains. "My daughter is very talented. It would not be an embarrassment for us to sell her work at Vie Bohème. André admires her and her work. A little too much, I think sometimes. He is the one who in the past has suggested that we put her in a show."

"You didn't agree?"

"No, I wanted her to find her own way."

"You could say that about me too."

"I could, yes, but our relationship is different from the one I have with my daughter."

"Obviously."

One of his hands, large and paw-like in the dark, smoothed the sheet over his chest. "I should tell you that you are not the only artist I help, Jayne," he murmured.

She felt a hollowing in her ears. "Are there other artists you're helping right now?" she asked.

"Yes." He took her hand in his. "I am, I guess you could say, a patron of the arts in a way that is different from how I am a patron of certain artists at the gallery. Those relationships are not the same because I earn money from them. I might earn money from the others, with time, but that is not my only concern." He paused. "We can talk about this when I am not so tired. I need to sleep now." He turned onto his side, ignoring or else not seeing her look of alarm.

"Laurent," she said. "Please don't spring this on me and then go right to sleep. Who are they?"

He reached for the glass of water on his night table and drained it before looking at her again. "There are two women and one man, but please, let's go to sleep now, Jayne. Je suis crevé. Toi aussi, tu dois dormir. Maintenant il est très tard."

He wanted her to go to sleep too, despite a moment ago having done the emotional equivalent of setting off a string of firecrackers in their bedroom. She stared disconsolately at the curve of his back before she got out of bed and went into the living room. She wasn't sure what she was feeling besides jealousy and disorientation, and that she'd somehow been duped. He was helping two other female artists. And one man, he claimed. What did they give him in return? And what did he expect from her, Jayne wondered, that he hadn't already asked for?

From behind the dark, rippling curtain of her unease, she felt a deep weariness with herself. Who was it that had said the problem with being alive, being a person, was that wherever you went, there you were? You never had time away from your petty, roiling sackful of insecurities, your sagging body, your covetous, senseless ego. Before she'd left for college, Jayne remembered overhearing her parents arguing in the kitchen about how busy they always were, how tired her father felt after a frustrating day at work, he returning home long after the dinner hour. "What's the point of all this?" he'd asked Jayne's mother sharply. "I don't know, Lloyd," she'd replied, exasperated and exhausted too. Jayne had always thought that the point was, for better or worse, to be a success, to be able to support yourself, and to help other people when possible. Every tool she needed had been handed to her. The price was that she ignore some of the more immediate demands of her hungering ego.

Your self-respect, you mean, she could hear her sister saying. *Abase yourself for now, and you'll get what you want.*

Put in those terms, it sounded a little like Dr. Faustus's deal with Mephistopheles, but as was the case for Dr. Faustus, the immediate rewards were all but irresistible.

> Hi Jayne,
> Thanks so much for writing back. It's okay that you didn't tell me you were moving before you left. I'm guessing that you had a million things to do.
> It looks like I'll be coming to Paris later this summer, probably sometime in August. As soon as I know for sure, I'll email you. Or text you? Can you get texts without being charged an arm and a leg? It'd be great to see you and maybe you could show me a couple of your favorite places.
> Yours, Colin

CHAPTER 14

Rue Merlin

On the way to Jeanne-Lucie's apartment on Saturday, Jayne stopped at a sidewalk vendor to buy a bouquet of sunset-orange and pink roses near the Gare Saint-Lazare, where she caught the Metro, which would whisk her across the city to the eleventh arrondissement in about a quarter of an hour. From there, she would walk the short distance to meet her cagey lover's ex-wife Anne-Claire and their second-born child. The other luncheon attendees she wasn't sure about—Jeanne-Lucie's husband, Daniel, Marcelle, and one or two more Frenchwomen close to Jeanne-Lucie's age, which was Jayne's age too, more or less?

Laurent had not wanted to say much more about his role as patron of the arts, but he did tell Jayne that he gave monthly stipends to the artists he helped support, and had been doing so for a number of years, though he had not been supporting the same artists all along. A few had stopped making art, and another had gotten married, and her husband had not wanted her to accept Laurent's money, which had caused both marital friction and financial hardship, but the husband had prevailed, and the last Laurent had heard, the couple was still married.

"What if the artist had been a man?" Jayne asked. "Would his wife also have insisted that you stop giving him money?"

Laurent was eating bread with raspberry jam in the kitchen while he read the paper at the table. She sat across from him, her own bread and jam untouched. "No, I am guessing not, but I think you understand why," he said.

"Yes, because a wife is property. A husband is not."

He took a bite and chewed for a few seconds. "That is one way to say it, I suppose. But what if you were married to a man who was being given money by a female patron? Would you accept this arrangement?"

"I don't know. Probably not," she admitted. "But it would depend in part on how well we were doing without the patron's money. How do you know that your artists are actually working? Do you go to their studios?"

"Yes, usually."

"They live in Paris?"

"Two of them do. One is in Marseille, but we are in contact from time to time."

"How did you find them?" she asked.

"Different ways," he said. "A few have come into the gallery to see if we would represent them. If they are not yet ready but I like their portfolio, I sometimes offer to help them for a little while."

How much do you give them? she wanted to ask but held her tongue, realizing that the conversation had become more of an interrogation than a dialogue. She didn't have the right to know what he did with his money, and to make matters more complicated, she depended on him financially herself. Even so, the existence of these other artists bothered her, as if he'd admitted to having a second lover somewhere in Paris. A second and a third, with a fourth down in Marseille.

On the Metro now, as she rode across the city to Jeanne-Lucie's apartment, Jayne wondered if she or her mother knew that Laurent gave money to poor artists. Were these artists-in-waiting really that good? Another question she wished she had asked: How many of them did become good enough for Vie Bohème to represent them? It was like baseball—Laurent with his triple-A team of artists, all of them presumably hoping to be called up.

On the train she glanced furtively at the other riders: fast-talking, cackling teenage boys in ersatz vintage Who and U2 T-shirts, hair greasy and uncombed; ponytailed, hunched girls in earbuds who tapped on their phones; dispirited-looking men in button-down shirts, some North or West African, some white, who tried to hide behind newspapers or else stared blankly at their reflections in the grimy windows; elderly men and women clutching net bags filled with leeks and peaches and raw meat tied up in clear plastic; tourists in their shorts, knees bald or hairy, speaking German, Japanese, English: "Why do we have to do so much walking, Steve? I thought you said we could take a taxi if I got tired."

"I thought that woman was a prostitute."

"I'm never going back to that restaurant."

She met the gaze of a lone unshaven man with a guitar case and a frizzy nimbus of hair that reminded her of Bob Dylan's. He smiled at her, chapped lips parting to show a crooked front tooth. Who knew where they were all going. If she asked each of them, said she was researching human happiness, what would they say they had done so far to sabotage their own?

Emerging into the glare of the midday sun from the Metro at Père-Lachaise, she oriented herself toward rue Merlin and almost stepped on a tiny pyramid of dog droppings. This would have been the second time since her arrival in Paris. A wiry, unshaven man in blue coveralls near the Metro exit saw her narrow miss and yelled "Merde!" as he chuckled at his cleverness and her distress. She had on her favorite sandals, silver and dainty, and looked down at her still-pristine feet to hide her angry blush. "Tais-toi," she said, too quietly for her tormentor to hear. "Tête de merde."

Laurent had given her the code to the front door of Jeanne-Lucie's building, which was five stories tall and looked like innumerable other apartment buildings on Paris's quieter streets: its facade of blond stone, the windows fitted with elaborate black-enameled iron grills. The windows above street level had narrow ledges onto which flowering plants might be placed, but none of the residents had done so. The building was blocky and wide and looked expression-less, as if withholding judgment from the people who glanced at it on their passage down the street. Two blocks east was the cemetery with its famous dead and hordes of tourists trudging the paths that led to Jim Morrison's, Gertrude Stein's, and Colette's graves. She wondered if this was where Laurent wanted to be buried. Or maybe he planned to be cremated. There was undoubtedly some skillful politicking required for the acquisition of a plot at Père-Lachaise.

Unlike the area surrounding rue du Général-Foy, with its busy train station a few blocks away and the innumerable cars and harried pedestrians, rue Merlin was almost peaceful, with its uncrowded sidewalks and the small park where dog owners exer-cised their energetic Labs and collies. Jayne could feel her body tensing as she pressed the bell for Jeanne-Lucie's apartment. An engraved brass plate read MCELROY/MOLLER. She hadn't been brave enough to punch in the code Laurent had given her and walk into the stairwell as if she were a privileged regular visitor.

Why had Jeanne-Lucie invited her?

Don't be so eager to believe the worst, Liesel had advised in an e-mail that morning. *I bet they'll be nice enough. They're probably just curious about you.*

At the end of the note, she added: *A kindly reminder: don't flatter yourself. Isn't that what you always say to me when I think someone's talking about me behind my back?*

Laurent, however, had seemed uneasy before she set off for his daughter's apartment. "I hope you will not reveal anything too personal," he said.

She laughed, shaking her head. "You mean about our sex life?"

He showed her what she called his sad-dog face, a smiling grimace. "No, I am not thinking you will speak of that, nor will my daughter ask you to."

"Will your ex-wife?"

He snorted. "No, she won't either, at least I do not think she will."

"What are you worried I'll tell them?" she asked.

"I am not sure, but whatever you say, my ex-wife will remember it."

"I won't embarrass you," she said. "I'm not a child who goes off and tells all her parents' secrets to the neighbors."

His face reddened slightly. "I am not your parent, Jayne. Please do not say that."

The front door buzzed, the lock releasing with a quiet click. No voice called through the intercom to make sure the person ringing was welcome inside. Jayne pushed open the heavy exterior door and made her way into the unlit stairwell. She sneezed twice and wondered if someone had just swept the stairs. Above her on one of the landings she could hear someone opening an interior door.

"Jayne, c'est vous?" a woman called. It didn't sound like Jeanne-Lucie. Anne-Claire?

"Oui, c'est moi," Jayne called back. She was five minutes late but wondered if she was the last to arrive. How prompt were the

French? Laurent liked to be on time and grew impatient if she was slow getting ready. She looked at the bouquet in her hand and wished she had also stopped for a small box of macarons; the colorful, chewy cookies were as beautiful as they were delicious.

She glanced down at her hemline to make sure her slip wasn't showing before remembering that she wasn't wearing one. She also realized that she didn't know Anne-Claire's last name and wondered how was she supposed to greet her. Laurent had said that Anne-Claire had not remarried, but this did not help Jayne with the last-name problem.

On the third-floor landing a thin, glamorous woman in a knee-length taupe skirt, matching heels, and a silk blouse the color of orange sherbet awaited Jayne. She had the defiant air of an actress who had not yet accepted that younger women were being chosen for all the better roles. Her skin looked soft as a child's. She was blond and wore false eyelashes, expertly applied, along with creamy coral lipstick and pearls, her expression more impassive than welcoming. She was used to being listened to, Jayne sensed, to having the last word, though this desire had likely cost her allies.

"Madame Moller?" asked Jayne, offering her hand.

"Non," said the woman, with a brisk shake of her silken head. "Madame Parillaud. Mais tu peux m'appeler Anne-Claire."

"Bon, d'accord," said Jayne. The older woman was using the familiar form of address, tu instead of vous, which Jayne had been taught was inappropriate between strangers, unless one was a child, the other an adult.

With a faint smile, Anne-Claire stared at Jayne for a moment before stepping aside to let her into the apartment.

As soon as she crossed the threshold, Jayne smelled something delicious—a stew or a roast, its scent rich and heavy. She wondered how Jeanne-Lucie managed to keep the apartment cool with the oven on. Did she have that rare object, an air conditioner, some-where in her home?

"Follow me," said Anne-Claire. "Nous allons boire un apéritif dans le salon. You will have a drink, yes?"

"Yes, but a small one please," said Jayne, not sure why Anne-Claire hadn't yet acknowledged the flowers. Surely she wasn't annoyed that she hadn't thought to bring some herself—her daugh-ter could hardly expect her own mother to appear with a bouquet or some other hostess gift. At least Jayne didn't think so. She still knew so little of practical value about the French, and she had all but squandered her semester abroad by staying with her American classmates instead of befriending French students; going to the movies, bad American ones in most cases; mooning over the boyfriend she had left on campus in D.C. before he dumped her and she leaped into bed with a guy named Cédric who turned out to be married, although he claimed to be her same age and had looked and acted it too.

Jeanne-Lucie still had not appeared, and Marcelle was nowhere to be seen either; she was likely keeping an eye on her mother. Or else she was somewhere with her father, whom Jayne was curious about. Laurent liked his son-in-law but had told Jayne that Jeanne-Lucie was more than Daniel could probably handle. What Laurent meant by this specifically, he hadn't said.

"Yes, me too. Un tout petit apéritif." Anne-Claire turned to look at her and finally nodded at the bouquet. "Les fleurs sont très jolies. My daughter will like them. Très gentil aussi. You are kind to bring them."

"Merci," said Jayne, embarrassed now, though she had been waiting for the compliment.

Anne-Claire took the bouquet and motioned for Jayne to sit on a leather armchair, one very similar in design to the pair in Laurent's salon. In front of the chair and its mate was a glass-topped table with four long-stemmed glasses, a highly polished silver ice bucket, and one bottle each of Perrier, crème de cassis, and white wine. The room with its armchairs and matching sofa was bright with the midday sun. On the wall adjacent to the streetside windows hung a large faded tapestry of a unicorn in a forest, a good copy of *The Unicorn Defends Itself*. Jayne had seen the original at the Cloisters in New York two or three times, once with her sister, who had pronounced the tapestries boring. ("Medieval art," Stephanie had said with visible irritation. "Sorry, but who cares about a fucking unicorn when people were dying at thirty back then from TB and impacted molars?" "That's probably why they put unicorns in their tapestries," said Jayne. "To forget how miserable they were." "No," said Stephanie. "They were just repressed guys who drew horses instead of naked women because the church forbade it.")

The room's built-in bookshelves housed a colorful jumble of French and British novels, biographies of politicians, scientists, and writers—the ones Jayne would have asked to borrow if she had known Jeanne-Lucie better were fat volumes about D. H. Lawrence, George Orwell, the Curies, and Winston Churchill, and slimmer biographies of Sylvia Plath and Camus. There were many art books too, ones heavy enough to smash all ten toes if dropped from the height of the middle shelves. She spotted the first volume of *Maus*, primly encased in a cellophane jacket. The room did not look like the kind of space where Marcelle would be allowed to spend much time. No toys were scattered about or tucked into a basket, though it was probable that Jeanne-Lucie had had someone in to clean before Jayne's arrival. She remembered Laurent shaking his head over his daughter's housekeeping abilities; surely she had a cleaning woman too.

Maybe she also used Pauline, and Pauline reported back to her about what was going on in her father's household. What would she say? *Judging from the wrappers in the trash, the American girl, or maybe it is Monsieur Moller, seems to be eating a lot of chocolate.* Or, *Your father bought a new bread knife and threw out an old pair of running shoes last week.* Or, *Someone has been making frequent trips to Galeries Lafayette.*

Anne-Claire disappeared with the flowers, leaving Jayne alone to wait for whatever arrived next. Jeanne-Lucie's apartment was larger than any place she could imagine herself ever being able to afford. Whatever her husband did, he made a good living, unless like Laurent's pet artists, it was Laurent's money that financed their lifestyle too. The revelations of Thursday night had threatened her sense of her role in his life, in part because there seemed to be so many people he had relationships with who she would probably never meet or have more than a passing acquaintance with.

Marcelle appeared in the doorway and stared at Jayne with a shy smile. She was wearing a pink sundress, satin ribbons tied into bows at her shoulders, and matching pink sandals. With Marcelle as an example, Jayne could see why most women wanted children, though she could not imagine herself as a mother. ("Good thing," Liesel had teased her. "Because unless he's lying, Laurent won't ever be up to the task of impregnating you.")

"Bonjour, madame," said Marcelle.

Jayne smiled. "Bonjour à toi, mademoiselle."

"Maman est dans la cuisine avec Martin et Grand-mère."

"Bon," said Jayne. "Should I stay here? Je dois rester ici?"

The little girl nodded. "Oui, restez là."

Maybe Jeanne-Lucie had burned the roast, and that was the reason behind her continuing absence. A burned beef roast might be one step removed from a catastrophe in France. Jayne remembered her Strasbourgeois host mother spending several hours on Sundays preparing a midafternoon meal for the family, one frequently as elaborate as a Thanksgiving feast.

And who was Martin—Jeanne-Lucie's husband? Jayne had thought his name was Daniel. It didn't seem likely that Marcelle would call her father by his first name, but Jayne hadn't expected to find a man at their luncheon, only a small gaggle of women, one or two of them inspecting her through their lorgnettes, as if she were the poor relation, still dusty and rumpled from her trip in from the vulgar countryside.

Martin, the mystery guest, materialized before her a few minutes later, Marcelle trailing after him, Grand-mère a few paces behind, the roses trimmed and now in a crystal vase that Anne-Claire set on a small cherrywood table next to the leather sofa (*canapé!* Jayne chided herself), its back low enough not to block the windows it hulked beneath. The way he held his chest lightly forward, his shoulders pulled back, Martin looked like a dancer just past his best days. Jayne guessed he was thirty-five, maybe a year or two younger. He stared at her long enough, half smiling, to make her look away. He was wearing slate gray pants and a blue dress shirt that matched his eyes. She wondered if he was Anne-Claire's boyfriend.

"You're Jayne from Grandpa's gallery, Marcelle tells me," he said. "Nice to meet you."

He sounded American but didn't look it, not with his fashionably disheveled dark blond hair an inch past his collar, his manicured hands, the tailored shirt that might have been plucked from one of the men's boutiques in the seventh and eighth arrondissements where Laurent shopped.

"Yes," she said, offering her hand. From where she stood mixing their drinks, Jayne could feel Anne-Claire watching them. "Nice to meet you."

"Very nice to meet you," he said, squeezing her hand twice before letting it go.

"Martin knows Laurent," said Anne-Claire. "He used to work at Vie Bohème when he was still in art school."

"Really?" said Jayne. "Were you one of his assistants?"

"Yes, he put up with me for two years."

"You speak such good English," she said.

"My father's American. I was born in a suburb of D.C. It's my mother who's French."

"Which suburb?" asked Jayne. "I went to college in D.C."

"Bethesda. Did you go to George Washington?"

She shook her head. "Georgetown."

"Well, good for you," he said with a smile. "I didn't even bother applying. I didn't think I'd get in."

"I liked it there," she said. "I like D.C. too. I stayed and worked there for a couple of years after graduation."

"Before moving to New York," said Anne-Claire.

"Yes," said Jayne. She wasn't sure how Anne-Claire knew this. She didn't remember talking about it with Jeanne-Lucie when they'd had dinner the other night, but maybe she had. Or else Laurent had told her.

Anne-Claire had moved over to the table with the drinks and was pouring crème de cassis and white wine into four glasses.

Martin settled into one of the armchairs and crossed his legs; he had chosen the same chair Jayne had been sitting in before he'd come from the kitchen.

"Where's Jeanne-Lucie?" Jayne asked. "Does she need help with anything?"

He shook his head. Anne-Claire gave a small burbling laugh. "Ma fille est très têtue," she said. "Comme son père. Et son frère."

"She's stubborn," Martin translated. "Like her father and brother. She doesn't want our help, but I'm pretty sure she could use it."

"I told her to order everything from a traiteur, but she refused," said Anne-Claire.

"She's making roasted quail," said Martin, "with grilled potatoes and carrots, and a *tarte aux abricots* for dessert."

"Et un bouillon aux champignons pour commencer," said Anne Claire.

"I love mushrooms. It all sounds delicious," said Jayne. "It must have taken her hours and hours."

Anne-Claire handed Jayne a kir. The glass was almost full, her earlier request for a small apéritif forgotten or else ignored. "Yes, it has taken her all morning and some of last night too," she said.

"She must be an excellent cook," said Jayne.

Anne-Claire smiled. "She tries. She is sincere, I think you could say. Not everyone who tries to cook is."

Jayne noticed that Martin had turned to look at the unicorn on the wall; she wondered if this was his way of disagreeing with Anne-Claire. The older woman gave him a kir too, her fingers brushing the back of his hand. "Merci," he said, his glass also filled nearly to the rim. "Jeanne-Lucie is a good cook," he said, looking at Jayne. "But it's hard to compete with Anne-Claire. Aside from my mother, she's the best cook I know."

"Your mother? I thought I was the best," said Anne-Claire. She smiled. "I am joking, Martin. Je sais que ce n'est pas un concours."

"Tell that to my mother," said Martin, returning her smile. "She thinks everything's a competition."

"Most women feel that way," said Anne-Claire. "But I am sure you know that already. Jayne does, yes?"

"Maybe, but I would like to think that it's not true," said Jayne.

"I would too, but in my profession," said Anne-Claire, "it is never a good idea to ignore the truth."

"She's a psychologist," said Martin.

Jayne nodded. "Yes, I heard."

"Did Laurent tell you?" asked Anne-Claire.

"I think it must have been him," said Jayne. It had been him, but her perverse instinct was not to admit it to this disconcerting, feline woman.

"You think," said Anne-Claire with a trace of a smile. "Ah, oui."

"J'ai faim," said Marcelle, "Et tu dois parler français, Grand-mère. Je n'aime pas parler anglais."

She didn't feel like speaking English. Jayne looked at her and smiled; she didn't always feel like speaking it either. How precocious, a little pugnacious too, Marcelle was in her own home, very different from the subdued little girl of the other night.

"Marcelle," said Anne-Claire sternly. "Sois sage, s'il te plaît."

The little girl gave her grandmother a mulish look. Jayne hadn't thought Marcelle was behaving badly, but she was used to American parenting, where children routinely bossed their parents around, choosing their own diets and bedtimes. Here, from what Jayne had seen, children were mostly children, and parents were the adults in full command of the family rule book.

Anne-Claire continued to look steadily at her granddaughter. "Le loup aime bien manger les enfants gâtés," she said.

Marcelle's expression darkened further.

Jayne blinked, wondering if she had heard Anne-Claire correctly. The wolf liked to eat spoiled children?

"Don't say things like that to Marcelle, Maman," said Jeanne-Lucie, who had at last appeared in the salon. She looked so sleek and pretty in her sky-blue sleeveless dress, waist cinched by a matching belt. Her hair was pinned into a bun at the nape of her neck, and tiny silver hoops adorned ears. She seemed to have just stepped off a cloud. "She'll have nightmares." She glanced at Jayne and smiled. "Bienvenue chez nous, Jayne. I'm sorry that I have been in the kitchen for so long. Our luncheon is finally ready. Please come into the dining room."

"Moi aussi?" asked Martin.

"No, you must wait for our scraps," said Jeanne-Lucie.

"Comme un chien," said Martin. He winked at Marcelle and barked once. "Your mother told me that I can only have the scraps."

"Maman, pourquoi tu es méchante à Martin?"

"In English, Marcelle." Jeanne-Lucie looked at Martin and made a face. "Don't encourage her."

"Marcelle doesn't like to speak English?" asked Jayne. "If her father's British, does he mind?"

"He doesn't, not really," said Jeanne-Lucie, "But I do. She's being lazy. She speaks French at her nursery school and Daniel speaks French with her too, though I wish he would always use English to help her practice. He's fluent in both English and French." She glanced at Martin. "Like Martin."

"And me," said Anne-Claire.

"Oui, Maman," said Jeanne-Lucie. "Toi aussi. Et moi."

Anne-Claire gave Jayne a tart look. "Always forgetting her mother."

"No, Maman," said Jeanne-Lucie. "Never. How could I?"

The older woman laughed, but Jeanne-Lucie did not.

"Your husband isn't joining us?" asked Jayne.

"No," said Jeanne-Lucie. "He's in Manchester until tomorrow. For his business." Her skin glowed from her work in the kitchen. She had a kind face. Here in her home she was a much softer version of the aloof, slow-to-smile woman who had introduced herself to Jayne at Vie Bohème four days earlier.

How pretty you are, Jayne wanted suddenly to say, but was too shy with their audience of Martin and Anne-Claire.

CHAPTER 15

A Critique

When they sat down to lunch, Jayne had trouble forming a sentence for the first few minutes: the meal Jeanne-Lucie had prepared was better than any of the entrées and plats principaux in the restaurants Laurent had taken her to, the best she had eaten since coming to Paris. Although the restaurant meals had all been delicious, Jeanne-Lucie's cooking was extraordinary and personal, the flavors so refined, almost symphonic in their layering, the game hen and sautéed vegetables melting in Jayne's awestruck mouth. How lucky the absent Daniel was! Did he even realize it? she wondered. When she found her voice again, she could not stop complimenting Jeanne-Lucie, which incited Anne-Claire to skewer her and her daughter with sharp little glances as she ate her food in dainty bites and chewed each forkful far longer than seemed necessary. Jeanne-Lucie kept her eyes on Marcelle or Martin or else on Jayne instead of engaging in a contest of tacit one-upmanship with her mother. Along with her culinary skills, Jayne silently marveled over Jeanne-Lucie's self-restraint, especially when her mother took a bite and murmured, "Not bad" or "A little too salty, chérie" or "Not enough garlic" or "My bird is fine, but next time, you should roast them for one or two minutes more."

Whose idea had it been to invite Anne-Claire? Or was it she who had planned the luncheon and used her daughter as the decoy to lure in the ex-husband's unsuspecting new girlfriend? The conversation was desultory for much of the meal, touching on the rumors of a postal workers' strike, of the best variety of apples for tartes, and an accounting of the artists Martin admired most—de Chirico and Dalí, and lately the protean Gerhard Richter and another German artist, much different from Richter, Anselm Kiefer. Jeanne-Lucie also liked Richter and Cézanne and Bonnard, because they were geniuses, and why did it matter if they were popular? She also admired one of Martin's former art-school classmates, a realist painter who had been featured in the most recent Venice Biennale, Émile Tôti-Frère. Martin rolled his eyes over this, but Jeanne-Lucie ignored him. Jayne thought of her own former classmate and the next Biennale, but kept quiet.

"I admire Kara Walker's work," said Anne-Claire. "It is so political and striking."

Jayne looked at her in surprise. "I like her work too."

"I was in New York in the spring, and I visited the gallery that represents Madame Walker. Just marvelous."

"You were in New York?" asked Jayne, wary.

"Oh, yes, I was there in late March. Laurent must have told you?"

For a second Jayne felt as if she'd been splashed with cold water. "I think he did," she lied. "But I don't remember."

Anne-Claire paused, seeing through her subterfuge, Jayne knew. "You don't?" she asked. "Interesting. We met for dinner at an Italian restaurant that is on Prince Street. I always—"

"Maman was there for a conference," said Jeanne-Lucie, cutting her off. "She goes to New York often. I do not, not with Marcelle now. Daniel has so much travel for his own work too, and he doesn't like us to take Marcelle out of her little school now that she is used to going to it."

Martin smiled, his wineglass raised to his lips. "There are worse places to be than in Paris, in any case."

Jayne looked at her plate with its tiny bird carcass and streaks of rosemary-laced butter from the spring carrots and grilled potatoes. Why hadn't Laurent told her about meeting his ex-wife for dinner? Did he not think that she would want to know these things? This was the same tendency, she believed, that had kept him until last night from revealing his patronage of other artists. But why he seemed to believe that she wouldn't find out some of these things on her own, especially if he was permitting her access to the people who knew him best, she couldn't guess.

"No, I agree, but it is nicer when we did not to have to stick to such a strict schedule," said Jeanne-Lucie.

"Your life is not so bad," said Anne-Claire. "You can take Marcelle on shorter trips."

The little girl hiccupped. Martin looked at her and raised his eyebrows comically. She giggled and covered her mouth.

"Marcelle," scolded Jeanne-Lucie. "Don't be rude now."

"Le loup mange les enfants qui ne sont pas sages," said Marcelle.

"Maman," said Jeanne-Lucie. "See what you've done? She's going to have nightmares for sure."

Anne-Claire shook her head. "No, she is too smart for that."

Jeanne-Lucie gave her mother a frosty look. "I still have nightmares," she said. "And I'm smart."

Anne-Claire opened her mouth, but it was Martin who spoke first. "Jayne, I'd love to see your work sometime. I'm sure we all would."

"Have you studied formally?" asked Anne-Claire.

"I did, but after college I was so busy trying to pay my rent that I didn't have much time to get my paintings into galleries."

"Now you have much more time, yes? And with my ex-husband and his two galleries, not to mention the fact that he must be taking care of the bills, nothing stands in your way now but yourself," said Anne-Claire.

A hush came over the table, an expectant, awful silence that in the kinds of films Jayne didn't like usually preceded the moment when the storm felled the house, or the masked madman leaped from behind the door. She could feel Martin, Jeanne-Lucie, and Anne-Claire all staring at her. Jayne looked at Anne-Claire. "Yes, nothing but my own limitations," she said. "By the way, you have such amazing eyelashes. Are they real?"

Out of the corner of her eye, she could see Martin look down, hiding a smile. Marcelle was pushing a piece of carrot around her plate, oblivious to the tension at the table, or else already having learned to ignore adult bickering. Jeanne-Lucie was still, watchful and alert. Jayne wondered if she had offended her, but talking back a little to Anne-Claire had felt so good that she hadn't been able to stop herself.

Anne-Claire's smile wavered but was quickly restored. "My ex-husband has always had good taste," she said. "For as long as I've known him, he has been very skilled at picking talented women for his lady friends."

Jayne didn't reply. The only thing she could think to say was "Fuck off."

"Maman," said Jeanne-Lucie, fatigue in her voice.

Anne-Claire laughed in a short burst. "He's a funny man. He has always thought of his women as projects. Even me. Maybe especially me. His daughter too, more so than his son. Men are supposed to find their own way, but women need to be shown, according to Laurent."

"Maman," Jeanne-Lucie repeated, her anger a sudden hot wind sweeping across the table. "Don't say that about Papa. That's ridiculous."

Her mother shook her head, her face fixed with a fierce smile. "No, it isn't. Your father should have become a teacher. It is his natural mode." She paused. "But there are worse things that he could be, of course. He can be very restless, which I'm sure Jayne already knows."

Jayne said nothing. She knew that if she spoke, she would tell Anne-Claire to fuck off, which she was certain would please the older woman.

"What do you think, Jayne?" asked Anne-Claire. "Is my ex-husband trying to educate you?"

With effort, Jayne forced herself to bite back the words she wanted badly to say. "I don't think of him as a teacher," she finally said. "He doesn't act like one either."

Well, sometimes he did. But it was no one's business but her own how Laurent treated her.

"Isn't he telling you what to wear and what to think?" Anne-Claire asked sharply. "I'm guessing he's also lecturing you about art and politics and the way you should look at the world, as if it is a canvas on a wall."

"Maman, arrête," said Jeanne-Lucie.

Anne-Claire turned to her daughter with an expression of feigned innocence. "Why should I stop? Jayne can speak for herself." She looked again at Jayne. "You can, yes?"

"Laurent has been very kind to me," said Jayne. She refused to be baited. Whatever Laurent's ex-wife was after, she would not give it to her.

Anne-Claire's eyes glittered with exasperation. "That's excellent for you, but you are not answering my question."

"Maman, arrête," repeated Jeanne-Lucie, raising her voice. What followed was said too quickly for Jayne to understand. Martin picked up his water glass and hid most of his face behind it as he drank. Marcelle was still pushing food around on her plate and singing softly to herself.

"I think we learn from anyone who's important to us," Jayne finally said.

"All right," said Anne-Claire. "That is a good answer."

Jeanne-Lucie stood up and snatched her mother's plate from the table, almost knocking her fork to the floor, before turning to Martin, who shook his head. "I'd like a few more potatoes," he said. "If that's okay." He reached for the serving platter where several tiny golden potatoes remained, small, still-fragrant islands in the congealing butter.

"Yes, of course," said Jeanne-Lucie. "Have the rest."

"Moi aussi," said Marcelle. "Deux pommes de terre."

"Please, Martin," said Jeanne-Lucie, looking at her daughter.

"Please, Martin," Marcelle repeated.

He forked two onto her plate and the remaining three onto his own.

"Let me help you," said Jayne, standing up, her own empty plate in her hand.

"Thank you," said Jeanne-Lucie. Jayne picked up her silverware and followed her out of the dining room and into the kitchen, where afternoon sunlight and heat from the oven had made the room several degrees hotter than the rest of the apartment. She had had the same problems in her kitchen in New York. Throughout the summer, she had gone as long as she could without using the oven, making do with the microwave and stovetop, but stir-fry, pasta, and Lean Cuisines quickly became monotonous, and she always broke down to roast a chicken breast and bake a potato, sweating and dehydrated, dressed only in her underwear as she ate them, but so happy for the more flavorful food. She could picture Kelsey, her left-behind roommate, and the woman who had taken over Jayne's part of the lease, one of Kelsey's classmates, sweating in their fraying bras too, waiting for their frozen pizzas to come out of the probably now-filthy oven.

For a moment she felt homesick for the life she had left there— her friends, her reliable nightly fatigue, the Joe café near her office's subway stop where she had guiltily treated herself to cappuccinos that she couldn't really afford until she met Laurent. When he'd found out how much she looked forward to them, he had given her a large gift card. His thoughtfulness, his willingness to spoil her, from the beginning, was almost breathtaking, but he did not think it so remarkable. If you could afford to be generous, why was there even a question? "Once you get into the habit, and it should not take long, it is second nature to give gifts to the people you care about," he said.

"How did you learn to cook like that?" Jayne asked Jeanne-Lucie, surprised to see the other woman's flustered look.

"I'm not very good," she said, embarrassed. "But most of what I know comes from cookbooks. Some of it my mother taught me too."

"However you've learned it, your cooking is amazing. I don't think I've had a meal that good in years."

"You're so kind. But my mother was right. It could have been better." She paused. "She isn't usually so unpleasant. I'm not sure what's wrong with her today."

"It's okay," said Jayne. "I've been having a good time." She stood a few feet from Jeanne-Lucie, who was at the sink, rinsing dirty plates beneath the gushing stream of hot tap water. Jayne gently touched the skin beneath her eyes; her fingertip came away clean.

She was surprised that her makeup hadn't run in the heat of the kitchen or the argument at the table.

"Next time, it'll just be you and me. Marcelle too, unless she's at the crèche." She glanced at Jayne. "If you'd like to have lunch with me again."

"Yes, for sure," said Jayne, flattered. "It's kind of you to suggest it. I know I've only been here about a month, but I don't really know anyone in Paris yet except for you, Laurent, and André."

"Now you know Martin and my mother too."

"Yes."

"Don't worry about anything my mother said today. She can't resist saying things that she knows will upset my father."

"I probably won't tell him what she said."

Jeanne-Lucie looked at her levelly. "I don't see how you couldn't. I would."

"Do you think she's right? That he thinks women are projects?"

Jeanne-Lucie exhaled softly. "Yes, to some extent, but I think many women think of men in the same way."

"I don't know if I do," said Jayne.

Jeanne-Lucie glanced at the window next to the sink. It over-looked a sunny, dusty courtyard where Jayne could hear a little dog barking bossily. On the outside ledge a gray-and-white pigeon was roosting, its beady, unblinking eye trained on her through the glass. "I understand why you were drawn to my father," said Jeanne-Lucie. "He enjoys his life, and he treats the women he spends time with very well."

"Yes, he does treat me well," said Jayne. How many women are there? she wanted to ask, but she knew the question would make her sound desperate, possibly unstable. She watched Jeanne-Lucie loading the lunch plates into a small dishwasher that smelled of lemon detergent, a hard knot in her stomach now. "What can I do to help you?" she asked.

Jeanne-Lucie shook her head, dumping dirty silverware into the utensil basket. "Nothing at all. You can go back to the dining room, Jayne. I must serve dessert. Marcelle will be waiting for it."

"I'd be happy to help you serve."

"No, no, you're my guest. I'll serve you at the table. Please go ahead. Do not worry about me." She smiled and shook her head again, a wisp of dark hair falling into her tired eyes. She hastily pushed it back.

Later, as Jayne walked home from rue Merlin, the subway too crowded and claustrophobic for her unsettled mind, she worried that she'd behaved tactlessly in the kitchen with Jeanne-Lucie, and again during dessert when Anne-Claire asked her daughter if Laurent had been to his family's vineyard since he'd come back from New York. Jeanne-Lucie said no.

"I'm sure it's beautiful," said Jayne. "I don't know why he wouldn't want to go."

"What has he told you about it?" asked Anne-Claire, turning from her daughter to meet Jayne's inquisitive gaze.

Jayne took a bite of the apricot tart Jeanne-Lucie had served her a large slice of, bigger even than Martin's. She didn't know if she could eat it all, but it was as delicious as everything else Jeanne-Lucie had already set before her. "That Vie Bohème keeps him too busy for much leisure travel," she said, "and that his sister comes up to Paris a couple of times a year. He said that he usually sees her then."

"That's partially true. They have a—" She paused. "I suppose you would call it a complicated relationship. Perhaps he will tell you more if you ask."

Jayne had asked him, but he had never spoken at real length about his sister or their family's winemaking business.

Martin poured more dessert wine into Jeanne-Lucie's glass and offered to refill Jayne's glass too. She shook her head. "Thank you, but I'd better not," she said. She wanted to be clearheaded enough to defend herself against Anne-Claire's insinuations.

Laurent's ex-wife only unsheathed her sword one more time, but it was then that she delivered the deepest cut of the day. Jayne was at the door saying good-bye and exchanging cheek kisses with Jeanne-Lucie when Anne-Claire said, "You might not want to hear this, but it is my nature to offer help to other people, especially to women. You should not expect much from my ex-husband, beyond his financial support. You can enjoy his home and his money, but other than that, I wouldn't be—"

"Maman," said Jeanne-Lucie, quietly fierce. "Leave Jayne alone."

Jayne stared at Anne-Claire, awed by her rudeness. She opened her mouth to reply, but only a brittle laugh of affront emerged. Probably sensing that the luncheon was about to plunge at last into disaster, Martin thrust his hand toward her and said, "Jayne, it was so good to meet you."

She could feel everyone looking at her. "Thank you, Martin," she said, smiling mechanically. "Nice to meet you too." She needed to escape into the fresh air and quell her angry, bewildered thoughts.

As Jayne descended the stairs toward the hazy sunlight of midafternoon, the apparently indomitable Anne-Claire called down with her final parry: "Mind your step, ma chérie!"

What she meant by this, Jayne could not bring herself to speculate.

CHAPTER 16

Bach Suite

Her mother and sister had both sent e-mails during the luncheon at Jeanne-Lucie's. She stopped a few blocks from rue Merlin to read them on her phone.

J, her sister wrote,

> I'm coming to see you in August, I hope! Just have to get the dates set and buy my ticket. Cannot wait to get out of here, even if it's a long, long flight and I can only be gone for a week. Are you sure that your old man won't mind if I stay with you?
>
> Love, your (much) cuter little sister
> P.S. Do you want me to bring you some peanut butter? I heard that the French don't have it.

After the verbal abuse Anne-Claire had just inflicted on her, Jayne thought it would be a relief to spend time with someone whose abuse she at least understood the reasons for, even if she wouldn't be able to get as much work done in the studio as she wanted to during Stephanie's stay.

Her mother's note was briefer, and slower to arrive, than her usual e-mails:

Hi sweetie,

Sorry that it's taken me a few days to get back to you. I'm glad to
hear you're doing lots of painting. You of course know that Paris
has a long history of inspiring young artists, writers, and
composers to create their most marvelous work (e.g. George
Gershwin, one of my favorites). But don't let yourself get as fat as
Gertrude Stein did. (Just kidding—you know that, I hope.)

I keep forgetting to ask if you'll be coming home for Christmas
this year. If so, I'll start looking for a good deal on a plane ticket.
Your father thinks it might be too expensive for you to bother
unless you're planning to stay with us for a couple of weeks. I told
him it didn't matter if you could only stay a few days because it
would be worth it to have you here. The man is hardly one step
away from the poorhouse but for as long as I've known him, he
insists on acting as if he were.

Love, Mom

Jayne read her mother's e-mail twice, trying to decide if she
should worry about the dig at her father. She didn't know if she had
the energy to worry anyway. All she wanted to do was hide out in
her makeshift studio for a while, finishing her sketch of Colin's
friendly, open face. She also intended, for what would be only the
second time in her life, to buy her own plane ticket home for
Christmas, with money she saved from her Vie-Bohème paychecks.

In her building's crepuscular vestibule she was greeted by an arresting sound: strains of a cello suite drifted down from one of the
high floors, startling and alive. She knew that it was Philippe, not
someone's radio turned up to an unneighborly volume. He must
have thought that all of the apartments were vacant on a weekday

afternoon, because he had said that he didn't practice in the building, not wanting to intrude on the lives of the other tenants.

His playing was both melancholy and contemplative. Jayne paused on the first-floor landing, one shoulder pressed against the cool wall. She felt tears sting her eyes, her nose prickling from the wave of unexpected, unfiltered feeling.

The piece was by Bach, one of the cello suites that her father had listened to on his stereo many times during her childhood. She wished that she had paid more attention, that she could mention it by name to Philippe the next time she saw him.

Dear Paris. Dear Philippe. Dear Laurent. Did you bring me here to break me apart, to see if there is anything inside? How brief I know my time here will be. Even if it is the rest of my life.

At the door to her and Laurent's apartment, she rested her forehead against the frame, unwilling to go inside while Philippe was still playing, but after another minute the music stopped, the silence abrupt as a slammed door. Dust motes drifted in the sunlight pouring hotly through the stairwell's windows. She waited a little longer, but he didn't start again. Later she would realize that this was the most purely peaceful moment she'd had since moving to France.

Whatever Laurent might be keeping from her, she could almost say in that moment, with conviction, that she didn't care.

She realized that she had no real idea of how his mind worked, and she had no idea how his daughter's worked either. The luncheon invitation had been so unexpected, and with a mother like hers, Jayne had to wonder why Jeanne-Lucie would ever allow Anne-Claire near her and Marcelle. Jayne was also curious about

Jeanne-Lucie's marriage, because two things had been clear during the lunch: she wished for more freedom, and the lion's share of Marcelle's daily care was left to her.

Jayne had felt Jeanne-Lucie's absent husband's presence in the books in the salon, and in the ceramic, brick-red ashtray that she'd spotted on a small table in the corner, off to the side of the bookshelves. The ashtray held a carved cherrywood pipe like the one her maternal grandfather smoked, a few shreds of tobacco still in its bowl. Very likely it was Daniel's; she laughed at the idea of Jeanne-Lucie smoking it, her cheeks puffing like bellows. The pipe made Jayne wonder whether Daniel was quite a bit older than Jeanne-Lucie. In the two photos she had seen of him with Jeanne-Lucie at Laurent's apartment, he didn't really look it, but depending on the light and the lens, she knew that years could be taken off a person's face. And Laurent had never mentioned an age difference.

It was almost five o'clock by the time she'd taken a shower and gotten dressed again, the evening's meal a looming obligation, but on many of the days that he spent at Vie Bohème, Laurent was unlikely to return home before eight. For herself, after the five-course lunch Jeanne-Lucie had served, she wanted nothing more for dinner than a small green salad. She thought about calling Laurent to suggest that he pick up something for himself on the way home, but instead she went into the study and worked on the sketch of Colin for an hour before moving to her easel and the painting of Joanie in Salinas, the sky behind and above her human subject a pale orange with streaks of yellow. She'd been thinking about doing a series of portraits with desert settings; the quality of light in the desert, how it was refracted by sand—this elemental form of glass had always appealed to her.

Whatever she did, she wanted to be thought original. In college art classes, everyone she knew would have admitted to this desire without irony, but now, long past art school and youthful hopefulness, what many artists in the gallery scene seemed to want most was to be rich and famous. (Originality was nice too, but it didn't pay the electric bill.)

And how could it be different? Laurent had asked her one night during her first week in Paris. They lay naked in bed, the lights off. Outside on the narrow, becalmed street, an occasional car slipped by, the sound of urban low tide. "You are aware that money makes the laws in the art business, as in every other business," he said. "Genius is secondary to profit. This is a fact, one for adults, not children."

She made a sound of disapproval.

"Genius is to be coveted, of course it is," he continued, undeterred. "But from my point of view, it matters less than salability. If you can sell your work, then making art can be your only job. Does genius matter more than the ability to put food in your mouth and clothes on your back?"

"That's why I have you," she said, half serious. She felt the leaden weight of these words, the truth hiding behind the teasing facade.

"Yes," he said, nonchalant. "I know, but commerce aside, you seem to think that if an artist creates, for example, a beautiful sculpture of a dancer that many people will want to have in their homes, it isn't likely to be unique and fresh."

"I don't really think that," she said. "If a lot of people like something, it doesn't mean it isn't good. Georgia O'Keeffe and Edward Hopper were still brilliant, even if their work has been co-opted by greeting card companies."

"The only rule, as far as I'm concerned, is that you do not create something lazy and thoughtless."

"I wouldn't do that."

"I know you wouldn't. Brilliance will come if it is supposed to."

Was this meant to comfort her? Because it didn't, though she didn't say so. He had to know this. Maybe that was his intention—to challenge her to move toward her greatest work.

What will you do? Laurent seemed to be asking. Now that you can do whatever you please?

CHAPTER 17

The Use of Light

When Laurent returned home a little before eight, she had stopped painting for the night. The study was often the warmest room in the apartment, and she'd had to take another shower to cool off. She heard him in the hall and called out a greeting as she dried herself with one of the pearl-pink towels he'd bought before she moved in. At pink toilet paper, she was glad he had drawn the line. She'd forgotten since living in Strasbourg that some of the paper in France was the same color as Pepto-Bismol. "Why on earth is it that obnoxious color?" she'd asked.

Laurent had said that he wasn't sure, but maybe the intention was to add color to the proceedings. "Or perhaps it is someone's idea of comedy," he suggested.

He stood now in the bathroom's doorway as she toweled off. "How was it?" he asked, a wary smile flashing across his face.

She went over and kissed him hello, pressing her nose to his warm cheek. Her work in the studio had helped to erase much of the sting of Anne-Claire's behavior at lunch, as had hearing Philippe play.

Laurent's face glowed with a thin glaze of sweat. He had walked home, something he did a few times a week instead of hailing a cab or taking the Metro. "You mean lunch?" she said, though she knew for sure that he did.

He lifted her chin and kissed her; one of his hands smoothed down the unruly hair at the back of her head. "Yes, of course. Did you have a good time?"

"Your daughter is a wonderful cook, and her apartment is very nice, but your ex-wife was, to put it gently, hard to take."

He raised his eyes to the ceiling, showing her the pale scar beneath his chin from a boyhood bike accident. "What did she do?"

"She kept criticizing Jeanne-Lucie's cooking, even though everything was delicious. It really was perfect. She's like a gourmet chef."

"I don't know if I'd say that, but she does cook well. Anne-Claire isn't very good at giving compliments. Not to our daughter, and certainly not to me. With Frédéric she's a little better."

"You're nuts," said Jayne. "Jeanne-Lucie is an amazing cook. You should both be able to say it to her without reservations."

He leaned against the doorframe, watching her pull on a black tank top. She wore the top to bed sometimes, or had in New York, when she'd still slept alone on some nights. "Jeanne-Lucie doesn't know how to accept compliments."

Jayne gave him an arch look. "I wonder why."

He looked tired and older than usual, despite his fitness and his beautiful clothes—the light gray summer suit and brown loafers, highly polished. She couldn't remember if this was what he'd been wearing when he left for the gallery around midday. The morning felt very distant, as if since then she had traveled to another country and returned to find things subtly but noticeably altered.

"What else did you talk about?" he asked.

She felt a knock of defiance in her chest and blurted out the words she hadn't been sure she should say, certainly not so soon. "Your ex-wife told me not to trust you. She also said that she was in New York in March and that you took her to dinner."

There was no trace of evasion or guilt on his face. "Anne-Claire and I have known each other a long time, Jayne. More than thirty years," he said. "We are friends, and that is all. I didn't think to tell you she was in New York because it didn't mean very much to me."

She looked at him steadily for a few seconds before turning to hang her damp towel on the hook next to the tub. "She took such pleasure in telling me about seeing you there," she said. "She knew that you hadn't told me. I felt like an idiot."

"I'm sorry you felt that way, Jayne. It was rude of her to tell you, but there really is nothing between us anymore. Maybe some old resentments, but most of the time we avoid arguments."

She slipped past him into the hall. A few feet away were Sofia's family of portraits. Looking at the one of the father, she called to Laurent. She could hear him peeing now. "I met one of your former assistants at lunch," she said loudly. "Martin Donnell."

There was silence.

She repeated herself, raising her voice a little more.

"Yes, I heard you," Laurent called.

"He seemed nice," she said.

"He and my daughter are good friends." He paused. "A little too good, you could say."

She heard the water running in the sink before Laurent appeared in the hall. He passed by without touching her and went into the bedroom. She glanced again at the portraits, the father's expression shifting into a question: *Do you really need to . . . ?*

"What do you mean?" she said, following him into the bedroom.

He had his shirt off and was hanging it in the closet, oblivious to or else not caring about its gaminess. "I think they spend too much time together, but from what my daughter has told me, Daniel does not protest."

"I thought Martin might be your ex-wife's boyfriend."

He laughed. "No, no. Not Martin."

Why was he being so vague and smug? "What does that mean?" she asked again.

"Martin is in love with my daughter, not my ex-wife. You must have noticed at lunch."

"No, I didn't," she said. "Anne-Claire made sure that we paid attention to little besides herself."

"That sounds familiar, but it is still true about Martin."

"He seemed very kind. I liked him."

"My daughter used my apartment to meet with him while I was in New York," he said. "I am almost certain."

"No. Really?" she said. "Doesn't he have his own place?"

"Yes, of course he does, but it is nicer here, and I think he has a roommate. He did when he worked for us."

"If I were her, I wouldn't want to meet my lover at my father's apartment."

"You are not her, Jayne. Do not look so surprised. It is comfortable here, and I am sure this building is more private than the one where he lives. That is what is most important."

"Privacy," she said.

He shook his head. "No, comfort."

"Did they use your bed?" The thought bothered her, as if she were being forced to wear a stranger's unwashed clothes.

He wavered, noticing her discomfort. "I don't know. I assume they used the guest bedroom."

"If they came here at all."

"Oh, I think they did."

"How do you know this?" she asked.

"They left a few things here—a letter addressed to him from his mother, a hairbrush and a shirt that Jeanne-Lucie admitted was his. I think they intended to remove them before I returned from New York, but they must have forgotten."

In bed a little while later, when Laurent had her pinned beneath his sweating, lean-muscled body, her arms captured at the wrists and gripped hard above her head, she looked up into his shadowed face, where only headlong purpose could be deciphered. She too was close to the final ecstatic leap and found herself begging, "More, Laurent. Please." Then she said it again, her voice ragged with pleasure.

He paused, eyes flickering, before tightening his hold on her wrists. Leaving her behind, he came in a seismic, angry roar.

Her sleep that night was erratic—her parents and sister, Jeanne-Lucie, Martin, Colin, Laurent, and André fading in and out of her dreams in half-awake leaps from one face, one image, to the next. She woke herself up sometime before dawn when she cried out, though she wasn't sure what she had said, and it was possible that the sound had only been a gasp, loud in her dream but little more than a whisper in the darkened bedroom. Laurent shifted onto his side, sighing softly as he resettled his head against the pillow. She could feel her heart knocking fitfully in its cage as she got out of bed and went into the study to look at the painting of Joanie. She was having trouble using light in the way she intended, to bend or extend line, but she hoped that she was making progress.

Sofia understood the principles of light and line; each of the six portraits in the hall was as insightful and skilled as the larger portraits by Bernard Ferriss that Jayne had seen and reluctantly admired at Vie Bohème–New York on the night she met Laurent.

Perhaps André had tried to kiss Sofia too—or, who knew, maybe he had gone so far as to fall in love with her, though Jayne's impression was that he was too much of a womanizer to permit himself to be vulnerable enough to fall in love. She knew not to trust him, but she still had not yet told Laurent that his partner had kissed her. If André told him first, she had no idea how he would slant it. In the morning, whether or not she felt ready, she would talk to Laurent after his first espresso and Gitane of the day, when his mood was usually good, though in truth it was rarely ever bad.

CHAPTER 18

A Beautiful Woman

"Do you guys have paint-by-numbers in France?" asked Jayne. "I used to do those when I was a kid."

Laurent looked at her over the top of his newspaper. They were in the kitchen, sunlight muted by the sheer white curtains, he at the table eating a piece of buttered baguette while she flitted about, sponging off the countertop next to the sink. Someone was whistling outside in the courtyard; it sounded like a Journey song Jayne's sister used to sing in a falsetto to make her laugh. Jayne heard corny 1980s pop songs, played without a trace of mockery as far as she could tell, everywhere in Paris, songs that she had been taught to deplore in grammar school by the boys she'd had crushes on.

"What is paint-by-number?" he asked.

"I guess you'd say it's a kind of toy," she said. She was going to tell him about André and could not quell her nervousness. "You fill in a picture with different colors according to a numbered code."

"Oh, yes, I have seen those. You are like a vacation tour with everything scheduled in advance."

"Kind of, yes." She paused, her anxious mind registering that the whistler was moving away, taking the Journey song with him. "Laurent," she said.

He glanced up again from Le Figaro, the headline trumpeting more funding for TGV train lines. "Yes?" he said without curiosity.

It looked for a moment, unbelievably, as if he would laugh after she told him what had happened in the back office with André. Something shone out from Laurent's eyes and then abruptly was gone—it had the startling gleam of mirth.

"I am more annoyed that he told you first about the vernissage than I am that he kissed you. I wanted to be the one to tell you about the show, mais alors, sa bouche. He can never keep his mouth closed."

"I'm sorry about what happened," she said. "I felt ashamed that he thought he could do it at all." Saying this now, she wondered if this was a lie. She'd felt embarrassed, but shame had been harder to locate in the tangle of conflicting feelings that had assailed her.

Laurent did not reply for several seconds and turned the crinkling pages of his newspaper before setting it down next to his crumpled breakfast napkin. "You are a beautiful woman, Jayne. Of course he wants to kiss you. He also believes that I was seeing his ex-wife for a time. He will always be seeking revenge against his imagination." He put a hand on her forearm. His fingers were disconcertingly cold; she nearly recoiled.

"Were you seeing his ex-wife?" she asked.

The brief rogue glint appeared again in his brown eyes. "Not really," he said.

"Were you?"

"We were never a couple," he said.

Who else should I know that you slept with! she almost snapped. Instead, she said, "What about Sofia? Is she your mistress?" She tried to laugh, wanting to make a joke of her doubt, but the sound came out choked.

"No," he said. He looked again at his newspaper, one hand on the crease, ready to return to its oily, ink-shedding pages. "She is my friend."

"Is she pretty?" She knew the answer, having already studied the half dozen photos she had found of Sofia online, but wanted to know what he would say.

His expression didn't change. "Yes."

"Prettier than me?"

"Jayne, please."

She said nothing and stared into the sink, at the drain basket with its bloated bread crumbs.

"You are different," he said. "I do not compare you to each other."

"I'd like you to introduce us."

"I am sure you will meet her if you stay here long enough."

"Do you want me to leave?" she asked.

He pursed his lips. "No, of course not. Do not do that, Jayne."

"Do what?"

He sighed. "Jump so quickly to suspicion of me."

She looked at him, his furrowed dark brow, his gaze now turned away. She was disgusted with herself, but her jealousy of Sofia in that moment was almost unbearable.

"I'm sorry about André," she said softly.

Laurent shook his head. "I know that you were his victim." He paused. "Am I correct in thinking this?"

"Yes, of course you are."

He regarded her dispassionately. "Good. Then that is that."

She nodded but said nothing.

PART TWO

Laurent, Fall and Winter

CHAPTER 1

The Frames

*U*nattributed, *anonymous* . . . The people mentioned here will no doubt know who I am if they take the time to read what I have written, but any person who does not know me, I am thinking, will probably not regret this fact. These pages are an attempt to explain how I have so far chosen to live. It is similar to what I intend to ask my artists to compose for me after their work has been exhibited at Vie Bohème. Long after their paintings or sculptures have been sold or packed away into storage, long after the closing date of their shows, there should be something left—just as a diary remains after someone dies, whether the dead like this or not.

Not having been able to make a career as a painter, and later, in a sense, having failed as a husband (though that failure was a joint effort), I realized a number of years ago that I needn't also fail at retaining some claim on the past, of making sense of what has happened to me and what I have caused to happen.

For example, I am no longer young, and in recent months I have been thinking that there are few men and even fewer women whose lives and legacies have continued to be remembered in our modern age, to be celebrated or cursed: Napoleon Bonaparte, Abraham Lincoln, Adolf Hitler, Catherine the Great, Attila the Hun.

Men and women who oversaw violent upheaval, who were responsible to a significant degree for millions of deaths and millions of
liters of blood shed on their soil and the soil of countries they
conquered or tried to conquer.

We have also Beethoven, Da Vinci, Michelangelo, Tchaikovsky,
Tolstoy, Vermeer, Rembrandt, Bach, Mozart, Montaigne, Shakespeare,
Voltaire, Manet, Picasso. Jonas Salk, Thomas Edison, Louis Pasteur.
Anton van Leeuwenhoek and Gregor Mendel. Marie Curie too, yes,
but our history has been dominated by men and their ways of seeing,
unfair as this might be. I am, after all, the father of a daughter and a
lifelong admirer of women.

What is the point of any life? This is what Jayne—not my
daughter, but my girlfriend and protégée—has asked me more than
once. She asked me this question not long after we met, when I was
already smitten with her, more than I expected to be, and more
than she expected too.

There is the old philosopher's answer: The point is to be.

There is the pacifist's: To live and let live.

There is the hippie's: To love.

There is the Zen Buddhist's: To be present.

There is Jayne's answer, as it was at the time: To be someone.

There is another answer, maybe the best one: To be kind.

And another: To regret nothing (but that is impossible, no?
Unless you have no conscience or else have been endowed with
such a charmed life that no trouble ever enters through your front
or back doors).

For years I have held on to love letters and old photographs. I have
held on to receipts and IOUs and the occasional regret, but not too
many. I have made lengthy notes, kept track, kept things straight, in

my mind at least, if not always in body and deed. It might sound cold, but these pages are not meant to be read by my son or daughter. They would not be happy, I suspect, with what they would discover here, although no honest accounting of any mature life is without its shadows, its trapdoors and dirty cellar floors, its attic rooms with all the cobwebs and blind, floundering bats.

There is the chance, however, that I will decide to throw all these pages away and no one will ever read them, unless I die suddenly, but I don't believe that I will. It might seem foolish to declare this here, but I have never been superstitious; ordinary life is not without its mysteries, of course, but to assume there are malevolent forces at work—something other than human beings in angry, destructive collectives, or dictators, or pillaging captains of industry—that, I have to believe, is a waste of time and energy.

Jayne has had many questions for me in the time we have been together—more than a year now, six months in New York, eight months in Paris. We have weathered changes of season—summer to fall, fall to winter. We have weathered visits from her younger sister and parents, from her friends Liesel and Melissa, with their floppy summer hats and bright red toenails and newly blond-streaked hair (both of them, and Jayne's sister, Stephanie, too! It was comical, though comedy was not their intention, I do not think). During Liesel and Melissa's visit in particular I had a headache more nights than not, the two of them, with Jayne, laughing and squealing so often, as my daughter Jeanne-Lucie had done at fourteen when she carried a torch for the actor Olivier Martinez and met him one afternoon when he appeared at Vie Bohème to look at everything with what seemed a discerning eye but then, to my dismay, he bought nothing.

We have also withstood visits from Jayne's friend Colin, though she does not know how much I know of her outings with him. She left her phone at home one afternoon when she went out for a long walk, and I read the text messages he'd sent to her, at first inadvertently, the iPhone chiming on the table next to where I sat looking at e-mail on my phone, no code to lock her own against intrusive eyes, I discovered then (though this has since changed). Colin had written to confirm an assignation later in the week, and when I opened the text window, a long thread unspooled before me, many exchanges over several months, numerous unequivocal facts about their ongoing liaison. This man from her life in New York has been coming to my city for business, and for pleasure. I will admit that you should not come to Paris if you have no talent for pleasure. That his pleasures are taken with Jayne at his side, I am not so thrilled about this, but it is to me she returns every night, and she only sees him every couple of months. How much, realistically, can I expect from her? If you look at this state of affairs in a harsh, truthful light, she has been with him six, maybe seven afternoons out of the last year.

If you are practical in this manner, even about perceived betrayals, maybe they are not so hard to live with.

This was one way my ex-wife and I tried to justify ourselves when we did something that upset the other. An hour or two with someone else, here and there. Why should this matter as much as it always ends up mattering? Why is the body such a faithless, straining beast? But that second question belies a bias—that it is wrong to please the body, and also, that what pleases the body, in my experience, sometimes ends up hurting some other body.

If you look at your life, you see that it is filled with routine tasks and obligations—with phone calls and dishwashing and cooking, with tooth brushing, showering, driving, dental appointments, food shopping, standing in line, typing, walking, waiting at stoplights, opening umbrellas when it has just begun to rain. How not at times to submit to temptation, to an occasion to veer off from the rote and responsible?

I for one do not want to die thinking about the beautiful women I had a chance to be close to but turned away from. No one who loves women would want to die that way. Because surely that is a miserable fate, perhaps the most miserable.

This is not to say that I am leaping every hour from one bed to the next. Nonetheless, if an attractive opportunity presents itself, I think you are indeed a fool to turn it away. I do not mean every opportunity. Only the best ones. I see the libidinous glint in my son's eyes too. He should understand me better, being in possession of his own blunt instrument of passion and occasional dishonor. He thinks I am the one who deserves the blame for his mother's and my divorce. Not true. Anne-Claire, like many beautiful women, had more admirers when she was younger than she knew what to do with.

Some of Jayne's questions for me, ones she has asked sometimes with a catch in her voice:

What were you doing in Paris during the six days that I was waiting to fly here from New York?

What is between you and Sofia?

Who are the other women in your life that I haven't met, besides your daughter and ex-wife?

Who was the woman who went with you to the nudist beach in Italy?

Why do you not go home more often to see your sister and the vineyard where you grew up?

What do you get from the artists you support, other than a pledge to continue making work?

What took you so long to get home tonight?

What happened between you and André's wife?

How many other women have lived here with you before me?

What do you really think of my paintings? My future as an artist?

What are the real reasons you asked me to move to Paris with you?

And again, always: What is the point of any one life?

Those are the frames and the following are the pictures that fill them.

CHAPTER 2

Young Artists

*I*f you have money or uncommon good looks, if you are healthy and good company, if you attract the kind of attention that other people alternately envy and admire, you possess the sort of advantages that may permit you to enjoy a happy life. Even so, permission is not the same as a guarantee. Money and a handsome face make things easier, but this does not mean that easier is always better or enough. I am not claiming to have lived through terrible hardship or to have failed at finding love and friendship. But I have enjoyed some of the advantages noted above, and have lived contentedly for most of my adult life in Paris, first alone in a two-room apartment in the attic of a bookstore on rue Gay-Lussac, and later with Anne-Claire in a five-room apartment on rue de la Montagne Sainte-Geneviève when she was still at the Sorbonne and I was painting the canvases I succeeded in hanging on few people's walls but our own. Frédéric and Jeanne-Lucie were born on this sloped street, with its disheveled students streaming in and out of the universities and lycées on the adjacent avenues and boulevards and narrow, crowded passageways.

We lived in the fifth arrondissement for several years before moving to a larger and sunnier apartment in the sixth near place Saint-Sulpice, a building with a concierge who stood for hours most afternoons in the courtyard doorway, waiting for her husband to return from the antique postcards and stationery stall they ran with their grown son at the *marché aux puces* near the Porte de Clignancourt. She was also there to watch the tourists and delivery boys and residents coming and going, her greying hair combed and curled against her pink-rouged cheeks, her fingers stained from many daily cigarettes. This was Madame Latour, whose real surname was Lasky, which I learned after a year or so of living above her and her family, when a letter meant for her was mistakenly placed by the postman in Anne-Claire's and my mailbox.

When I gave it to her that evening, asking if she knew whose it was, she nodded. "Mine," she murmured with a small, embarrassed laugh. She didn't meet my eyes. But what did I care if she and her husband, having emigrated from Poland forty years earlier, as I eventually learned, had chosen a more French-sounding name? Isn't everyone, to some extent, trying to leave behind their past, their former selves, with all the ancillary pain and doubts? Madame Latour could have asked me to call her Madame Mitterand for all it mattered to me. She was kind to my children, to Anne-Claire and me. Kindness is not so common, you realize, as you leave behind childhood and move farther into adulthood, with its treacherous landscapes, its ambushes from enemies known and unknown. There is also the aging body and the sense at times that you will be crowded out, or worse, trampled, by the sheer mass of other people alive at any one time. Of a hundred people, two hundred, a thousand, how many names, how many faces, will you remember a day later, a month later, a year?

Among the two or three hundred faces that passed before my eyes in New York on the November evening when André and I were expecting rainstorms and poor attendance for our new gallery's vernissage, Jayne's face was the one that stood out among all the others. "I would like to paint you," I might have said if I were still a painter. How many men have used that line to lure a beautiful woman into bed? It is not a bad line, as these things go. There are certainly worse: *You remind me of my daughter.* Or, *May I buy that zucchini for you? And afterward buy you a drink?*

She had an alert but soft look, her eyes a little tired, as if she had spent some time that day being scolded by a boss (or a therapist?). She was unsure of herself and her beauty. Whatever it says about me, I like that. I admire confidence but am more impressed by modesty, or maybe it is humility. In any case, the awareness that one has limitations, while at the same time believing they might be overcome—this is a quality that I find both rare and good. Her hair had been cut recently, I also remember thinking. Its satiny ends gleamed a rich dark brown. She stood very straight, her posture a dancer's, though she told me later that the only dancing she had done as a girl had been in her room to pop music, alone or with her little sister, and later with her girlfriends, the door now locked against annoying younger siblings. I could sense too that she did not sleep soundly every night—her mind seemed to be clicking away with unsolved or unsolvable problems. It was clear to me that she did not have a lot of money, despite how well-groomed she was, how carefully her blouse and skirt had been chosen, how well they fit her young, lithe figure. Having money yourself, you often learn to spot its absence, and the gestures toward it, in others.

Perhaps the most interesting detail about the way she circulated through the gallery: when she looked at the paintings, she knew something about how they had been made. The fingers of one hand tapped her thigh, a nervous, impatient motion she might not have realized she was making. In profile, I could see that her breasts were not large, but they were high and round, and I could imagine their weight in my hands, their softness too. These thoughts and impressions form so fast in a man's mind—much faster than it takes to write them all down. Her face reminded me of some of Renoir's young models, her cheeks flushed, her skin soft and clear. I wondered for a moment if she was already married but could not see a ring.

Then, unexpectedly, twice I turned to find her looking at me too. The first time you exchange a meaningful glance with a beautiful woman, well, I suspect it is obvious—this is the sort of thrill it is difficult to imagine yourself ever tiring of. I was in that gallery to sell art, and I was certain that she wasn't there to buy any of it, only to judge it, but I didn't care. Other people would buy it, and that night, several did.

I also felt sure that if I asked her to dinner she would say yes. She would say yes to most everything I asked, once she trusted me. Or rather, once she trusted me enough.

Something that is not often discussed: when a person falls in love, this does not mean he (or she) will no longer be in love with someone else. Love is an expansive element, and like helium and other gases, when fire is applied, it becomes volatile. But these concerns were all far away on that evening. When you meet an exciting new woman, you think about her, not the other woman or women you love, wherever they are. I sound guilty of something, I'm guessing, but I wasn't. I wasn't married anymore. The woman I was last close to, Sofia, was across the Atlantic, traveling through Italy and Spain with a friend, a man who was more than a friend, though Sofia claimed she did not take him seriously. He was a banker, not an artist, not a gallery owner, not an actor, or a director, or a fashion designer. "How can I take a banker seriously?" she asked me, laughing at my jealousy.

"You don't have to," I said. "But you do take his money seriously, I am sure."

"Oh, Laurent," she said. "Always thinking the worst of me!"

Did her banker know how talented she was? Did he know that if she did not allow herself to get pregnant and distracted, she would have an important, maybe even a tremendous, career?

One of the reasons I have allowed myself to become close to Jayne is because she is not interested, at least not at this juncture in her life, in having a child. We had a minor argument about my view that artists, especially female artists, should put off childrearing for as long as possible, or at least until they and their work are firmly established, although that often takes many years, and there is of course the risk that an older woman will not be able to conceive when she makes up her mind to do so. Last July, Jayne and I went to see Sidonie Clément, one of the three artists to whom I give a couple of thousand euros every month. She lives in an apartment off the boulevard Vincent-Auriol and paints in a closet-size second bedroom, its graying white walls fissured with cracks.

When we arrived at her door, she threw it open before we had finished knocking, startling Jayne and me both. Sidonie greeted us with a nervous smile, dressed in blue jeans, a paint-streaked black blouse, red flip-flops. I could see as soon as I set eyes on her that she was pregnant. Almost five months along, she confirmed, her thin laughter an apology of a sort as we followed her down the gloomy hall to her studio with its low ceiling and one dusty window that faced the neighboring building's eastern wall. Her boyfriend was living with her now, an Austrian boy named Stefan who works in the kitchen of a restaurant near place Pigalle—Chez Patric or Pascal; I haven't had dinner there yet, and can't ever seem to remember its name. He is training as a chef, and is responsible for the soups and broths, an important role in any kitchen, needless to say, and I was impressed when Sidonie told me this but have learned to keep my enthusiasms about my artists' personal lives to myself. If I portray myself to be a friend more than a patron (I am thinking of the French meaning of the word, "boss," more than the English meaning, "benefactor," though I am that too), my artists tend to expect more leniency when I express displeasure with their productivity or the directions in which they are taking their work.

Sidonie was not making the lush, deeply personal paintings she'd been working on when I began giving her money a year or so earlier. She was wasting her time and talents on foolish-looking wood carvings and thematically related paintings. In her studio, scattered on two rectangular worktables, one gouged by the chisels and carving knives she was learning to use, were wooden animals about ten to fifteen centimeters high, in various states of evolution—a leopard, an elephant, something that resembled a llama, a horse with a foreleg cast onto which ROBERT + CAROLE had been carved. The llama-like creature had one large bulging eye, the other eye a question mark. The elephant had an open umbrella for a trunk.

The new paintings in progress were other breeds of strange animals—one creature half tiger, half jackrabbit; another a black cat wearing the frilly neck ruff of an old-fashioned clown, its tail a pig's. The series was called La loi naturelle—"Natural law," she said, glancing from Jayne to me. "Our environment has many problems, and people have no sense of the sacred anymore. We are changing all our genes with chemicals and the scientists in the labs who want to clone everything. Pretty soon there will be no authentic creatures."

"And of course we're told that it's all in the name of making the world a better place," said Jayne. "These are so good."

"Thank you," said Sidonie, smiling and relieved, it seemed to me.

I said nothing.

"Money is an exciting word, but a dirty one too," she added.

I made a small coughing sound. I couldn't help it.

"The more money, the fewer moral questions asked," said Jayne, ridiculously agreeable.

"Exactly," said Sidonie, still smiling at Jayne, before glancing over at me. Her large, pretty brown eyes were so anxious that I made myself say something.

"Your new paintings are okay," I said. "But your landscapes and the portraits are better."

"Oh, yes, I know," said Sidonie, crestfallen. Her hands fluttered over the horse with the cast, over the llama with the goggle eye, brushing off flecks of sawdust. "I am still working with those paintings too. I have not abandoned them."

"I hope not," I said.

She looked at Jayne, as if for support. Jayne met her eyes and smiled again. I didn't think that I was being too severe, but I was not going to encourage Sidonie either. Was she wondering if I would withdraw support if I didn't approve of her new interests? With time, if she kept on this trajectory, I very likely would.

"I like working with the wood right now. It's a risk, I know, but—"

"That's fine, Sidonie. We'll see how it goes," I said, looking down at her disintegrating flip-flops. Her toenails were unpainted and badly in need of attention, but I suppose I could be grateful that she had not made an appointment at the salon, as this would not be the best way, in my view, for her to use the money she received from me twice a month. But we did not have a contract; our agreement was only that she keep producing thoughtful work. If she stopped working, I stopped sending money. Tacit in our unofficial agreement was also the fact that I had to continue to like her work too.

With each of the dozen or so artists I have helped over the past eleven years, it is usually apparent within a year and a half that they have a real future as an artist or else are better suited for something else. One painter became a graphic designer and has done well designing logos and other corporate materials. Another, a sculptor of beautiful and alien female bodies made from small household objects, decided that she would be better off spending her life designing haute couture hats for the atelier of Yves Saint Laurent when the opportunity was offered to her. Another stopped making art altogether and moved to Saint Lucia to open a café with her mother, who had recently been remembered fondly in a long-ago lover's will.

But most of the artists I have helped have continued to make fine art, even after my patronage ended. Some teach in art academies to supplement their earnings from the sale of their work; one is a guide for part of the year for a company that sells vacation tours in Morocco and Tunisia. Another creates and oversees large-scale mural projects for different municipalities and arts organizations.

As we were leaving Sidonie's apartment, her boyfriend came out of the kitchen to look us over. He was not tall and had a bulldog's neck and shoulders. He shook my hand with his ruddy kitchen worker's hand, one that he had probably burned many times while learning his art of boiling broths and simmering potages. We stared at each other for a few seconds. In his dark green eyes I could see his fear of the future, his need for reassurance, but I knew that I was not the right person to offer it to him. He smiled and turned to look at Jayne, who had dressed up for the visit, unnecessarily, in a a black miniskirt and a tight black-and-white-striped top, worrying, I suppose, that Sidonie would be more glamorous than she turned out to be. Not every pretty woman is the enemy that other women, pretty or not, old or young, assume she will be. But I am aware of these rivalries; I am aware of the jealousy and willingness to perceive slights and the outright hostile obstructions that pit women against each other. They should not blame men for all their troubles, however—we who are said to make every rule for how a woman is supposed to look and act. If this is true, why don't more women protest these circumstances?

In the taxi back to rue du Général-Foy, Jayne and I had a disagreement over Sidonie's condition.

"Did you know before today that she was pregnant?" she asked.

"No, I did not."

"I thought you seemed surprised," she said, regarding me with suspicion.

Did she think that I had something to do with Sidonie's pregnancy? Because I certainly did not. "I was surprised," I said.

After a moment she said, "I like her work. She seems very nice too."

"I am not very happy about the wood," I said. "I think it is a waste of time."

Jayne did not agree. "I thought that what she's done with it so far is interesting. I doubt you have to worry about her crossing over to a kind of craft-fair art. Knickknacks, that kind of thing."

"We will see," I said.

"You were a little grouchy up there with her."

I looked down at Jayne's legs, her miniskirt riding far up her thighs. She had gooseflesh from the taxi's air conditioning. Outside it was a hot day, 33 centigrade, maybe even a little hotter. "Sidonie should not be having a baby," I said. "She and Stefan cannot afford it."

"I'm sure they'll figure it out. Their parents will probably help them if they can."

"I do not want my money to be used for baby clothes and diapers," I said, irate. "And those wooden circus animals. Is she planning to make art for children now?"

"I thought they were good," she said flatly.

"Yes, for a nursery," I cried. A song was playing on the radio loudly, one by a band my son was crazy about in his adolescence; the musicians were all screaming American males and barely talented. I asked the driver to turn it down, and he did without a word.

"You can't expect to be able to tell her when she can or can't have a baby," said Jayne. "It's just not something you can do, whether you're giving her money or not."

"I really do not understand why people are in such a rush to have children when life is so much easier without them. And frankly, better."

She laughed. She was angry, but instead of raising her voice, she poked me in the side, hard. "You wouldn't say that in front of your own kids, I hope," she said.

"No, I wouldn't, and while they were growing up, I didn't think it, but now, looking back, I see that this is the truth. Everything is easier if you do not have to worry about a child." I glanced at her. She was listening, and to my surprise, without condemnation in her eyes. "You must know this too. You have told me that you do not think you will ever have a child."

"Obviously not everyone feels the way you do about parenthood," she said. "My friends with babies are nuts about them."

"You can love the child, but not the fact you are a parent. Those are two different matters."

"I don't know," she said.

"They are. That is the truth. I know this, but you cannot, never having raised a child yourself."

"Maybe someday I will," she said, annoyed.

"Yes, maybe you will." It won't be mine, though, I thought but didn't say.

• • •

One other exchange from our visit with Sidonie remains in my mind's eye and ear. My behavior was rather foolish, which I didn't really grasp at the time.

As we stood at the door of Sidonie's apartment, ready to make our way down to the street and leave behind her wooden animals and her tired boyfriend, who seemed to want nothing more than for us to go and not come back—my presence implied, I suppose, that he could not take adequate care of her on his own—Sidonie announced that they were getting married, most likely before the birth of their child. Jayne was happy for her and congratulated her with enthusiasm, before looking at me to do the same. I did wish her well, but I wanted to say aloud that she must not let her changing domestic situation keep her out of her studio for months at a time. Cold as it must sound, if she expected the checks to keep arriving without new work being produced in that sawdust-filled cell, I would need to let her know this would not be the case. I said nothing of it, though. As much as I wanted to, I held back the warning, knowing it would sound more like a threat. It was better to wait to see what she would do after she gave birth.

"We will call the baby Joie, boy or girl," said Sidonie.

"Joie," Jayne repeated. "That's very pretty."

"It means joy," I said.

"Yes, I know," Jayne said, her voice tight.

Sidonie laughed, though not out of spite; instead, I suspect she was trying to diffuse the awkwardness between us. I was sure Jayne would not forget that I had embarrassed her, but I was so disappointed by the visit and therefore unable to keep myself from forcing her to feel some of my displeasure too.

. . .

Why do I give money to artists I barely know, ones who might, as has been suggested by more than one friend, somehow be conning me?

I think of it in this way: if you have the means to make someone else's life easier, someone who is doing something you admire and want to encourage, why shouldn't you share some of your good fortune? I am not without self-interest either, obviously. I own a gallery and profit from the work of the artists I represent. Half of those whom I have helped financially over the last several years have ended up with their work in Vie Bohème. Some of my investment in their talents has paid dividends. But there is no guarantee that the artists I am currently helping will earn me anything in return, and although I admit that it would be nice if they did, I know that I won't spend years feeling angry about it if they don't.

You give to other people if you can, and you might end up making their lives better. They in turn might also go on to make someone else's life better. I have inherited money from my parents, who along with running a successful vineyard also invested in real estate in Italian, Caribbean, and South African resort towns. My sister and her husband run the vineyard, which is part of a Gevrey-Chambertin collective that produces one of the Bourgogne region's celebrated grands crus and a number of other good, less distinctive vintages. Camille and Michel are happy that I do not interfere with the family business, but admittedly, this has caused tension between us. Long ago, when I was nineteen and very arrogant and self-assured, I told my parents that I intended to make art, not table wine, and this did not go over so well, but there was never any threat that they would disown me. Camille stepped into my shoes at home, and she has never deviated from her devotion to Maison Moller. Any interest that I have expressed over the years in the vineyard's day-to-day operations, any request for information about the vines or the weather conditions or the state of the oak barrels in which the wine is aged, or about the harvest, which I know I am not truly a welcome participant in, even though I would gladly come down to help them each year—any question I might ask is construed as criticism, or worse, a desire to usurp her place as the loyal lifelong servant to and CEO of the family business.

When I sold off the several vacation properties our parents had left to me, the sum was significant enough, in addition to my share of the annual profits from the vineyard, that I would not have had to work another day if I chose not to. My sister has held on to the properties willed expressly to her, and she rents them out to vacationing Americans, Russians, Germans, Japanese, and Brits with a management company she hired to help her and Michel with the particulars. They do well with them, but I preferred to have my money in a lump sum. I started Vie Bohème with some of it, and met André shortly thereafter; his wife Caroline—now ex-wife—was friends with a number of good artists, some in need of representation.

Before long André and I set up shop on rue du Louvre (not my ideal location—that would be in the sixth arrondissement on rue Bonaparte, but through a school friend, André found our space for much less than what a smaller storefront in the sixth would cost). We had signed on artists whose work was more skillful and interesting than the imitation Monets and Renoirs that I had been painting and futilely trying to sell—romanticized landscapes of the people and countryside where I grew up. I was also painting Van Gogh–inspired interiors of hospitals and fromageries and garages. (Garages! What could I have been thinking when I tried to paint these greasy, light-deprived interiors in the style of the mad Dutch genius? I have no idea what was wrong with me. Or with Anne-Claire for not telling me to stop immediately. It wasn't until we were in our final ugly year together, insults flying aggressively and as often as the starlings outside our windows, that she told me how untalented a painter I'd been. If I had just continued faithfully copying the faces and objects from sales ads or photographs—which I had done when I first was learning how to draw and paint—she thought that I might instead have become a competent enough illustrator. Our daughter, ironically, went on to become one and is very good, but she does not have the work ethic she should have, and her husband also makes too much money, probably, for her to be hungry or ambitious enough. And for that matter, my own wealth did not, early on, encourage hunger in her either.)

The ego is good for some things, but in financial matters not always so much. I was able to add to the money from my inheritance because I stepped back and did not go into a self-pitying depression (not for long, in any case), over the fact that other artists were making work that people wanted in their homes, and I was not.

CHAPTER 3

Charity and Profit

Jayne is gifted. Without question I knew this when I first saw the delicate, precise oils of the strangers she had painted from scavenged photographs, and the street and hillside scenes framed by the windows of her parents' home in southern California. Some of these paintings were hanging in the dismal apartment in lower Manhattan that she had shared for years with a series of other destitute girls, and I thought, "I did not expect this," but I kept my surprise to myself.

Every other person I meet tells me with a smile somewhere between self-mockery and defiance that he or she is an artist or has always wanted to be an artist. I know that it's the same for writers, according to my oldest friend, Paul Ligault, who is a novelist of some repute in France, though it has been several years since his last book. How many fans or family members or former students have told him they're going to write a book one day, or they are in the midst of trying to write a book, or they have an excellent idea and would love some help writing a book and maybe he has some time, some suggestions, knows an editor, knows a filmmaker in Paris or Rome or Hollywood . . . ? When Jayne first told me that she had studied painting in college and still drew and painted a little in her scarce free time, honestly, I didn't think much of it.

Another surprise: she never asked me for a show—out of fear or a species of calculated, mercenary patience, or perhaps a failure of confidence? Nonetheless, I felt the gentle, constant pressure of her hopefulness. I tried baiting her a little, seeing what she would do when I praised other artists without also praising her. I was not cruel, but I wanted to see if she might say some unguarded thing, reveal the depth and intensity of her ambition. On the whole, however, she kept it reined in, and so I believed that she cared for me, for my confidence and kindness to her, for my foreignness, and for how I made her feel in bed. That I have money, that I am co-owner of just the kind of elite commercial and artistic enterprise she hopes some day to be an integral part of, well, that is mostly happenstance.

But even if it is not, I don't really mind very much. I think it's true that the people we open ourselves up to, whether as friends or as lovers—we choose these people with some calculation, conscious or not. Maybe they dress well and seem delighted by life all the time, things we wish we did too; maybe they are wealthy and will be generous materially with us because we are poorer; maybe they are beautiful and make us look closer to beautiful when we are with them, smiling and laughing too. Though sometimes these hopes do not work out so well; their wealth and beauty might underscore our relative poverty and plainness. We end up resenting them for not making us happier, for not making us look better, but this seems such a cynical way to view the world and how we interact with each other.

I asked Jayne to move with me to Paris because I was attached to her, but also because I knew that she would not fulfill her promise in New York. She could not afford to live there; few people can, despite the irony that it is the most densely populated city in America. Working those two miserable jobs she was wasting her life on, maybe earning thirty or thirty-five thousand between them, her share of the rent a thousand dollars per month, not a good rent-to-salary ratio—how was she ever going to find the time and energy to get her work ready and in the hands of someone like me, who could change these circumstances for her? Because again, if you can make someone's life better—without, I suppose, doing harm to your own—shouldn't you?

This, after all, is the ethos that bolsters a million different charities. If we think of charity on a more personal scale, we could do as much individually for a few specific people as any big organization like PETA or Médècins sans Frontières or UNICEF does for larger groups.

It is a rather extraordinary thing, though, I know—I opened my home and invited into my life in Paris a young woman I had only known for four and a half months. I gave her food and employment and leisure to make her remarkable paintings. Most important, perhaps, I eventually offered her a show in my gallery. I also introduced her to my daughter, who became her friend, and before long to my son, and to some of my own friends. I trusted her with my business partner, who in short order proved himself untrustworthy where she was concerned, though in fairness to André, I did not behave as nobly as I could have while he and his wife Caroline were deciding whether to get a divorce, a couple of years before we opened Vie Bohème–New York. But André was hardly the most loyal husband in the world, let alone on the little street near the Bastille where he and Caroline lived. She had real cause to leave him: the second e-mail address used for correspondence with his lovers, the gifts paid for from their shared account, the forgotten anniversaries and airport pickups and other minor but ultimately catastrophic disappointments he visited on his lovely wife, who is also quite a bit smarter than he is. He should have chosen a woman who is less watchful, less skilled at adding up discrepancies and detecting the reasons behind them.

The fact that I helped her come to a final decision about their marriage by making myself available to her in ways that perhaps I should not have is not a point of pride, but she and André were separated during the few weeks that Caroline and I were meeting at my apartment for late dinners and sex, and sometimes, rather than going back to her friend Clothilde's apartment, she would stay the night. The next morning we often took our time getting out of bed and having breakfast. And after I had cleared the table of our crumbs and dishes, she let me wash her long red-gold hair, closing her blue eyes in pleasure, her thin, strong, pianist's fingers gripping the side of the porcelain tub as the warm water coursed over her head and back.

Not until months had passed did André learn of our evenings and mornings together. Caroline had promised not to tell him, but he discovered our liaison from an old e-mail exchange he found on my computer in the gallery office when he was checking to see if I had paid the same bill twice. As it turned out, I had left for the day in absentminded haste to meet another woman, the caustic and brilliant Sofia. He had always suspected that his wife found me attractive, that I found her attractive too, and it was true, but until that time, on the eve of their divorce, we'd indulged in nothing more than light flirtation.

I remember now that it was more than a few weeks that Caroline and I were seeing each other; it must have been closer to six or seven. André was in New York during some of this time, looking for locations for our new gallery. When he returned to Paris, I had trouble meeting his eyes for a few days but forced myself to do so. I also made sure that I had errands and appointments outside the gallery whenever he planned to be there for more than a couple of hours at a time. This was not unusual—I often had to be away from rue du Louvre for one reason or another, and I knew that if I wanted to continue working with him, I had to stop seeing Caroline. It would have to be a gentle break though, nothing too violent or dramatic that would have her swearing revenge on me too. Ideally, I wanted her to be the one who called it off. By invoking my guilt, by reminding her of some of André's good qualities (his spontaneity, his tendency not always to jump to the most obvious conclusion, his playful sense of humor), I was able to make her pause and reflect, to feel some of the shame I also felt. It was possible that my tactics would send her running back to their marital bed, and although I wasn't thrilled about this prospect, our liaison needed to end before I did long-term damage to Vie Bohème and the trust we'd built among art collectors and the emotionally fragile, often insecure artists who were our cakes and ale, our raison d'être.

Before you make up your mind about me, slashing an X through the box of my murky character, you should know there is more to the story. My daughter was one of the women with whom André had his own idylls while he was married to Caroline. Jeanne-Lucie and André of course tried to hide this fact from me, but if you live long enough and are at all vigilant, most truths will be revealed, whether or not you'd like them to be.

This was about five or six years ago, before Jeanne-Lucie had met Daniel, or maybe just after, but they weren't a real couple yet, I don't think. To a certain kind of woman, André is quite appealing: he is attentive, confident, and gives the appearance of having quite a lot of money. He does have some, but at the time he and Jeanne-Lucie were meeting for trysts at the apartment she lived in off of Avenue de Wagram, one of the spokes protruding from the Arc de Triomphe—an apartment, incidentally, that I was paying for—a fair portion of André's money was Caroline's from her success as a musician, and from her father's willingness to connect us with artists we were interested in representing.

Upon learning that one of Jeanne-Lucie's lovers was my married business partner, I had a few different reactions. On the one hand, I was outraged and alarmed—What was she thinking? Where was her conscience? What if André, as unlikely as this was, ruined her chance for future happiness with a more suitable man? What if Caroline became unhinged and, in a jealous fury, murdered my daughter? (And her own husband too, though I wasn't as worried about that.) Conversely, I also felt something close to admiration. What chutzpah my daughter had. She had found herself drawn to an older, attractive man and had decided to enjoy him. She was twenty-two, André thirty-five. She told me later, after their fling was over, that she had never seen a future with him—not at all. She had wanted to have fun, and he had made her feel good about herself. In her view, it was uncomplicated. Though it was also risky. She professed to feel respect for Caroline and did not intend to let her find out. I don't think Caroline ever has, unless André himself has told her, but I doubt that. He likely thinks of it only as a footnote in his catalog of amorous adventures anyway.

A daughter is different from a wife, yes, but I don't believe that the feelings of trespass and affront are much different in the situations I have been describing. It's a rare husband who doesn't mind the thought of another man touching his wife's willing and supple body. But it is also a rare father who isn't upset by thoughts of his fair young daughter falling prey to a libidinous, deceitful man.

Even if, yes, it is two who must walk the path from the front door to the bedroom and its inviting confines.

My daughter, somehow, got a slightly more generous helping from Eros's bag of tricks and troubles than I believe my son did. She is a sensualist, which in general and within reason, I believe to be a good quality—why inhabit a world as sumptuous as ours and not enjoy its riches? (In the case of friends and lovers too, the sensualist generally makes a more interesting companion than an ascetic does.) When Jeanne-Lucie told me a few years ago that she intended to marry Daniel, I tried to dissuade her, but she was pregnant and sure that it was his. He wanted to be a father; he was five years her senior and ready to settle down, he'd told her. And so Jeanne-Lucie thought she should try and learn to like or at least abide the conventions of marriage and motherhood and monogamy.

But another M-word complicated things: Martin.

How surprised Jayne was when I told her about the trysts I suspected Jeanne-Lucie and Martin of conducting at my apartment, during the months I was in New York overseeing Vie Bohème's successful launch. Although I don't want to be a scoundrel, sometimes it is hard to resist testing the limits of her innocence.

An example:

More than once after she moved in with me, I encouraged her to keep a diary, which she alleged that she did, but I never saw her writing in one, and for a few months I wasn't sure if she really did possess one. One Wednesday evening, however, when she had taken herself to the movies after working at the gallery, I came upon it. It is a small green book with a black elastic band attached to either edge; she had left it on the desk in the study that I have turned over to her for painting and whatever else she sees fit to do in there. I am not in the habit of snooping in other people's private papers. One thing that I know, from mistakes made when I was first married: it is not a good idea to go looking for bad news. Plenty will reveal itself to you of its own accord.

There is also the well-documented fact that a person's desire to take stupid risks will lead to unnecessary complications—my ex-wife's risk taking, for example. I once came upon her in our salon, sitting very close to a man with whom we were both friendly at the time. His arms had been around her, I was certain of this— his lips pressed to her lips—only a moment before I had entered the apartment, returning home from a three-day business trip to Cannes. Anne-Claire denied any wrongdoing, but I knew she was lying.

I believe that the impact of the kind of bad news encountered in someone's diary can far outlast the impact of the bad news received through other channels of distribution, though—the words taking on special power in one's distorting, guiltily seeking mind. A diary read behind its owner's back is a deadly little object, its voice a Siren's, its words the shoals you are broken upon each time you revisit them on the page or in memory.

Most of what I found when I opened Jayne's diary, my heart sending out stern warnings as I rashly glanced at the pages of that little green book, was innocuous, sometimes charming. If I had kept reading, I'm sure that I would have come across some observation or confession too difficult to digest, but I realized I had been let off the hook, like the gambler who walks away with a few extra dollars in his pocket because he knows when to stop. I skipped around a little, glanced at sentences here and there, before I got to the following passage:

> 9 Sept. — A warm, sunny day after three miserable, rainy ones. I loved that this morning there were so many little dogs being walked on Bld Malesherbes, moving their stubby legs like robots on speed. A woman about my age with big silver hoop earrings was walking two short-haired dachshunds ("le teckel"—I looked it up the other day—what a strange word). They were so cute. I wanted to stop and pet them, but the woman looked like she was in a hurry.

I stopped to sit in Sq. Marcel Pagnol for a while too. I love that it's
only a couple of minutes from the apartment, and so beautiful, like a poem
made out of flowers (corny, maybe, but true), crushed stone, wrought-iron
benches. The little floral fountain with all the rosebushes growing around
its base is something I could probably stare at for hours. I keep being
surprised by intricate little things all over the city (Why don't I remember
them from when I was a student?)—sudden clamoring colors among all
the beiges, grays, and dirty whites, small recessed fountains in the walls
of old stone buildings, the way the city is lit at night—I can see why
so many people have come here to claim (at last!) the lives they've been
hoping for.

Whatever happens between Laurent and me, I have to thank him for
bringing me here.

I read this passage fast and afterward forced myself to put back
her tiny, grass-green book where I'd found it. I had to wonder, of
course, if she had left the diary out on purpose, wanting me to pick
it up and find something inside that she didn't have the courage to
tell me directly. I knew that she was still corresponding with Colin;
she had admitted as much after she'd been with me in Paris for a
few weeks, after I asked if he'd encouraged her to paint too. She
said that he hadn't, not really, but she hadn't talked very much with
him about art either—her own or anyone else's. What I didn't
yet know was that he had managed to find a job requiring him
to come to Paris from time to time, and he was trying to steal her
back from me.

What had Jayne told him about our life together? What did he
think her true feelings for me were? What had she told him they
were? I tried to see myself through his young, covetous eyes: an
older, wealthier man from an elitist country (we know what the
world thinks of us, just as many Americans I've met are aware they

are considered loud, self-indulgent, but contrarily puritanical), an art gallery owner, a fool to believe that a woman Jayne's age, as lovely as she is, as talented, could truly be interested in me as a long-term lover, or eventually a husband.

She might not have told him that I'd made it clear before we left New York that I did not see us marrying—which is not so much a reflection of my feelings for her as it is a reflection of my feelings about marriage. Once was enough.

She doesn't seem eager to marry anyone, though, and I think she felt this way even before she learned that a marriage she has long believed to be stable—her parents'—is not an inviolable institution either. For a number of days this past October, she was very upset when she learned from her sister that their mother had left their father, not for the first time, and moved into a nearby friend's house, but after ten days, Kendra Marks apparently returned to Lloyd Marks because he promised to take her to Paris to see Jayne in the spring, and he also vowed to help more often with the laundry. He intended to pick up after himself more regularly too, and pledged not to begrudge her every eight-dollar pair of socks or pantyhose that she decided to buy. I wondered how long their truce would last, but did not ask this question aloud. Anne-Claire and I had had similar détentes in our own marriage, and needless to say, they had not lasted.

As an older man with a talented, attractive younger woman, I know that I am playing a game with long odds. Even if she is coming home to me every night, even if she is telling me she adores me, there are forces at work I cannot hope to control. I don't think about this very often though because what is the point? The Buddhists seem to have it right—be present, forget yourself, the goal is in the path. The Buddhists also say that life isn't about pleasure; knowledge and wisdom come instead from the experience of difficulty. I am not a Buddhist, but I have known some—my friend Paul Ligault, for one. I admire what I have learned about his practice without embracing it myself, although with time, I do think that all men find religion—whether it is in a church or a tavern or a whore-house or the natural world.

Paul met Jayne after she had been living with me for a little over four months when he dropped by unexpectedly one night after he'd returned from a long stay in Japan with a woman he knows there, another Buddhist, a priest, in fact. We had been talking amiably for a little while when he called Jayne by Sofia's name. He'd had had a few glasses of wine and lay stretched out on the living room floor, one of the purple throw pillows from the *canapé* under his head. I was teasing him about his dislike of chairs, an old argument. Neither of us ever gives in. The posture they force us into is destructive and unnatural for the human body, Paul always says.

"I believe you," I said, as I always do. "But how to stop using them?"

He laughed at me and turned to Jayne. "You can stand or lie down. It's as simple as that, isn't it, Sofia?"

Jayne looked from him to me, a smile trembling around the edges of her lips, her eyes stricken. A nervous laugh escaped her. (The next morning she would ask me why he had said this, though she knew by then that Sofia and I had once been lovers.) Paul looked at her, bewildered, not yet having realized his mistake. She and Sofia do resemble each other, something Jayne discovered on her own by finding photos of her perceived rival online.

"Her name is Jayne," I said to Paul.

"Oh, yes," he said. "Sorry." He laughed now too, embarrassed. "Well, you keep me on my toes, don't you, Laurent."

"As you do me," I said calmly. He couldn't have known that he had chosen the name of the one person he should not have mistaken Jayne for.

He glanced at her, his smile sheepish. "I apologize, my dear."

"It's okay," she said, her voice too cheerful. Her hands were gripping her knees. I could see her knuckles straining.

The apartment smelled like sauteed garlic, the odor suddenly asserting itself in this moment of distress. Jayne had made us a very good simple marinara sauce for dinner, one that I loved and she was happy to make frequently because it took so little time and had only a few ingredients: plum tomatoes, garlic, dried chili flakes, olive oil, salt. Paul had come in sniffing the air an hour earlier and had eaten all of our leftovers. I loved him as I would have loved a brother—maybe more. We've known each other since we were nine years old, and his parents also owned a vineyard in the Gevrey-Chambertin collective. He was more involved with his family's business than I, but as a working novelist (although not so much in the last several years), and as someone who had recently decided to study to become a Buddhist priest himself, he had left its care more and more in the hands of his aging father and a younger brother.

"Are you enjoying Paris?" he asked Jayne.

I couldn't tell if he wanted to know or if he was trying to make amends. He was not one for conversational hot air, for How are you? and Nice weather today and Tell me what's new. We might go months without speaking and a year or more without seeing each other, and he will show up on my doorstep and announce that he is tired of socialism but isn't sure if there is anything more humane, or that he has decided he wants his ashes scattered at the base of Mount Fuji.

"Yes," said Jayne. "This is my favorite place on earth."

"You need to see more of the planet then, I think," he said with a flirtatious smile. "Come with me to Japan next time. I will show you some beautiful places too."

She laughed but said nothing. She looked down at her hands and seemed to notice then how tightly she'd been holding her knees.

"How did you and Laurent meet?" he asked, glancing at me, maybe to see if I was upset with him. I wasn't, but I was ready for him to leave.

She answered the question, and I listened closely, not sure what I would find in her tone. "I wasn't planning to go out the night I met Laurent," she said. "It was a Friday, and I was tired from work, but my friend had a crush on one of the artists who was in the very first show at Laurent's gallery in New York." She went on to describe the suit I was wearing, how she'd been keeping track of me across the room, how before long I came over to her and tried to get her drunk.

"That is not what I was doing," I said, laughing.

"Oh, of course you were, Laurent," said Paul.

"I don't need to get a woman drunk to make her talk to me," I said.

"No, that's true. He just has to open his wallet," he said, winking at Jayne. "That will do the trick faster, and no drunk woman to worry about stuffing into a taxi later either."

"He has taught me well," I said to Jayne. "He opens his wallet, and any woman he wants will be going home with him in no time."

"Well, if it works . . ." he said, winking again at Jayne.

When he finally left, an hour and a half later, having consumed an entire bottle of grand cru from our collective as he ate our leftovers, including the chocolate torte I'd picked up on the way home from the gallery and was looking forward to having a piece of for breakfast, Jayne said that she liked him, that he had helped her get to know me better. "I wouldn't have expected someone like him to be your closest friend," she said.

"Oldest friend, not my closest," I said. "Not after tonight."

She laughed. "He's a flirt, that's for sure."

I smiled. "Yes, he is."

She regarded me, perhaps not sure what to think. I was speaking so noncommitally, in part because I was tired, it was almost midnight, and Paul has always had the irritating habit of showing up without warning and expecting to be welcomed with open arms—even now, after his Buddhist training, which I think is supposed to make a person more mindful, but it appears that nine years of study can't preempt the habits of the forty-four preceding years.

After Jayne and I went to bed that night, she asked why I hadn't invited him to stay over. Maybe he'd been expecting it?

I shook my head. "He has his own apartment," I said.

As her fingers played lightly with the hair on my chest, she asked, "Doesn't he live on his family's vineyard? I thought you said he works down there."

"He does live there, but he has an apartment here too." I remembered that she did not have the habits of mind of someone who has grown up with money. She had not been poor or deprived, but she had not, I knew for certain, been brought up in a home with acquisitive parents. If anything, they seemed to have taught her and her sister to regard material pleasures with suspicion or maybe, more likely, with dispassion. Jayne had lived in a middle-class Chicago suburb until her parents moved her and her sister to California, to a sunnier middle-class suburb of Los Angeles, the year she turned fourteen and began high school. I had not understood why she later left L.A. for the gloomier East Coast and, eventually, crowded, expensive Manhattan, where, as it turned out, her shy knocks on the art world's locked doors were not answered. She tried to explain that she was waiting until she had more work she felt confident about, that she wondered if she needed to apply to M.F.A. programs and make more contacts, but I reminded her that she needed only to make art to be an artist. And she had a mentor in Chicago, her Art Institute summer studio teacher Susan Kraut, whose work Jayne introduced me to, and which impressed me: her oil paintings of interiors (as if recently vacated by a quiet man and his quiet wife—elderly, childless, their dinners prepared and eaten, the dishes washed and put away by six o'clock every night) and a series of serene pears and persimmons on window ledges that looked out upon muted blue or gray skies.

I decided to contact her to ask if she had representation in Paris; if she did not, I wanted to include her—if she had new work she was ready to share—in the March show that Chantal Schmidt and Jayne had been scheduled for. I had decided not to include Jeanne-Lucie. Some other time, I thought. It seemed wisest to put my daughter and my girlfriend in separate shows, and I did not bother to ask André for his opinion. In general, he approves my decisions because the work I choose sells.

I wondered whether Susan Kraut would ask for a solo show, being an experienced painter and instructor of note at the School of the Art Institute in Chicago, but she was accommodating and so flattered by my call, and she spoke very fondly of Jayne and her work. She asked if she might take a look at her newer paintings and get back to me the next day. I suppose she wanted also to look into Vie Bohème to reassure herself that I was not a con man, about to try, by some circuitous means, to bilk her of thousands of dollars—or worse, I have to think—of her sensitive, beautiful paintings.

As we agreed, I called Susan back the following day, and she said yes to my proposal that we show five or six of her paintings with Jayne's and Chantal's. I admit to thinking, almost immediately, "How happy this will make Jayne. How good I am to her."

But how foolish it is to let oneself think these things, even if they are true. Self-congratulatory, self-deprecating, self-effacing, self-obsessed—whatever a person's proclivities are—I have to believe that they are no small part of what determines our fate.

CHAPTER 4

Daughters and Wives

*W*hen he met Jeanne-Lucie, Martin was married to a young woman from Neuilly, one of Paris's most wealthy suburbs, a place where as its mayor for nearly twenty years, Nicolas Sarkozy had sharpened his skills as a politician before marrying his singer/fashion model third wife and moving into the Palais de l'Elysée. Martin's father-in-law—a member of the cabinet of the Neuilly mayor who succeeded Sarkozy—was a magistrate by training who oversaw local public works. He did not like his daughter's choice of a husband, because not only was Martin half American, but he had left medical school in his third year to enroll in art school. It was there that he made friends with one of Jeanne-Lucie's friends, who before long, introduced Martin to my daughter, but she has told me that she is not the reason for his divorce, only a symptom of it.

I think of Martin, when he was newly smitten by Jeanne-Lucie, trailing behind her into Vie Bohème—he is three years her senior, but I think that she has always had the upper hand. He stared at all of our paintings as if intending to imprint them on his brain and go home to attempt to duplicate them. Jeanne-Lucie soon asked—no, in fact, she demanded—that André and I hire him as our assistant; I owed her that, she said. I was always owing her things, mostly because she saw me as the villain who had tied her innocent mother to the tracks as the divorce hurtled toward her and obliterated her life.

Well, hardly so. Her mother had and still has her own productive life. She also had her own lovers during our marriage. At least two—an older psychologist who mentored her when she was first seeing clients, and Paul Ligault's younger brother Georges, though of the latter liasion I am not wholly certain. If they did meet, it was infrequent, their affair conducted during holidays and on our rare visits with the children to Bourgogne to see my sister and her husband, and before then, my parents, who died when Anne-Claire and I were in our thirties.

It has been a curious experience to witness my daughter and Jayne's evolving friendship—my daughter who didn't speak to me for nearly a year when her mother and I were in the midst of divorcing, who resisted my advice not to marry Daniel or to wait a little longer if she didn't feel ready to, regardless of her pregnancy. It seems almost spiteful of her to befriend my girlfriend, when before now Jeanne-Lucie rarely took an interest in the women I have dated since her mother and I separated. Yet, Jeanne-Lucie has always been capricious. She appears genuinely to like Jayne; she has commented to me on Jayne's kindness and lack of artifice, and her talents as a painter. My daughter also, I suspect, likes Jayne's willingness to adore her.

Without realizing it, Jayne has inspired Jeanne-Lucie to become more restless than she already was—Jayne having no child to worry about and the freedom to explore her talents as a painter, to open herself up to new opportunities in a city celebrated for its long, romantic history of artists and their affairs, both personal and professional. I worry about Jeanne-Lucie's restlessness because my granddaughter senses her mother's inattention and must not know what to think of Jeanne-Lucie when she kisses Martin on the mouth as they say good-bye, longer than she should, I am sure, and Marcelle is at the age where she will start to make comparisons between how Maman acts with Martin and how Maman acts with Papa.

After Jayne's first luncheon at Jeanne-Lucie and Daniel's apartment, I asked my daughter why she had permitted her mother to join them. Jeanne-Lucie claimed that she hadn't invited her, but she admitted to having made the mistake of telling Anne-Claire about the date, and true to her aggressive character, her mother had insisted on attending. Why my ex's prurient interest in my private life continues, I am not sure, but I suppose it is mostly because she considers it a tasteless spectacle that allows her to continue to feel superior to me, even though on the surface, we are friendly to each other and manage to have an amicable dinner together now and then.

I do not like it at all that she never seems to tire of poking fun at me for my involvement with younger women. "Why are they so young all the time, Laurent? Don't you get bored?" she asked recently, her sharp eyes laughing at me. "What do you talk about? Which nail polish color to use next?"

"You don't have to be jealous anymore," I said. "You're free to go off and date younger men too."

She snorted. "Oh, yes, of course I am."

"You are. What's stopping you?"

She shook her head, pursing her pretty red lips. We were having dinner two evenings before Jayne was scheduled to arrive from New York. Anne-Claire had heard I'd returned home and had stopped by the gallery to see what new art was on our walls and criticize it, one of her favorite hobbies when we were still married too. "Younger men do not want to date older women, unless they are twenty and the women are thirty," she said. "But even then."

"I'm sure you could change a few of their minds," I said.

She ignored this. "How is that Sophie girl? Are you still with her?"

"Sofia," I said. "No, we are not together anymore. I told you that I'm seeing an American woman now. Sofia is in Italy, traveling with a friend."

"A friend," Anne-Claire repeated. "That girl doesn't have friends."

I wasn't sure what she was getting at, but I knew that it couldn't be very pleasant. "She doesn't?"

"No, she has slaves." She turned from the painting of two young black-haired women lying on yolk-colored beach towels, both of them suntanned and naked to the waist. It was a breathtaking painting, and I would sell it within a month to an Austrian collector who paid the sixty-five hundred euros we were asking for it in cash and also bought two other paintings by the same artist, an Italian man named Giulio Pardí who lives much of the year in Nice.

I laughed, but not loud.

"What did you say?" asked Anne-Claire.

"Nothing," I said.

"I thought I heard you say something under your breath."

"No, I was laughing. I didn't say anything."

She continued to stare at me but said nothing. She had been seeing patients before coming to meet me at Vie Bohème and was dressed in a black skirt and a short-sleeved poppy-red blouse, her arms and legs still sleek and girlish. She was a devoted custodian of her beauty and had told me more than once that she suspected it kept some of her patients from relaxing around her, but she had no interest in downplaying it, and there was also the fact that her patients kept their appointments. I had no idea how much they were actually helped by their visits with her. I couldn't believe that she became someone else, someone softer and more nurturing, when she closed the door to her office and sat across from her clients, strangers who had come to her for advice on how to cope with a lazy, directionless son or a wife who wanted to invite another man to live in their home.

"You'd be happier if you dated women closer to your own age, Laurent. I know I've said it before, but it doesn't hurt for you to be reminded." She spoke softly and dabbed her dinner napkin at the corners of her mouth. She had ordered a salad and a small bowl of squash bisque. I had been the gourmand in the marriage, the midnight snacker, the one who used to court heartburn and restless sleep. "I also wish you'd stop chasing girls around and pay more attention to your children," she said. "Frédéric told me that you didn't want him to come to Paris when he asked about visiting the other day."

I could feel anger rising in my chest: that old, perverse comfort, that sense of being wronged and misunderstood by the woman I had been married to for twenty years. I took a quiet, deep breath and reminded myself how happy I was to have escaped twenty more years of her intimate daily scorn. "I did not tell him he shouldn't visit. What I said was that I thought it would be better if he waited another week or two before coming with Léa and Élodie. I needed some time to settle in after being away for a year."

"That's not what he said when I spoke to him this morning."

"Well, then, I suppose either he misheard me or he was lying." She regarded me. "Why would he do that?"

"I have no idea." I continued looking at her until she glanced down and reached for her wineglass. One glass of Languedoc Chardonnay was all that she would have. She would be content with it too. I wanted two glasses, three—the entire bottle—but stopped myself after two. There are so many ways of classifying our tendencies, but I think one of the most telling must be this: there are those of us who do not wrestle very often or for very long with our appetites, who can simply say, Enough, and walk away, and those of us who are constantly at odds with how much we desire and what we actually allow ourselves. The gap between desire and restraint: here rages the river of discontent, one that often threatens to overflow its banks.

"You know very well that they prefer to stay with you when they come," she said. "Your extra room is larger, they say, but I think the real reason is because you let them keep whatever schedule they want. I don't like Frédéric watching television until two a.m., and he knows this."

"Yes, I'm aware of all that, but I told him he should still consider staying with you if they really do want to visit this weekend."

"Tell me what happened with you and Sofia," she said, refusing to be deterred from her wish to provoke me. "You wouldn't tell me when I saw you in New York last time."

"I wouldn't?" I said. "I don't remember."

She shook her head. "No, you wouldn't."

"Nothing happened, not really. Why do you ask?"

She smiled. "Just curious, Laurent. What else?" How ready to pounce she looked. I had no idea what was wrong with her that evening and wanted to find a way to end our dinner before the cheese course arrived, and especially before dessert—the mousse au chocolat that I would order and Anne-Claire would watch me eat, teasing censure in her eyes.

"We were always friends," I said. "Sofia and I were under no illusions that there was more between us than friendship."

My ex-wife laughed. "Oh no, nothing more. Of course not."

"Anne-Claire," I said. "Really. I don't see why you keep asking me about Sofia. Why are you so interested?"

"Women like her always interest me."

"You met her once," I said.

"Twice. I saw her again one day last fall when I was at the Cojean near my office, having lunch with Jeanne-Lucie."

"I see," I said. No one had told me about this encounter. Not my daughter, nor Sofia, nor Anne-Claire until now. "Did you speak to her?"

She gave me an amused look. "Yes, of course I spoke to her! She came over to me first, in fact. She remembered me from the day I came by the gallery, when you and André had left her there by herself."

"We often do that with our assistants," I said. "That's why we hire them." I had told her this how many times? And still, for reasons I couldn't understand, she would not let it go.

There are three main qualities that bother her about Sofia, I suspect:

- She is not afraid of other women, and Anne-Claire is the type of woman who often inspires fear in her gender (not to mention mine).

- She is as stylish as my ex-wife, when Sofia decides to make the effort.

- Sofia is a very talented painter—and because this talent is apparent in every painting she has made in the past several years, it cannot be explained away as a fluke.

A woman such as this—it is the world's good fortune that she was born. About Jayne, I think I can say the same, but her potential is still being plumbed. Sofia's is too, though, of course. They are both so young, just a year apart, Sofia born the spring before Jayne was. They could, perhaps, be sisters with their dark eyes, shapely ears, and long hair that is often held back in a band—Jayne's hair the color of dark chocolate, Sophia's of anise-flavored licorice. I describe them as if they are edible, which, in a sense, they are.

(Am I like Hemingway in that I might be accused too by Jayne of devouring women? I hope not. I try to give back as much as I might take from them. More, I hope.)

CHAPTER 5

Origin Story

*I*t has been more than twenty-five years since I've called myself a painter. Half my life. When friends asked why I wanted to be an artist, I could give them several reasons, but it wasn't until a while later, several years after I quit painting, that I realized the foremost reason was that I hoped to impress women. I wanted to impress other men too; of course I did. We want our friends to respect us (and envy us a little too) and our rivals to be threatened. I wanted to be able to say that I could produce things with my hands, things of beauty and intelligence that people, women especially, would have trouble tearing their eyes away from.

The idea that you want to master a skill purely for the joy of doing or being—well, I have trouble believing it. Humans are social creatures, we live and move in herds, we fight for attention and affection, even those of us who say we are loners and prefer our own company to other people's. I know that true hermits exist—men, rarely women—who leave society and have no wish to return, but I am not one of these people. I want to be among other people, to look at and talk to them, to kiss a lover's lips and touch her smooth, warm skin.

My parents were responsible in some ways for my adolescent desire to be an artist. When we came to Paris at Christmas each year and walked through its crowded, cold, exquisite streets—the storefronts bejeweled with expensive, closely guarded gifts—we also went to museums and churches to look at the stained glass, Sainte-Chapelle the one my father kept making us return to each December, until I started to be grateful for what seemed to be this Catholic shrine's immutability, how no matter what had happened in the twelve preceding months, it would be there, looking the same as it had the previous year—only the other tourists were different. As a boy, I spent the year between visits drawing from memory what I had seen on those trips. We did not take photographs; my father instructed Camille and me to remember with our mind's eye instead, and I took him seriously, teaching myself to record in pictures some of the rooms and museum galleries we had entered.

There were the streets too, and the girls who caught my eye. I drew their pink, wind-burned faces, their long legs in thick stockings, feet in buckled shoes and boots with heels. The girls I was most attracted to walked with their backs straight and chests thrust out, arms linked with another girl's, their expressions alive with laughter. These laughing, glamorous girls seemed agonizingly unattainable, but within a few years, when I was fifteen and at a birthday party for my friend Etienne Rivard, his older sister Fabienne took me into her room, locked the door, and offered herself up in all her womanly, eighteen-year-old splendor. She tasted of wine and garlic and let me press my nose to the soft, fragrant skin behind her ear and breathe in her warm, intoxicating scent until I found the courage to do what she wanted me to do. The elastic of her black silk stockings that reached up to mid-thigh, their tops just visible beneath the hemline of her miniskirt, was so tight that it had scribbled angry pink bands around her strong, smooth legs. She rode horses, and when I'd see her on some afternoons riding her chestnut mare Loulou on the road near my house, I thought that she was the sexiest girl in all of France.

In bed with her that first time—her parents, oblivious to our disappearance, were drinking the new vintages that night—my fingertips kept returning to the imprinted flesh of Fabienne's thighs, these temporary scars irresistible. I had the sense there in her bedroom, the Rolling Stones playing on the turntable, of finally waking fully to my life and its possibilities. I knew that women were going to be an important part of the story, maybe the most important part. That is still being decided, I suppose, but I'll risk saying that more likely than not, it's true.

Fabienne had a slim, limber body that she was already comfortable with, more so than I was with my own, with its occasional embarrassing eruptions and pimples and recent, coarser hairs. She showed me where to put my hands; she whispered and coaxed and told me gently how to use my mouth on her, one of her hands pulling hard at my hair whether I was making her sigh or moan or cry out, "Non, là . . . oui, oui, très, très bien, Laurent, oui . . ." I worried that someone might hear us, hear her especially. She seemed to hold nothing of herself back; I still remember my shock and pleasure in her cries and convulsions. I'd had no idea that girls were really like this—the movies, even the little bit of pornography I had seen, often showed women in submissive positions and attitudes, or else in cartoonish dominatrix roles. She didn't want to talk very much, not until afterward, and then she expressed surprise when I admitted that she was my first. "But you're so handsome," she said. "I'm sure other girls have offered themselves to you?"

Yes, I admitted, but not as boldly as she had, not without fear, not with so much feline confidence. I had kissed other girls; there had been some groping and a botched attempt at fellatio, but not what Fabienne had offered and also taken for herself.

I probably fell in love with her that night. Maybe I have always fallen fast. For three days I walked around in a haze of remembered carnality. I could not control my body, the impromptu erections after I sat down at the dinner table, or when I was at the lycée supposedly learning algebra or reading about the resolution of the War of 1812, or even worse, changing after school for a soccer match with my friends. At eighteen, Fabienne might as well have been living in another country. In the land of fifteen-year-old boys, there are curfews, no driving privileges, many locked doors real and virtual, and the unnerving sense that everything is meaningful and momentous. It took me a while to figure out that everything is not momentous, and a little more time to understand the fact that this relative lack of gravity is a gift handed down from above.

On the fourth day Fabienne appeared at my school, waiting for me with a heart-stopping smile by the gate. Every cell within me leaped toward her, but I stopped and stared at her sly, vivid face, making sure that she really was there because I had had her almost ceaselessly in my thoughts since being invited into her bed. She had borrowed her mother's car, and she drove me to her house, asking on the way how I felt, laughing when I stuttered an indistinct reply. Who at the school had watched us leave? I wondered. Her brother would surely know before long what we were up to.

We walked in through the back door into the kitchen, which smelled of stewed tomatoes and roasting lamb, and went straight upstairs to her room. Her parents were in Dijon doing household errands, and Etienne was with his girlfriend at her own house, Fabienne reported, smiling at me as if he were a coconspirator and would have approved of our new relationship, but I was certain that he would feel betrayed. I knew that he adored and admired her, though he wouldn't have said as much to me or any of our other friends.

She was not wearing stockings this time; she wasn't wearing any underwear at all. I could not believe how fearless she was, how daring and hungry. Within three, maybe four, minutes it was over, but Fabienne did not laugh or get angry with me. At that age, an amorous boy belongs to the same cadre of marvels as a circus sideshow character, and she knew that it was only a matter of minutes before I'd be ready again. I remember that it was early November, warm outside her bedroom windows; she had left them open, and I could look down at Simon, the family dog, a hairy, aging German shepherd mix. He was sleeping peacefully on the lawn, oblivious to the fact that my life had changed, that Fabienne was teaching me how to be a thoughtful lover, something I remain deeply grateful to her for. If I had had the same passion for painting that I do for women's bodies, I would have been a success.

As a painter, I was merely able to copy what I saw—faithfully but without, I finally had to admit to myself, finding the soul of my subject and capturing or imaginatively reinterpreting it. I might have made a good illustrator, but I knew that I would never approach anything like John Waterhouse's genius with his perfect *Ophelia* and the *Lady of Shalott* paintings, or *My Sweet Rose*, his female subjects so flawless and idealized that I could imagine lovestruck men losing their wits if they stared at these images for too long. When I first saw Waterhouse's paintings in a book my father's older sister, Aunt Cécile, gave me for my thirteenth birthday, hoping to encourage what she considered to be my artistic promise, I had trouble believing that women such as these walked the earth, but if they did, how to find where they lived and convince them to let you kiss them and touch their luxurious hair? How to inspire them to love you too?

I was mocked by artist friends who were firm in their belief that art was something more than a reflection of an artist's sexual desire, which I hadn't realized was the view I was embracing, not until they made this clear for me, though I don't think this is true for everything I painted—only, perhaps, the most elemental motive behind my wish to be an artist. I had moved to Paris at nineteen and began to lurk around the École Nationale Supérieure des Beaux-Arts, to which, a few years later, I did not succeed in gaining admission. Twice, a year between each attempt, I took the entrance exams and presented my portfolio to the admissions jury, and twice I was turned away. You are only allowed two chances, and so, that was that.

It was crushing—probably the worst pain I had ever felt, my self-doubt a savage, clawing force that left me wrung out and bleeding internally. By my second attempt, I had met and was close to marrying Anne-Claire, our parents disapproving of such an early leap into marriage from their homes far from Paris, far from the city that is the self-appointed arbiter of all that is beautiful in the world.

Maybe our marriage was doomed from the beginning; maybe Anne-Claire could not help but see me as a failure too, even though I came from a wealthy family and we and our children-to-be would never starve. And before long the idea also arrived that I might be able to sell the work of my artist friends, who had succeeded in gaining admission to ENSBA, but had no clear idea how to make a living from their talents. I conducted self-directed studies for a couple of years, reading the business plans of companies of various sizes and missions, talking to a number of gallery owners who were willing to share with me a few of their mistakes and successes. I put away the canvases and brushes and paints. With time, I learned how to make money from art rather than how to make art itself.

I did not undertake this change with a light heart, however. It took me years to accept that I was more skilled at imitation than at creation and interpretation.

As for Fabienne, she and I continued to meet for a few more months, into the new year, but after that she left Bourgogne and went abroad, married a man from New Mexico, divorced him several years later, and eventually resurfaced in France. She was the woman who took me to Italy, to the nudist resort that worries Jayne. Fabienne and I have kept up with each other, and meet from time to time when she is passing through Paris or I am traveling somewhere she also happens to be, and one or both of us is free. The friendship between her brother and me faded away after he learned that I was his older sister's lover; we had a fierce argument, one that ended with him driving his fist into my hotly blushing, defiant face. In any case, his and my paths have not crossed for years.

Perhaps he has forgiven me by now, but it isn't important anymore—these things happened almost forty years ago, which in itself seems to me the bigger injustice: how hastily our lives pass. Fabienne is still my friend, and her brother is not. I am sorry to have caused him distress, but at the time I wasn't sorry. I regretted nothing. She was one of the great joys of my life up to that point, possibly the greatest. A boy's carnal education, those earliest lessons especially, I believe most of us will remember far into our lives, the suspense and urgency we experienced, the mute awe. And what gratitude I felt toward Fabienne, her willingness to take what she wanted, to let me know that other girls may have felt about me as she did. There are people who live chastely, who think they can get by without wanting or needing sex, who say that it causes too much trouble, that it is dangerous and shameful, and that, like the value of one's bank account, this aspect of our lives should never be discussed. I do not believe them; I have to think that they have not been with the right person, or that something awful has happened to spoil it for them, whether it was abuse or shame over their appearance or too much religious dogma.

I can see ahead to a time when it will not be so easy for me to find a willing partner, beautiful and youthful (Anne-Claire can make as many snide remarks as she'd like to). This question should be considered too: would it be better to die than to live without this most instinctive and elemental of pleasures?

No, nothing that extreme, but I suspect that it would be like losing your ability to see color, to taste your favorite foods, to hear the nocturne that sometimes lulls you to sleep. I am not some kind of sex maniac or slavering addict—what I am mostly saying is that there are limits to what a person should learn to live without, that deprivation is yet another kind of sadness, possibly the worst kind.

CHAPTER 6

Other Women I've Known

*L*iving with Jayne is different from living with the women I have shared my home with in the past. Most days she is so quiet, never stomping from one room to the next or leaving her dirty clothes on the floor or talking loudly on the phone or watching the television at an unpleasant volume; she watches so little television at all. She would rather read and paint and draw or take naps in the quiet hours of the afternoon when the motorbike messengers are more scarce, when the boisterous students are locked up inside the lycée with which we share our street. Some days I have come upon her lying on the *canapé*, the curtains drawn on the tall northeast windows, a book facedown on her chest. She sleeps with head tilted toward her left shoulder, her face and brow pale. She is so lovely in these moments, sweetly childlike, as she is when she tells me a joke from when she was a girl, one that she must patiently explain to me, her expression growing tart, her eyes turning fiery with disbelief that yet again I do not understand! Her drawings—of human hearts with muscular aortas, of cats with owlish faces (or owls with feline faces), of dachshunds in little blue shoes—convey her sense of humor, these mementos she leaves for me on my pillow, a line or two written beneath each picture:

For you, mon amour, because we all need an owl in our lives!
You have my heart now (please take good care of it).

She must understand somewhere in this young heart of hers that our situation will not last, that her life with me will come to an end before long; other men here will catch her eye, or it will be Colin with his broad shoulders who succeeds in seducing her back to New York. Even then, I can see ahead to what she will experience: eventually she will find someone else, even if she marries Colin, has his child. Her essential restlessness is something that she is only beginning to admit to herself. We have many things in common, whether she believes this or not.

Hand-to-mouth circumstances in Manhattan kept her marching in place for a while, along with fear of losing the little she did have—her independence, such as it was, her place in a New York apartment with its interchangeable roommates. There are so many young women, from what I have observed, who live this way, waiting for the right person—lover, boss, dying relative—to come along and rescue them from the indignities of budget meals and inconsiderate neighbors and oppressive crowds, the near-ceaseless noise from the street and inside the claustrophobic buildings where millions of city dwellers are trying to live meaningful, mostly peaceful lives.

If it is nothing else, money is the escape hatch from the constant tyranny of other people's bad behavior. This is part of what I have offered her by taking her away from East Second Street in New York—the space and leisure to make art. It is what I offer the other artists I help support, something I started doing without Anne-Claire's knowledge near the gasping, exhausted end of our long marriage. Those ENSBA friends led to other artist friends, ones whose work I wanted for the gallery, and sometimes succeeded in acquiring and selling.

Over the last twenty-five years or so, there have been a few men and more women to whom I have given money for art supplies and food. My parents were stingy while I was growing up, paying the bare minimum to the housekeepers and handymen we employed over the years, and I felt deep shame over this. I told myself that I would never be so stingy, that when I had money of my own, I would worry less about it running out, which I believe was the main problem for my parents, even though neither of them had ever gone hungry. They feared another world war, having lived through the horrors of the second. I think they believed that they had to squirrel away as much money as possible and buy property on other continents, in case they were ever forced to flee their land and start over somewhere else.

Although I have profited from the free market and complain at times about the money I earn that must be sent to the government's tax treasury, it doesn't seem right to me that there has never been a functioning collective, whether state-run or otherwise, that has truly embraced economic and social equality. The poor continue to remain poor, and the rich remain rich. Jayne wonders why, if I feel as I do, André and I do not show overtly political art. I suppose it is like this: you might admire the people who bake bread for a living but do not want to bake it yourself. Similarly, I admire the people who speak loudly against injustice, but I prefer to conduct my protests in private, giving to artists who are not supported by their families or an arts council, or by employers who permit them enough time and energy to devote to their studios.

What I ask of the artists I support is nothing sordid or extortionary, only that they keep working. Some of the women I have lived with have also been artists, but from them I also expect friendship and ardor, respect and loyalty.

Anne-Claire was the first woman I lived with, for a little over two decades. I think of that now and wonder how we did it without one of us ending up in an asylum. It must have been because we had two children to raise and had to keep the household in order for their sake, and because we had careers we enjoyed and friendships outside of the marriage. We each also had the confidence that we were always right. Our occasional flare-ups and entrenched resentments kept us more or less sane too—anger is more clarifying and motivating by far than depression or melancholy—even if these resentments rotted the marriage from the inside out.

Agnieska was the second woman who lived with me. She stayed for seven months, a few years after the divorce. She eventually became a Vie Bohème artist, and is a painter of both male and female nudes. She is also the firstborn child of a French father and Polish mother and was a friend of my son's, older than him by three years; her younger brother was Frédéric's friend.

I think that my son was briefly interested in blond, impulsive Agnieska a year or two before she moved in with me, but she has told me that she has always preferred older men, and my son never spoke of his feelings for her to me—it was his sister who did, and angrily too, as if I had stolen Agnieska from him, which was not at all the case. I don't believe that Frédéric would have made her happy, and I don't know if he makes his wife happy either. (They have been married for four years; he was only twenty-six, Léa twenty-five, when they married. Your child's marriage is something you regard with both curiosity and a little doubt—you know this child's flaws, his tendency to find fault where there is none, to forget to say thank you, to believe the worst, to get angry when he does not get his way.) Agnieska moved to Montpelier to help her sister, who had had twin girls; it was supposed to be a temporary situation, but Agnieska stayed on, after discovering how much she liked warm weather and sun. She teaches painting classes down there and continues to paint and exhibit at Vie Bohème from time to time.

My third domestic companion was Brigitte, for about year, two and a half years ago. She is a friend of Fabienne's too, but we are the same age—she is not an older woman like Fabienne is. Brigitte and I met on a day in late April so perfect, the air so light on our skin, it seemed as if nothing in our lives had ever been or ever would be dull or frustrating or tiresome.

One night toward the beginning of my relationship with Brigitte, she, Fabienne, and I had quite a good time together in my home. This is not the sort of event that has occurred often in my life—one attractive and willing woman is plenty to keep me happy—but Fabienne is hard to deter once she sets her mind on something, and Brigitte wasn't afraid or skeptical, nor was I. We had some wine and good food, and soon there was some laughter and teasing, and Brigitte, who is an obstetrician, twice divorced and sexually adventurous, was as fearless as Fabienne.

After several months of living together, Brigitte began to speak of marriage, noticing that I had not, and when I gently made it clear that I did not intend to marry her, a few more months passed before she was able to remove the renters from her apartment in Montmartre and reinstall herself inside its sunny top-floor rooms. We still talk from time to time and meet for lunch or a glass of wine if she stops by the gallery near closing. She has since married for a third time, this husband also a doctor, but a psychiatrist rather than a deliverer of newborns.

Sofia lived with me too, for three weeks, when she was between apartments, just before I left for New York. I should not count her as a cohabitant, because, in part, she regarded my place as she would a hotel—temporary lodging with certain useful amenities. A good place for sex, for indulging one's appetites for fattening foods and throwaway movies. She loves to eat and walk around naked and laugh at silly films and television shows. She is, I suppose, a true Bohemian, and although she preferred me to André and his sweaty, grasping style (he is a man who will swallow nearly whole something that should instead be savored), she bestowed a few of her favors on him too. I was jealous, one of the few times in my life where I strongly felt this airless, ugly urgency. But having had such affectionate relations with his ex-wife some years earlier, I tried to convince myself that a little time with Sofia was his due.

And presently I live with Jayne. It is a month now before her March show at Vie Bohème. When she flew home to Los Angeles to see her sister and their truce-observing parents over Christmas and New Year's week, I stayed here and felt my home's sudden stillness settle around me during the hours when my son and his family were visiting with Anne-Claire and Jeanne-Lucie, and I knew then that I would not want to live alone anymore. I have wondered often if Jayne will be ready to leave my home after her show goes up at Vie Bohème because that is my hunch.

Why have I not already shown her the door, knowing that she has met her old boyfriend on a few isolated afternoons and returned home to rue du Général-Foy with the vague, dreamy look of a teenage girl who has just been kissed by the golden boy of her fantasies? And knowing as I also do that she has been painting this boy's portrait in the studio that I have made available to her, a portrait she readily admitted was of him when questioned, her honesty something I admired in spite of myself? And why, if I would prefer that Jayne forget Colin, have I not sworn off my own occasional meetings with other women?

What I know is that we cannot always do the things that our better judgment dictates we do, not all the time, and certainly not with joy.

I worry that Jayne has become an addiction for me: her soft skin; her ascending, girlish laughter; her powdery, clean scent; her shyness; how the tender flesh between her legs sometimes tastes slightly of brandy; her awakening belief in her talent as an artist. She is more grateful than Sofia was for what I have done for her, and more generous in her opinions of other people. If not for the threat of another man reclaiming her heart, I would be content— or as content as it is possible for me to be.

Jayne will have five new paintings in the March show, which André and I decided to name *Intérieurs intimes*. She wasn't sure at first if she liked our choice of a name, but eventually she agreed that it seemed fitting because Susan, her mentor, is showing six canvases that are all part of a series of paintings based on photographs of a maternal aunt's Manhattan apartment, and Jayne is showing two interiors— one of her childhood bedroom, the other of her maternal grandparents' kitchen—as well as one painting with a window view onto a verdant yard and two portraits of people whose expressions I'd describe as contemplative, as if each subject has recently received disappointing or worrisome news. Chantal Schmidt will show five paintings of three different couples—Chantal and her girlfriend, two young men, and a heterosexual couple—lying in their beds, nude or partially clothed, the sheet or blankets kicked to the end of the mattress or missing entirely.

Colin is planning to attend. Jayne's phone revealed this fact on the day I read the long thread of their clandestine communications. I am still trying to decide if I should tell her that I know about him.

Sofia will also attend; it doesn't surprise me that she is curious about Jayne. I think, under different circumstances, they would like each other quite well. Maybe even under these circumstances, but I have to doubt it.

The Intérieurs intimes opening is on March 21—the same day that Beethoven, one of my favorite composers, debuted his Quartet no. 13, op. 130, in Vienna in 1826. It is also the day on which, in 1859, the Scottish National Gallery opened in Edinburgh. Jayne was especially pleased by this latter coincidence. "That museum is still open," she said. "It seems like a good sign, don't you think?"

"Yes," I agreed. "If you are looking for a sign."

"Oh, of course I am. I think we all do. Don't you?" She smiled, but her dark eyes were clouded with doubt. Why was she so worried, I wondered. Her work would attract attention. She would make her former teacher proud, and her parents, who would not be able to attend the opening but planned to come to Paris in early April, when her mother would have her spring school vacation.

"I don't think I look for signs," I said. "If I did, it would mean that I am waiting for something to happen, yes?"

She regarded me. "I suppose it would."

"I am happy with things as they are," I said, but even as I said this, I knew that I didn't mean it, not fully.

CHAPTER 7

Final Questions

Something I have begun to notice with increasing frequency: why is anger so often the first emotion we reach for?

I heard Jayne murmuring in her sleep a few nights ago, after we had gone out to see an American movie that we argued over in the taxi on the way home—she thought the female lead, who was having an adulterous affair with her brother-in-law, was treated much more unfairly than the brother-in-law by their respective spouses and most of the film's other characters. I thought they were equally miserable by the time the movie ended—both had been forced out of their houses and were in the process of getting a divorce. He had more money, and his parents were still speaking to him, but I wouldn't say that he was any happier than the woman was. "He might be just as unhappy," said Jayne, "but he's not as badly off. She lives in a shithole apartment and never gets to see her kids and can barely afford to eat and pay her rent!"

Did it bring back memories of your own awful apartment in New York? I almost asked, but knew she was talking about something else.

Very early the next morning, she startled me from a sound sleep when she called out, "Where is it?" At first I thought she was awake and talking to me, but when I looked over at her, her eyes were closed and I could see that she was still asleep. In the morning she had no memory of this outburst.

"Where is it?" she repeated, bemused. "I have no idea what I meant. Have I done something like this before?"

"No," I said. "Not that I've noticed. Have other men told you that you talk in your sleep?"

A peculiar look crossed her face. She was deciding if she should lie, I realized, but I didn't understand why; I hadn't asked her to tell me who it was, or what she had said. "No," she murmured, brushing away the hair that clung to her sleep-creased cheek. "But I once accidentally hit someone in the face."

"I hope you won't do that to me," I teased.

"Me neither."

"Did he hit you back?"

She blinked. "No. Thank goodness."

"Well," I said. "I hope you didn't hurt him too badly."

"He was fine. After he got some stitches."

"What?"

She laughed, her voice croaking. "I'm kidding. I didn't hit him hard at all. It just woke us both up. But we did break up not long afterward, for other reasons."

"I guess he was afraid he'd wake up one night and find you standing over him with a knife."

"Ha-ha," she said.

"Or a baseball bat."

"That's not funny. Things like that freak me out," she said. "I watched too many scary movies when I was a kid, I think."

"I could put you in a straitjacket before we go to bed, if you'd like me to," I said.

She sat up, her body rigid, her expression one of unequivocal distaste. "That's so creepy, Laurent. How can you say something like that?"

"I am only kidding, Jayne. But how could I resist? You're like Jeanne-Lucie. She is easily frightened too. The things her brother would say to her when they were children. If you think I'm bad—"

"Poor Jeanne-Lucie. You and Frédéric were so hard on her. She's told me stories."

"She lived through it all just fine," I said.

"Barely." Jayne gave me a scolding look. "Has she told you her idea yet?"

"What idea?" I asked, sensing controversy.

"She wants to go to New York with me after Intérieurs intimes opens. We'd go for four or five days, see a couple of plays, visit a few museums, do some shopping. She said she could get Anne-Claire to help Daniel take care of Marcelle while she's gone. And Martin too. She said he'd help out."

"How nice of him," I said, dryly. "Is she paying for everything?" I wasn't sure why, but I did not like the thought of my girlfriend and my daughter on the loose together in New York.

Jayne hesitated. "No, I don't think so. I'd pay for my share."

"You would?" I asked, interested. "How?"

"With my savings," she said, not meeting my eyes. "You don't have to sound so sarcastic."

"I'm not being sarcastic," I said. "I'm just a little surprised that you two have been talking about traveling together. Especially when I'd think your show that's opening in a few weeks and the arrival of your former teacher and your parents soon after would be more than enough to occupy your thoughts right now."

"It is occupying my thoughts," she said. "But I miss my friends in New York. I'd like to see them this spring if I can. When I couldn't get together with Liesel and Melissa over the holidays, I told them I'd try to come in April or May."

"Then I suppose you should go. As soon as you can arrange it."

"Laurent," she said. "Please don't be mad."

"I'm not mad."

She didn't reply. It was almost eight thirty, and I hadn't yet gone out for my newspaper and morning espresso. My mood would only deteriorate further if I waited much longer. "You do what you want to do," I said. "You and Jeanne-Lucie can go to New York whenever you'd like. But your parents are coming soon too, aren't they? You must be here for that."

"We'd go after their visit. Mid-April, probably."

"I'll help you pay for the trip," I said.

She must have heard the sigh in my voice because she shook her head. "I have money saved. You don't have to pay for any part of it."

She said this, but knew that I wasn't likely to permit it.

It bothered me more than I let on that my daughter and Jayne were considering flying across the Atlantic together, but Jayne must have guessed this. It also bothered me that when Frédéric called and Jayne answered the phone, he liked to talk to her for several minutes, and it was usually she who had to suggest passing the phone to me. From the next room, I could hear them talking, she laughing at almost everything Frédéric said. When had my son become such an entertainer? With me he was sometimes sulky, replaying in his mind our unresolved disagreements, I imagined, probing ancient wounds to see if they still throbbed. He could have called my mobile too, but he stubbornly preferred the landline. Frédéric and Jayne had met in early August when he came to Paris for a weekend with his wife and daughter, a week or so before Jayne's sister and her two girlfriends from New York descended on us, each of those two visits lasting for six days, Jayne's mood pensive and a little glum after their visits ended. She spent more time alone in the study painting, making up, she said, for some of the hours she had lost while entertaining her guests.

And then she had her first rendezvous with Colin—at the end of August, I think it was, but of course I didn't know this until the winter afternoon when I broke my own rule of not invading another person's privacy (because I know how it feels to be the one whose e-mails and call logs have been looked at with increasingly furious eyes, assigning blame, assembling clues without being able to see the whole picture).

What would Jayne have found out about me, if she had known where to look? If she still wanted to look—that impulse should be considered first. Would it be worse to live with a lover who isn't ever concerned that you are thinking of someone else when you lie together in your sanctioned bed?

Before anyone judges me, I hope she (or he) will think of all the things she has done in secret. The purchases made on a tertiary credit card and buried in the closet or hidden in the trunk until she could no longer keep herself from wearing the new shoes or the new dress or serving dinner on the new porcelain plates the night that guests were dining with her and her family? How many times has she passed judgment on a friend with a guilty conscience but in her most harshly honest moments realized that she wished an attractive and passionate man would come to sweep away her boredom and to look with lust upon the body her husband began to ignore after their third year together? Or perhaps once or twice, maybe more, on a business trip or on a vacation with college friends, she met an attractive stranger and spent the night with him, and all it truly meant was that someone still desired her.

I have heard that men regret the chances they've missed, whereas women regret the ones they took that did not turn out so well. There are exceptions, I am sure, but it seems to me that the women I know who have alluded to such a thing do wish they had behaved more chastely. Men, without much variation, seem to wish the contrary.

Have I gone off to undisclosed rooms and taken Sofia into my arms during the months that Jayne has lived with me?

Have I gone off to meet a visiting Fabienne in her hotel near the Hôtel de Ville, her miniature greyhound, Fiona, locked away in the bathroom while I am naked in the clean white bed with her equally naked mistress?

Have I ever thought, No, I will not, but at the last minute changed my mind?

Have I gone off with any other woman whose name Jayne has never heard me or anyone else, as far as I know, mention?

Have I had any regrets about these choices, these opportunities?

One other question, some variation of which we never stop asking:

What will happen next?

PART THREE

Jayne, Spring

1.

Laurent suggested, cajoled, and finally insisted that I write down some of my impressions after the opening of *Intérieurs intimes*. I was skeptical when he gave me the assignment; wasn't our work supposed to do the talking for us? It felt similar to the times when I was told as a child to think over something I'd done that had upset someone else (such as stealing my sister's Barbie doll and throwing it into the street), even though I knew that Laurent hadn't made the request to punish me. He was handing me a chance to relive the event, he said, to see myself as both artist and spectator. I hadn't been very disciplined about writing anything but e-mails in a long while, and so this extended artist's statement, of a kind, wasn't an undertaking that felt second nature to me.

He was passionate about it, though, and said that he and André planned to start asking each of their artists to record their thoughts within a week or so after a vernissage, no matter how many or how few shows the artists had already had. Our remarks should be something like a hybrid of exhibition catalog copy, an artist's statement, and a diary. Coincidentally, *journal intime* is the French term for diary—so close to the name of our show, which I didn't really like at first, because it made me think about the actual interiors of a body—the blood and veins and laboring organs—but the name has grown on me.

"Do you want me to do this in some formal way? Or should I just write down thoughts as they occur to me?" I asked Laurent.

"Just write something true," he said. "You can interpret my instructions in any way that you want to."

"Maybe I could draw my impressions instead of writing them down."

He shook his head. "I want your words, Jayne. Eventually we would like to put together a book, after we get enough of these statements or whatever it is that we call them."

"It does sound interesting."

"You will be a star, Jayne," he said. "Isn't that what you want?"

"Yes, of course it is," I said, pretending to be serious before I laughed.

"Why do you make a joke of your ambition?" he asked. "It isn't a joke."

I paused. His irritation was obvious, his mood a sudden cloudburst. "I'm not," I said. "Not really."

At first I tried to think of my essay/artist's statement/diary mash-up as I would have an assignment for an art history or theory of art course. I thought I should try to sound like someone who contemplates every brushstroke before she makes it, even if this isn't always how I work. I wanted my response to sound like me, though, not as if I were talking from behind a magic velvet curtain or calling down prophecy from the top of some snowcapped holy mountain.

Laurent had more advice when I came out of the study after another false start and gave him a dirty look. "Just tell the truth," he advised.

"As I see it, you mean," I said, tired and irascible.

"Yes, of course," he said. "How else?"

2.

Opening

This didn't happen to me when I was in shows in the past, not as it has this time: I'll be going about my daily business—putting on my shoes, combing my hair, eating an apple while looking out the kitchen window—when I remember that my work is hanging in a gallery a few miles from where I live. It is being subjected to the critical, sometimes hostile stares of the strangers who enter the space and stand in their high heels, on their bowed legs or flat feet, before my paintings, thinking that they could do what I've done. Or maybe, more generously, thinking the opposite: they wonder where my ideas come from, how I choose my subjects, and how I learned to paint a face that looks more brooding and melancholy on the canvas than it probably would in person. Equally disorienting is that I am responsible for this relationship, as short-lived as it might be, as glancing an impression as my work might leave on the gallerygoer.

Susan Kraut, Chantal Schmidt, and I, along with Vie Bohème's owners, Laurent Moller and André Séguy, were relieved that so many people—around two hundred, by Laurent's estimate—passed through Vie Bohème on the night of the spring equinox, March 21, which was unseasonably cold. Maybe it was the promise of free wine? Whatever their reasons, people emerged from their homes and delivered themselves to rue du Louvre at the appointed hour, and we were grateful. We smiled, we shook hands, we looked into each other's eyes, my own eyes—I'm sure—hopeful, but nervous too.

The night was a difficult one, even with the high spirits and all the hands reaching for other hands; it was filled with specters, suppressed but roaring expectation, people from our pasts and futures. We had spent so long preparing for it, thinking about it, worrying, doubting, wanting. I was showing my work with my adored painting instructor but did not believe that I deserved to. My paintings looked fine, even good, I think, but I had spent so much time staring at them that I could no longer really see them, like the view from the window you have looked out of for half your life. It is like the face in the mirror: the known latitudes, the no longer suspenseful flaws and strengths.

Inquiry

In college, one of my painting instructors said during a critique, "Each completed painting asks: who was the artist when she started? Who is she now?"

When I arrived an hour before the opening officially began, Susan was already there, standing several feet back from her paintings, each mounted perfectly plumb. Susan was an emissary from my past, from my bubbly, foolish earliest twenties. She looked so pretty, petite and smiling in turquoise beads and a black tunic dress embroidered with small blue, green, and red flowers, her light blue eyes taking everything in. We had seen each other twice in the three days that she had so far been in Paris; I was shy in her presence, but talked too much. I felt something like rapture too, bewitched again as I had been years earlier by her gentleness, her sincerity, her steady hand on the brush, her sympathy, her eye for the whole, intricate picture, no detail neglected. I looked at her the night of our opening and felt winded. It was how I'd felt during the first several weeks that I was seeing Laurent.

I think this might be the exalted state, a celestial plane, its air dizzying, the heady altitudes that are visible from our earthbound stations but are mostly unreachable.

That she felt as happy to be there as I did was immediately apparent, and also, I have to say, humbling. Here we were, looking upon concrete proof that it was possible to make it through the grinding sameness of most days, the self-doubt, the exhaustion, the worries that no one would ever be interested in your work again— all the feelings I had been living with on and off for the last twelve years, three or so years shy of half my life. Yes, we were in Paris, where I have been living for the past nine months—but call me an ingrate, I had gotten used to many aspects of my life here, and this ability to adapt both saves us and does us in—if everything felt new all the time, there would be much less restlessness, fewer crimes (of the heart or otherwise), but would we ever get anything done? I could only guess at Susan's feelings about her life as an artist, but I wondered if they weren't much different from my own, even with her huge talent and record of previous successes and exhibitions.

On the early fall afternoon when Laurent told me that Susan would be one of the other two featured artists in Intérieurs intimes, I remember staring at his right ear. How oddly pale it is, I thought, compared to his sun-brown face. "Susan Kraut, my teacher?" I asked stupidly. He nodded, and I said, "Would she really want to be in a show with me? Shouldn't it just be her work?"

"Maybe next time," he said. "We will see how it goes."

We will see how her work sells, he was saying, not, We will see how we like her. I knew he and André didn't like all the artists they represented. Some were almost absurdly demanding: the opening must be on a Sunday, not a Friday night, and go from 11:00 p.m. to 4:00 a.m., with purple lightbulbs instead of white ones in the gallery fixtures, and a hip-hop deejay, and Cristal served by the case. Some were querulous and ungrateful, blaming their inability to sell every single canvas or sculpture on Laurent and André rather than on the whims of art collectors and the faltering economy.

Later, I thought about the student-teacher relationship, how it is said that the best teachers want their students to surpass their own mastery of painting or sculpture or pastry-making. From my own minimal experience teaching art at community centers and retirement homes, I know what it's like to feel that jolt of recognition, the almost corporeal thrill when you meet someone whose work shows irrefutable promise. Susan had acted as if she felt this about me, and for a few years I got by on the memory of her praise and kindness. This is the kind of thing that sends a student off to make a life as an artist rather than as a bookkeeper or a dog walker or a librarian.

But even with Susan's early encouragement, I had given up on trying to make a career as a painter until Laurent appeared in New York and offered a hand up and scolded me for not trying harder, for feeling sorry for myself. There is also this fact: I have been enormously lucky. Few artists have been given what he has given to me.

Student, Teacher

Susan said a number of things when I was her student that I recorded in the journal I kept during those summer weeks in Chicago, when the air felt like heavy, damp cotton you had to scissor through with your arms and legs.

— *You have to love this because there are far easier ways to earn a living.*

— *Not so much orange, Jayne. Save some for the construction cones!*

— Composition in a painting is usually instinctive, but if you keep working, if you study how other painters handle it, you'll get better. Like you would if you were baking bread or building a house—one day you'll realize that you've gotten the hang of it.

— This can be lonely work, but it connects you to other people in ways that many of the things we could do with our lives do not.

— Vuillard is the artist I find my thoughts turning toward most often. At least ten times a day, probably more.

— Remember to soak your brushes!

The night of the show, she said, "You and Laurent . . . goodness, Jayne. I'm still speechless. Do I look tired? Because I haven't slept more than five hours a night in the last week, I was so thrilled about being here. My husband thought I was drinking too much coffee, and didn't believe me when I told him that I wasn't. You think you know what's ahead, and it's certainly not someone calling from Paris with an offer to put you in a show."

"When I was still living in New York, I felt like nothing was ever going to happen with my work," I said.

"Oh, come on," she cried, putting her hands on my shoulders to give me a good shake. "You're too young to feel that way."

I laughed. "I wasn't painting very much there—that was the problem. I felt intimidated, but here I don't feel that way as much. Maybe because I'm not French?"

She nodded. "Yes, probably so. It's important from time to time to remove yourself from a place you're familiar with."

Whenever I caught sight of her that night, I'm sure I started smiling like an imbecile. Several times we looked at each other from across the gallery and started laughing, confusing the people who were standing with us, trying to talk to us, to flatter and flirt or express their suspicions about whether we knew what we were saying with our brushes and tubes of paint. "What's so funny?" they'd ask, but we didn't know. "I'll try to paint it for you sometime," I said to one man who reminded me of my father. "Because I can't describe it in words."

"Really," he said, miffed. "Is that so." The furrow between his emphatic black eyebrows deepened, but he ended up buying my Joanie painting, the first I'd completed in Paris.

Where would he put her? I wondered. What would he do in front of her, she looking on with her mournful eyes?

These were the pages that I gave to Laurent, but he wanted more; he was certain I had more to say. Over the next several weeks, I went ahead and wrote more pages, many more, but I only gave some of what follows to him.

3.

What about Chantal Schmidt, the third artist to round out our trio intime? I liked her paintings, even if I wasn't sure I liked her—she didn't look me in the eye when we met to do our walk-through, a couple of days before the opening. She seemed always to be smirking or twisting her mouth into something between a grimace and a pout, an affectation or tic I hadn't noticed in other Frenchwomen. Maybe she was nervous, or high? Did she possibly have some kind of nerve damage? I wasn't going to ask, and I started wondering if she thought I was a hack, even though I knew there wasn't anything wrong with my work, and two nights later, at the opening, no one seemed to be sneering at it.

I could see why Laurent was all riled up about her work, though. Her paintings were overtly sexual—the women's breasts so idealized and voluptuous, their skin and hair infused with a mellow, dusky light, their drowsy eyes half-closed and long-lashed. Her male models had daunting muscles, but their faces were languid and sated-looking. Each of her couples seemed to be resting after an energetic but affectionate rendezvous, their cheeks flushed, their bodies curving protectively into each other. I thought of Gustav Klimt and the lavishness of his palette—all that gold! and his forest greens and rich reds and browns—but most of all his sensuous models, their ethereal faces and long hair and bared breasts, their intricate patchwork gowns.

Klimt, like Marval before him, has become in the last year or so my Vuillard. He was only fifty-five when he died, a victim of a stroke and the flu epidemic of 1918, and I remember being moved when I first read about the tragic facts of his premature and probably painful death, as commonplace as it might have been in an age before vaccinations and penicillin, all the medical advances of the last hundred years that have allowed us so quickly to overpopulate the planet (not that I want to return to the age of death by tetanus and abscessed tooth). As a student during the spring term that I spent in Strasbourg, I took the train to Vienna with two friends, and we went to the Belvedere Palace, which houses The Kiss, and stared at it as if we might brand the two lovers onto our eyes.

Chantal studied at the École des Beaux-Arts, where Laurent had tried to enroll, and where François and Nathalie are currently enrolled. Among the people milling about at the opening, I saw the boy from the art supply store off rue Bonaparte, the one with the stoplight tattooed on his hand. He made an attempt to remember me and listed some of the items he thought that I'd purchased, but they weren't accurate. He was friends with Chantal, and also knew the two men who were one of the couples in the paintings Laurent and André had chosen for the show. This couple looked like brothers—they were about the same height, with close-cropped dark hair, and the same powerful chests and shoulders beneath their wool sweaters, one in black, the other in charcoal gray. They loved my paintings, they said, and stood before them with solemnity. They seemed truly to be seeing them. Looking at my paintings with them, I felt such a wave of self-consciousness and maudlin emotion that after a few seconds at their sides, I went off in search of a glass of water.

There were several other people at the opening whose presence I want to record, along with Susan's and the boy from the art supply store (whose name is Nicolas, something I learned when Chantal introduced us. "Mon petit frère," she said, her lip and eyebrow rings catching the light as she leaned over to kiss his cheek, her tar-black hair swinging forward, a liquid curtain that, contrary to the photos I had seen of her online, now reached past her shoulders. "I'm not really her brother," he said, his smile placid. "No," she said, "But I wish you were instead of the one I have. You're here, and he's not." "Maybe he's sick?" asked Nicolas. Chantal made a face and shook her head. "Maybe he's drunk.") Chantal's brother might not have shown up, but Colin did, having managed to arrange a business trip to coincide with the show, though he was embarrassed to admit this. I would never have thought poorly of him for not paying for the trip out of his own pocket; it wasn't as if I could spend much time with him, and airfare was so expensive. I hadn't encouraged him to come to the opening; the thought of him there had made me nervous. I didn't want to have to introduce him to Laurent either, who I was sure would sense my skittishness. Colin also knew that I'd painted his portrait—I'd told him one afternoon when we were lying in his bed at the hotel where he usually stayed, hoping this would make him happy. Now I realized that he would see that this painting wasn't in the show, but I knew he wasn't likely to say anything about its absence.

I wasn't looking forward to introducing Colin to André either, whom I had kissed a second time, and it was as unasked-for and unsettling as the first time. It happened on his birthday, January 25, which I remember as a blustery but sunny day that had also made world headlines because some teenage pranksters from Prague climbed to the top of the Arc de Triomphe and dumped a large sack of miniature chocolate bars onto passing cars and the heads of the oblivious tourists below. No one was injured, but the police roped off the area for a couple of hours, snarling traffic for many blocks.

We'd had birthday cake at the gallery in the afternoon, and champagne, and despite my protests, Laurent went out to buy a third bottle after we drank the first two. André knew that I'd had too much to drink when he asked me to kiss him. I shook my head, but was a little unsteady on my feet, which were tired from wearing heels all day, and I stumbled toward him, only slightly, but he took this as a yes. Nathalie had left a few minutes before Laurent did, and André and I were alone again in the gallery, but in the front this time, with all the windows and curious passers-by. I think, like the first time, we only kissed for a few seconds, but I remember his body's humid heat, his short, muscular legs and chest pressing into me before I pulled away. Just as Laurent had predicted, I had not been faithful to him in Paris (by saying this, I wonder, had he fore-ordained my behavior?), and I volleyed between feelings of self-loathing and self-righteousness.

I mumbled to André that this wouldn't happen again, but all he said was "No, of course not." He laughed and turned away to cut himself another piece of cake while I went to the bathroom to stare with fury and embarrassment at my messy hair and chewed-off lipstick. I had mostly sobered up by the time Laurent returned with more champagne, and I told him that I didn't want another glass. André also declined, and with Nathalie already gone, there seemed no need for our party of three to continue. "I have dinner plans," André informed us, looking entirely at ease with himself. "And I had better get ready to go."

Laurent put the champagne in one of his desk drawers, and there it stayed until I noticed a couple of weeks later that it was missing. When I asked where it had gone, he told me that he had given it to one of his favorite clients, a thank-you gift for a recent purchase. He said this without looking at me, and I had trouble believing him but said nothing more. My immediate thought was that he had taken it to some other woman's home to drink with her in her bed, the shades drawn against the gray afternoon sky. I still felt guilty for not telling him that André had kissed me again, and although I worried that André might report this news, with gleeful malice directed at me as much as at Laurent, I didn't really believe that he would.

Nor had I told Laurent that, since the previous summer, I had seen Colin in Paris five times—on a Friday afternoon at the end of August, on two afternoons in mid-October, and twice more at the beginning of December. We met for only a few hours each time, but these meetings may as well have lasted several days considering the amount of time I spent reflecting on them afterward. One thing I learned is how quickly secrets accumulate once you start collecting them.

When I saw Colin last August, the first time since the previous February in Manhattan, when we were both cold and he was in a bad mood, we met for ice cream at Berthillon on Ile Saint-Louis, a place he had read about in his guidebook. (In the days before his arrival, I'd missed him even more. I kept remembering his sense of humor, his playful pranks. One of my favorites was a voice mail he'd left on my work phone: *I am calling to inform you that the extra-large polka-dot girdle you ordered has just arrived, and will be held in the Macy's lingerie department for two weeks.*)

Quite a few other people had read about Berthillon in their guidebooks too, judging by the line that snaked out the shop's door and around the corner. I knew this wasn't his first visit to Paris, but I wasn't sure how many times he'd been there before now. There were so many things I didn't know about him, and it occurred to me then that we had spent most of the time we were dating talking about other people, or the cost of food, clothes, coffee, and rent, the difficulty of owning a car in Manhattan if you weren't a millionaire, the movies we liked, the books I thought he should read instead of only buying collectible copies of, along with the feats he had performed on the basketball courts of his adolescence and early adulthood, courts he had played on with other aggressive, half-feral boys and men.

I had a little trouble breathing, which I had not anticipated, when I first saw Colin among the other tourists standing outside the ice cream store. He had a summer tan, and his expression was calm as he waited for me. I wondered if he'd expected to be stood up, and I knew that I didn't deserve what seemed to be his still-strong feelings for me, especially after I'd ambushed him with the breakup the previous November, in order to be free to glide off on Laurent's well-tailored arm.

Outside Berthillon, I didn't wave or call Colin's name; I wanted instead for him to find me at his side without having seen my approach—the idea of walking toward him, holding his gaze, or looking away in shyness, was too much to feel in that moment. It struck me later that compared to being with Laurent, it had been much easier to be Colin's girlfriend, even if I'd sometimes been bored when he'd talked about sports or irritated when he'd been reluctant to go to a gallery or a new exhibition at the Met or MoMA with me. I hadn't worried when we were together that I would say or do something foolish, or that he was interested in other women. If he did have a wandering eye, I'd never noticed it (though of course we hadn't dated for very long).

I stood next to him for a few seconds before he glanced down and found me at his side, and it was then that he let loose a great whoop of laughter. Several people turned to stare at us, their tiny, expensive ice cream cones dripping in the afternoon heat. Seeing Colin's face relax into a smile of such pure joy, I laughed too and stepped into his arms. He held me hard against his white-and-blue-checked shirt for a long time, maybe inappropriately—but right then, his warmth and strength were more of a comfort than an erotic argument. He had been my friend for a year or so before we started dating, and seeing him again made me realize how much I'd missed him, that painting his portrait was a way for me to keep him near me, in a different way, one more immediate somehow than e-mailing or calling him. I also realized that I was probably more homesick than I'd wanted to acknowledge, more in need of the reliable comforts of the friends and routines and familiar places I had left behind in New York. What if I had stayed with Colin, resisted Laurent's advances last November? I wouldn't have come to Paris, for one; I wouldn't have been offered a show at Vie Bohème either. But I might have been happy anyway; I might also have forced myself to start painting again in earnest and found my way into a New York gallery, if I'd tried harder than I had during the year or two after I'd moved up from D.C.

"Jayne, you look great," Colin said softly, his lips touching my hair. "It's so good to see you."

I could smell the minty shoulder ointment he favored, his lime deodorant, along with the traces of some smoky cologne. My throat constricted with desire and misgiving.

"How tall you are," I said idiotically, smiling up at him. "I forgot."

He looked at me in silence before bending down to kiss my forehead. I didn't remember him ever doing this when we were together in Manhattan. I stayed there in his arms, cheek pressed to his chin, not squirming or laughing; I was breathing in short, quiet gulps. When he leaned back to look at me again, he blinked as if dust had blown into his eyes. Then he turned away, embarrassed. I wasn't sure what I felt; my conscience and heart were sending conflicting, strident messages. On that afternoon the sky was a vast seamless table of blinding blue light. People were milling around us, gingerly holding their hazelnut and raspberry cones, taking careful, greedy bites. It was discombobulating to be assailed by such strong feelings for Colin, stronger than any I'd had when we were still together. If I'd felt more confident about Laurent's feelings for me and my place in his life, I have to wonder if I'd have responded to Colin in the way that I did that afternoon. Would I have been as interested in seeing him again when he came back a month and a half later, in early October? On that day, instead of meeting for ice cream, I went to his hotel and climbed directly into bed with him, almost as shy as if it were the first time, no agreed-upon pretense of a drink or a sweet beforehand. But this was still several weeks away.

"Let's go inside," he said that first afternoon outside Berthillon. With one long-fingered hand at my lower back, he steered me into the dark-paneled store and ordered us both three-scoop cones: bittersweet chocolate, pistachio, vanilla.

Watching him devour the melting ice cream after we were outside again—standing with several other couples and a German family of five, two parents, two teenage sons in black T-shirts and shorts, a younger daughter in a purple sundress, the sun easing into the west—I tried to turn back the abrupt, vivid memory of Colin's wet mouth on my breasts, his hairy, forceful knee parting my legs. I remembered his uneven, strained breaths against my ear and had to look away, down at the street where a piece of scrap paper had lodged in a melted puddle of pale pink ice cream. How did we get here? I wondered. Where will we go?

"It's delicious, isn't it," he said, wiping his ravenous mouth with a crumpled napkin, innocent of my careening, X-rated thoughts.

"Yes," I said, too brightly. "It was nice of you to find the time to take me here. I'll have to come back."

"Are you kidding? I was really looking forward to it. Except that I thought you might bail on me."

I shook my head. "You know I wouldn't do that," I said. "You were the one who used to cancel on me at the last minute."

"I did?" he said, doubtful. "I don't remember that."

"When your boss had Knicks tickets. You remember, don't you?"

"Oh," he said, making a face. "That only happened once, I think. No, wait, maybe twice."

"It's okay, Colin. Water under the bridge."

"No wonder you dumped me." He smiled.

"Oh, come on. Let's not talk about that."

He touched my hand lightly before closing his fingers around my wrist. "Can I take you to dinner? Make it up to you?"

I laughed. "Right now? But I'm not done with my ice cream yet."

"We could walk around for a couple of hours," he said. "Work up an appetite."

I remember my ears ringing, the sidewalk seeming closer when I looked down. It felt as if a window had been opened in my chest and the air blowing in was ransacking a carefully ordered room. What if I were the one to make the move, to say that I could think of another way to work up an appetite? I was pretty sure that I knew what his answer would be, though sometimes he could be shy. But I wasn't going to do it—I wasn't confident or brazen enough yet to do these sorts of things. Even if Laurent wasn't going to ask any questions about where I'd been, or with whom, I wasn't in the habit of sleeping with two men in the same day. It would take me a little while to realize that I would have sex with Colin the next time I saw him. This first, sunny meeting in August, the idea of being in bed with him again was a possibility my mind, like a frightened bird, kept darting away from.

I realized something else later, after he was asleep in his hotel room and I lay next to Laurent, wide awake after midnight:

My erotic history, if I ever took the trouble to write it down, probably wouldn't fill more than half of a single-subject notebook. Nothing about it is impressive or intimidating or sordid, but it is incredible to me how much time I spent thinking about the boys I had crushes on before I knew anything about how their bodies worked. How much time I spent worrying before I started having sex that the condom would break or the pill would fail, and I would end up pregnant and ostracized by my gossipy classmates, a disgrace to my parents and family, my life never again the same more or less steady ride toward something good and meaningful it had formerly seemed to be.

Despite these fears, of course I went ahead and lost my virginity anyway, and in a different sense, my life never *was* the same again. I didn't get pregnant, and even if I had, I certainly wouldn't have been the first girl in my high school that this had happened to. I know too that, growing up only with a sister, I was curious about my friends' brothers, especially their older brothers.

Slinking past their bedrooms, their doors locked and festooned with posters of surly-looking rock stars, I wondered what they were doing in there, their stereos sometimes playing so loudly we could hear the bass thumping throughout the house; who were they thinking about, and did they ever think about me, but I was sure that they didn't, at least not until I was sixteen or seventeen and less gawky and flat-chested than I'd been before they'd left for college. When they returned home during breaks, they seemed to keep their visits as short as they could without permanently offending their loving, harried mothers. I felt what must have been awe for these boys' private lives, for their new sideburns and hard biceps and messy rooms and deepening voices, for what I believed to be the constant sexual uproar and suspense they lived in, and, as I later imagined it, for their shy infatuations with girls they wanted to protect almost as much as they wanted to undress, bookish girls that their macho friends would have teased them about savagely if they'd been privy to these more soulful boys' private feelings.

I think sometimes about the immutable fact of our bodies—how inviolably strong and resilient we believe ourselves to be when we are sixteen, twenty, twenty-four, how each of us, with our egos and animating consciousness, is walking around in an envelope of bone and sinew and skin that to a significant degree determines how the rest of the world responds to us.

Your beauty or plainness or homeliness—your eyes, your hair, your voice, your sadness, your feet, your hands, your nose, your thoughts, your fears, your fragile happiness. There are quiet parts in each of us that can only be gestured toward with light and color and shadow. This is one reason I am trying to be a painter. I think I understood this for the first time as we were organizing *Intérieurs intimes*. If a painting is going to be good, if you are going to remember it after you no longer stand before it, it has to hint at its subject's inner life, whether this subject is a middle-aged woman or an elm tree or an empty room.

In the last year and a half, I have gotten so many of the things I have hoped for. Laurent keeps asking me how it feels. He has a quality that I haven't given him enough credit for, not until now— he genuinely wishes people well. He wants to be a force for good, for pleasure too; he wants to make people happy. I have never known anyone quite like him. It is a kind of compulsion, I think, this desire to see everyone so happy, to have them look upon you with favor, with affection, possibly love. What was his childhood like? What determined that he would go in this direction rather than another?

Because it seems to me that it is easier for most of us to be selfish, to turn in rather than out. You risk less disappointment that way, I have to think; by not giving so much, or anything at all, you can't reasonably spend your time wondering what you will get back. Laurent does wonder what he will get in return—I know that he does; he might not expect anything tangible, but those grateful, adoring gazes, those thank-yous, how important they are to him. He wants to be the godfather, the rainmaker, the prince. I get jealous sometimes, of course, and in my worse moments, cynical—What sins is he atoning for? I wonder angrily. Where are the balance sheets he must be keeping? And why does he now have two cell phones, along with the landline at home, not to mention an office phone? He claims that the second cell phone is simply an indulgence—a newer model of the iPhone he has had since I've known him. He is too lazy to change his number over and transfer all the data from one phone to the other, he says, but will get to it at some point. I offered to do it for him, but he did not accept my offer.

One of the other artists he supports, Sidonie Clément, came to the opening. She had had her baby, a little girl, Joie Hilaire, over the holidays and had already thinned down, her baby weight probably not registering much beyond the extra fifteen pounds that Melissa once told me wistfully is at the lowest end of the pregnancy spectrum. (Melissa gained thirty and is still trying to shed the last seven, her own and her husband's spectacular skills in the kitchen not exactly helping her cause.) Joie's grandmother was at home with her, Sidonie said, because Stefan was working at the restaurant. Her face was tired, but her eyes lit with fervent curiosity for the paintings Chantal, Susan, and I were proclaiming as representative of our best selves, our best recent decisions as artists. I liked Sidonie so much, I wanted to kiss her. I wanted to kiss almost everyone that night, I suppose, which Susan later told me wasn't unusual. Many of us, I had to think, on the night of our openings, must ping-pong between wanting to throw up and wanting to throw our arms around everyone who has made the effort to come when there are countless other galleries or concert halls or theaters or living rooms to go to on any Friday night of the year, so many other people clamoring for attention and time and money.

"Jayne," Sidonie said softly. "I love this one." We were standing in front of *Owls and Starlings*, a three-by-four-foot canvas, a perspective of a yard with a big pine tree and a smaller one a few yards away. The trees are seen from the inside of a house, its occupants absent; in front of the window there is a table cluttered with breakfast dishes, a half-eaten loaf of bread, a fruit bowl with browning bananas and a few green apples, two brass candlesticks without candles, four disheveled blue cloth napkins. "I like that we cannot see any birds," she said. "There is only the suggestion of them."

"I hope I'll soon be looking at your work on these walls too," I said.

"Thank you for saying that. I am trying." She gave me a timid smile. Her profile was doll-like, her cheeks plump and pink as she grinned and looked again at my painting. "Joie is not so good for my work, but Stefan has been doing very much with her. He wants me to do well. He is acting like a boss."

"A good boss, I hope."

"I don't know," she said with a small laugh. "Sometimes, maybe. He is saying that I should not be working with wood, only paint, but he doesn't understand that I cannot pretend I want only to paint if I do not."

"I hope you won't listen to him," I said, "It's like someone telling you that you can't eat apples anymore, even if they're your favorite fruit."

She nodded. "That is exactly what I am trying to say to him." She paused. "Will you come see me again? Maybe we can talk about what I am doing with my work. Would you have time?"

I was so touched by her invitation that for a second I couldn't reply. Other than Jeanne-Lucie, who had shown me some of the ink drawings of table lamps and old desks that she worked on sporadically, and François and Nathalie, who had let me page through their sketchbooks at the gallery a couple of times, no one else had asked me to look at her work. "Yes, of course," I said. "I'd love to."

"And you can meet Joie."

I nodded. "That'd be great. As soon as we can arrange it."

"Thank you," she said quietly. "I am so glad you will."

I wondered if she felt like a shut-in now with Joie, though I was sure that she wouldn't admit such a thing to me. Nonetheless, I think she had sensed that day last summer when I went with Laurent to her and Stefan's apartment that I could be an ally. I hadn't gone again because Laurent hadn't welcomed it. It was easier for him if he stopped by alone when he was out doing other errands. No need, in his view, to make such an occasion of it.

Aside from Jeanne-Lucie and my camaraderie with Nathalie from Vie Bohème, which had led to a few movies and a couple of meals with two or three of her own friends, I didn't have any girl-friends in Paris, but I'd been so busy with my work the last several months, I hadn't had much time to try to cultivate any other new friendships.

I was curious about the other two artists whose bills Laurent was helping to pay. I hadn't met them yet, and they didn't attend the opening. The female artist lived in Marseilles, and the man was in Paris, but apparently he'd been attending to a sick mother in Bordeaux for the past few months, and so he wasn't here either, if in fact Laurent had bothered to tell him about Intérieurs intimes.

4.

Liesel and Melissa have a hard time with the fact that Jeanne-Lucie and I have become friends, and they wonder what kind of daughter would willingly make room in her life for the girlfriend of her father, a girlfriend who happens to be only a couple of years older than the daughter. What I have tried to explain to them, and to myself, I suppose, is that Jeanne-Lucie is attracted to controversy. She is complicated, sometimes contradictory, but I think most people are. She loves her husband and her daughter, but keeps a lover she has no plan to give up. I know this through Laurent; she has not spoken to me of her affair with Martin at any length. But she knows that I am aware of it, and mentioned once that she wished her father hadn't told me—not because she expected me to gossip or judge her harshly—just that the fewer people who knew about it the better. Beyond this, we haven't discussed it.

The only way it will end, Laurent has said, is if either she or Martin meets someone else—and it would probably be Jeanne-Lucie, not Martin, because he has been in love with her since they met several years ago, and Laurent thinks he is biding his time until she leaves Daniel and agrees to move in with him. I wonder if he sees other women, casually, perhaps to keep himself distracted from thoughts of her lying next to her husband every night. Laurent says he doesn't know, but he suspects that Martin does go out with other women from time to time. Why should he sleep alone when Jeanne-Lucie doesn't have to?

"Because he loves her and doesn't want to be with anyone else," I said. "That's why."

He smirked over this. "Those thoughts do not keep him warm," he said.

I talked a little bit about Jeanne-Lucie's love triangle with Liesel and Melissa over Christmas when I was in Pasadena and we were online together; the two of them were at Melissa and Joe's apartment making sugar cookies. Liesel thought it was reprehensible. Melissa, ironically, the married woman in our midst, wasn't as judgmental.

"Why are French people so fucked up?" asked Liesel. "Do they all cheat on each other? Is it written into their marriage contracts or something?"

"I'm sure they don't all cheat," I said.

"Right," said Liesel.

"Even if they don't, maybe they still have the option to," said Melissa. She was speaking softly because Joe was in the next room. "That might not be so bad," she whispered.

"I wouldn't stand for it," said Liesel.

"Wait until you're married for a little while," said Melissa. "Then tell me how you feel about it."

Liesel glared her. "Do you want to cheat on Joe?"

"Sssh," she hissed. "No, I don't, but I can see how it could happen if the conditions were right."

"Jesus, you too?" said Liesel. "You guys are crazy."

"I'm not crazy," I said.

She widened her eyes. "You cheated on Laurent with Colin!"

"That doesn't make me crazy," I said. I had only told Liesel and Melissa that I'd slept with Colin one time. I'd decided to keep our meetings to myself after that first confession because I didn't want to deal with their disappointment or censure. "Laurent and I have a 'don't ask, don't tell' policy," I said. Finally, this fact, if little else, I was sharing with them.

"What?" Liesel cried. "You do?"

"Yes."

Melissa said nothing, but she looked at me closely, her eyes wide with surprise and what might have been approbation.

"Well, let me know in a few more months how that's working out for you guys," said Liesel.

I have said nothing to Jeanne-Lucie about Colin, and cannot imagine myself ever doing so. In my most honest moments, I cannot see our friendship continuing for long if I were to leave France. Other times I think that this feeling is probably a reflection of my own insecurities more than anything she has implied in her behavior toward me. Sometimes I worry that she considers me little more than an amusing oddity, and perhaps she goes off after seeing me and laughs with her real friends about missteps I have made without realizing it.

Nonetheless, in her defense, she has never been petty or rude to me. If she were, I don't think I'm so desperate for female companionship that I'd continue to meet her for lunch or go to the little parks near her apartment with her and Marcelle, to the little stores where Jeanne-Lucie knows the slender, brisk saleswomen, where we shopped for leather boots and jeans and thick wool stockings when the weather grew cold. I thought that I might adore her forever too one afternoon, when we were buying fruit at an outdoor market and Sofia's name came up and Jeanne-Lucie gave me a wry look and said, "She's so vain and annoying. I know I can be vain too, but not that vain, I hope."

"Do I need to worry about her? I think Laurent still sees her."

Jeanne-Lucie shook her head. "No, don't waste your time thinking about her."

I said nothing and adjusted my scarf, my heart beating hard.

"You don't need to worry, Jayne. My father respects her work but he knows she's very calculating and selfish. He wants to be with you, not her," she assured me.

Without knowing it, Jeanne-Lucie has also taught me to stop apologizing so often for my Americanness and occasional homesickness, for my doubts about my talent, and for the fact that her father is doing so much for me. Hearing me speak about these feelings a couple of times, she finally said, "Do you think most other people would think twice about taking what he has offered you? Why should they? Do you think I feel bad that I was born into a family with money? Because I do not, and these two things don't seem so much different to me. You are lucky, and so am I."

We were walking in the Jardin du Luxembourg a few weeks before *Intérieurs intimes* opened. It was cold, but the sun was out, and we were bundled in scarves and warm coats. Marcelle was riding in her stroller, which she doesn't really need anymore, but Jeanne-Lucie still uses it on long walks because Marcelle always gets tired and is ready to go home before her mother and I are.

"People said I shouldn't have married Daniel because I was too young and not ready to settle down. They thought we would get a divorce within a year, but we didn't. When we had Marcelle, they said it was too soon, and I was going to be miserable and maybe I was, and still am sometimes, but it isn't her fault or Daniel's, and we are all fine most of the time. And who knows, I might want to have another baby someday. Daniel would like this, but I'm not ready yet."

"I don't think I want any kids," I said, "but most women I know do." I glanced at her in her red wool coat and black knit cap, the ends of her hair framing her cold-pinkened face. Marcelle was asleep in the stroller, her head tilted down, her chin buried in a lavender-and-white scarf that matched her hooded lavender coat.

"It's good to know this about yourself. It would be hard if you had a baby and then wished you hadn't. I think some women feel this way but would never say it."

Your mother? I wondered, but didn't ask.

"Men feel that way too," she added. "Maybe more of them than women."

Later that day, Jeanne-Lucie said something else that I have probably thought about too often since. "My brother was disappointed when you were not here for Christmas, when he and Léa visited," she said. As she spoke, I remember watching her bend down to check on Marcelle, who was awake now but still looked drowsy. I wondered how much of our conversation the little girl understood. "He likes you," said Jeanne-Lucie. "He hasn't liked the other women my father goes out with, the few he's met before you, anyway. Maybe my father has told you this. Or maybe Frédéric has?"

"No, neither of them has," I said, flattered but wondering now why Laurent had never said anything to me about it. I liked Frédéric too. He was funny and good-looking and full of energy—the kind of man women generally respond to. I suppose that if I were single and he were too, I'd probably want to get to know him better. He looks like his father—even their voices sound similar—but until Jeanne-Lucie told me this, I probably wouldn't have thought twice about Frédéric. I knew that André coming on to me was one thing, but Laurent would not have been able to overlook anything of the same nature between his son and me. "I like your brother and Léa too," I said. "And their daughter's so cute." Élodie was three months older than Marcelle; the two cousins got along well, Jeanne-Lucie had told me. "Much better than her father and I used to when we were little."

"Frédéric likes to flirt," she said now. "His wife puts up with a lot. I know that I wouldn't be as easygoing if I were married to someone like him." She made a silly face. "But who am I to talk, considering my friendship with Martin."

We rarely confided in each other this way when we were together. We talked about New York and food, our artmaking, and a little about the French political landscape, along with American politics, about which she knew almost as much as I did, and sometimes we discussed her father, though she did not say much about his past girlfriends, or her mother, and I didn't ask about them very much either. I didn't want her to feel as if I were taking advantage of our friendship. She had done so many things to make me feel welcome in Paris, and I was grateful.

I wondered that afternoon what had happened to summon all the conversation about her brother and Laurent and the mention of Martin. Although she never said it, it seemed to me that she was probably in love with Martin too. I wondered what her mother thought of the affair—surely she didn't approve, despite the fact she liked Martin and was friendly with his parents too, when they came to Paris a couple of times a year. Laurent told me that Jeanne-Lucie did not confide in Anne-Claire about her feelings for Martin. She and her mother had grown apart in the last few years, something Laurent attributed to Jeanne-Lucie's increasing awareness of her mother's innate coldness. These were his words, of course, not Jeanne-Lucie's, and I wondered if whatever bothered her about her mother was more complicated than Laurent made it seem. If I stayed in Paris long enough, I hoped that she would eventually talk about it with me.

She knew that I worried about my parents' marriage and having lived through her own parents' divorce, what she had to say about the subject was reassuring, though mine were not getting a divorce, not yet, anyway. "You have to remember that you have never wanted them to live your life for you," said Jeanne-Lucie. "You must try to act the same way with their lives."

"That's what Laurent told me too, more or less," I admitted.

"We think we cannot survive certain things if they were to happen," she said, "but we can. At least, that is what I say when I have dark thoughts."

"Laurent thinks it's because I want to stay a child, that I want the world to be what it seemed to be when I was a little girl. If my parents got a divorce, it obviously wouldn't seem that way anymore. But it's more that I worry they won't be able to take care of themselves if they're on their own. My father, especially."

"Oh, Jayne," she said, looking at her phone to check the time. We were having a mid-afternoon coffee, but Marcelle would need to be picked up soon from a friend's house. "Americans are so dramatic. All your television programs are about nuclear bombs exploding and the people next door making methamphetamines. No wonder you think everything that happens, big or small, is a catastrophe."

I smiled. "Is that why?"

She nodded, very sure of herself. "Of course it is."

Of Daniel, Jeanne-Lucie's husband, I can say this: he is pleasant—not as bland as that word implies, but reliable and even-tempered, from what Jeanne-Lucie has told me, and from what I gathered on the few occasions we've met. One afternoon when I stopped by their apartment to meet Jeanne-Lucie before we went out to buy Christmas gifts for Marcelle and Laurent, I saw Daniel smoking the cherrywood pipe I'd spotted on an end table in the room with the unicorn tapestry, months earlier, the day I first had lunch in the apartment. At the sight of him, fair and curly-haired, several years older and more weathered than his pretty, unfaithful wife, with that old-man pipe in his mouth, plumes of smoke rising from its bowl, I felt an unexpected rush of protective tenderness for him. I had to look away, but I think he caught something in my expression before I averted my face. He smiled at me when I met his eyes again, and we had a silent exchange, as if he was acknowledging that I believed him to be vulnerable and undervalued, and was politely dismissing my concern. He could take care of himself when it came to his wife and his marriage. There was no anger there, only what I sensed to be an abiding, calmly tended patience. Perhaps he'd known before he married Jeanne-Lucie that he wouldn't be able to keep her from other men's beds. Maybe he had decided that he could live with this, provided that she also lie willingly in his bed each night. I wondered if he and Laurent were, in this one sense, cut from similar cloth.

Sometimes I envy Jeanne-Lucie's and Laurent's risk-taking nature, their unapologetic self-interest, but in the next second, I realize that we are not so different, that here I am in Paris, and I have taken a lover too, one, oddly enough—or perhaps it isn't so odd—from the life I left behind in New York. At some point I will ask Jeanne-Lucie what happened between her and André. It could be there is something still between them, though this would surprise me. Even if since meeting Laurent, many of the things I am learning about myself and other people have surprised me, my instincts are that Jeanne-Lucie was done with André not long after whatever relations they shared began.

And on the whole, he and I now give each other a wide berth at the gallery when we are together there. He goes about his business, such as it is, Laurent allowing him to take money from the gallery accounts as he wishes, and Laurent, I know now, doing the same, though not as much money, from what I can tell. Laurent also moves funds back and forth between his personal accounts and the gallery's, as needed. These are my *droits de seigneur*, he once said to me, laughing but serious too, I knew. It is none of my business; in both senses of the expression, this is the truth.

5.

I have not yet said much about Sofia Baude, a gifted painter who also happens to speak four languages, a fact Laurent revealed after I pestered him for more information about her. He told me too that her Italian mother is a poet, her French father a distinguished linguistics professor. Sofia came to the opening, but she didn't stay long, no more than thirty or forty minutes. While she was there, I could feel other people looking at her too, and although he would have denied it, I knew Laurent was keeping track of her graceful movements around the gallery, as if she were a rare and wild creature not to be let out of his sight. She was wearing a sleeveless black dress, its hemline just above her shapely knees and bare legs, despite the cold night, winter still in the air on this first day of spring. Her necklace of interlocking silver discs, matching earrings, and two thick cuff bracelets were heavy and expensive-looking and gleamed like polished armor. She was clearly used to people staring at her and she moved within their capacious attention with queenly poise, her toned arms bent slightly at the elbows, her dark hair pinned up in a lush, disorderly bun to expose her long, elegant neck. I instantly felt a queasy fascination with her beauty and self-possession. She was someone I could learn from, someone who like my college quasi-nemesis Pepper embodied many of the qualities I wanted so badly to claim for myself.

This was my show, these were my paintings on the wall that night, but of course she knew that six of her own paintings were hanging in the home I shared with the man who I could see still desired her. Her understanding of light and color, her meticulous brushstrokes, her sympathetic, intuitive eye: how long had it taken her to master these talents?

Without knowing it, Susan gave me the reserves I needed to withstand my jealous feelings that evening. Susan and I were standing together near one of her paintings, Central Park West Window (oil on linen), waiting for a server to reappear with two glasses of cold water, when she glanced from me to Sofia, who was standing several yards away, flirting with André and François. "Is that your sister?" she asked, nodding toward Sofia. "You two resemble each other."

I laughed, too loudly. Susan's benign expression wavered; she knew instantly that something was going on, but didn't press me.

"No, no," I said. "That's Laurent's ex-girlfriend."

Whatever Susan really thought of this, and by association, of Laurent and me, she managed to keep it hidden. "Well," she murmured, "don't tell her, but you're the prettier sister."

I laughed again, more softly than before, and glanced at her painting, feeling a little better. Whether or not she believed her remark was true, I could have said then in all sincerity that I loved her. That I needed and appreciated her and wanted desperately, for the rest of my life, to be her friend, to be able to call her on any day that I had the urge to, but I couldn't string the words together. She might have sensed how I felt; she squeezed my shoulder and smiled and shook her head, glancing toward Laurent, who stood talking to several people I didn't know near the table where emptied wineglasses were being placed by the caterers until they could be carried into the back. Susan looked at me expectantly, but instead of unloading my romantic insecurities on her I looked again at her paintings, which were, almost paradoxically, both mysterious and very personal. I asked how long had it taken her to complete *Central Park West Window*. Did she work on several canvases at once? What was her studio space like?

Soon Colin walked through the gallery doors, looking like an anxious, excited boy sneaking downstairs to the grown-ups' party. I can only guess what Susan thought, seeing me turn toward him with such abrupt focus, my whole body alert in a way it hadn't been before he came in off the street and looked apprehensively around the noisy room, his brown hair, which needed cutting—it had grown past his ears about half an inch—springing up when he pulled off his gray wool hat.

Before he spotted me in the crowd, I noticed his eyes landing on Sofia—only for a second or two, but long enough for me to know that he had registered her presence. I knew he was there to see me, but I still felt a tremor of jealousy. I wanted unequivocally at that moment for Sofia to disappear from my life and Laurent's, for her to retreat to some remote island with her perfect paintings and artfully messy bun and glamorous silver adornments, for her to grow fat and uncertain. Yet I knew it wouldn't matter how far away she went if she retained her place in Laurent's erotic imagination. What had happened between them, and what continued to happen between them? I could recognize the irony here; I had no right to feel injured when I was playing both sides too.

It was then that André brought Sofia over to where Susan and I stood, his hand at the small of her back as they walked toward us.

Colin was lingering in front of Chantal's paintings, not yet having come over to say hello. Laurent was still with the group by the empty wineglasses. If I had a picture of this scene and had decided to do a detail instead of painting the whole, I would have chosen Laurent's face: the watchful expression, the dark, fathomless eyes. I saw him looking over at us at one point, pretending to listen to what a man in a burnt-orange sweater was saying, his hands gesturing as he spoke. Laurent might have noticed that Colin was there, but he would not have made a scene, even if he had a right to. We rarely spoke about Colin, and in January, I finished the painting I'd started of him last fall. He now sits with some other canvases, his face against the wall, though I look at him sometimes, trying to decide what to do with him. I knew that Laurent wasn't thrilled when he first saw that I was painting my ex-boyfriend, but he had not really protested. "The muse," he'd said, his voice laced with irony. "How wicked she is, Jayne, don't you think?"

"I'm sorry," I said, my heartbeat very loud in my ears at that moment. "I guess it's rude of me to be painting an ex-boyfriend."

Laurent had looked at me for several seconds before saying, "No, not really, but I hope that you will choose me as your subject before long too. I would like that."

I promised him that I would, but so far, I haven't. I want to paint one of the framed photos of him that he keeps in the apartment, but I haven't yet been able to decide which one.

About a month after this conversation, on the morning before I flew home to California for Christmas, Laurent asked, strangely, if Colin would be there too. "Of course not," I said, wary. "He doesn't live in L.A."

"He doesn't have to," Laurent said. That was all he said, and I didn't press him to say more. If he'd wanted to pursue it, I thought, he would have. But from then on, I was more on guard, more aware that he probably knew I was keeping something from him, and that my sneakiness, my selfishness, whatever he thought it was, surprised him more than he'd expected.

"I like your paintings," Sofia said. Her French accent was a little more pronounced than Laurent's when he spoke English. "The one of the couple standing near the ice cream cart is my favorite, I think. The way you expose the man to us, I can see that he is worried he will lose her."

"You really see that?" I asked. "I thought I'd made sure he looked happy."

She shook her head. "It is a very thin happiness that he has."

"I noticed that too," said Susan. "I can almost hear 'Moon River' playing in the background."

"The song from *Breakfast at Tiffany's*?" asked Sofia.

"Yes, exactly," said Susan. She glanced from Sofia to me and smiled. I couldn't remember how the song went; I smiled back at her but said nothing.

"Someone once told me that I look like Audrey Hepburn," said Sofia. "But he said that to other women too. He was such a terrible flirt."

Susan studied her for a few seconds. "I can see a resemblance."

"You are kind to say that, but I don't see it," said Sofia.

"Sofia is as beautiful as Audrey Hepburn was," said André, leering at her before he turned to me, as if challenging me to disagree. God, I disliked him. For a second, I worried that I would say this aloud.

"Don't be ridiculous," Sofia scoffed. She didn't blush, nor did she seem to be acting coy, which I must admit impressed me. I think she must have seen through André too, through his paper-thin flattery, his mercurial moods, straight through to his insecurities and unflattering competitiveness with other men.

"Jayne here looks like Catherine Deneuve, don't you agree?" he asked, laughing in a loud burst.

Sofia glanced at him. "Don't be ridiculous," she said. "She looks more like Audrey Tautou than Deneuve."

"One of my friends said that once," I said. "But really, who cares?" I said, trying not to raise my voice. I really did want to yell *Why are we talking about this?*

"Do you mind holding my glass for a minute?" I asked, turning to Susan. I needed to use the bathroom but didn't want to announce it to everyone. "It was nice to meet you, Sofia," I said, ignoring André, who was now leering at me. "Thank you for coming tonight."

"I was looking forward to it," Sofia said, her voice warm. "See you again soon, I hope."

I paused, taking in her eyebrows raised in inquiry, her right hand at her throat, fingering her gleaming necklace. I had no idea what she was talking about. "Of course," I said. "See you again."

When I returned from the back office, I walked straight to where Colin was now standing in front of *Sarah with Cat-Eye Glasses* and put my hand on his sleeve. His arm was so solid under his coat, and I wanted to throw my own arms around him but hesitated, imagining both André's and Laurent's eyes on us. Sofia had completed her tour of the show and stood now with Laurent, her coat on. Colin turned and enveloped me in his long, hard-muscled arms. I pressed my cheek to his shoulder for a few seconds, breathing in the cold night air he'd carried in with him, the smell of damp wool. "Your paintings are stunning," he said. "They really are, Jayne." In the next second, his mouth very close to my ear, he whispered, "I've missed you so much. When are you coming home to New York?" We hadn't seen each other since before Christmas. More than three months. I had missed him, but we were in touch often; we e-mailed and texted, and I spoke to him on Skype some-times when Laurent wasn't home.

"I'm not sure," I said softly, stepping away. "I missed you too." I paused. "I'm so glad you like my paintings. That means a lot."

He searched my face. "Jayne, if you move back, you could think about moving in with me."

I took another step back. "What?" I said. I could sense two women a few feet to my left turning to look at us, but I kept my eyes on Colin.

"If you wanted to," he said.

"Thank you," I murmured, unable to think of anything else to say. I wondered if he'd been drinking, but I couldn't smell any alcohol on him.

"I mean it," he said. "I wanted to wait until we were alone to ask you, but I was so happy to see you that I couldn't keep it to myself."

I looked up at his earnest, clean-shaven face. I could hear people talking and laughing all around us. I was afraid to look for Laurent. By now he must have noticed that I was standing with Colin. "Yes, let's talk about it when we're alone," I said.

"I'm sorry to put you on the spot here," he said, contrite. "Tonight of all nights."

"It's okay. I'm really flattered." I made myself glance around the room for a second, but I didn't see Laurent or André. The gallery was crowded now; fifty or sixty people, maybe more, were stand-ing around, talking in noisy, animated groups.

"Let's talk tomorrow," he said. "If you can?"

"Yes, I should be able to."

"Okay," he said. He was pale, and his face looked thinner, his cheeks less full, than the last time I'd seen him. "You know where I'm staying. Same place as always." His eyes were on the floor as he spoke, and when he raised them again, instead of looking at me, he focused on the wall where my paintings were mounted.

I had the feeling then—as if I had woken in the night, certain that something I'd long feared had come true—that Laurent knew about us, and had for a while. It wasn't fear or guilt that I felt, though. It was probably something closer to relief.

"I knew you were good," said Colin. "I saw the paintings you kept in your apartment in New York, but these are—these look like they should be in a museum."

I managed not to scoff at him. "It's so sweet of you to say that, but I still have a lot to learn," I said. I was pretty sure that I could paint a human body with the suggestion of a real person awake inside it, but I wasn't in any danger of having a curator from MoMA come looking for me.

"I mean it, Jayne." He reached for my hand, his palm a little damp. "Your paintings are beautiful. Congratulations."

We were still standing in front of *Joanie* and *Owls and Starlings* when Laurent came over to introduce himself. He stood looking at us for an uncomfortable moment, neither Colin nor I knowing what to say, before he offered his hand to Colin and said, "I'm Laurent Moller, one of the owners of this gallery. You are Jayne's friend from New York, yes?"

"Yes," said Colin, shaking Laurent's hand. "One of her friends. My name's Colin Fuller."

"I thought so," said Laurent, with a cryptic note of finality—no, of assessment. He was taking the measure of this interloper, just as I had done a moment before with Sofia. "How long have you known Jayne?" he asked.

"About three years," said Colin.

"Ah, not so very long then," said Laurent.

Colin glanced at me, his expression hard to read. "Well, no, I guess not. But longer than you've known her, I would say."

Laurent laughed. It was an odd, forced sound, like someone ripping cardboard. "Sometimes I feel as if I have known Jayne for all my life," he said.

"That would be difficult, wouldn't it? Considering you're more than twenty years older than she is," said Colin.

I could feel my stomach clench with apprehension. They were looking at each other harshly, a faint smile on Laurent's face, his eyes cold; Colin's face was burning. "I need a glass of wine," I said, willing my voice to stay level.

"How do you like Jayne's paintings?" Laurent asked, his harsh gaze still on Colin.

"They're terrific," he said.

"Yes, they are terrific," Laurent repeated. He glanced at me and blinked deliberately, as if having decided something—to save his displeasure with me for later, I think—before he looked toward the back office. The caterers were using it that evening as their make-shift kitchen, the four of them circulating in and out, shoving open the heavy door with their white-shirted shoulders. "I think it is time for champagne," said Laurent. He turned toward Colin. "Good to meet you, Mr. Fuller. At last."

I said nothing, but Laurent wasn't looking at me anyway.

"And you," said Colin. Neither he nor Laurent smiled.

It was not until the next morning that Laurent said, his gaze flat, almost incensed, that before he had come over to introduce himself, he had noticed Colin and me talking at the gallery about something that had looked serious to him, and he wondered what it was. Had Colin had a death in the family? Had he lost his job? Was he ill?

"No, nothing like that," I said, wondering if he was mocking me. If he was, I would surprise him by telling the truth. "He was trying to get me to come back to New York."

"Why would he do that?" asked Laurent, watching me closely. "Because he wants to take you from me?"

"Yes, I guess he does," I said.

"Do you want that too?" he asked.

"No."

He said nothing for several seconds. When he finally spoke, his expression was meditative. "Are you sure that you want to stay here, Jayne?"

"Yes," I said. "I am." I didn't ask if he wanted me to stay.

In Vie Bohème on that cold March night, my favorite teacher, my boyfriend, my lover, my boyfriend's lover, his resentful business partner, his daughter, his daughter's husband, and her own lover were all in attendance. It is a wonder we all remained somewhat civil to each other, that there were no histrionics. I wondered about Anne-Claire, why she hadn't come to stir the pot too. As it turned out, she was in New York, visiting a man she had started seeing a few months earlier—another psychologist, an American she had been introduced to by Martin's father.

6.

The vernissage of Intérieurs intimes might have been a fraught event, but the show was a commercial success. All but one of the paintings I had shown sold within the week, along with most of Susan's and Chantal's paintings. (Who were these buyers, I wondered—men with inherited money, or ones who had made their fortunes on the stock market? Old dowagers with young lovers who had convinced them to buy our emotional paintings of haunted-looking rooms and people in the grip of melancholy or the torpor that sometimes follows sex?)

The afterglow from the opening remained for several days, but then normal life, with its questions and lack of satisfying answers, returned. Laurent got up at eight each morning and later went to the gallery. He ran his errands, visited artists' studios and who knew who else—women friends mostly, I felt sure—on the afternoons when he took long breaks. When he later returned home or to the gallery, he was often humming under his breath, something I began to think of as a tell. I could never detect any lingering scent of another woman's perfume, but I suspect he would have taken a shower after he'd finished rolling around with whoever she was. He was a seasoned philanderer, a belief that I had become increasingly more susceptible to as my months living in his apartment and sleeping in his bed passed. But when I weighed the costs of challenging him, of constantly fighting and accusing him of bad behavior, they seemed too heavy. I was painting the best work of my life so far. I was living in Paris rent-free—and I had my own secrets to hide. There was also the fact that I cared a lot about Laurent, that although I didn't know if I really did love him, I often loved being with him. It was my conviction too that he was turning me into a less fearful, less insecure person—because what did it matter, in the barest analysis, what he did when he wasn't with me, if he acted no differently from one day to the next when he was?

My jealousy did rear up out of its dark, hot cave and make my life unpleasant sometimes, especially in the early evening when I was alone and often wondering where he was. Is it a mark of sophistication or maturity if you have learned to stifle the impulsive, explosive feelings that come with being betrayed? Because that is what I believe I was learning to do. And I had to think Laurent had also learned to do it, long ago, when he and Anne-Claire were both, from what I gather, seeing other people and their marriage was falling apart. The wish to be all things to our intimates into perpetuity—friend, confidant, lover, therapist—is there something fanciful and unrealistic about this? Perhaps we should have more than one friend, more than one person, to fill all those roles.

Learning to be more sophisticated, if that's what it is, learning to channel your energies into pursuits more productive than jealous speculation, takes time. On some days I sensed something in Jeanne-Lucie's manner toward me, a hint of pity, a habit of looking too long and intently at my face, her mind, I was convinced, cycling through a litany of reasons to tell me or not tell me what she knew of her father's secrets. I remember a day not long after Colin's October visit, the first time since the previous year that I had been in his bed, when she asked me if her father ever failed to come home at night. I was unbalanced by the question and said no with too much vehemence, and then laughed to try to cover up my distress. "Why wouldn't he?" I asked. "Does he have another apartment in Paris with some other girl he takes care of? Does he think he's François Mitterand?"

She smiled and laughed softly. "You know about Mitterand, with his two families?"

"Yes, I do," I said. "What a lot of hassle and work, frankly."

"You are so funny. The French do not think that way so much. It is pleasure he was after, comfort too. I doubt he thought of it as work. He was in love with both women, I'm sure."

"Very nice for him," I said. "Not so nice for the women."

"Maybe not," she said. "But I suppose they got used to it. He was a great man, and they were happy that he wanted to be with them."

"I'd rather have a less great man all to myself."

What did I truly think of Mitterand's domestic arrangement? I wondered later—if I could have two homes, both welcoming and designed to meet my whims, would I want this?

No, I didn't really think that I would. Seeing Colin, even infrequently, left me feeling emotionally fractured and guilty too, because even given Laurent's leniency and his own probable affairs, I realized that I didn't have the temperament to live parallel amorous lives. You have to be a natural risk taker, I think, to thrive in such unpredictable conditions, to ignore the probability that someone you are close to is getting hurt, and you are the cause of these hurtful feelings.

Whatever she might think of Jeanne-Lucie's affair with Martin, Liesel, for one, showed herself to be a risk taker. When she and Melissa flew over to see me last August, Liesel met André for a drink one night and ended up going home with him. She didn't get back to Laurent's and my apartment until four in the morning. I was awake, lying next to Laurent, who as usual was sleeping soundly, oblivious to the night's provocative events. The next night Liesel was supposed to see André again, but for a while it looked as if he intended to stand her up. At ten thirty, he finally texted to suggest that she take a cab over to his place, where he was now ready to receive her. Like Jeanne-Lucie and Daniel, he lived across the city in the eleventh arrondissement, near the Théâtre de la Bastille.

I was jealous, even though I knew that André was a rat. This was several weeks before I leaped again into Colin's arms. I could imagine that André was a capable, maybe even a ferocious lover. Without much trouble, I could also picture him naked, and I knew that Liesel had had the time of her liberated-woman's life. All day after that first night with him, she spoke of little else when she spoke at all. Melissa and I teased her, waving our hands in front of her dazed, glowing face when we could see that her thoughts had again drifted away. "How was he?" Melissa asked, giggling. This was one of her many questions. I hadn't asked any; Melissa's curiosity was irrepressible, more than enough for us both. "He was pretty kinky. We had fun," Liesel said, solemn. Then she too giggled. "I'll never be the same again. I think I'm going to have to move to Paris," she said.

"Are French guys really that great?" Melissa asked.

"I don't know, but this one's damn good," said Liesel.

It was after the next night, however, when Don Juan André made her wait until ten thirty, after having promised that he'd be free by seven, that she realized what kind of punishment she'd probably be subjecting herself to if she did move to Paris intent on bringing him to heel. "I can get booty calls in New York," she said. "I'll save myself the moving expenses and the job search over here. He was fun, but he doesn't want a relationship. When he comes to New York again, he said he'd call me, but I'm not sure I'll answer."

Melissa looked at her and laughed. "You'll answer."

Liesel hesitated, wrinkling her brow. "Yeah, because if I don't, you will."

"Ha-ha," said Melissa.

"Ha-ha," retorted Liesel. "I know I'm right!"

7.

When my sister came to visit, she had trouble with blisters on her heels, the bolster-like pillow in the guest bedroom, the meat that figured prominently on so many restaurant menus (she had been a vegetarian since freshman year in college), the exchange rate, jet lag. On the first four of the six mornings of her visit, she was nearly impossible to pry out of bed, because in spite of feeling exhausted by nine thirty every night, when she did go to bed a little later, she would lie there staring at the ceiling until two or three a.m.

"I've never had anything like this happen before," she'd croak each morning when I'd finally get her up at ten or ten thirty. "It's midnight in L.A. I'd just be getting to sleep now if I were home." Her brown eyes were bloodshot and sleep-crusted, as if she were recovering from a bender; her hair stood up in little wings all over her foggy head. Once or twice I crawled into bed with her and put my arms around her and rested my head on her skinny shoulder, as I'd done when we were little girls. She was so thin, thinner than she should have been. For the first few days, her skin looked chalky too, despite all the Southern Californian sun. Further proof that her life at the record company, her long commute, her high rent, and her sudden intense fear of skin cancer (she wore a hat whenever we went out to walk in the Parisian sun, as she now did in L.A.) were wearing on her.

"Why do you have to live so far away?" she asked as we lay in bed on her third morning in Paris. "It's amazing here, of course, and Laurent seems nice, but I miss you. Don't you miss me?"

"Of course I do," I whispered.

Her laugh was a throaty rasp. "You'd never know. We haven't lived in the same city for more than twelve years."

"I'm working on an invention," I said. "Not sunglasses for dogs, but a teleportation device. Don't tell anyone. I don't want anyone to steal my blueprints."

She croaked out another laugh. "Don't forget to bring me some cheese when you use your device. And a baguette. You'll have to make sure you figure out how to bring luggage too."

After she took a shower and had some coffee, along with a *chausson aux pommes*—the flaky apple pastry she preferred to a plain croissant or a *pain au chocolat*—she was usually revived, and we would set off for the museum or neighborhood or shopping district she wanted to see that day. I took her to the Porte de Clignancourt to visit the sprawling flea market near the city's northern periphery, where I would also take our parents—who were more affectionate with each other, on the whole, than I'd seen them be in years—when they came in the spring, but Stephanie was bored after an hour of looking at antiques and knick-knacks, and I took her back into the center of Paris to walk along the narrow streets near the Sorbonne and through the Jardin du Luxembourg.

During our wanderings around the city, she grilled me about my life with Laurent, whom she liked, she said, but thought was too old for me, as I knew our mother also did. "He reminds me of Uncle Hugh," she said. "Around the eyes, and his voice. They kind of dress alike too."

Hugh was our mother's younger brother, and he spent a lot of money on his clothes and hair. He was divorced, no kids, lived in Dallas, and was probably gay, but he had never come out to anyone in the family.

"I don't think so," I said. "Hugh's voice is more nasally, for one."

"No, but there's still something about the way Laurent speaks that reminds me of him."

"I don't hear it," I said.

"Well, I do," she said. "You just don't want me to compare your boyfriend to our gay uncle."

"Compare them all you want," I said. "Doesn't matter to me."

"Really," she said. "Could have fooled me."

I knew before she'd arrived that we'd probably bicker during her visit, out of lifelong habit, but also because of her unhappiness with her own life, her job and feelings of stagnation.

She wasn't dating anyone seriously either, and here I was—more or less well rested, not worrying about money, working on paintings that I was interested in, enjoying some success in my chosen field, living in a city I loved. I hadn't told her about my suspicions that Laurent saw other women. I didn't want her to have this on me, even if it might have made her feel better. What I recognized was how much importance I'd begun to place on people no longer pitying or feeling superior to me. I'd had enough of that, probably enough to last my whole life, when I lived in New York.

Stephanie was thinking of going to law school but didn't know—as I'd also felt about getting an M.F.A.—if she wanted to take out more loans and go back to the shabby-genteel student life-style. "I'm almost twenty-nine," she said. "I'd be the oldest person in the class."

"I doubt it," I said. "And that shouldn't stop you, if you do want to go."

She shook her head. "Easy for you to say. Your sugar daddy would pay your bills if you wanted to go."

"He's not my sugar daddy," I said.

"He's not?"

"No, he's my boyfriend."

"If you say so, Jayne."

Don't be such a bitch, I almost said, but knew we'd launch into a full-blown fight if I did. This was her last morning and instead, I forced myself to change the subject. "Do you want to go out for dinner tonight?" I asked. "Or I could make a big salad and some penne with asparagus and peas."

"Look at you," she said. "The master chef." To my surprise, she didn't say this maliciously. She was smiling now, her mood swinging back to amiable. "Let's eat here. That sounds good."

"But we can go out for lunch," I said. "Falafel sandwiches. I'll take you to rue Montorgeuil. It's a fun street with a lot of little shops that you'd probably like to browse."

"I'm ready," she said, though she was in her robe and her hair was still wet from her shower.

"Ten minutes," I said.

"Fifteen," she said.

"Twelve and a half. I'm setting a timer." I waved my phone at her.

She laughed. "I wouldn't put it past you."

After lunch, as we were walking past Saint-Eustache, Stephanie asked if Laurent liked her. He'd been nice enough but hadn't really tried to talk to her. Hadn't I noticed this too? I had noticed, but it hadn't bothered me very much. He didn't like small talk, in part because he was required to make a lot of it in order to stay in business. I told Stephanie that he did like her, which is what he'd told me.

"Really?" she said. "Because he's only had dinner with us twice."

"He wanted us to have time to ourselves," I said. "He wouldn't know most of the people we talk about anyway."

"I thought it was because he didn't like me."

"No, Stephanie," I said. "That's not the case at all."

"Maybe when you move back to the States, if you ever do, you could live in L.A. again," she said.

"Or you could move to New York."

She shook her head. "No. I don't do winters. Do you think I'd put up with all the bullshit in L.A. if I didn't love the weather there so much?"

I'd only been living in Paris for a little more than two months when my sister came to see me, and was just starting to internalize that this wasn't a vacation, that I was an inhabitant, not a visitor. It made me pause. I think I felt afraid, almost—as if I were a refugee and would never be able to return to my country of origin. I knew this was foolish, like how I'd felt as a small girl when the tub was draining after my bath—I'd been afraid that I'd go down into the pipes with the dirty water. Foolish, yes, but it was how I felt sometimes.

8.

At certain times of day, midmorning or early afternoon usually, when I am walking alone, down the sloping streets of the eighth arrondissement toward the Seine, passing the sleek fortresses that house the most powerful politicians in France, I feel my skin prickling with possibility. I am closer to my twenty-year-old self here, closer than I am at home. Almost no one knows me here, and this feels like a gift. It is true that hardly anyone knows me in New York either, but I could not have started over there as I have here. The plane trees along the Seine, their leaves' coin-like rustling, the light that threads its way through the gaps between the branches and each perfect, ephemeral leaf—I know that I will only feel this way here. I might feel like this for the rest of my life if I decide to stay. But of course I can only know this if I do.

I still wonder if what has happened during the months I've lived with Laurent should simply be considered a kind of adult education, training for the rest of life, like a college program that teaches you to become a more fully developed person. My jealousy, unease, and suspicion, along with the physical and material comforts, the affection, the leisure, the time to paint, the enormous generosity he has extended to me by showing my work along with Susan's, the boost he has given me into the hierarchy of artists—I know, oh, I know. There is nothing I could ever do for him that would be even half as meaningful.

It's been several weeks now since the opening. My parents came over for the second week of April and got along fine (for my benefit? I hope not—they seemed so much themselves, and if this was all subterfuge, they should be auditioning for Hollywood movies) but my father, predictably, was alarmed by how expensive everything was. This was the first time they'd visited Paris together, and even though I asked them to stay with Laurent and me, they didn't want to impose, and decided to reserve a room in what turned out to be a flea trap up by the Gare du Nord, the kind of place my friends and I paid forty dollars a night for during our semester abroad. My father justified his ingrained cheapness by saying they would have a more salt-of-the-earth experience ("But you'll be in Paris, which is not a salt-of-the-earth kind of place," I said) if they stayed in a dive, not realizing a French dive is different from a mostly clean Super 8, but after the first night, my mother had said "Enough," and they reserved a room at the Hotel Esmérelda on the Left Bank, just across from Notre Dame. It isn't the fanciest place either, but it was cleaner, and the room was bigger; it was also three times as expensive as the Gare du Nord flea trap.

My mother cried when she saw my paintings at Vie Bohème. She once wanted to sing and write songs like Joan Baez, and she has long claimed responsibility for my artistic leanings. "Jayne, honey, this is wonderful," she said, her eyes filled with tears. "Your father and I are so proud of you. I'm glad you kept pushing us to send you to that summer class in Chicago. It was a good investment."

"Did I really push that much?" I asked, a little ashamed. I'd minored in studio art in college too, but I didn't remind her of this.

"No, you didn't," said my father, who was looking closely at Joanie. "Do I know this woman?"

"I don't think so, Dad," I said. "She was in a photograph taken forty-five years ago in Salinas with a guy named Jim."

"She looks like one of my high school English teachers," he said. "It could be her, but I don't remember if her first name was Joanie."

"You grew up in Danville, Illinois," my mother said. "I doubt it's her."

"She might have been on vacation in Salinas," he said.

My mother gave him a derisive look—her mouth half open, ready to laugh—that I had seen on her face many times before, and I cringed. But instead of reacting to her, my father looked back at Joanie, and my mother turned to me. "We weren't sure what to expect from your show here," she said. "You wouldn't tell us much at Christmas about what you were working on."

"Kendra, come on," said my father. "We knew it'd be good."

"You've seen my work," I said. "You know that I do figurative and narrative paintings, not abstract ones. There's nothing really inscrutable about my work."

"Yes, but how did we know that you wouldn't be trying something else this time?" she said.

My father gave me a look of commiseration. "Is Laurent going to show your work in his New York gallery too?"

This would be the first time I'd spoken of the possibility with anyone but Laurent. The idea of it made me almost sick with anticipation and fear that it wouldn't happen. "Sometime next year, maybe," I said, "but we've just started talking about it, so I'm not sure if it'll actually happen."

"That would be marvelous, wouldn't it, sweetie?" my mother exclaimed. "You've always wanted a show in New York." She grabbed my arm and squeezed it, her face glowing. She looked very pretty in her pink dress and cream-colored raincoat, her thick, silver-streaked brown hair pinned up, pearls in her ears and at her throat. My sister and I have always envied her long, healthy hair; ours is like our father's—finer and flyaway if not conditioned enough.

Mom was charged up on coffee and sugar from the pastries we'd had before coming to Vie Bohème around four o'clock. Dad, the skin under his eyes loose and violet-tinted, looked as if he needed a nap. It was their first full day in Paris, and their trip from California had taken all day and night.

"We'll see," said my father. "Let's not get too carried away."

"No," I said. "I'm not holding my breath." But I suppose that in truth, I was. If Laurent had suggested showing my work in the Chelsea Vie Bohème, I knew that he wasn't kidding. The four of my five paintings that had so far sold had earned respectable sums, and he had told me the day before my parents' arrival that someone was interested in the fifth.

They knew very little about my life in Paris, I realized. They stumbled around, half listening to my tour-guide narrative, staring up at the rooflines, at the hovering golden dome of the Hotel des Invalides in the distance, at the eerie, skeletal Eiffel Tower. Each time my mother spotted it, she murmured hopefully, "Oh, there it is," as if it were a herald of her future too.

I knew that I wasn't ready to leave Paris yet as we walked together or rode the Metro around the city, emerging from the subways into the sunlight or the benign glow of the streetlamps. Even though many days still felt as fresh as my first day here last June, it's hard to understand how much your city, adopted or native, means to you until you show off its treasures to someone for whom the landmarks and cafés and shops haven't become common sights, or, in some cases, all but invisible. I intended to stay in Paris, at least through the summer; I decided this as my parents and I walked down through the north side of the Left Bank on our way to the Jardin du Luxembourg.

Whatever he might have felt in his secret heart, Laurent seemed in no hurry for me to leave his apartment. He liked having me there, painting in his study, working at the gallery too; he liked eating the food I was teaching myself how to cook with more pleasure and inspiration now that, for the first time since college, I had the time to do it properly. I could feel, however, that by small increments, Laurent was receding from me emotionally. It wasn't just the unacknowledged infidelities. He was uncomfortable with my friendship with Jeanne-Lucie; he did not think it appropriate or else was simply jealous and wary of our regard for each other. When I mentioned that she wanted to travel with me to New York, he was instantly resistant to the idea but tried to make it seem as if I shouldn't be away from my painting for so many days at a stretch, as if I was in danger of missing a deadline. He also implied that he would not pay for any part of it, that I was on my own in this respect. What I didn't tell him was that Jeanne-Lucie had insisted that she pay for our hotel room, and I need only buy my plane ticket. Food we didn't discuss, but I could cover that too, provided she didn't intend for us to go to Per Se or Le Cirque (or, God forbid, both).

"What are you going to do next?" my father asked as we rode the train to the airport on the morning they left Paris. "Graduate school?" he said. "Do you want to get an M.F.A. now?"

"It might be a good idea," my mother said, glancing down at her purse, which she was gripping tightly in her lap. No one had been pickpocketed during the visit, but she would not decrease her vigilance, even on this final leg of their trip. "If you want to teach," she continued. "Isn't that what a lot of artists do to support themselves?"

"Yes," I said. "If they can find jobs. There are so many artists with M.F.A.s who want to teach."

"It's worth looking into," my father said. "You should be able to get some scholarship money too."

"You could go to UCLA and live with your sister," my mother said. "She needs a new roommate. She and Jill are at each other's throats constantly now. Jill's boyfriend is always over. It's just terrible for Stephanie, who needs peace and quiet when she's home."

"You could probably also go somewhere here in Paris," said my father.

"I'm too old to get into the national art school here. The age limit is twenty-four for new students."

"What?" said my mother, scrunching her face in surprise. "Why is that?"

"I don't know," I said. "But those are the guidelines on their website."

"So you were already looking into it," said my father, his expression guarded.

"Yes, just out of curiosity."

"Your French is good," said my mother. "You speak it like a native now."

I shook my head. "No, not even close, but it has gotten better. Hearing it all the time helps, of course, and I speak it at the gallery and when I'm in the stores, but you know that Laurent and I speak English mostly."

"His English is very good," she agreed. "I like him, Jayne." She glanced at my father, who said nothing. He was looking out the window now, pretending not to listen to us.

"I thought you would," I said. "He's easy to like."

One of the few times she and I were out exploring the city by ourselves, my father having decided to stay behind for a nap at the hotel, she had asked me what sort of future I saw with Laurent. What if I wanted to start a family? "I don't think I want kids," I said.

I could tell that this wasn't the answer she was hoping for. "You might change your mind, Jayne, but your thirties are going to go faster than your twenties. You'll see," she said. "And I wouldn't wait until you're in your forties to have a child and settle down."

"If I want to do those things," I said.

She hesitated, a smile quavering on her lips, her face so familiar to me, almost as familiar as my own, but here in Paris I found myself looking at her differently, trying to imagine how other people saw her. Was there another man tucked away in the most private rooms of her life? Was he the reason she had moved out for those few days the two times that Stephanie and I knew about? I had asked her this, over the phone and in person, but she always denied it. "You just get tired of things never changing," she'd said. "There doesn't have to be someone else. You don't know this yet, but at some point you probably will. I don't wish this on you or your sister, though."

She was aging well—Did my father see this? She wore sunblock and hadn't gained more than a few pounds since I was a child. She liked going to yoga and Pilates classes at the gym; she also liked being a high school English teacher. She did love my father, she said, she did, and she loved Stephanie and me. A few years after college, New York roaring all around me, its expensive pleasures not within my reach, I'd thought that my mother had the knack for happiness. From my wobbly vantage point, I peered hard at her and my father's lives, the choices they'd made alone and as a couple, wondering how I could ever acquire the things they had in Pasadena, both material and immaterial. That these things weren't enough for her (and maybe not for my father either, but he was even more tight-lipped than she) was, I eventually realized, part of why her problems with their marriage bothered me so much.

"You might want a child one day," she said. "You and Stephanie are the biggest joys of my life."

"I hope not," I said, laughing.

"Why do you say that?" she asked, genuinely puzzled. "It's true, Jayne, and your father feels the same way."

My humble, pensive father, an attorney who helped people negotiate their way out of unjust debt, who helped immigrants bring over other family members, who lent money to friends and did not expect to be repaid, whose car nosed into the street from its gloomy lair in the garage at six thirty every weekday morning, sometimes before the L.A. *Times* had been tossed heedlessly into the hedges that flanked the front door: how hard he worked, and how decent he was. How angry he became when he heard about people being treated unfairly, being robbed by their employers or by trusted politicians, or sometimes when he was stuck in traffic, mute with fury over the time being wasted (in L.A., nonetheless, where you had to cultivate a certain stoicism if you were going to drive a car, but it didn't matter, he still got mad), or the neighbor left his German shepherd in the backyard, where it barked and whined inconsolably for hours. Were Stephanie and I really his biggest joys?

"Thank you both for coming to see me," I said. "I know it wasn't cheap, and Dad said you need to repair the roof."

She waved a hand in front of her face. "The roof isn't that bad. Your father worries more than he needs to, and we haven't had real rain in so long that it almost seems unnecessary."

"It'll rain again though," I said.

My mother's expression was skeptical. "Yes, but it probably won't be enough to make any difference."

When I hugged them both good-bye at the airport, my father looked at me for a long, thoughtful moment and said, "I guess we won't be seeing you until next Christmas."

"Maybe before then," I said. "I'm not sure."

"I'd say you have a pretty good deal here," he murmured. "If you're enjoying it, I wouldn't rush back to the States."

I waited, listening for a qualification, but he said nothing more. All along I'd been assuming that he was worried about my lack of an engagement ring and no talk of a more binding commitment between Laurent and me.

"No, I agree," I said.

"You seem to be hitting your stride here, Jayne," he said. "If you get the show in New York, that'd be very nice, but until then, take it one day at a time. Laurent seems like a decent man. I just wish he weren't as old as I am."

"You're almost two years older," I said.

"Yes," he said, laughing a little. "Thank you for reminding me."

"Laurent really should be with someone closer to my age," said my mother.

I hesitated, not sure what she really meant. "Maybe," I said, "but for now, he's with me."

"Yes, I know," she said. "At least he's taking good care of you. That's apparent."

"Yes, he is," I agreed.

9.

For a number of days after the opening, I woke up thinking that friends who might have underestimated me before now would henceforth consider me a more serious person, and that whatever happened, I could handle it because I'd had a successful show in Paris. One very pleasant surprise was that Pepper emerged from the mists; somehow he had found out about *Intérieurs intimes* and had gotten in touch to say that he'd seen my new paintings on Vie

Bohème's website and was impressed. When he was in Paris next, if I'd still be there, he wanted to have lunch. How it pleased me to know that he remembered me.

Maybe he wanted a favor—an introduction to Laurent. It isn't impossible. There is something I've realized this spring—to have the ability to bestow this type of favor: that in itself is a kind of privilege.

Yet my happiness was undermined by the conflicting feelings I had in the aftermath of Colin's visit. I called him the day after the opening and went to see him that afternoon at his hotel. He looked tired and said that he'd had trouble sleeping the night before and had read through our old e-mails, everything I had ever sent him. He'd reviewed our conversation at the gallery too, and had come to the conclusion that I wasn't ever moving back to New York to live with him. I hadn't texted him after the opening the night before, and I hadn't e-mailed either—I would have done one of those things if I wanted to leave Laurent for him.

He went over to the window and looked out over the street, where traffic streamed by in frantic bursts dictated by the stoplights. "I should never have said anything last night," he said into the window. "I don't know why I couldn't stop myself. It was the biggest night of your life. I acted like an idiot." His voice was gravelly with fatigue and regret.

"You're not an idiot," I said. "I thought it was very romantic."

He shook his head. "You're nice to say that but—"

"I was really moved, Colin. You just caught me off guard."

He put his arms around me, and we stood there for a while. He knew that I wasn't feeling any sense of normalcy right then, and his suggestion that we live together had done little to reduce my feelings of disorientation. I had just had lunch with Susan, who was going back to Chicago on Monday—it was the middle of the spring semester at the School of the Art Institute, and she had already missed close to a week of classes. We had gone to La Cantine de Quentin near the Canal Saint-Martin in the tenth arrondissement, where Jeanne-Lucie had taken me the previous fall because she had wanted to look at the selection of wines they sold, along with a few delicacies she and Daniel liked: apricot preserves, a jar of mustard made with white wine, a bag of caramels that she surprised me with when we were parting ways. "You don't have to share them with my father," she said with a mischievous smile.

Being with Susan, talking to her as we ate roast chicken that dissolved like honey in our mouths, I knew that we were becoming friends, that I was no longer only a former student to her. Without fanfare or fuss, she seemed to be welcoming me into her orbit; she spoke of her artist friends' current projects and said that one or two would be in Paris at the end of May. They planned to stop by the gallery to say hello. Our show would be coming down by then, the paintings shipped to their buyers, but Laurent might be willing to hold them over for another week. I told her I would ask. I didn't mention any of this to Colin, but these thoughts were in my head as he and I stood with our arms around each other in his hotel room near the Place de la Concorde. Eventually he leaned back to give me a look that I didn't bother pretending I couldn't read.

"Yes," I whispered.

I stood on my toes to meet his lips, his hand already at the small of my back. Shivering, I pulled him closer. His hair smelled of the hotel's verbena shampoo; I kept a bottle at home, having taken it with me during Colin's last visit. His athlete's body with its heavy, muscular legs and long white feet was younger than Laurent's by more than twenty years, but I couldn't say that I loved one more than the other, and I wondered if Laurent felt the same way about my body and those of the women I imagined him touching and pressing his mouth to, parting their legs with the same skilled intensity that I knew well. More vividly than I wanted to, I could picture him doing these things to another woman, a sexy Frenchwoman, expensively perfumed, diamond studs in her ears, when he was supposed to be running errands or meeting with clients. How different were he and I, really?

Colin and I left the curtains open, the sky overcast but brightening in the east. We didn't speak, but each time I opened my eyes, his were open too, his gaze uncharacteristically direct; most of the time he kept them closed when I was on top, pinning him to the disheveled bed, my hands on his warm, freckled shoulders.

Afterward, I didn't want to leave, but I'd been gone for several hours and even if Laurent wouldn't ask what I'd been doing, I'd sense his unasked questions, and it was likely that he'd be in a querulous mood.

"You should go out for some fresh air," I said as Colin hugged me good-bye.

"I will in a little while. Right now I need a nap," he said. We could hear sirens outside, moving away. "Thank you for coming to see me. I know it wasn't easy to get away."

I shook my head. "It wasn't that hard. And I wanted to see you. You know that."

"No, I'm never really sure," he said.

I saw him once more before he left, but I didn't answer his question about whether I'd return to New York, and to him. He didn't press the point, though. I think we both knew what my silence meant.

For a few days after he went back to Manhattan, I was fine, insulated by career-related happiness, I suppose, but then I started to feel his absence, and Susan's too, and I wondered if I should be back in New York, if that was where I really belonged. It felt a little as if a wall had cracked in half, the subsequent repairs inadequate. A number of weeks later, Colin sent me an e-mail:

Dear Jayne,

It's been so rainy in New York for the last three weeks. Not much of a spring. I might go to Cabo with my roommate and one of his friends from college for four or five days the week after next. We found a package deal that looks pretty good.

What I'm really writing to tell you is that my boss said the other day that starting in July, they might want me to move to Paris for a year or so. Maybe you and I could talk when I'm there next.

I miss you.

Colin

I didn't know what I thought about him moving to Paris, even if I recognized it as a gift that he still wanted to be with me. He had always been kind to me. I was sure that writing again had not been easy for him, but I waited nearly a day to write him back, needing some time to let his message settle.

Dear Colin,

My parents just left, and I feel a little strange now, like life is going too fast. Do you ever feel that way? I never used to, not that I can remember.

I bet you'll have a fun time in Mexico with Jamie and his friend. It's good you're going. All that rain sounds so depressing.

Yes, let's talk when you're here again.

I miss you too,

Jayne

When I lived in New York I believe that I felt differently, but in Paris, I realized that I didn't want my life to be, above all, about the men in it. I wanted them to be an important part of the story, but not more important than my work as an artist. Would it have been different if there hadn't been any men who wanted to be with me? It's possible, even probable, and maybe before long I would find out, whether I wanted to or not.

10.

Wikipedia

Liesel made good on her promise and wrote us both Wikipedia entries that one day she believes the gatekeeping editors of the site will publish.

Jayne Marks (born 1983, in Oak Park, IL) is an American painter. She has an undergraduate degree from Georgetown University (2005) and an M.F.A. in painting from Yale (2017). Her work has twice been included in the Venice Biennale (2017 and 2019). Marie Walsh Sharpe Foundation Space Program grant recipient (2015). Fulbright Scholar 2016–17, Corsica. Personal portrait artist for President and First Lady Obama. Winner of the Rome Prize from the American Academy in Rome (2021).

Liesel Freund (born 1990, in Madison, WI) is an American supermodel. She is also an architect, attorney, master gardener, and financier. Her hobbies include hang gliding, particle physics research, quilt making, boxing,

seeing-eye-dog training, equine therapy, and sculpture.
She is a vegan and weighs 115 pounds; her measurements
are 34-26-34. She speaks fluent Japanese, Chinese, Urdu,
German, French, Italian, Spanish, Swahili, and English.
She graduated summa cum laude from Harvard University
(2012) and double-majored in calculus and biochemistry.
She is also a millionaire and a good cook.

11.

The Last Painting

Sofia's banker turned out to be the buyer for my painting *Vicky and Sheldon at the Brown County Fair*, the one canvas in *Intérieurs intimes* that didn't sell within the first several days of the opening. Laurent informed me of this purchase, his expression neutral, and my first thought was, "Good. Now one of my paintings, if not six, will haunt the house where her lover lives."

I was at the gallery when the banker came to claim *Vicky and Sheldon*. He wanted to pick up the painting himself instead of using the delivery service Laurent and André contracted with. He was younger than I expected, around forty, maybe as young as thirty-five. Of course he was very handsome; Sofia surely wouldn't have settled for someone she didn't enjoy looking at. Her artist's sensibilities wouldn't have permitted it either, perhaps.

The banker had black hair and gray-green eyes—a color I'd rarely seen, almost the color of pine needles. His face had a feminine delicateness—prominent cheekbones, full lips, tended eyebrows—but he was also broad-chested and taller than Laurent. He wore a navy blue suit, a light blue shirt, a green silk tie with tiny yellow and blue flowers. Laurent was at the gallery that afternoon too, and when the banker came in from the street, Laurent greeted him by his first name, Serge. They talked for a minute before they looked over at me; I was sitting at the desk that the assistants usually occupied, pretending to read a book. I had no idea if Serge knew that Laurent was a rival for Sofia's affections.

"This is the artist, Jayne Marks," said Laurent, walking over with Serge, who smiled and nodded once, very polite and proper.

I climbed down from the desk's high stool and offered my hand, conscious of both men's assessing gazes. I wanted the banker to find me as talented and as attractive as Sofia, but I was embarrassed by this impulse. One of the lessons I'd been learning during the year and a half with Laurent was that I probably wouldn't ever feel confident that I knew a man's true thoughts and feelings, not the ones I was attracted to.

"Very nice to meet you," said Serge. "I am looking forward to seeing more of your work soon."

"Thank you," I said. "That's so nice of you to say."

"It is the truth." He smiled.

"We both thank you for buying Jayne's painting, as does my business partner, André," said Laurent.

"It is a gift for my girlfriend," said Serge. "You know her, of course."

Laurent's expression didn't change. "Yes, I know Sofia." He sounded so patient. It was costing him, I thought, to be so agreeable with this good-looking younger man who also had the money to spoil his sexy girlfriend as much as he cared to.

"It's for her?" I said, trying to hide my surprise.

Serge nodded. "She came home after your vernissage and told me how much she liked your paintings."

"I had no idea if they'd sell," I said. "And not as quickly as they did, that's for sure."

"I knew they would sell," said Laurent. "But that is part of my job." He glanced at Serge. "The painting is in the back room, packaged and ready. I can help you take it to your car if you would like."

"No, no, I think I can manage it on my own," said Serge.

I could see that Laurent wanted Serge to follow him, but the banker stayed where he was, looking at me inquisitively while Laurent disappeared into the back office. He was gone for no more than a minute, Serge asking me during Laurent's absence if I minded the rain, which we'd had all week, and who were the artists I'd been most influenced by?

"Gustav Klimt," I said, "and my coexhibitor, Susan Kraut. Jacqueline Marval too."

"Klimt, really?" said Serge. "But your work isn't very much like Klimt's."

Laurent reappeared then, carrying my painting, which earlier in the day had been packaged for light travel and handling. "It doesn't have to be," he said, answering for me. "An influence is often like a spice in a stew that you do not know you are tasting, but without it, there would be no depth."

Serge reddened slightly. "Yes, I suppose. You can see that I am not the artist in this room."

I smiled. "You should be relieved about that."

"Oh, I am," he said, his grin foxy. "Bankers have almost no talent. We are only good at counting money."

"Or losing it in bad investments," said Laurent.

Serge paused. "Yes, some bankers do," he said. "That is true."

After Serge left, carrying off Vicky and Sheldon to their new home with Sofia, a revelation I was still reeling from a bit, Laurent presented me with a check for my percentage of the painting sales.

It was more money than I'd ever been given at one time, but I tried not to ogle it. "This should make you happy for a little while," he said, suppressing a smile.

I laughed. "Yes, for an hour or two at least."

"What is the expression? Don't spend it all in one place?"

"That's the one," I said. "I won't. Two places, for sure. Maybe three."

"Good," he said. "Then you will be just fine." He put his arms around me and kissed the top of my head.

"Thank you, Laurent. Thank you for everything," I said.

"*C'est mon plaisir, ma chérie.* It is what I am here for."

Within an hour after Serge left, it was time to close the gallery and go home. I had a big check in my handbag, money that I'd already decided to put away for the future. We rode home in a taxi, through the streets of the first and eighth arrondissements, and I stared out the window at the stone buildings already illuminated for the night ahead, at the people in their soft spring coats, some of them hatless and smiling to themselves in the light evening rain. I had tears in my eyes, joy washing over and through me. It was a temporary state of grace, this upwelling of suspense and happiness, but I knew that every feeling I'd ever had was and would be temporary.

POSTSCRIPT

About a week after Serge picked up *Vicky and Sheldon* at Vie Bohème, the intercom buzzed around nine o'clock. Laurent and I had finished dinner a half hour earlier, and he was now watching some news program while I worked in my studio on a painting I'd started a couple of weeks earlier, one of Jeanne-Lucie and Marcelle from a photo I'd taken at Place des Vosges the previous fall, Marcelle staring into the camera from where she stood a few inches in front of her mother. Jeanne-Lucie was looking to the left, toward what I remember to be a group of Japanese tourists, the men in dark suits, the women in hats and pretty silk dresses, all of them having just laughed in a loud, jubilant burst.

Laurent got up to answer the intercom, and I froze as I heard the cheerful, static-riven voice that charged into our apartment from the street: "C'est moi, Sofia." Then a very short pause before she added, "Et Serge aussi."

Laurent buzzed them in without a reply.

Above all else, I remember feeling irritated. I was not dressed to receive visitors, especially ones as beautiful as Sofia and her banker boyfriend. I stuck my brush in the jar of diluted solvent that I kept near the easel and called to Laurent, "Were you expecting them?"

"No," he said. "I was not." He did not sound bothered, though. When I went into the hall, I saw him still standing by the intercom, and he seemed only to be distracted, perhaps a little perplexed. He hadn't yet changed out of his work clothes—a black cotton-and-silk shirt, slate-gray pants. He was in stocking feet and had made no move to put on the shoes he'd left in the hall by the door.

I was in jeans and the ratty blue T-shirt I frequently painted in. I felt resentful of Sofia for dropping by unannounced, and wondered if Laurent was lying, if he'd known they were coming but hadn't thought to warn me, though I didn't really think he had. I went into the bedroom and pulled off the T-shirt, flinging it onto the bed, before putting on another blouse. I chose a grape-colored V-neck, thin and close-fitting. I quickly looked in the mirror over the dresser and pulled my hair up higher in the clip I had subdued it with earlier.

Soon Sofia and Serge were ringing the doorbell and Laurent was letting them in, their laughter and greetings carrying down the hall as I came out of the bedroom. Sofia was wearing an emerald-green dress, and as she had on the night of my opening, expensive silver jewelry; she looked like a starlet, her face shining with almost belligerent good health, and it wasn't hard to imagine the admiration of everyone who saw her. Serge was in jeans and a black sweater; he was also aglow—in his case, in the lone, bright light of Sofia's regard. "We're not going to stay," she announced after I said hello and pretended to be happy to see her. "But I wanted to give this painting to you, Jayne. I made it just for you." She offered me a small square brown-papered package.

I glanced at Laurent. He was looking at her, his face relaxed with pleasure, and although I tried, I couldn't catch his eye. It all felt like an ambush, and I was so jealous of her, of the feelings Laurent obviously still had for her. At the same time, I hated myself for reacting this way and knew that I didn't deserve his fidelity. It bothered me too that she didn't seem at all threatened by me, even here, in what had become my home.

"You made me a painting?" I asked dimly.

Why? I thought, pulling off the package's wrapping, all four of us silent. The thick paper was heavy and intractable in my hands.

Sofia's painting was of a little black-and-auburn dachshund, its eyes deep brown and expressive, almost entreating. It was perfect— adorable, really—but how strange that its creator would think I would welcome her gift wholeheartedly, as if I had no idea of her history with Laurent.

"Her name is Madame Tussaud," said Sofia. "She belonged to my grandmother. Laurent has told me that you like dachshunds. They are my favorite dogs too."

"She's beautiful," I said slowly, not looking at Sofia. "But are you sure? You should sell this painting. Someone would probably pay a lot for it."

She laughed. "Oh, no, no, no. Sometimes I like to paint for my friends. I love your painting, the one Serge bought for me, and I wanted you to have one of mine."

There were, of course, six of her paintings in the hallway already, just beyond where we stood, but I didn't mention that. She knew they were there.

"For your studio," she said. "Or the bedroom?" She laughed, darting a look at Laurent. "The kind of dog that will not wake you up in the middle of the night."

He laughed too. I looked at Serge, who was smiling, oblivious, it seemed, to any subtext.

"You will have to come and visit her," said Laurent. "Maybe you can both come for dinner later this month. Jayne likes to cook."

"Do you?" said Sofia. "I do too."

Of course you do, I almost said. "I do like to cook, but I think we'd be better off going to a restaurant. I'm not sure I want to subject you to any of the new recipes I've been trying lately."

Sofia nudged Serge's side. "He will eat anything," she said. "And I at least will taste anything."

They left soon after this, refusing Laurent's offer of a drink. They were going to see a movie, a new Almodóvar film. "Would you like to come too?" Sofia asked, looking at me before Laurent.

"No, but thank you for asking," I said. "I should get back to work."

"Oh, yes, go back to your work so that you can make me another brilliant painting," said Sofia, her smile unforced.

After they left, I looked at Laurent for a long moment, waiting for him to say something for himself, but he only made a show of admiring Sofia's painting of her grandmother's dog. "Very meticulous and honest," he said. "As always. Very nice of her to give it to you too, don't you think?"

"I don't understand why she would," I said, exhausted by her clever act of one-upmanship, or whatever it was supposed to be.

"Sofia is your fan," said Laurent, "and naturally, she hopes that you will like her work too."

"There are six of her paintings here already," I said.

"Yes, but this one is yours. The others are not."

For a moment I considered leaving the apartment, going to Jeanne-Lucie's, but even though I believed that she would have welcomed me, I did nothing but go down the hall and into the study. I thought of Colin in New York and wondered if he was thinking of me too, lying in his own bed—alone or with another woman. I knew that he could very well be seeing someone new— his bedside lamp off, the tiny basketball hoop perched like a bird of prey on the back of his door, his new girlfriend's head against his shoulder.

I was too tired and distracted to paint, and I didn't feel like sketching either. I pushed my easel against the wall and lay down on the rug in the center of the room, first pulling off the drop cloth I always covered it with when I was working. For a pillow, I wadded up the old sweatshirt that I'd tossed onto the desk chair earlier and lay down with a bitter lump rising in my throat, the door locked against Laurent, but I knew that he wasn't likely to come to check on me. Eventually, maybe after twenty minutes of brooding, I fell asleep.

It was very late, the middle of the night, when I awoke with a stiff back and my right arm tingling painfully. I got up and pulled my easel away from the wall to look at what I had so far finished of the painting of Jeanne-Lucie and her daughter. There was no movement on rue du Général-Foy, no sense that there ever had been or would be again. Morning felt as distant and unreachable as the life I had left behind in New York. I stared at the faces I had begun to paint on the canvas and hoped that they would become what I wanted them to—I loved the hint of annoyance in Jeanne-Lucie's profile and the candor of Marcelle's stare; in it was her absolute desire to shield her mother from influences she could feel but not yet name.

Down the hall, I imagined Laurent in bed, still as a corpse, but when I went into the bedroom, he wasn't there. I looked in the other rooms, and he wasn't in them either. I stood in the dark hallway for a long time, looking at the outline of Sofia's six portraits, each obscured in shadow. I stayed there until my heartbeat slowed and I knew that I would be okay, that I could stand it all, for now. The bed I had slept in for the last eleven months was comfortable and harbored its familiar scents. I could see that Laurent had been lying in it for a little while before he'd disappeared, and I wanted very badly to be able to go back to sleep; it seemed important that I not be awake when Laurent came home from wherever he had gone, from doing whatever he had done.

ACKNOWLEDGMENTS

*N*ancy Miller at Bloomsbury deserves at least a year off after all the work she has done with me on this novel, as does Lisa Bankoff at ICM, who helped to shape it from the very beginning. Sheryl Johnston remains a most patient, generous friend and role model.

My parents, Susan Sneed and Terry Webb, and Melanie Brown continue to offer their steadfast love and support.

Thank you to Susan Kraut, who is an extraordinary painter and a giving friend. I feel very fortunate to have been able to write about her work (though the events described in this book are fictional).

Thank you to Francis Noel-Thomas, who read early pages and offered helpful suggestions and details.

I must also thank the kind and supportive people at Bloomsbury, among them George Gibson, Lea Beresford, and Sara Mercurio; Daniel Kirschen, Dolores Walker, Leonard Sneed, Floyd Skloot, Stuart Dybek, Anita Gewurz, Denise Simons, Adam McOmber, Chrissy Kolaya, John Buckvold, Randy Albers, Randy Richardson, Mike Levine, Alison and April Umminger, Bob Bledsoe, Carolyn Kuebler, Noelle Neu, Beth Eck, Dorthe Andersen, Melissa Spoharski,

Ruth Hutchison, Greg Fraser, Melissa Fraterrigo, Paulette Livers, Patricia Grace King, Taigen and Naomi Leighton, Patricia McNair, Cindy Martin, Cindi Rupp Rand, Don DeGrazia, Julie Deardorff, Barry Benson, Mary Dixon, Debra Gwartney, Bill Hageman, Bill Weber, Ann and Tom Tennery, Karri Offstein, Angela Pneuman, Jason Klein, Kim Brun, Ross Werland, Dave Wieczorek, Lauren Klopack, Melanie Feerst, Debra Stephens, Peggy Shinner, Gina Frangello, Robin Bluestone-Miller, Mare Swallow, Javier Ramirez, Felice Dublon, Don Evans, Suzanne Clores, Joel Drucker, Mona Oommen, Marlene Garrison, Natalia Nebel, and Alexandra Sheckler.

My students and colleagues at Northwestern University, DePaul University, and the University of Illinois at Urbana-Champaign— thank you too, for your friendship and support.

Thank you to the Chicago Public Library Foundation, and to Marilyn Berling, Ann, Amy, Andy, and Richard Tinkham and their families.

And thank you again, dear Adam T.

A NOTE ON THE AUTHOR

Christine Sneed's story collection *Portraits of a Few of the People I've Made Cry* won the Grace Paley Prize and Ploughshares' John C. Zacharis Prize, and was a *Los Angeles Times* Book Prize finalist. Her debut novel, *Little Known Facts*, won the Society of Midland Authors award for best adult fiction and was named a top ten debut novel of 2013 by *Booklist*. She lives in Evanston, Illinois and teaches for the graduate writing programs at Northwestern University and the University of Illinois-Urbana-Champaign.